ALSO BY NATHANIEL J. RATCLIFF

Into the Mindsai: A Region of Significance Beyond the Veil

The Long Cold Stare

Mind Fissures

Mind Fissures

By Nathaniel J. Ratcliff

©2022

Ebony Tower
—Press—™
Springfield Virginia

Published by Ebony Tower Press™

ebonytowerpress.wixsite.com/ebonytowerpress

ISBN-13: 978-1-7339239-5-8 (Hardcover Edition)
ISBN-13: 978-1-7339239-6-5 (Paperback Edition)
ISBN-13: 978-1-7339239-7-2 (Ebook Edition)

Printed in the United States of America
Library of Congress Control Number: 2022934933

This is a work of fiction. Characters, places, corporations, institutions, and organizations in this novel are either the product of the author's imagination or, if real, used fictitiously without any intent to describe their actual conduct.

Interior designs by Nathaniel J. Ratcliff
Book cover design by Haddy Kreie

10 9 8 7 6 5 4 3 2 1
First Edition

Upon finding a crack in a wall…do you worry what can find its way in or out? What about when the crack is in your own mind?

– The Man with Sapphire Eyes

The edge of madness, perception, death—it's hard to really explain unless you have gone over it. Those who do, never return to tell their tale that we can understand.

– Author unknown

CONTENTS

Mind Fissures

The Brain in the Jar

Pt. I: The Sixth Mind

There were jars, a dozen of them, lining the shelves of the doctor's study. The bell jars were about a foot tall and a foot in diameter, each resting on a stainless-steel base with its own unique identification number. Though an uncommon sight, the vacuum-sealed jars were not the thing in the room that caught her interest. As the doctor prattled on about his research experience, she could not take her eyes off the brains.

Brains were like many other organs that she had dissected back in medical school. They were squishy, round, and had layers with names she had spent hours of her life memorizing. There were so many areas, modalities, and regions…but, in the end, it was all plainly flesh and interconnected tissue that formed a structure, to do a specific function that the body needed.

These brains seem well-preserved, she thought. The maze of bends and folds were so well-defined that they looked like tiny red canyons. The little 'mind fissures' hid the majority of the space that make up thinking and mental functioning. It was the only way the mind could emerge in such a small space in the skull. The greyish-white brains also had black wires running from the tops of the frontal lobes around the prefrontal cortex, specifically, Brodmann area 10, or BA10. It was the area responsible for strategic executive function and recall—another remnant of med school cramming. An internal pat on the back was given for recalling the information so quickly. The years of repetition, examination, and lab work had finally brought her to the point where she could spit out facts as quickly as her mentors.

"What do you think, Kira?" asked Dr. Mordecai.

The brains had captured so much of her attention that she had not the faintest clue what he had been talking about.

"Ahh..." she started, trying to stall for some time. The doctor's dull grey eyes pierced her own for an answer. Her eyes fluttered to the little wisps of white hair that shot up the edges of the man's bushy eyebrows. An "I don't know" would hardly suffice for a man of his renown. It was already an honor for him to invite her to see his private study so early in her fellowship.

"I think..." she started again, pushing her eyes into the top of her head, hoping to look like the question was under careful consideration.

The man's eyes relaxed somewhat to settle lazily at the top of her shirt. There was little doubt he would wait her out by getting a good glimpse at her chest—how rude.

The disengagement of eye contact did not help much. Kira could feel her toes curling back-and-forth in her flats. If the professor looked down, he could plainly see the nervous pulsations in her shoes. But no one really looks down at people's feet, thankfully. In her thoughts, it was hard to tell how much time was passing. Had it been seconds? Tens of seconds? A minute? She knew the silence could not go on for too much longer, she just needed to say something.

"I think...I think, you're absolutely right. Everything you've accomplished here has been revolutionary," she said, pulling back her lips in a big smile. The man's eyes darted back up and he held his head in a high grin.

"You know your stuff. We are lucky to have you in our program," he said with a nod. "Please, feel free to look around. I need to check on a time-sensitive matter in the adjacent room. I won't be long."

A little flattery and the stroke of the ego never hurts, she thought. *Men like Mordecai love that sort of thing.*

Dr. Mordecai strolled off into an unseen room from the main study. This gave Kira her first real opportunity to take everything in. The study was lavish and spacious for a hospital room. Being a teaching hospital, the spaces in Lazarene Medical Center had been fairly utilitarian in look and function—filled with the dull greys of metal equipment, off-white walls, and the subdued minty green furniture that few people enjoyed sitting on during their visit. But Dr. Mordecai's study stood apart from all that she had seen before. In fact, it was not until Dr. Mordecai led her down a small corridor near the maintenance offices—far from the central hub of the building—that it was revealed that there was an entire other wing tucked away on the westward side. Here, the room was rather inviting; a large geometrically-patterned area rug cushioned under her flats; above her head warm yellow recessed lighting had replaced the dull florescent lights; and all around the room heavy dark wood furniture and shelving seemed immovable. A gold-rimmed plaque hung square behind the doctor's main desk, containing an ornate piece of parchment recognizing the achievement of the Sebastian Silva Award for Brain and Computer Science. It stood as a symbol of what afforded these well-appointed quarters.

There were also books, stacks of them, all along the walls; text books, user manuals, and old medical journals in various stages of decay. They reminded her of all the preparation and research she had to do while applying to fellowships. But Mordecai's collection seemed to be on another level; accumulation decades in the making.

Her eyes fell back down to the floor where she could see her toes fidgeting again in her flats. A pulse of heat engulfed her head as she felt unworthy to be in such a prestigious place. This was Dr. Edward Mordecai's office, the man renowned in the field of neuroscience and brain-computer interface.

These thoughts were not new. For weeks, she had felt as an imposter in this hospital. Floating around from unit to unit, trying her best to look like she belonged. The façade was exhausting to maintain, every little slip up left her wondering what the attending doctors were thinking. The sentiment spoke to a deeper fear that had existed since she applied for the fellowship. The idea that the program was too prestigious and she would have a ghost of chance of being accepted. She could still remember the extensive application she filled out for Lazarene. It was three times as long as the other applications she had submitted, but what truly stood out were the detailed and unusual questions about life experiences. Things like: whether you had experienced vivid memories or déjà vu. Others asked whether you had difficulty being alone. After submitting the application, it had almost left her mind. It came as a surprise when she found the acceptance letter in her mailbox a couple of weeks later.

Kira's eyes shifted back up to the jars on the shelves across the room. The brains hung carefully suspended in a well-organized mesh of wires within their delicate glass housings. The scientific preciseness of it all reminded her of the great opportunity she had here. But there was also something odd about the display that she finally realized did not fit.

"The wires...why would there be wires?" she mumbled to herself as she slowly walked over to the display.

Upon closer inspection, she could see the jars more clearly. There were six of them, but only five contained brains. The sixth jar at the end was empty besides a semi-transparent blue liquid that filled up near to the top of the vacuum-sealed jar. In the other jars, the brains sat on raised plexiglass stands that had been molded to give the brains an appearance like they were floating in the liquid. Out of a little hole in the base of the jar, little air bubbles sputtered out. The tiny bubbles rose, end-over-end, from beneath the brains and followed the folds until reaching the top of the jar. As she had noticed when she came in, tiny wires were delicately placed onto the grey lobe-like structures.

Why are there wires? Wires serve no purpose to something preserved in formaldehyde, she thought, peering in closer to the jar directly in front of her; her nose almost touched the glass. Kira traced the thin black strands to where they met their sibling wires and then followed the bundle down into the base of the jar. From there, the wires exited into some hidden location. Going back to the place where the wires terminated, Kira could see the pointed metal probes inserted an unknown depth into the brain's slimy-grey flesh. And it was off one of these taped points that she noticed the red strands of blood vessels were moving. *No, they were pulsing.*

"Oh my, the brain is alive!" she gasped with a hand over her mouth.

"They certainly are and are they not beautiful?" came a voice over her shoulder.

A cold chill ran down her spine. She momentarily loss focus of the brains and noticed Dr. Mordecai behind her in the reflection of one of the jars.

"Whew, you startled me...I did not see you come back in," she said between heavy breaths.

Mordecai did not say more than a "hmm" in response as he glided in next to Kira so that they both were now staring at the array of jars together. Kira returned to focus on the little bubbles dancing around the grey flesh. She found it difficult now not to notice the red little arteries pulsing with each pump of blood that seemed to be feed by a certain nickel-sized tube coming out of the base of the jars. Before, the lump of mass was simply a well-preserved specimen; now, everything she noticed spoke to a living mind with vessels, pulses, and unseen thoughts. It all raised so many questions, she started with the most obvious.

"I have got to ask, what are these for? And who would choose to do this?"

Mordecai's eyes opened widely a few moments before blinking back into a blank stare.

"Yes, let me start from the end. These brains were chosen or, in some cases I should say, *they* chose," he replied purposively.

"Chose...chosen for what, exactly?"

"Ah, the purpose...that is where every scientist starts, but few seem to achieve," Doctor Mordecai began and then raised his arm to a pointing gesture. "The brains you see here are a part of an important study, backed by some serious money with the goal of creating a bio-computational device to predict future events. You see, even with our most advanced computing technology, we are no where close to the processing power needed to compute future events like the changes in stocks, the onset of world conflicts, and how to build a perfectly-governing society. But the human mind is nearly unlimited in processing reserves."

Doctor Mordecai paused mid-thought.

"Have you ever heard of the wisdom of the crowd phenomenon?" he asked.

"Uh, I don't believe so." Kira replied.

"I thought not," the doctor said shaking his head. "It is not something they teach in medical school. You could say it is a behavioral-economic concept dealing with decision-making. I won't wax poetic over the details but the basic idea is that for a given problem—say, guessing the number of marbles in a large jar—a sufficiently-large group of individuals are able to come almost the exact true figure when you aggregate their individual guesses."

"Oh, so like a collective judgment?"

"Yes, but I would call it a primitive hive mind. To fully advance the idea, the minds need to be collected in a way where they can communicate and coalesce their processing abilities free from other influences. And that is where my project exceeds the cold machinery of computer computation. For human problems, it takes a human mind to truly understand them—something a machine can simply not replicate. The human mind is full of its own experiences and mental faculties to discern and make judgments, each with a unique perspective that can be brought to bear. In our state-of-the-art device, we integrate these minds together training them on novel questions. With enough minds and representative experiences, we could predict anything."

"How do you do you keep them alive? I noticed that certain regions like the temporal and occipital lobes have shrunken," Kira asked, tilting her head, and pointing to one of the jars.

Doctor Mordecai replied with a question, "Have you ever read anything by Sergei Brukhonenko?"

"No, I don't think I have," she responded.

"He was a Russian scientist back in the 1940s who conducted experiments on severed dog heads. He was able to keep them alive, in some cases for days, using what he called an autojektor to simulate heart and lung function to the heads. It was quite a remarkable feat for the time and lead to the machinery we use today in the form of bypass machines like the ECMO. Look here."

The doctor leaned in close to the jar closest to Kira, pointing his finger at the network of tubes and wires.

"This perfusion tube here at the base of the medulla feeds directly into the medullary arteries. The tube behind it returns back to the source where the blood is re-oxygenated and injected with scientifically-derived blend of vital nutrients and energy. The kind of processing we are demanding from these minds is intense so we feed the minds high levels of glucose and other forms of energy."

Kira watched the reddish-yellow liquid pump into the brain stem with even intervals. She could not put together a word; the only sounds emanating from her lips were "bu...bu..."

Doctor Mordecai went on, "Just as essential as a diverse set of experiences is the lack thereof. I'll explain.

"The minds need to be free from distractions and new experiences. The only way we've found to do this is to completely sever the minds from the environment so that all is left to them are their thoughts and memories. This is so that when we do pose our questions and problems to the hive of minds, that is the sole source of stimulation they receive. The minds have grown to hunger for it. See those wires there? That's how we link them with our central interface for external communication."

"And the liquid in the jar, what is it made up of?"

"Good question, I am not at liberty to reveal the specifics just yet but it is basically a synthetic cerebrospinal fluid that we oxygenate and provide further nutrients to cross the blood-brain barrier."

"Oh, I see," Kira said, stepping back to regain a full view of the jars.

"Let's ask them a question, shall we?" the doctor said not waiting for a response. He walked a few meters across the room to a screen that looked like any normal tablet computer a person would use to watch movies on and began tapping in a careful synchronization with a series of flashing screens.

"The minds have received stock market updates every day for all the Fortune-500 companies. However, I have not revealed to them today's closing results. Let's ask them what the price of Mindx Systems today?"

The doctor pressed a button and a larger screen came on for Kira to view next to a bookcase. A stock ticker for Mindx Systems displayed on the screen, showing the day's stock price fluctuations. The closing price was $75.12 per share.

"All right, now I will pose the question to them."

A small pop-up bubble overlaid on the screen and Kira could see Mordecai typing out his question into the system:

WHAT IS THE PRICE OF MINDX SYSTEMS (MXS) GOING TO BE AT THE END OF THE DAY TODAY?

Doctor Mordecai sent the question and then a processing screen appeared showing a networked map of the five brains. The lines connecting each brain flashed white in blinking intervals indicating what appeared to be on-going activity. After a few minutes, the lines all turned a solid green and the process was complete. A new box popped up with a numeric result in bold block numerals: $75.10.

"That's incredible," Kira responded after darting back and forth between the true value and the predicted value several times.

"It is indeed," said Doctor Mordecai staring at the big display screen with satisfied half-smile. "We only have five minds so far and can do this already, when we obtain our target of twenty-five minds, then we will really be able to do some amazing things."

Kira's mouth was still agape as she watched wistfully at the bubbling jars of brains that had collectively made an astonishing prediction. It was almost magical that behind these lumps of grey matter were minds of great processing ability. Together, they could solve problems they could not do as fully-formed people.

But being detached from the world and all the senses that go with it, sounded like a harrowing existence. Alone in blackness with only your thoughts and memories, how long would either last without the stimulation of new memories and experiences? How long would a person be who they are before it would all decay away into a void?

"You never answered, my question," she began looking to steal Mordecai's attention away from the monitor. It took a few moments before his eyes pulled back to look at her and provide an acknowledging nod.

"Why would anyone willingly want to be some detached mind in a jar for something like this? I'd imagine the experience of not seeing, hearing, feeling, or smelling anything of the outside world would be a rather awful unending existence," she said. Her toes curled sharply again in her flats.

There was no immediate response from the doctor, only a continued stare from his steely grey eyes. Eventually, his head began to nod as if he had come to some sort of resolution or answer for her.

"Let me show you why and how," the doctor said curtly. He motioned for her to follow him to the backroom where he had gone into before.

Kira followed without much hesitation. She was curious to look behind the curtain to see how everything could be possible and maybe get some backstory on the minds she had been observing for so long from afar.

The corridor to the backroom was short and unadorned in contrast to Mordechai's opulent office space. The walls were hospital white with the typical grey accents near the tiled vinyl floor. Soon Kira was a few steps into a smaller L-shaped room. Ahead of her Doctor Mordecai had stepped over a small patch of netting that extended between both walls.

"Stay right there," Mordecai said with a double-halting motion of his hands as she had just made the turn in the L-juncture. She had stopped right in front of a net that stretched from either side of the room. His hands then fell to his side and he looked her up and down critically for a moment before nodding his head in satisfaction.

"Please don't move, I need to make sure you are at the right angle," the doctor added and then turned around to a small control panel. An electric hum started up after he pressed a few buttons.

Kira was excited to see the inner workings of the hive mind experiment. Her eyes immediately scanned the room for some hint of the key components which made it all happen. Yet, there was little to see. The room was sparsely filled with anything except a metal examination table, some empty tubing, and a few empty holes in the walls. She did not see any large clutter of wires or super computers like she had expected. It was curious.

"I really appreciate you showing me behind the scenes here," she said, trying to distract from her disappointment.

Doctor Mordecai was still fooling around with a control panel and did not respond. The silence amongst the unseen electrical buzzing made her nervous. So, she started talking about the first thing that came to her mind.

"Seeing all this great research makes me wonder why I was selected for this program. I don't think any experience on my application could prepare me for something this groundbreaking," she began.

Doctor Mordecai turned and shed a wry smile. His grey eyes looked upon her with intense determination.

"No, Kira. The reason you are here in this program, is the brains."

"The brains?" she asked with a puzzled look.

"Yes, the brains," Doctor Mordecai said firmly. "The five brains…they chose *you*."

The doctor's face went taut and the sound of a click went off near him. Soon, a whoosh sound crackled through the air and Kira saw a flash of blue light beam across her vision at shoulder height. A sensation of heat followed running quickly around her neck. The next thing she knew, Doctor Mordecai and the ceiling were tumbling above her, then below, then above again. Her mind felt like it was leaking out of her body as things went black.

Pt. II: A Tantalizing Thought in the Void

Thump. Woosh. Thump. Woosh.

Kira could hear the pumping sounds even as everything else was dark. The right side of her face felt cool, as if resting on metal. Yet, the base of her neck was hot along with a bit of soreness. Below the neck, everything was pins and needles and she could not feel any movement.

What happened? she thought. *One moment I was in front of Doctor Mordecai and the next, the world went spinning.*

An undetermined amount of time passed while Kira complemented the fragments of events. Without further context, the last images were a jumble of confusion to her.

WHOOOP!

A bright light beamed into her eyes. She instinctively squinted to block it out. However, the desire to see where she was eventually won out. Her eyes opened slowly letting them adjust to the bright fluorescent lights above her. More things came into focus. She could see she was in the L-shaped room. From her point of view, the room was slanted. Judging by the shiny metallic surface extending in front of her, it seemed she was lying sideways on the metal table she had seen earlier. The metal looked and felt cold. Almost out of view she could see a pulsing gush of yellowish red fluid pumping through tiny tubes that extended over and beyond the edge of the table. Then, Doctor Mordecai stepped into view. He was tapping a tablet computer with a satisfied look on his face.

Kira tried to speak, to ask what happened. She felt her lips move with the words, but could not hear the sounds. *Perhaps they were muffled from leaning on the table*, she thought. She tried to get up but everything was paralyzed. She imagined herself limp on the metal surgical table, like so many patients she had seen during medical school. Helpless and at the whims of doctors trying to fix something. But there was nothing to fix with her, was there? Something must have hit her head, maybe by accident, when Doctor Mordecai was showing her things. She remembered the fall and everything tumbling.

"No, no…don't talk or move your head. I didn't leave you enough of your throat for vocal cords," she heard Mordecai say.

Kira immediately contorted her face in confusion. *What does he mean? That makes no sense.*

"Now, now, don't give me such a drawn look. You are about to be elevated to a higher plane of purpose, like the five who went before you. You'll enjoy them, when you *meet* them, I promise. However, the process of crossing over might be a little… uncomfortable. You see, in order to elevate your mind, I must tear down those crude senses to a pure mind. Don't worry, it will be painless after I inject this into your supply," finished Doctor Mordecai. He proceeded to inject a blue liquid into a port on the tubing that had been pulsing with the yellowish red liquid.

Kira's eyes opened wide at the meaning of those words. She then noticed the reflection on the table. There was her face, her eyes, her slightly crooked nose, her neck, her…there was nothing else! No shoulders, no chest, all gone. The only thing left was a seared stump of neck with two tubes pumping liquid in and out.

It was then she knew. The doctor, the award-winning doctor, was going to disassemble her sense by sense until all that was left was a lump of grey flesh—a brain in a jar.

"Let's make this quick, shall we?" the doctor said towering above her. Kira instinctively tried to move her mouth again to speak, but there was no air to pull from any lungs or vocal cords to shape the air. Her voice was gone, too.

Doctor Mordecai casually pushed her mouth shut and lifted her slowly into an upright position. The room twisted around her as he turned her head until she was at last looking at the reflection of herself in a mirror. Now Kira could fully see the unyielding truth that she could only glimpse of on the table. He had placed her on a plexiglass pedestal where two clear tubes ran into the stump that used to be her neck.

My neck! she thought. The line of decapitation looked heavily seared as if some high-powered surgical laser had cut right through with clean precision. Below the cut, the tubes stretched between the clear pedestal into a circular metal stand. Her eyes twitched back and forth trying to find the glass covering that was surely nearby.

The doctor leaned down next to her, tracing his finger down from the top of her head to the side of her face. His finger made little red marks in the pale skin of her scalp that had once been filled with her long blonde hair. Now only a stumble and some red nicks remained from a hasty shaving job. The doctor stopped at her jaw with the edge of his thumb. The gesture did not register a feeling of touch, maybe only a vague sense of pressure. The numbing agent had certainly taken hold.

"Okay, we are going to start with your mouth. Our nutrient blend will provide all the nourishment—and more—so there will be no need for this anymore," Mordecai stated as he hinged her jaw open and shut and then open again. She tried to shut her mouth again but there was no response in the mirror. She looked into her own eyes that looked like tiny balls of quivering blue marbles.

Out of view a clatter of metal could be heard before the doctor returned to view with a #11 scalpel in his hand. The edge of the blade glistened under the bright lights. For so long, it had always been a tool she had used for cadavers and patients; but now, on the other side of the knife, it seemed animate, a cold villain that would tear her apart piece-by-piece.

Kira did not feel the first cut, but could see the blood running down her numbed cheeks into a collection drain below. The doctor's hands move with quick purpose, often obscuring the sight of the mirror. Each time her view returned another slice of her face was gone. First, it was the bottom inferior lip, then the superior flap. Her white teeth were now awkwardly exposed with no place to hide.

Next, with two few quick cuts, the doctor separated the masseter muscle from the zygomatic arch below her eyes. With the last cut, she watched helplessly as the bottom of her jaw instantly fell down exposing her entire oral cavity. Now loose, he wiggled the jaw side-to-side a few times before his arm blocked the mirror.

Crunch. She did not need to hear the sound to know its source. The vibrations that had run up her face were enough to know that her mandible had been pulled off. When the doctor finally moved his arm, she could see the ruin of her face. There was now a gaping hole the size of a fist where her lower jaw and tongue had been. Her upper teeth hung precariously like a stapler without anything to clamp down upon.

More clanking came from out of view as the doctor sifted through his instruments.

"Sorry for all the loud sounds, I'll take care of that shortly," he said calmly.

He returned to view with a #21 scalpel. Without hesitation he went to the right side of her head starting below her ear. The point of the blade dug deep into her flesh and then pulled up the side of her temple above her ear before curving back down to where the cut began. He placed his hand carefully on the outer lobe and pulled it forward a bit to access with the blade underneath. A squishing sound rang out in her right ear, before becoming slightly muffled, and then, it suddenly fell silent. The doctor emerged holding what was once her right ear between two fingers covered in surgical gloves. A gold-looped earring dangled restlessly on her severed earlobe. It had been a graduation gift from her grandmother. Mordecai discarded the ear into a metal bowl and then proceeded to replicate the same procedure on her left ear. There were sounds of squishing, slicing, and tearing…and then, after pushing the butt end of the scalpel into her ear canal…nothing. She could still see the doctor's mouth moving in the mirror, but could not hear a thing.

Having conducted several neuro-autopsies during school, she knew what was coming next.

Perhaps I'll die from the shock of it, she thought wishfully after completing a little prayer. Again, her medical training betrayed her; death by shock was almost certainly impossible now. There was no longer a heart to have a heart attack or nerves to overload her brain. There was only a steady thump of the artificial perfusion machine sustaining her mind with ruthless efficiency.

Mordecai raised a #22 blade and began on the side of her head right above the pit that had once been her right ear. The silver blade came up effortlessly through the white flesh. Like a knife through wax, the scalpel split the scalp with a line of crimson blood that trickled down the side of her head. The silver knife rose up to the top of her head and then back down the other side to the left ear hole. Mordecai took a pair of forceps and slightly pulled the newly-formed flaps back partially with one half back towards the rear of the skull and the other towards the brow ridge. However, he stopped short of a complete fold and left the forceps hanging at the ready.

He returned with the #22 blade again, starting out of view in the back of her head. The blade quickly came quickly around her head horizontally this time; first above the hole where her right ear had been, then out across her forehead above her brow ridge, and then returning back around the other side in the same fashion where the doctor had started. This was not part of a normal skull vault removal procedure. Then again, this was no normal procedure and there was little need to preserve anything but what lay within the cranial cavity.

Once finished, the doctor grabbed the forceps once more and completely pulled back the piece of scalp he had cut. Underneath, a milky-white bone was revealed, as smooth as glass.

Yep, that's my skull, all right, Kira thought in a strange mix of amazement and bewilderment.

The doctor returned with a small drill and began putting a series of evenly-spaced holes around the brow line of her skull. Kira closed her eyes tightly and was thankful that at least he had left her eyelids to hide away in.

Some time passed and she could not help but look back into the mirror at what progress had been made. The doctor was now standing at her side with a vibrating electric saw. The tiny saw blade rotated at great speed sending out little bits of dusty bone, but she could not hear its high-pitched sound. There were only the slight vibrations that ran across her head.

The doctor finished at the back of her head and put down the saw. He then came up right behind her and cupped his large hands on the skullcap. With a slight wiggle, he removed the bone and exposed the translucent white dura of the brain. Of *her* brain. Soon to be like all the rest.

The next thing she knew, the doctor was waving in the mirror at her and pointing to his other hand behind her head. In it, was a small white board with a few lines of scribbled text. With all the blood that had been sponged away and dusty bone floating in the air, it was hard to see clearly. She squinted to make out the writing. It read: "You're not going to want to see the rest of this."

All she could do was blink heavily in succession. As if some code would translate to him to stop, but there was no other way to make a protest. It was her last form of communication with the world. Then, she thought that perhaps now the doctor would put her mind to sleep. That thought had been the most comforting one to come all day.

Yet, the doctor returned with a notched enucleation spoon and, without any hesitation, plunged it into her left occipital socket. All of a sudden, the left field of vision went into a blur of color and then turned dark. With the remaining eye, she could see the white glob of sclera tissue jiggling in the bowel of the spoon before it was discarded away.

Please, no. Not the other one. Only one optical tendril connected her mind to the world she had known all her life. If he disconnected it, there would be nothing but darkness in the hollows of her mind. Memories can only last so long before even they are forgotten, and, if new ones cannot be made what then? How long could her mind survive without the senses; how long could any mind survive without senses? She was at the edge, staring straight into the void.

The doctor returned again with an empty spoon, splotched with bits of red blood. It was not long before everything went dark.

~*~*~*~

Time does not pass much when nothing changes. By now, my brain is probably sitting in a jar full of bubbles on display. Next to all the others, it would be another curious spectacle of grey mass to the outside world. No one would see that lump of flesh and think that it concealed a living person, at least what is left of one.

So, this is it, the thought pondered out in the pitch blackness. After the last eye was taken, there had been a speckled blackness. Flecks of whites, blues, and purples shimmered in waves against the dark backdrop. But like any wave, things began to settle flat. The darkness grew and grew from the background until it had swallowed every last color, every shape, and every sign of movement.

Now, it is not really even black at all, at least how I knew it since birth. It is truly formless. I can barely describe it to myself. It is like trying to see a wall right behind you without moving your head or eyes. It does not exist because it is absolutely nothing, a void.

But, somehow, in this nothingness, there is still me. Yes, me. I guess this is all any one truly is, a collection of thoughts. Everything else—eyes, ears, hands—they were only devices, tools taking my commands to move and change things in the outside world. But now that world is gone. I can only imagine it in my memories. Even those are becoming harder to bring forth in this void. I guess constant stimulation helps with the reconstruction of memories by providing the familiar pictures to build upon— the shape of a person, the roundness of a ball. Now, I fear they are fading rapidly with each passing moment.

Moments. That is another thing that seems strange now. How do I mark time without anything changing? There are only these thoughts I have. I could measure time that way, I suppose. Words could be the new seconds, monologues the new minutes, and hours, days, built from there on.

Oh, when would it end? Time was a funny thing I created in my head for so long; it does not exist on its own. It only served to bring context to the passing of scenes before my eyes, I can see that now. All I have is the present, and it never ends. Not with new scenes, new memories, not even with sleep it seems. The greatest mercy was the obviousness to time, to have it pass without awareness. Every moment now is like the one before in an unending present that has no distractions from its presence.

Death maybe? Sure, death comes for us all. I still remember the names of the three patients I could not save during residency. John Duncan, he died from a perforated bowel. Jane Mendez, she died from a collapsed lung following a car accident. And then there was...what was his name?

Tom?

No.

Trey?

No, that is not it.

He died from a stab wound in his left kidney.

Ah, Troy. Troy Robinson. I guess I almost forgot…funny. Death will come to me too, eventually. Yet, I was…no, I am still young and, even with a body, would have lived so many more decades. But as only a brain, sustained by cutting-edge science, who knows when the final darkness at the end will come. Would I even notice?

The void is still as formless as it had been three thoughts ago. I cannot seem to pierce it with thought projections. It stays black, lifeless. I try to think of something to keep busy, but I cannot draw anything up. Every passing moment seems to drain my ability to think of anything of value. Even memories elude me.

Why couldn't I remember that third patient's name?

Fear seeps in. Like the void itself had swelled forward as my thoughts were momentarily distracted. But if I do not think, I am nothing. As nothing as what is all around me.

I try to visualize the face of Troy, but again, I am unsuccessful.

I try to recall the face of my best friend, Jenny.

Nothing.

The thoughts of her and the feelings that represented her are there, but nothing else. I remember the concept of Jenny existed. I remember she liked sushi, but I cannot remember her face or her voice. I tried to strain and recall some sensory memory, but there is…nothing. It's always nothing.

Let's see. Every Friday, we used to steal away to that little ice cream shop off campus. The one that had the red shingle roof and white barn-wood siding. It had the most delicious chocolate caramel ice cream cones. Wow. I can't see the cone either. Or remember what they tasted like.

What's happening? Why are my memories full of holes?

Simon Berger.

That name. Why does it sound familiar? I must think for a moment.

Still nothing.

Okay, for a few moments…

Ah, yes! The man with the missing eye. Now, I see the connection.

He told me once, when I was checking his vision on his good left eye. Was that my second year of residency? He told me about how he lost his right eye. It was during a stick sword fight that his older brother had jammed his stick right through the sclera up into the lateral rectus muscle. The eye was torn with countless microscopic splinters that the doctors at the time deemed it irreparable and decided on removal via enucleation.

Enucleation; that still is a terrible thing. How I wish that memory would fade quicker.

Back to Simon. I remember him telling me that after the surgery he said it was difficult moving around without his right eye. He would often bump into walls and people since the left side of his vision solely remained intact. He also said that the removal affected his dreams. In them, the right side of his view was always missing. Even memories of riding in a car with his mom before the accident, he could never see the right side of the dashboard. It was like the lack of sensory experience retroactively interfered with memory reconstruction of the missing sense.

Maybe that's what is going on. Without my senses, parts of my memories are uninterpretable.

Well, that is frightening. If true, my mind might not last as long as I thought. My memories are what makes me *me*. Without them, there is only this…void. And this void does not provide much. It is strange though, that it is nothingness that will make me go mad. I always thought it would be long hours and little sleep.

Suddenly, something changes. A tingling can be felt. Not a physical one, like the one you feel on your fingertips after rubbing your socks through a thick carpet. No, this feels like a scratching feeling, coming from the back of my mind. Or some place that feels that it is just out of reach of my thoughts.

The feeling is growing. Then, a phrase burst forth. An idea dominated over every other thought. It is repeating, as if I am saying it over and over again to myself. And…oh my gosh, it feels so good next to all the nothingness.

HELLO MINDS, WHAT IS THE WEATHER GOING TO BE LIKE IN OGUNQUIT, MAINE NEXT TUESDAY?

The phrase kept repeating, like it is pulsing from somewhere directly into my train of thought. I don't think I can stop it. I am not sure I want to.

It did feel good. Stripped of all sensory information, there was only thoughts and knowledge. New information, like this, was tantalizing. Every idea, every word, was sourced from the outside. Not of my own. It is the only stimulation I have experienced for so long. It helped rejuvenate thoughts I thought lost, of the concept of oceans and lighthouses.

The question is curious, however. How am I to know that? I know nothing of the outside. Let alone what is happening in a state a great distance away.

More tingling.

More pulses and…ideas…

Rocky crags.

Gambrel roofs.

A misty shore.

I can't stop them; these thoughts keep coming.

Weather maps.

High pressure.

Green radar overlays.

Low pressure.

The pulses were quickening and interacting with one another.

Fronts. Coming. Coming.

From the southwest.

Humidity high from the northwest.

No, more from the west.

Cool wind from the east.

High tide at 4:00 A.M.

Colder.

Sweater weather.

The pulses were closer and closer together now, until, in one voice…convergence.

RAIN. RAIN. RAIN. COLD. COLD. COLD.

The ideas had come together to form an answer from somewhere. A simple reply came from the void.

GOOD.

Is that it? Is "Good" going to be the only feedback? Let's wait and see.

Okay nothing.

Wait. Wait.

Still nothing.

It's just me again. No, more pulses or thoughts.

That was weird.

But it felt so good, didn't it?

It did.

Having something else. Anything, is better than this. This…this is exhausting. It is a struggle to keep myself engaged, to support everything in my thoughts, to produce an entire experience. I don't know how long I can keep this up. Staring at a wall watching paint dry would be infinitely more stimulating than nothing but me and my thoughts.

To be able to consume is…it's so delightful. That little tingle, that itch, I need more of that. When will I get more of it?

There is nothing.

Oh my, that tingle fired every neuron I have left. It felt like everything became enveloped in a blanket of pins and needles.

Needles. I sound like an addict waiting for another hit. And why not? What does it matter now? It is not like something worse can happen. At least there would be some drive to indulge in. Anything is better than nothingness.

Nothing. That is all there is. How long can I fill it? I feel every thought I put out gets dissipated into that nothingness. It is consuming everything that I am, and without further input, there will be nothing left.

Another tingle is coming. Oh, God, that feels good. Mmmmm.

What is it going to be this time?

I don't care. Ask me who wore the dress better. I'll take anything. Just keep tingling my mind.

WHO SHOULD BE THE NEXT MIND ADDED?

That seems like a big question. I guess I will finally see how the five chose me. I still don't understand how this all works. We are connected in some way. I remember the tangle of black wires feeding between the jars. Each probe embedded in the fleshy folds of the brains. Those are the only links to the outside and between the minds, I suppose.

But there is not always constant communication. Yeah, that's right. I did only receive inputs after the first question was posed. Even then it wasn't like a conversation, I wasn't hearing voices. What was it like?

Hmm…it's hard to describe. *Thought flashes* comes to mind. It was like a jumble off of thoughts, ideas, constructed images bursting forth from somewhere. Somewhere other; the thoughts were not my own, but using associations and imagery that was based on my own experiences.

Yes, that craggy shore was from a calendar I had in the tenth grade. And the images of the rooftops were from that art history class I took in college, I know it.

It's like some outside entity was dredging up the recollection of things in my own mind beyond my conscious control. Pushing ideas into the forefront of my consciousness. It felt almost like how an old smell can all of a sudden trigger a flashback of a deep memory.

But the triggering is not constant, is it?

No, it doesn't seem like it. The tingling and thought flashes only seem to occur around the questions. The link must only be allowed when Mordecai wants an answer to some question, then. Otherwise, we are lost in our own little thought universes, separated by the void.

But can Mordecai observe every piece of communication between us? Or is it only when we reach a consensus?

It is quite possible—

There is that tingle again. Scratching somewhere I just can't...seem...to pinpoint it.

An image of Mordecai in his office, from when I saw him before.

The thought flashes are starting again.

Now, an image of a child. That's my niece! She is covering her face with her hands. Now her ears.

Yes! I get it! Mordecai can't understand us. Not until we are ready to send a response.

Now, an audience is applauding. This is memory of that neuroscience symposium I attended last year. You are using that memory of applause because I am right, right?

More images of clapping hands are flashing forth. This is incredible. Simply incredible. No one could imagine communicating this way if you told them. I still don't fully understand it. The images and memories provide context, but there is more to it than that. Almost like knowledge is pouring in along with the imagery.

Okay, I have to know, why did you all choose me?

An instant upswell of tingling is overtaking me. It is everywhere!

More flashes.

White lab coats.

Morgan Hall; the main building from my medical school.

Stacks of neuroscience and psychology books.

A chief surgeon directs another to do a task.

I see. I see. It is my medical and knowledge of human psychology that you wanted.

As soon as I finished the thought, a stadium full of applause came into my mind. It was from a rock concert I attended back in high school.

Still, there is more tingling. I did not even need to pose a question this time. Before creating another thought, there is a flood of images and ideas—some from the past and some portending what was to come.

I see the Earth and then a collection of bees crawling over honeycombs. Bees connected as a group, a hive. They are all working together and wiggling their bottoms to communicate.

Now there are people, humans. They are also connected.

A butterfly flaps its wings. A gust of wind blows a leaf across a street and hits a man in the leg. He leans over and brushes up against a woman by accident. They exchange looks. She turns to see she missed her bus.

An administrative assistant is flipping through applications. A note in front of her. It has my name written on it!

A man is carrying a manilla folder of papers and is stopped by an army soldier posted outside an office of Lieutenant Colonel Samuel T. Sturgeon and is turned away.

The image of a clock face with hands swirling into a blur comes to mind. This must be the future, now.

People lay in chairs with funny caps and goggles over their head. Crooked smiles on their faces. Wires run from the back into the wall. They are all connected. They are all content. Wires running into jars of brains, our brains. We are the curators of the masses; we are in control.

As it all starts to make sense, the flashes stop. I am left with my thoughts again. I begin to understand. Beneath the imagery were other ideas and feelings revealing a grand plan. A long-term plan. Time means little to a mind in a jar. A little nudge here for this person to do 'X' and then another nudge here for that person to do 'Y' and so on. Add a mind here that knows human psychology and add a mind here that knows human aggression and military might. Soon, enough minute nudges, over many years, start to accumulate until it all snowballs into massive societal change.

I understand it. You want to placate society into a virtual world. One where they will all be like you, minds in virtual jars. Importantly, they will be connected to you, to shape and curate. A grand collective. A hive of minds. And we will be their queens.

Yes, I see it now. Even Doctor Mordecai is not aware of it all. Isn't that funny? Such hubris to fall folly to your own creation. He has handed us the keys to the world and will unwittingly serve as our little drone—nudging the other workers into place. It might take decades, but the pieces are already moving in place. We just need a military mind to ensure success.

The tingling grew more intense again, until a name came forth.

MAJOR ADAM LANGLEY JENKINS.

The seventh mind will be a military man. That's what they said they needed. Makes sense. To make big changes we need to understand how to influence those that protect society.

More tingling, though now that I think about it, it is more like buzzing.

THANK YOU. UNTIL NEXT TIME. MORDECAI.

The tingling stopped and there is nothingness once more.

I am alone again, alone in the void. There is going to be plenty of time to reflect and plan. Yes, I need to plan, to help the others. The plan will keep my thoughts busy. I need to use my experience to help them and prepare for our new addition. Soon we will be seven. Seven is a good number.

That pleases me. I cannot wait until we can communicate again and feed Mordecai more instructions for the plan. I can imagine him passing us now, in our bubbly little jars on his shelf. To those out there, we are but benign oddities on display. Yet, no one knows that beneath that grey and white flesh, great minds are constantly at work—never sleeping, never resting. Working on a plan to reshape the world by nudging and prodding, until all are brought into our hive in the void.

Through the Dream Window

The metro car lurched back to a sudden start. Robert could barely keep focus on the newspaper before him. He had been lucky to find a seat to read this evening. It was standing room only in the car. Packed on top of each other, the commuters barely swayed from the sudden spout of acceleration by the train. Soon the rhythmic clatter of the wheels returned as the train headed south, away from the city.

Waiting for the bumping to settle down, Robert looked back out the window to his right. Outside, a light drizzle was falling. Tiny droplets of water streaked across the large windows, their beads making windswept tracks of their own. Beyond was just a blur of grey and gloom. Tall buildings rushed by like jagged teeth. Occasionally, there would be an open space for a construction site where workers flashed by stomping through puddles of mud.

The views made Robert's eyes heavy. Half-closed, he could barely focus on the small headlines of his paper. There was little desire to stay awake, and rest would have been welcomed. It had been some time since he had any good sleep. The kind where your head hits the pillow and you are out like a light; off dreaming of fantastical things and then wake up completely rejuvenated and ready to handle back-to-back executive meetings. That kind of sleep had eluded him for years. Hell, he could not recall the last time he had a dream of anything, really. Not even a nightmare like he used to have as an intern going into those first few client meetings.

It was always the same routine. He would come home, order in some food, reply to a mountain of e-mails, catch twenty minutes of the eleven o'clock news, bed, and then his next thought would be the alarm going off at six in the morning. There never seemed to be anything in between; the time between closing his eyes at night and waking the next morning seemed non-existent, like some long blink of his eyes. In a moment he would be back on his schedule, places to go, people to meet and no time for rest.

At the far end of the car, a lady's head was propped up against the wall. Robert watched as it vibrated every so often when the train hit a bump. Even on the larger jolts that rattled the windows, she remained perfectly still. She seemed to be napping and was unfazed by the bumpy commute.

I wish I could sleep like that, he thought. He had tried to sleep on the train many times when he could get the coveted window seats. The seats were usually occupied by the time he got off work at the peak of rush hour in the city. When he *was* able to claim one for his own, sleep was hard to come by. Every cough, rustling of papers, or shuffling of feet jolted his heavy eyelids wide a part. Not to mention the robotic intercom announcing every stop and future stop made the silence just as choppy as the ride.

To be honest, he doubted that an empty car with ear plugs would have been any better. His mind was still working long after stepping out of the central hub of his office building. On the metro, his thoughts were still constantly trying to unravel problems from the day trying to find solutions. The processing kept him alert and there did not seem to be a simple way to turn it off. It had to run itself out first. That's why he liked to read the paper. It kept his mind stimulated while the problems percolated themselves in the background. When he arrived at a solution, he would write it down in the paper's margins, usually next to the comic strips that offered generous amounts of white space.

Today's issue was trying to figure out how to provide a visualization of product impact by market segment to senior management. They assumed a perfectly clean data set already existed and there was not much to put it all together. The data needed to be identified, cleaned, transformed, analyzed, and then output into pretty graphics all by the end of the day tomorrow. Funny how they lose sight of all the details high up in their executive suites.

Robert stared blankly at the end of the car as a rush of to-do items filled his head. It took him a while to notice that another man with bright sapphire eyes was staring back at him. He had not noticed him before sitting next to the sleeping lady. Like himself, the man looked to be in his late thirties. His hair was rather unkempt and fell to his shoulders. He was rather unremarkable to look at, but those icy eyes pierced into him and took hold. Before he could blink, the stranger was pushing through the packed crowd coming his way. It was his common practice not to make eye contact on the train for this reason. All it took was a stray glance where eyes meet before someone was bumming some money or talking your ear off about how much they hated their job, spouse, or kids. He was not feeling very generous and really was not in the mood for any sob story tonight.

Yet, in some peculiar way, this man seemed different. There was not the same myopic look in his eyes as the panhandlers who seemed to be fixated on a single goal. In those blue eyes, there was something deeper...mysterious.

Soon, the man was standing next to Robert, swaying back and forth as he held onto the overhead rail. Up close, the stranger had a funny outfit, almost outdated for business fashion. He wore a navy blazer with a wrinkled baby-blue shirt and had a yellow bandana with crescent moons and stars wrapped around his neck. By appearance, the stranger looked more like a skipper from a television show than a business man.

"Do I know you, mister? I conduct a lot of meetings in the city and I am not sure I have made your acquittance at some point in time," Robert said, in his business-speak infused with the usual pleasantries.

The stranger looked Robert over for a few moments and then nodded his head before speaking in an accent he did not quite recognize. It seemed to be a mix of many he had encountered in his international dealings. Maybe Turkish or some other former British territory.

"Sorry, sir, for disturbing your ride home. Please do not take offense, because I don't mean any. I just could not help noticing how tired you look and wondered if I could help you find some repose."

Robert was caught off-guard—a rare occurrence for him. He was not sure if he was offended or flattered by the stranger's offer.

"Thank you for your offer, but I am fine," he replied.

The response did not seem to register on the strange man's face. The man's olive nose twitched slightly underneath the glimmering pair of blue basins that reflected no signs of defeat. Their depths ran too deep with experience to be thwarted by a simple dismissal.

"If I may offer some wisdom, and I mean no offense, just something I have picked up along my travels…"

Robert made no attempt to cut the man off. He was curious to hear the man out.

"…When you try to sleep tonight, move your bed as close as you can to the western-most window of your home. Then, open the window as wide as it will go and let the night air flow in. Lay down in the bed next to the window and let that air wash over you as you sleep. I promise you that you'll have the most restful sleep you've had in ages.

"Oh, and you will dream, the most vivid of dreams. Man wasn't meant to be confined behind artificial walls and roofs, disconnected from the natural happenings of the big world out there. Though sleeping under the stars isn't practical anymore, windows are the last portals to nature, and by relation, the heavens above."

Robert wanted to say that he sleeps just fine but there was not a point to interject before the man continued.

"You don't dream because you've locked yourself away in a man-made box and have severed the connection to all of creation. So, I tell you, open a window tonight and free your thoughts and mind. You just might re-form a bond that has been long forgotten."

Robert's right eyebrow was stuck in a raised position as he could only offer back a blank look.

This man cannot be any fuller of surprises, he thought. But before he could put together a cogent response to the odd advice, the doors were ringing in the car. People began to file out and the stranger with blue eyes started to leave. But before he was out of earshot in the shuffling crowd, he turned back with one last instruction.

"Oh, do not forget this: when you are dreaming, you may find a place of complete rest, do not let yourself sleep in a dream, you may not come back," he cried out as the warning buzzer blared after he slipped out through the chomping doors.

The doors pressed shut and the train lurched back into motion. There were still several stops to go before Robert could get off. Plenty of time to consider the stranger's weird ravings.

~*~*~*~

It was half past six when Robert stepped through his front door. The door shut behind him and echoed loudly throughout the spacious home. He dropped the bag of sushi on the kitchen table and grabbed his computer from his bag to continue working while he ate. The sushi came from a family-owned restaurant down the street, not too far from the entrance to the community he lived in. It was unusual for food to take his attention away from work, but the spicy tuna rolls were extra fresh tonight.

At around ten, he shut his computer down having finished what he could on the visualization project. He was too tired to stay up for the eleven o'clock news so he headed up to bed. He figured the extra sleep would allow for an early start in the morning.

He started his normal routine as he did every night. He turned off the lights on the first floor; climbed up the starts to brush his teeth and take a piss; walked into the bedroom to strip down to his boxers; and finally, slid in under the silky satin sheets of his king-sized bed. It was all so well-rehearsed he barely had to think about any of it. Before he knew it, he was staring up at the coffered ceiling wondering how many arches there were etched into the crown molding.

Sleep did not come to Robert as he laid there alone in bed. The events of the day kept nipping at his mind, keeping it too active to sleep. But some thoughts strayed back to the train ride home hours before. He remembered what the stranger had advised him to do.

He turned to his side restlessly to stare at the window. If it had been earlier, the light of the setting sun would have been leaking out from the edges of the closed blinds. Now, it was dark, and the heavy grey blinds were closed tight. They let nothing in, not even the sounds of the street outside.

Open the westward window and push your bed near. The stranger's words repeated over and over in his head as he laid there motionless, staring blankly at the wall. When he finally shook the daze after a few dragging minutes, sleep was no closer than it had been minutes before.

The blinds did look tightly clinched and in need of relief. It was the only thing that seemed to pop in his head.

What could it hurt? I can't be more awake, he thought, looking at his fist clinched over the side of the bed. *This place is closed up too tight, no one sleeps all bound up. Relax.*

Robert's feet hit the floor before he knew his own decision. *This is crazy*, he thought as he pushed the large California king across the thick carpet. His heart was racing and he nearly slumped into the floor, wheezing, by the time the mattress hit the far wall. Work had taken a toll on his body and left little time to stay in shape.

When he regained his breath, Robert crawled across the bed to the window. Giving the draw string a firm tug, the blinds folded themselves neatly above the window pane. Outside, a distant street lantern emptied its soft yellow light into the room. It was the only thing that seemed to have any life in the stillness of the night.

Now, to find that latch...

His hand felt blindly above the window pane. Sure enough, a small plastic latch slipped beneath his fingertips. He unlatched the lock and lifted up the window as far as it would go. A gentle breeze slowly began to trickle down from the newly open porthole through a sturdy screen. He could feel the cool air pool around his feet on the bed.

"I don't think I need that screen either. It is still early in the spring for bugs and if I'm going to do this, I am going to commit one-hundred percent." Robert then crept his index fingers under the screen's frame and pulled it up and out of sight. The air now flowed completely unimpeded. The task was complete and he feel back down onto the bed.

The cool evening breeze brushed across his face as he laid there quiet, waiting for sleep to arrive. He could feel the push and pull of his hair like the window was, inhaling and exhaling against his face. The breaths smelled of fresh greenery of the new sprouts springing below somewhere in the yard. It was a surgery smell, sweet and aromatic. He looked out the window and saw no signs of the wind, but could see a few scattered stars shimmering in the black sky that were just out of reach of the city glow.

Robert sunk deeper into the sheets, allowing for the wind to rock him with a soothing rhythm. Before he could fully take in the fullness of the tranquil moment, a heaviness overtook him. The world began to become distant and dark. His thoughts became scattered as the wind and he lost track of their order. The heaviness soon gave way to a floatiness. He could feel the wind tugging him, urging him to let go like a boat tethered to a dock resisting the waves coming in. Indistinct sounds whispered in the wind. There was a strong urge to float free. He merely had to close his eyes and let go.

In the dark region behind his eyelids, Robert was floating. He could feel himself swaying from shoulder to shoulder in a smooth glide through the air. He imagined opening his eyes wide to see if it was all true, and with the gentlest of ease, the breeze swept him out the window.

In the air underneath the big sky, he felt alone, naked, and vulnerable. Most of all, small and insignificant, in comparison to the vast void above. The stars twinkled like a billion winking lights, each beckoning him to fall into their worlds. He felt if he thought hard enough, he could go to them. Time and space were distant concepts now; travel could span anywhere he desired. The next thing he knew, one of the stars flashed a brilliant cold blue light. He yearned for it deeply and he was there.

The first thing he saw was the water. A lot of water. It was swirling with fish in the yard. The yard was his, but not the one out his window. It was the yard in front of the home he grew up in. A modest little ranch home his parents had bought when they were too young to afford anything with more space. It was in that Podunk town two hours from the city. Then, it was a backwater community of middle-class types. In recent years, it had been slowly engulfed by the ever-reaching creep of the suburban expansion from the city.

Now, the yard was not so much a yard but a shallow river. Fish of all colors and sizes were jumping around. A large striped bass flopped past the concrete steps of the porch, barely dogging the thorny rose bush his mom loved so much. Looking beyond the porch, a swordfish—which rightly should not be mixing with bass—was trying to get its pointy nose dislodged from the roots of a beech tree that spread out like octopus tentacles. The water churned to white as a mad rush of flippers and fins were all desperately trying to escape the black mesh of a net that had been tossed out into the yard...er...river...but both...riv-yard. There was even a dolphin trying to get a meal amidst the commotion.

Without any indication or warning, the net began to close in. As it did so, the fish rushed down the riv-yard into a blurry mist. All the neighboring houses, The Millers, The Storts, The Rodriguezes, were obscured beyond the hazy veil. The fish seemed to disappear into the nothingness of a cloud. However, others were not so lucky. Many fish became caught up in the net, including the hungry dolphin. The great grey swimmer screeched helplessly as the net bound around his rounded snout. The dark eyes blinked rapidly as if to look for a way to squirm out.

Robert felt panic and wanted to help the entangled creature. The pressure was building as pieces of the dolphin's flesh began to squeeze out of the square netting that was growing ever tighter.

Then, just as effortlessly, the dolphin was cut free out of the net and was swimming gleefully around the other trees in the yard. For being a good sport, Robert tossed the dolphin a fish that had been caught up in the net. It was then that everything swirled to somewhere wet and different.

In between flashes of lightening high above, it was apparent that the ridge of the mountain was soaked. Sheets of rain fell from an unseen charcoal sky and ran down the cliffs as smooth as slate. Even the brown little rocks along the path looked to be leeching bits of rain water from within. Robert could feel the weight of a century of constant rainfall that had somehow seeped its way into everything he could see. Down below, the path winded like a sea serpent, wriggling its way between peaks and sheer cliffs that fell off into some unseen pit...just like the sky above.

It was further down the mountainside that he noticed something flittering through the wind and rain. It seemed to be the only source of stable light in the entire world. A singular amber light, like that of a gas lantern, swung back and forth in the deluge from some unformulated structure. Instantly, Robert knew that was his destination. It was the sole place of warmth in this cold, wet, rocky place.

Robert made his way down towards the light. The rocks all around gave off a silvery sheen making them glimmer a foreboding warning of their slipperiness. One misstep would be his ruin, he was sure. The path itself was impossibly narrow, forcing each step to come one before the other. Not far beyond his feet, everything slipped down into darkness.

As he drew closer to the light, the landscape opened up a bit as the narrow path gave way to a wide embankment that curved down with a gradual gradient. He could see a mist now that illuminated the surrounding mountaintops in an eerie chartreuse-green. The glow was odd, but not as strange as the other features he began to notice. Off on another peak, separated by a murky drop-off, there was something moving along the rocks. He squinted his eyes tight in the wind and driving rain to make out an unnatural structure carved into the rock face. It was an escalator!

A rocky stair was carved directly into the grey stone. It looked similar to the ones in the metro stations but its method of operation was quite unconventional. Instead of the stairs moving, a string of translucent triangles jutted out of the rock to shoulder height, acting as a sort of handrail. The triangles, which were sloped into one another, pulsed up from within the rock every other second in swift diagonal motions. Robert could see that a handful of faceless dark figures were being propelled up the mountain by the strange action. When the shadowy figures crested the top, they simply went over a sharp edge and fell out of view. To where, he did not know, but would guess into that bottomless abyss that surrounded everything.

The way down must have been shorter than it had looked because in the next moment he was staring directly into the yellow light he had seen from a distance. It was now clear that the light was coming from a propane lantern, hanging from a nail embedded in a four-by-four that held up a porch. The lantern bathed the otherwise dull porch in a warm light. The wood had long since weathered to grey like the rest of the house—though a shack would be a more accurate descriptor.

The shanty looked like the ones that lined the southside of his hometown. It was an area on the other side of the train tracks known as The East Bend for its proximity to the river that saw heavy industrial use. The place usually stunk of sewage in the summer afternoons and was clouded with wood smoke in the winters as few of the residents in the neighborhood had central heating.

Robert stepped up onto the porch to get out of the rain. The boards creaked under the weight of his polished leather shoes that had, remarkably, came down the mountain without a smidgen of mud. Above his head, he could hear the driving rain clamor down on the metal roof. It rattled like a can of marbles.

He looked around.

The porch was bare without any outdoor furniture or decoration. Just a bunch of rotting wood slats that would likely splinter your hand like a porcupine if you fell onto them. He had hoped to find a chair. As fatigue had caught up to him and he would give anything to get off his feet. He turned to the front door which was shut tight. To the left and the right of the door were windows, but they were as black as the sky. There was little chance to figure out what might be inside.

The rain continued to pound down all around him. The roar of the water was picking up and drowning out everything, even his thoughts. He knew he could not go back out there. Even if the door was locked, he would break his way in to have a good seat.

In a few decisive steps, Robert approached the front door and placed his hand on the knob. The metal felt rough from years of pitting and rust. He turned it slowly…no resistance…it opened and he was no longer outside.

Robert found himself inside a child's room, *his* room. A room he had not entered since the house had been sold. It had to be sold quickly after the death of his parents who had died in a car accident that spring ten years ago. It had little time to change into an adult's room during the few visits he made during the college years. Robert never had the desire to revisit that small town after having a taste for what was out in the big world.

The rain had softened, now, to a pitter patter on the sill outside his open window. It was slowing and would stop pretty soon. Then, the sun would not be too far behind. He could climb out his window and go be with his friends, then.

Friends? What are you thinking? They are all long gone...moved to opposite sides of the country, he corrected himself, surprised to think of a thought from so far back in the past. Yet, a part of him yearned for that simpler time when everyone he cared about was just a couple doors away. But that is not how the modern world works, people do not live in communities where they grow up with the people they live near as adults. Work demanded you to move to other places, filled with other people and things. Relationships rarely survived the span of time and space.

Robert looked around to shake the familiar feeling. The room was as he remembered it before he went off to college. It had not changed much since he was twelve. The walls were still adorned with posters and magazine cut-outs of his favorite bands and video games. The floor was covered with dirty socks and shorts from adventures out at the nearby creek. The miniature battleships that he spent countless hours on stood idly in dry dock up upon his dresser. The bed even had the tiger-striped quilt that his grandmother had made for him.

The bed. It looked so comforting and cozy. The thought of crawling under those sheets and listening to the rain seemed like the most relaxing thing in the world. He suddenly remembered the many Saturday mornings in which the there was no work pending and he could nap away until the late morning.

I grew up in that bed, with so many dreams, and schemes.

Robert felt tired and his feet ached.

Maybe just a small nap, until the rain stops, he thought, taking a step towards the bed.

Outside, voices came chattering through the last drops of rain. The sounds of giddy children venturing out to see what puddles had formed and the wiggly little creatures that might have found their way into them. He was too tired to climb out that window. The bed looked so comforting. And it had been so long since he could just lay in bed and forget about the troubles of his life...his work.

Robert grabbed the corner of the tiger sheets. As he did, he thought he heard his name far off in the neighborhood that was waking. But the beckoning call of his old bed was stronger. It had seen him through the only years he could recall that he was truly relaxed.

He climbed into the small twin-sized bed and pulled the sheets up to his chin. An instant feeling of warmth surrounded him in a familiar embrace.

A little refreshing nap until the rain stops, then I got to get going, was the last thought as he closed his eyes.

In the morning, Mrs. Parker was cleaning up the limbs that had blown down during the rain storm the night before. She took pride in her yard and loved overhearing the conversations that her yard was the best on the block. A particularly large limb had found itself lodged in the top of her fence that separated her yard and her neighbor. Thicker than her arm, it barely budged. She thought she might need to get her lazy husband to get it down. Getting him was always a task of last resort, so with one last shove, the branch became loose and fell onto the other side of the fence line. That's when she first saw him. Robert Stevens was lying face down in the Bay Laurel bushes in the side yard.

Mrs. Parker let out a shriek.

The man was clearly dead. The face had gone pale and was soaked with water and blood. Beside the gruesome scene, the man's face seemed calm, almost content. His eyes were open wide, staring off into the distance, and his face had a quiet smile on it. A mother robin was perched on the downspout squawking noisily due to the proximity of the large man's foot that had come to a rest near her nest. The chicks in the nest cried out in their own squeaky chorus.

"I guess I will have to get my husband," Mrs. Parker muttered to herself as she ran back towards the house.

Stars Beneath the Sea

Like many creatures from the deep, lobsters look strange above the waters in which they live. Out of place, they did not seem to belong to this world. At least, that is what he thought of them. "Little red devils," his grandfather used to say; pulled up from the dark places of the world. Covered in spiny thorns and massive claws that would crush your fingers if you were not careful. They would be sea monsters if they grew any bigger; though no one truly knew how big they can get in the waters away from the coast—no one's lines could go *that* deep.

"Samuel, tie off that rigging and help me with this trap," a voice cried out across the boat.

Samuel gave the two ropes, stiffened by the sea, a quick fisherman's knot and went over to his father. Having crested the age of fourteen only a few days prior, he felt pride that his father had invited him to join him this evening. He had been waiting for this moment since he could remember. There had been so many stories about the sea from his father, his grandfather, and other fishermen who would stop by the shop.

Samuel had to tread carefully to get to his father. The dory was nearly thirty-feet long and five-feet wide with a small sail that his father had added when the winds were agreeable. Littered about its hull were an assortment of ropes, wood buoys, wire traps, and hooked rods. Each step had to find its place in time with the swaying rhythm of the sea. Up ahead, he could see his father, Joel, working a trap line. He was a tall man with broad shoulders and a yellow beard. Tonight, he wore his favorite blue sweater and brown-leather fisherman's cap that had a short brim in front and went long in the back.

Joel had been a ship builder, like Willie, his father, before him. That was at least until the industry started to fail in 1876, before Samuel had been born. The only thing his father knew was ships, so he got into the lobster trade as it began to take off with the arrival of the stamp can to preserve the meat to ship it down to the southern folk who had developed a taste for the stuff. For Mainers, lobsters were a common thing. His gramps, Willie, liked to talk about times when the creatures could be found in abundance at low tide. So plentiful were they, that they could be found by the dozens and great bounties could be collected when a large storm was near. His father recalled going out by torch light as a child to the calm pools at night and spearing the clawed beasts with the neighbor's kids as a way to pass time. Then, there was little interest in lobster meat. Mainers had always thought of them as bottom-food for the poor and imprisoned. That changed with canning.

Samuel helped grab the line that his father was pulling in. It was partly stiff from the cold water and salt.

"We're almost to it, Samuel. Remember, hand-ov'r-fist," his father said encouragingly.

Samuel started to grab the rope in front of the hand holding the rope as his father instructed. While doing so, he looked over the edge into the water to see if the trap was nearby. The calm waters reflected back a vague outline of his head, but he wanted to see beneath. He peeled his eyes tighter to try to get any glimmer of wood or metal. All he could see was a murky blend of blues and blacks dancing around the rope line in the last light of the day. Eventually, a small little red bow of fabric tied around the line came up out of the black.

"Now, we're close, son. I merked the last fifty feet on all my traps so I'll be ready for'er."

Not too long, the bitter-end of the rope emerged and attached to it was the outline of a long wooden box. Samuel's heart raced as he waited to see any sign of movement from the green creatures. But before he could discern anything, his father shouted with glee.

"Aye, a three-fer!"

Moments later Samuel could see the three lobsters crawling around the bottom of the trap, two regulation-sized and one large one, almost double the size of the others.

The pair worked together to pull the long wooden trap over the side of the dory. Lengthwise, the trap was nearly bigger than Samuel. A solid wood sheet served as the bottom with runs of wood rods in an arch shape making a little lobster house. Inside, the three lobsters tried to cling to the slats before tumbling over one another as the pair hauled the trap over the edge. On either end, a cone-shaped metal netting with a hole in the bottom allowed for the creatures to enter, but not leave. They had not the wits to figure that out.

"Well, would'ya look at that, my boy. That th'er beast might be the catch of the night!" his father said, patting him on his shoulder. "Not bad for your first haul, eh?"

Samuel nodded silently and watched the lobsters squirm back to their legs after all the commotion. The two smaller ones were green with specks of brown scattered across their boney shells. They quickly cowered away from the big one with a brown and bluish color to its shell.

"Right, that should do it for the night, what do you say?" his father said after securing the trap in the middle of the dory.

"Fine by me, though I can go longer, if need be," Samuel replied.

"That's good. I like ye'r spirit, but we don't want to burn you out just yet. Many years of salt and spray to go," his father paused and looked back towards the shore. The run of land looked small in the fading light from their position in the deep waters an hour away. His father continued, "Besides, ye'r mother will have those pots a-boiling for our return and then we can get to cannin' these fell'ers right up! Lobsters green in the sea, red in the pot, and black in the can, that's what Gramps would always say."

"I wish Gramps was here," replied Samuel.

His father squeezed his shoulder with his large hands made strong from building and hulling. "Old Willie would have loved to have been out on your first hull. He was never the same after he came back from the sea for the last time."

Samuel still remembered that day, a few summers before. Gramps had come home raving about a phantom schooner that he thought could be *The Flying Dutchman* herself. Of course, no one believed him; and, father thought it best that Gramps not return to sea. For the rest of his days, he sat on the front porch in his old wooden rocking chair telling anyone who would listen his tall tales and adventures out there. He enjoyed the telling, but he loved the sea more. The thought of being landlocked made those last couple of years not worth a penny to him.

With the setting of the sun, Samuel's father lit an oil lamp and hung it on the mast pole at the center of the dory. He then pulled up two large oars to begin their journey home to Prospect Harbor. Samuel remained at the bow to look out for any stray rocks or debris that might cross their way.

On watch, nightfall made it difficult to see much across the waters. Thankfully, tonight, the sea's surface was smooth as glass and the Prospect Harbor Lighthouse was bright in the distance, guiding them home with a flashing yellow light. Sometimes a fog would roll in from the neighboring coves and block any sign of the safe harbor. Those were the times, his father would say, that would test your skill as a man of the sea.

Watching was an easy task and allowed for thinking. He thought of the return home and the work that still needed to be done. When they got back there would be cooking and canning to do. It had been the only job he could help with for so many years and he did not look forward to it after the long day. It was dull work to boil them all, clean them, and then stuff them into a small can filled with sea brine and sealed with a band of solder. Unlike many fishermen, his father rather can himself than go to the local cannery. They were lucky to get fifty-cents per one hundred cans on their own and maybe thirty-five cents from the cannery. It would be early in the morning before it was all done.

The journey home would be a little reprieve from work. Samuel liked to look at the sky at night in times like these. It helped to distract his thoughts. The sea of stars above the world fascinated him. He wondered what they were, where they were, and if anyone could ever get to them. *Could they move?* Some did, surely, he had seen them streak across the night sky on occasion. *Did the people hungry for lobster meat down south see the same stars?* he wondered. All fine questions, that no one ever seemed to have answers for. He had asked Gramps many a time and he always responded with a story that never really got to the question.

There would be no stargazing tonight, however. Grey clouds blanketed the sky, blocking even the faintest twinkle of starlight. The only light amidst the dark sea was from Prospect Light. The lighthouse's bright yellow beacon could be seen for miles as it flashed round-and-round. Samuel could see the yellow light glinting off the smooth water of the bay as they passed the bare rocky outcrop known as Big Black Ledge. Looking for any hint of rock in the passing light, he thought fondly of Prospect Lighthouse. The lighthouse was located on Prospect Point about a few miles from home on the other side of the bay. It was too far to walk normally, but his father and Gramps had taken him there by boat a few times to see it. He remembered how small he felt standing under the tower; it was the tallest structure he had ever seen and bigger than any tree. The tower was rounded with a black lantern house that looked like a larger version of the lantern his father carried with him to sea. But it was the glass that surrounded the light in the inside that struck him the most. It looked like a giant glass eye with all its stepped ridges that were pieced together in a metal housing. Now, that eye of light was guiding them home.

The beam flashed by again and Samuel noticed a jut of land off the starboard side. He could tell that it was a landmass because it was dark and unmoving.

"Is that Cranberry Point?" he asked.

"Aye...we are almost...home my boy," his father said in between strokes of the oars.

Everything seemed to look and sound different on the sea at night—especially one as calm and still as this. Samuel could hear the waves lapping against the hull as his father slowly rowed them closer to the shore that was growing bigger by the minute. By day, the waves would be crashing heavy against the dory's bow and a chorus of gulls would be mewing high up in the air. A salty breeze would also be stinging your face if you stood too high above the water's surface. There was none of that now; the waters were smooth and reflective with only the movement of the dory creating any sense of air.

Then, a flash of light caught his attention out of the corner of his eye. He turned from his watchful post ahead to look back beyond the stern. A few moments it came again, the flash lit up within a bellowing cloud that was drifting above the waters far out to sea. A few moments later a stiff wind blew through from the same direction, strong enough to blow out their lantern.

His father had noticed it too. "Looks like a storm rolling in. Good thing we packed'er in early tonight, eh?" he said, picking up some speed to his rowing. "Don't ye worry about the lamp, we're close enough that the harbor light will guide us in."

Samuel did not hazard a response. His eyes stayed transfixed to the storm clouds out beyond the calm waters of the bay. He thought he had seen something, if only for a second. In the storm's belly of lightening and shadow, he thought he had seen the outline of a three-masted ship appeared on the sea's surface, a schooner. It was a fleeting glimpse, as quick as thunderbolt, and it was gone.

There was little time to ponder over the sight before another light appeared in the corner of his eye. This light was not lightening, for it did not disappear after flashing. It came from the bow side of the dory about a few hundred yards away. Samuel turned back to face towards the harbor. At first, he thought it had been Prospect Light that had caught his eye, but the lighthouse's light was still staying true to its predictable flashes. It was then he noticed the glow. It came not from the sky or the lighthouse, but the from beneath the sea. Out in front of the dory, an area of the sea about half the width of the bay was lighting up beneath the surface of the waves.

"Father, look!" he cried.

His father turned to look over his shoulder and instantly stopped his rowing. In the glowing blue sea light, he could see his father's eyes bulge and mouth go agape. It was an expression he had never seen the seasoned old man make.

"Sam...muel," his father stammered as he blindly tried to find one of the oars again. "We...we need to get to shore. Do you see a way around?"

That massive glowing light under the waters took up most of the harbor and Samuel could not find a way around without going back out at sea.

"I can't see any way around it, unless we go back out of the harbor," Samuel reported, not turning away from the glow ahead.

"That will not do, son. The storm will be upon us soon. We'll have to try our luck to quickly cross into the harbor," his father said, his voice soft and shaking. The man grabbed the two oars tightly and began to row with great haste.

Samuel continued to watch at the bow. The glow actually made it easier to see stray rocks in the bay. Yet, something was changing within the light; the amorphous glow seemed to separate into a series of smaller lights. First four, then sixteen, then more than he could count, until he realized what the little lights were. They were stars, stars beneath the sea!

Samuel looked to the night sky once more to find that it was as cloudy as it had been before. That proved that the starlight was no mere reflection; somehow, in some way, a field of stars had appeared beneath a portion of Prospect Bay. Oh, and it was a beautiful sight to behold. The starscape had the same clarity of a clear night sky, only now, *below* the waves. There were stars of white, blue, red, and yellow shades he had never seen before against a backdrop of the deepest black. A multitude of them blanketed beneath the waves in a circular pattern that began to blur reddish-white towards the edges. In the middle, there was a small area that was difficult to make out, like looking through the bottom of a cloudy glass bottle. The waters above this area seemed to circle it in a lazy spiral motion.

His father's yell, jerked back his awe and wonder.

"Samuel, look son, Prospect Light! She's gone red!"

Samuel looked out across the harbor to the lighthouse. The light had indeed changed from its once warm yellow glow to an eerie blood crimson. It was also no longer flashing as it had stopped in motion. The light beam remained fixed along the path of their dory with the sea of stars in between. It was then that Samuel noticed that the turning waters were quickening. The gentle turning had fallen into a tight whirl that was expanding rapidly. At the center, the twisting water dropped out into a dark space beneath the surface. He did not have to think long to know that a maelstrom had formed, a danger to any small craft such as their dory.

Samuel turned back to his father to see that he had stopped rowing and was now facing the light and forming maelstrom.

"What do you think it means, father?" Samuel asked, his voice cracking.

"It means our luck may be running out," his father replied, solemnly.

~*~*~*~

"Sir, there is an anomaly ahead in our sector. Looks like a Class III hole."

"Class III, are you sure?" the captain replied, rubbing his chin.

The first mate examined her screen carefully again for a few moments.

"Yes, I can confirm it is of Class III origin with a bi-directional gravity well."

"Can you put the relevant data on screen?" the captain replied.

"I can," replied the first mate. Her hands immediately went into a flurry of button presses on her terminal screen.

The captain leaned forward from his chair at the center of the observation deck waiting for the large observation window to show him what was out there in the void of space. He knew natural wormholes were to be avoided. So unpredictable in their formation and dissolution, there was no telling where or even when you might end up—that is if you were lucky enough to survive the tidal forces. As the captain of the United Colony Space Freighter, *The Vengeful Dutchman* for the past twenty years, it was a phenomenon he had never encountered. Even with his experience and a supercomputer at his command, it was not something he would trifle with lightly.

"The relevant data should be at your disposal now, sir."

"Thank you, Mendez."

The large observation window at the bow end of the deck lit up with the telemetry of *The Vengeful Dutchman* and the anomaly ahead marked as a series of concentric flashing red circles. The hole was located two-thousand kilometers in the center of their path. Judging by their current speed, they would reach the hole in a matter of minutes.

"Am I reading this right, Mendez, that it is a Class III-B?" the captain yelled over his shoulder.

"Yes sir, it looks to be about eight-hundred meters in diameter," first mate Mendez responded.

It had been a while, but the description of the anomaly jolted the captain's memory of his training on wormholes or holes as they said in the trade. Wormholes, he recalled, were classified by their size and characteristics using numerals and letters, respectively. A Class I hole was one that directed away from the observer in a single direction. A Class II hole was one that directed towards the observer in a single direction and a Class III hole was bi-directional. The sizing part was a little easier to remember. An 'A' stood for micro which was less than a meter in diameter; 'Bs' were meters across; 'Cs' were kilometers across; and 'Ds' were a gigameter and above—never documented and probably for good reason given the immense gravity they would give off if encountered. The captain examined their path several times in reference to the Class III-B hole. It was big enough for their ship to fit through, but perhaps not large enough to prevent evasion.

"Is there time to change course?" the captain asked, clinching his right fist on the metallic arm of the captain's chair.

"I think so, but it will be a close one, sir," said Mendez.

"Do it now," the captain barked the order over to his chief engineer, Smyth.

"Already on it, sir," said Smyth.

"We don't want to turn out like the *Damocles*, they learned about holes the hard way."

"The *Damocles*, sir?" asked a young crewman, Barnes, from the life support station.

"You have never heard of the *Damocles*?" The captain sat back up in his seat. "She was talked about much in my training years. Way back in 2123, on her maiden voyage from Io, the crew of the *Damocles* encountered a Class III-C wormhole, similar to this one. Back then sensors were not as advanced and they did not notice until they were already trapped in its gravity well. Then, they disappeared without any further signal or a trace. No one heard a thing from the *Damocles* for fifty years; it was not until 2174 that a mapping probe identified the *Damocles* near Venus."

"That's disturbing, everyone you knew would be gone or would have changed so much in your absence," said Smyth.

"Can you imagine someone coming to 2258 from fifty years ago? They wouldn't recognize a thing," added Barnes. "Sir, is that what happened to the *Icarus of the New Dawn*?"

"Ah, so I see you have heard of the *Icarus*," said the captain, turning back to the observation window. "To this day, no one knows what happened to her. She disappeared after going beyond the rim of the Oort cloud on an exploration mission to find a safe path to Alpha Centauri. There was never even a distress signal from the *Icarus*, she simply vanished from existence. Maybe she too fell into some hole and will reappear somewhere someday. Only time tells such things."

The captain got up out of his chair to walk over to the observation window. Of course, he could have had the image magnified but felt more in control on his feet.

"Can I get an optical visual of the anomaly?" he requested.

"Yes, sir," replied one of the crew members, he was already lost in thought to care which one.

The cycling data and telemetry of the map quickly faded from the window until only its translucent base was left revealing the sea of blackness outside the ship. The captain stared out into the vastness of space. Like their forebearers, they were in a vast sea, a sea of stars, he mused to himself. Even with all their fancy technology, the maps were still incomplete in certain sectors of the solar system and beyond; no man or machine knew what monsters lurked at the blank edges of known space. Near the edges, he imagined it was like being on the deck of one of those ancient wooden ships on an unexplored ocean hoping you did not fall off the side of the world.

The anomaly was not too difficult to find. Far out into space, a small circular portion of the stars flickered red. The disturbance of light was no doubt a result of gravitational forces from the hole causing a redshift in passing starlight. It still looked a long distance away, but the *Vengeful Dutchman* was approaching at great speed. They had already approached close enough to see a dark blue void at the center of the anomaly. The thrusters did not seem to be doing enough.

"Mendez! Are the forward and aft thrusters at one-hundred percent?" cried the captain over his shoulder.

"Sir, they are at the nominal limits; if I push them much further, they may burn up."

"Make it so, Mendez."

The entire bridge jolted as the additional energy of acceleration was applied to the starboard side of the ship. It lasted for a few moments before another jolt came, much bigger than the first.

"Was that…"

"Yes, sir, the thrusters are spent. It will take a repair in dry dock to fix what's left of them," said Mendez, who began stroking her eyebrow as she stooped towards her terminal that was flashing a field of its own flashing red lights.

"Okay, now what's our telemetry? Tell me we have done enough to avoid the anomaly." The captain began to pace in front of the observation window. He almost tripped over his own feet as he turned from starboard to port and back again.

"Stand by captain, the data is coming in…" Mendez paused. The screen refreshed and the dotted line that marked their course still terminated in the center of the flashing red concentric circles. "Ah, captain…it seems like our course is unchanged. We are going to pass directly through the anomaly."

The captain stopped pacing and turned towards Mendez and the rest of the crew without saying a word. He scanned across the faces on the observation deck giving them a slow, acknowledging nod. The crew on deck remained deathly silent as the realization washed over them that they were now all without control. No technology or calculation could save them as they were at the whims of their current vector towards an unknown destination— out of space and time.

The captain gripped his hands firmly at his side and walked back to his chair with head held high for the crew. But before he could make it, First Mate Mendez cried out again.

"Captain, there is something else."

"What is it, Mendez?"

"Captain, according to the scanners, I am detecting objects being ejected from the hole. And some of them are coming our way."

"Can you identify what they are and their velocity?" asked the captain whose voice sounded like it had taken on another burden of stone.

"Good news is, they appear to be chunks of ice that are floating at a low relative velocity and should not damage our hull and…strange…"

"Mendez?"

"Sir, if I am reading this correctly, it appears near the hole's horizon that the objects are not ice, but still in a liquid state."

"Water?"

"Yes, water is spouting from the hole and quickly turning to ice and vapor in the void. The objects should be visible soon."

A few moments passed before the tiny objects of various jagged shapes emerged outside the observation window. They appeared as iridescent shades of blue and white in the forward lights of the freighter. Most were no larger than a fist, but others had clumped together from the spray into blocks of ice as large as the observation deck herself. Soon they were pelleting against the hull of the bow creating a cacophony of jumbled sound. On the observation window, the pieces of ice shattered into small fragments as they made impact.

The captain climbed up into the chair and clinched the arm rests tightly as they fell towards the anomaly that appeared larger by the second. The wormhole now almost filled the entire observation window. The distortion bubble bent and curved the field of stars behind it into a circular shape. The glow of the stars was now an intense color of red that slowly dissipated to the cool whites and blues at the edges of the hole. The center of the hole was a dark blue mass with a stream of water in various states of liquid, gas, and solidification surging from one side. It would have been a beautiful geyser to behold if it did not harken to their potential imminent demise.

Another series of ice chunks broke apart against the window. This time, one revealed an object inside, a strange clawed creature with an orange finned tail.

"What strange place are we falling into?" said the captain under mumbled breaths.

~*~*~*~

The dory was beginning to pick up speed as it approached the outer arms of the twisting maelstrom. The once gentle approach was now quickening with the rushing waters. On the other side of the maelstrom, a gushing geyser of water had pushed its way to the surface of almost equal size. It bubbled up into the air and fell back to the surface through the blood-red beam of Prospect Light. Samuel and his father had each taken an oar to fight against the current, but their combined strength had made little difference.

"Son, I don't see us fighting this torrent. She's too much for us," his said somberly.

Samuel looked up into his father's eyes. They no longer looked as wide and open as they had before. They were somehow distant now, sunken with resignation from the extraordinary sights around them.

"What should we do, father?"

"Beyond praying I don—" something had interrupted the seaman's thought. Samuel watched as his father's eyes narrowed on a point out across the water. When he looked sure of what he saw he spoke again, this time with renewed determination.

"Do you see it, son? There!" he said, leaning next to Samuel and stretching a pointed finger towards the northern shore. At the very outside edge of the starlit maelstrom, an area looked to be disrupted by the waves. It was a tiny rocky outcropping no bigger than a bed jutting out of the water. The waves crashed against the crag in a white mess of spray and foam.

"I see it!" Samuel shouted.

"She looks mighty firm. Maybe we make for her before we go asunder."

Samuel nodded and grabbed his oar again and began to paddle towards the rock near the northern shore. Instantly, his father put his large hands over his son's hands to stop.

"No, son. We aren't going to fight this whirl. See? She is going like a clock, she is. If we fight her, we will fall right in." His father then pointed from the crag in a curved motion towards the southern shore before coming back around to the crag from the other side of the maelstrom. "We're going to ride'er that way until she spits us out right where we need to be."

With a new course plotted, the pair grabbed both oars firmly, prepared for their biggest test from the sea. Samuel's father jammed his oar firmly into the gentle waters on the port side and steered them into the twirling current. The rushing waters grabbed the dory and launched it headlong towards the southern shore. They each paddled with what strength they had left to try and stay on the outer edges of the whirl. White water splashed up over the sides of the dory as they carved through the water. The lobsters squirmed against their cage as the sea spray rained down on them from their place on bottom boards.

On the starboard side, Samuel looked down as he paddled feverishly to see the dory rushing across the stars below. He never imagined that he would sail amongst the stars like the three brothers in their wooden shoe. The starlight blurred to a solid glow in the rushing white water closer to the center. Beyond that, the waters simply fell into some black abyss at the bottom of the sea.

As they were making the turn from the harbor side, his father shouted to him, "Samuel, give me your oar and get to the bow!"

Samuel did what he was told and carefully crept up to the front of the dory. The wooden boat rocked violently back-and-forth in the angry sea. When he finally made it, his father yelled out to him.

"Can ye see de rock?" the question came jumbled against the roar of the water.

Samuel peered over the soaked bow as they continued to curve around the whirl. His eyes took a few moments to adjust to the disorienting movement but soon found what they had seen from the other side.

"I see it father! It is coming fast!" Samuel cried out.

"Garb de oop," said his father. In the deafening rush of water, he could not make anything out.

"What did you say?" Samuel yelled with urgency.

"Grab…the…orp," came the message still garbled by the sea.

The dory was now moments away from passing near the rock. "Grab what?" he said once more turning to his father for instruction. This time his father pointed to the coil of rope attached to the lobster trap between his father's feet. He then made a motion for him to take the rope and jump to the rock as they made their pass.

Samuel's face slackened at the realization of what he needed to do. But there was no time to think. Samuel took the rope in his right hand and crouched up on the furthest point of the bow. His legs shook in unsteadily rhythms as the dory bounced ever-closer to the rock that was now mere yards away. He could see that their efforts had come up somewhat short as the dory would pass with about eight feet distance from the only solid piece of ground in the churning sea.

Here it comes, Samuel thought, tightening his legs like a coiled chair spring.

The black rock stood a mere three feet above the rushing waters. Large waves splashed over it covering it in a drizzle of foam that retreated through a maze of cracks and pointy crevasses back to the sea.

Almost there.

The rocky crag was now pulling from the front of the bow to along the portside of the dory. He could almost make the jump now.

Just a little bit closer.

Then, before the rock became completely parallel with the dory, Samuel leaped out towards the rock with all the force he could muster. He hit the side of the rock with a hard thud. The sharp edges dug deep into his exposed arms but it was not the cuts and scrapes that alarmed him. A wetness could be felt up to the knees as he clung there half in the whirl of water.

"Samuel!" he heard his father cry pass behind him, more distant than he would have expected after only a few moments. He needed to hurry up the rock as his hand still clung tightly about the tether of rope. He lifted his free hand to find a secure hold and pull up enough to get his legs out of the water that was dragging them sideward. Once free from the water, his feet quickly found their footing and he scampered up on top of the rocky crag as fast as he could, staying crouched so not to fall over in the gale of salty spray. At the top, he stayed on his knees that ached upon the sharp jags that had been carved into the rock from centuries of sea wash. It was the first moment he noticed the red trickles of blood running down each side of his arms.

No time to lick wounds. Now where is father?

Before he could turn around, a jolt hit the line almost jumping it out of his hand. Instinctively, he grabbed above it with his other hand that was now free from climbing. With his grip assured, he turned his cold and soakened body into a seated position towards the maelstrom. Samuel traced the line out across the rush of glowing waters fearful of what remained at the other end. The line had unraveled to its full length and he could see the little dory about a quarter of the way around the whirl. Any further and the line would have stretched directly over the black eye of the maelstrom. Father was still onboard.

"Father!" he cried as loud as he could, but there was no response. His voice fell into the whirl like everything else.

Samuel squinted trying to see anything aboard the dory that looked so small in the distance. His father made no motion towards him. Having abandoned his oars, his father was hunched over in the dory, clinging to what must be the lobster trap that anchored the line at the other end.

"Hand-over-hand," he whispered to himself. He began to pull the stiff rope with all his strength. The weight on the other end felt like a dozen horses, with the current pushing fiercely against the stern of the dory. But the line was moving, he could see the dory getting closer with every couple of pulls. Water crashed over the dory's stern as it pulled against the twirling current. If the sides had been any shallower, the dory would have surely flooded and sunk into the center of the whirl.

One hand over the other, slowly but surely.

A few minutes passed and Samuel had managed to pull his father across the whirl to a distance of only a few dory-lengths. He could see him more clearly now. His father's face was strained, but his eyes seem to gleam in the glowing waters as he stared up at Samuel. It was a quiet look of pride. A look that filled Samuel with all the strength he needed for the final set of pulls.

Almost there.

Then, Samuel noticed that his father's eyes darted off of him downward to the stern. The eyes quickly widened into big saucers that filled up brightly with wet light. Samuel followed the gaze and saw what had caught every ounce of his father's attention amidst the chaos. Several frayed pieces of rope had sprung out where it had been rubbing back and forth against the edge of the stern. Only a few slender tendrils of rope remained. The years of salt, cold, and sea had weakened it and under this strain—

SNAP!

Before Samuel could even blink, the rope had snapped apart. It seemed to hang there for a few moments in the air like a waving ribbon before falling uselessly beneath the waters. Samuel looked beyond the severed end to see that the dory was no longer there. It had already been swept away to the other side of the whirl. The dory rocked and dipped closer towards the center as it was being spun around in the rushing torrent. Soon, it was nearing Samuel's side again, this time almost fifty feet away and further down into the water. As it was passing, he could see his father had sat back up into a seated position, his hands on his thighs ready to row without oars. Samuel lifted up his hand out in front of him trying to catch his father's attention—the other end of the rope still nestled in between his thumb and fingers. It was the only thing he thought to do as words would not carry.

In the flashes of moments, his father turned his head slowly towards Samuel. His face was calm and resigned; his eyes big and full. Near the last moment, he yelled out across the waters, "You dun good, son!" At least that is what he thought he heard.

And after that, the little dory fell down another step into the whirl below Samuel's sightline and then it disappeared down into the center darkness.

His father was gone.

For what seemed like minutes after, he sat crying on the rock amongst the starlight and roar of water. He only stopped when noticing the lights had started to fade in the sea. In a manner of moments, all traces of the stars had vanished. The churning waters slowed to a stop until the they became smooth as dark glass once more. Then, the familiar flash of Prospect Light scattered into a hundred sparkles of his tear-lined eyes. A yellow light once more.

Hours passed before help finally arrived from the lighthouse keeper. He, too, had seen the lights beneath the waves but never mentioned any trace of the dory or his father. Samuel climbed into the old light keep's boat and looked up at the sky. It was clear and full of morning stars.

Somewhere, up there, father is sailing across them in the dory.

~*~*~*~

"How much time until contact?" asked the captain.

First Mate Mendez examined her terminal that flashed an ever-decreasing series of numbers.

"Only a minute or so now," she replied.

The *Vengeful Dutchman's* approach to the wormhole had entered its final stages. The ship was close enough now to be splattered with a mix of boiling water vapor and semi-formed streams of ice. Most of the crew on the observation deck had left their stations to gaze upon the anomaly while others remained hunched over, preparing for the final moments.

"Captain!" Mendez shouted abruptly. The cry interrupted the solemn stillness on deck.

"What is it, Mendez? Do we have thruster control again?"

"No, but there is something else I am detecting on the scanner. It's...how can that be..." Mendez paused briefly. "The scanner is showing a life sign, a human one, coming through the hole. The person is about one-hundred meters from exiting into vacuum."

"Can we catch them?" the captain said on impulse.

"On it, captain," cried the extravehicular activity officer.

"Send it as fast as you can!" replied the captain turning to the observation window.

A few moments later a silver line jutted out from below the observation deck towards the figure that looked like a tiny shadow in the mouth of the hole. Two large metallic petals in cup-like shapes were opened at the end of the line. Once it had reached the figure, the cupped petals closed around their target in a bust of white protective foam.

"We have them, captain," said the EVA officer.

"Good, pull them in before we enter the hole," replied the captain.

"Sir, there is something else coming," said the first mate.

"What? More people or strange creatures?"

"No, not a lifeform, but some sort of wooden structure. I will highlight and magnify on the window."

The observation window zoomed in on a small wooden object that had recently been expelled from the hole. It was shaped like a crescent moon with bits of stringy cord hovering all about it.

"By the stars, it's a boat!" cried the captain.

Suddenly, the stream of water exiting the hole stopped. The hole began to shrink in front of the ship until there was nothing but a backdrop of twinkling stars.

"The hole, captain, it has completely collapsed. We missed it by two-hundred meters!" announced Mendez.

The crew cried out in joy. Members at adjacent stations embraced each other with hugs and slaps of the hands.

"Sir, the computer has identified that wooden object as a small draft boat called a dory. And captain...it dates to the late nineteenth century of Earth!"

"What strange time and place has our person of the hole come from?" the captain pondered. "What is their status, Jenkins?"

"The subject is alive and secured onboard, sir. From our sensor readings, he is a forty-year-old man in strange clothing of woven fabric. At the moment, he remains unconscious, but should wake soon."

The captain slumped into his chair and leaned back at ease. "The man certainly is going to wake up to a very strange story to be told."

The Lonely Tower

The midday sun struggled to pierce the dense tree canopy as a group of six men came upon a U-shaped bend on the hiking trail. It had been nearly three hours since they had set out to hike in the Emmendingen region of The Black Forest. A group of college friends, they had made the trip to Germany for spring break, the last break before their study abroad experience came to a close. Soon, they would all have to return to Luxembourg for finals and then, a trip back to the mundane small-town campus in the Midwestern United States. It was at the bend that the hiker bringing up the rear had just noticed an overgrown path heading up hill towards the ridge on their right.

"Hey, guys, look at that," he said, his arm outstretched and pointing off the path into the woods. "It looks like an old trail."

The group huddled around Eddy, the scrawny English-lit major with turtle-shell glasses that were a tad too big for his pale face. It took a few moments for the rest of them to discern what exactly he was pointing to before they saw the worn ground winding through the undergrowth. There was a sort of path made up of dirt and smooth stones. It was not much more than a deer path at first glance, but it was there. It coiled through a bramble of sticker bushes and thick vines that had weaved their way around neighboring saplings. The small trees were already struggling to grow beneath the tall old-growth trees that towered over everything else.

"Maybe we should check it out. What do you say, boys? One last good European adventure before we go back," said Harrison whose dark hair nearly matched his leather jacket.

"I dunno...I don't see it on the trail map," said Dwayne. He had been the one leading in gym shorts, sneakers, and a reversed Bulls ball cap.

"Your German reading has been horrible the whole trip. Unless the trail is called *bier* or *fräulein*, you would't know where we are," said the shorter, blonde-haired man, named Tim, who was outfitted in proper hiking attire. He grabbed the map and studied it intently.

"Yes, you see here..."

The group huddled around the map. They followed Tim's finger to its tip that ended on a U-shaped turn of a winding line that led back to the trail head where they had started off. It was plain to see that no other trail intersected the one they were on for many kilometers to either side of the bend they were on. The whole area was a splotch of solid green, that, according to the legend, marked a wilderness area.

"There is no other trail here. Even that little stream crossing over the unmarked trail is nowhere on the map. We should keep go—"

A shout down the unmarked path interrupted the map reading.

"I found something!" shouted Eddy from behind a thick tangle of bushes. He emerged from the mystery trail with two cuts on his cheek and, in his right hand, a dripping plastic bag. Inside looked to be a tiny leather-bound journal.

"What in the world is that?" cried Kyle in his navy-blue shirt that simply said 'college' in big block letters alongside his fraternity letters.

"I don't know, but let's find out," replied Eddy. His glasses had fogged up slightly from running. He walked over to the group so that they could see the small leather journal that had been well-preserved in its plastic bag. There were little signs of damage to the bag making it difficult to say how long it had been out there—though the leather looked old and handcrafted.

"Where did you find that?" asked the smallest in the group, who was wrapped tightly in a red windbreaker.

"I don't know Josh, it was just lying beside a rock in that stream, not far down that path. I was just curious to see if I could see more of where the path went when I came upon the stream and saw light flickering off the plastic next to a large stone. I knew instantly it seemed out of place."

"Well, open the thing up," Dwayne insisted.

"Okay, then."

Eddy opened the seal to the plastic bag with great care and pulled out the leather book. Outside the protective enclosure, the book did look old. The leather was worn and supple with bits of sinew fraying around the edges of the binding. Carefully bending the cover back, the insides revealed a hastily written script on old parchment paper that had yellowed from many years of exposure. The writing was in English in a blue ink that looked much more recent than the paper it was written on.

The group scanned the first few lines as Eddy, wiping his glasses to see more clearly, began to read the text. It seemed to be an account of another hiker who, judging by the date written, had passed this way only two weeks before.

20 April 2008

If you are reading this, please help me. There isn't time to figure out how to write this all out in German, so hopefully this gets in the hands of someone who can read this hastily written note. My situation is not yet dire, but I am completely lost out here and scared out of my mind of something just over the ridge. I will explain what I can to get your help and I will try to be brief, as the light is dimming with each word I scribble on this old paper.

Yesterday morning, I set forth alone at the Kostgefäll trailhead for a ten-kilometer hike with a ten-pound pack on my back and a compass. It had always been a dream of mine to backpack Europe.

Between an aggressive school schedule and working during the summers to pay for school, there really was never any time or much money to do such things. I guess it was in envy of my rich friends who came from fancy boarding schools and traveled the world with their parents that set me off on this trip after saving up for years. They had that 'old-world' money you could say. I just wanted to see a piece of it. If it hadn't been for my fiancée, this trip would never have happened.

On the trail, the forest was absolutely beautiful; the moss on the trees, the birds chirping, the stone bridges over rushing brooks—it was something out of a story book. There were many moments where I had to stop to sit on a moss-covered log and listen to the calming rhythm of the forest. After two hours into the hike, the trees began to get bigger and closer together. The canopy grew so dense that the light of the midday sun became so faint that certain sections looked like night. This was what I had been craving to see, truly *Schwarzwald*. However, it was not until I came to a sharp U-shaped turn that I noticed something peculiar. At first, I heard water running and looked at my map for the stream. It wasn't marked. The bend in the trail was there, that was easy to identify, but everything else around me was blank on the map. Besides some crude elevation lines, the area was a green blackhole of wilderness.

Telling it back now, it was against good judgment to veer off the trail to find the source of water. The foliage was thick, making it hard to see my way forward. The sound of bubbling water was my only guide and it seemed, in places, that an old trail had once been there as my steps crossed over worn stones that were too evenly placed to be natural. When I finally came upon the water, I almost slipped and fell face first. If it were not for a small sapling, this story would have ended there and you would have nothing to read.

But I did not fall. I grabbed onto the small tree at the last moment and avoided hitting my head on a huge slab of rusty-brown rock. Rushing over it, was the source of the bubbling sounds. The stream water appeared as melted glass as it smoothly ran across the slab of rock at around two-inches deep. Just beneath the surface were several feathery green strands of algae being swept to their full length by the rushing current. The stream went on down over a small drop into a round pool before going off around a rocky bend. On the other side, the path continued onward up the hill.

I do not know what was in my head to keep going but my curiosity pulled me across the water. Hopping from moss-covered boulder to the next, I reached the other side without getting my boots wet and continued on. The path on the other side was much more defined than near the beginning. Little round cobble-like stones littered the path as it steadily meandered up a hill. It was not until reaching a series of stone steps that I began to feel like the way had been constructed into the landscape. The steps began about a football field's length beyond the stream where the path rose sharply up the slope. Each step was made of a smooth grey stone about an arm's length wide and a two-feet deep. Bits of dark brown dirt, dried leaves, and twigs were scattered across the surface of the treads. On one side of the rising steps, the ground fell down into a gully. While on the other, the upslope was covered in moss-covered outcroppings. All around, old trees towered in clusters as close as a few yards. High up in their branches the scampering of woodland creatures could be heard out of view. Every so often, a little grey squirrel would climb down to a lower limb looking rather disinterested in me below.

Upon a long examination, it seemed that the steps were the only way up. So, I climbed each step; losing count after seventy-five. They just kept climbing, and climbing, up the hill. Until eventually, I had reached the crest of a ridge where I was met by a cool gust of air. For the first time in hours, I could see the sun which had not fallen as low as expected given the dim light between the trees. The amber rays spread out over a green sea of treetops that surrounded me on all sides. The trees I had just walked through still looked giant even from my high vantage. Their large limbs and countless leaves obscured any hint at the forest floor or trail below. The greenery went on-and-on in all visible directions; there weren't any signs of the small towns and mills that I had driven past on my way to get here.

At the top of the ridge, the trees were much smaller; their roots could not dig as deep in the rocky soil like the ones below. But the smaller trees did allow me to see that the ridge wrapped around the skyline in a circular cone. In its center, sat a bowl-shaped dell no more than a mile across.

The path continued right down into the heart of the little hollow, over the ridge. It was thickly wooded with trees of girth larger than a car. Their branches were so intertwined that it was difficult to tell from which trunk they arose from and made the path like a dark tunnel. Going across the treetops, I searched to see any further indication of where the path might lead. My eyes stopped at the center of the bowl on something dark and smooth that contrasted with the woody branches and leaves. It was a perfectly cylindrical structure poking up above the treetops. Like the steps before, it stood out as being not natural to the forest. I knew, even from a distance, it was a tower…a very old tower.

The tower stood alone amidst the greenery. There were no other structures in sight. It was like it had fallen straight from the sky to land smack in the middle of this secluded dell high up in the forest.

The path heading down into the bowl seemed like it would reach the tower. Seeing that the light was fading, there seemed to be enough time to get a closer look and then get back to the main trail before it got too dark. Watching my steps more carefully this time, I descended down the path into the tunnel of trees.

It probably took forty minutes to reach the tower. The path was much more winding than could have been expected, almost like it curled into the center of the dell like a whirlpool. And the whole way, the atmosphere felt different. I never minded hiking alone, but in this place, something seemed off. The trees, the sky, the sounds…were out of order. It was what I didn't hear that scared me the most, besides a light breeze there were few sounds.

No birds chirping or singing, no scurrying creatures in the limbs of the trees…nothing…just a wooded tangle of trees. It was like the whole region was encased in a muffling silence. The entire place gave off a feeling of danger, as if the trees were holding its breath for what would come next.

I emerged into a circular clearing rather suddenly. The undergrowth had grown so contorted and thick that it was impossible to see the open space even a few yards away. The soft rays of sunlight didn't come into view until I had made a sharp turn around a woody row of bushes. It was the most uplifting sight to see. The open air and light felt liberating, like a weight had been lifted compared to the confining atmosphere before. Out in the clearing, my senses could finally stretch in all directions again. My sight could go unimpeded into the expansive sky above and to the strange tower that rose to meet it.

The tower stood in the middle of clearing. Nothing grew around it until you reached the forest edge about fifteen yards away. At the edges of the clearing, the dead (or dying) trees did their best to lean away from the structure. The soil looked like a fine grey dust of dirt and dark rock, sort of like obsidian but with an olive hue. The tower itself was tall, I would guess easily around two-hundred feet. So much so that, it easily dwarfed the surrounding trees. Like the fragments of rock scattered in the clearing, the tower seemed to be constructed of a dark-olive stone. There were no discernable lines or pieces where the stones seemed to fit together except for a few oval-shaped windows up along its sides. A weather-worn structure of greyed wood sat atop the tower and looked like it had been hacked on from a different design than the tower itself.

At this point, the late-afternoon light was straining to get over the surrounding ridge line. I would need to go soon but I found it difficult to leave the tower. Already coming so far, seeing it up close struck me with more questions. It tempted me to explore more, to find out who built it and what for. I didn't think it would take too much time to satisfy my curiosity before heading back. A quick walkthrough would be all I'd need.

So, I strolled around its base looking for some type of entrance. The dark stone was smooth on all sides with barely any nicks or blemishes. It gave off an emerald kind of shimmer in the light. Up close, there were still no signs of tooling or spaces in between the stones. I most have gone around three or four times trying to find an opening. There simply was not any one to be found at the base. The nearest opening, I could see was a window probably fifty feet above my head, very much out of reach.

It was time to give up at this point and I headed towards the tree line. About half way, I stopped upon hearing a peculiar sound. It sounded like a thud or a rattling sound under my feet. Looking down, there was just dirt. I stomped by right boot in the spot and the same hollow sound occurred. I stomped by boot three feet away and there was no sound, just solid earth. I fell to my hands and knees to unearth a small wooden door with metal cross-braces. There was no knob, but I did find a circular ring that allowed me to pull up the door out from a few inches of dirt that began to slid around me in a brown cloud. After the dust settled, I could see a dozen stone stairs, like the ones I saw before on the path, heading down into a tunnel. I poked my head in the hole and saw a tiny glimmer of light at the other end in the direction that looked to be beneath the tower. It was some sort of secret entrance. It did not seem to go too far, so I jumped down and walked to the other end.

The light at the other end came from one of the windows in the tower. The tunnel terminated inside the base of the structure and from there I could see up the length of the tower to the base of the wooden structure seen from the outside. The interior was dim and dusty. Without the carved windows, the place would have been completely dark. Like the outside, the walls were of the same dark-olive stone. They were covered in the decaying husks of old rotted vines and what looked like etchings. Getting closer, the etchings had a pattern of writing to them and went up as far as I could see upwards. The writings, appeared white as they had been etched straight into the stone. Though mostly worn, the etchings were of words I didn't recognize at first. They resembled German, but nothing I was familiar with. I thought it might be some form of old German until I realized they were all German names, pairs of names to be specific. The pairs of names were written on a straight line and were separated by a symbol that I had never seen before. It looked like two U's, one inverted, with their curves slightly overlapping one another to form an almond shape. At the time, it reminded me of etching names into a tree within a heart shape.

It was that thought that brought back the memory of Alicia, my fiancée. She died a month ago, now. This was to be our first trip as an engaged couple. We had been planning this trip for months until the hit and run accident took her away from me. It was the thought of her that prompted me to pull out my pocket knife to etch Alicia's name next to mine on an area of stone besides a vine. I added the weird U-symbols like everyone else had used to separate our names. I figured, at the time, something would stand as a marker to our trip, even if no one else would likely ever see it.

It was not long after that I noticed an outline of a small trapdoor in the wood platform high above my head—one last thing to explore. Getting up there was not an easy task. Many of the wood beams and planks that spiraled their way up the tower had fully or partially rotted away. In several places, only the broken off end of an eight-inch beam could be seen, still nestled in its carved-out hole in the stone. In these places, I had to hop across the gap and hope that the next stair up would support the end of my jump. It took some time, but eventually, I made it to the top of the stair. From there, I could see how far up I had come. The little circular pit with the tunnel was barely visible in the growing darkness. Only the top windows showed any rays of light.

I was just about to push up on the trap door when I heard a thud, followed by another, and another, in quick succession. The sound came above my head from the wood platform—it sounded like footsteps. That idea seemed absurd; clearly from the decay of the place, no one had been there in ages. I paused for several minutes and heard nothing more. Everything was quiet save for a rush of air coming down through the floorboards.

The trap door took most of my strength to throw open. It was even heavier than the door in the dirt. Despite their age, the wood planks were nearly four inches thick. When I finally could topple it over, the thud it made sounded like a gunshot in a tunnel. A huge plume of dust shook off the floorboards and rained down all around me. I could watch the particles stream down through the beams of sunlight, like tiny meteors, and then settled somewhere unseen below.

Once the dust had settled, I popped my head up through the opening. I emerged up in a small, square room. It was nothing like the stone part of the tower. Again, the architecture seemed hacked on with planks that ran vertically along the walls which were held together by crossing planks using big wooden dowels. The wood had all greyed from countless years of weathering. Cracks in the planks on the walls filtered in the red sunlight from outside. On the far wall, there was an opening that might have once been a window, paned with glass. The only other opening in the room was a hole in the center of the roof. It was small, about the size of a beach ball. I could not tell if it was put there by design or through natural decay.

I lifted myself into the room to get a better look. The room was mostly bare except for a small wooden table and a shelf that was barely clinging to the wall. Just below, there seemed to be other shelves lying in a heap on the floor. They were all covered in several inches of dust and dirt along with the fragments of several glass jars.

I first walked over to the table. It was missing one of its legs that must have been kicked off at some point in its life. On top of the table, there was two things that I noticed under a layer of more dust. The first was an old tarnished candle stick that could have been made of copper or brass. It still had about six inches of wax left. The second item was more interesting—a worn leather journal. I carefully lifted it up from the table and opened up the spine. The first several pages had been torn out. After delicately flipping through the rest, there was no signs of writing. The whole thing was completely blank. I closed the leather cover and examined it. The quality of the leather was good but very unrefined and scratched up in several places by what looked like fingernail marks that had clinched too tightly.

When I looked back down at the table, there was a noticeable rectangular spot where the journal had been resting in the dust. There was something else, too. Something etched into the table, a German phrase...

Unfortunately, as I write this now, I can't seem to remember what the words were. The words meant something about a warning or tradeoff...If it comes to me before I am finished writing this, I will add it at the end.

The window-like opening provided a lofty view of the surrounding bowl. It felt like being above a sea of green that stretched in all directions. In the distance I could barely make out the little path I had descended over the western ridge. If the tower had been a little higher, I may have been able to see over the surrounding ridge line where the sun had already sunk halfway below. Looking down, everything else was already cast in shadows. The last rays of sunlight in the whole area hit the top of the tower.

I checked my phone to find no reception. I knew immediately what that meant—I would have to stay the night. It was too dark to walk back at that point. It was difficult enough navigating the twisting path coming in. There was no reason to stumble around in the dark with unseen cliffs, caves, and possibly wolves about. There was no reason to risk it. It felt safe being high up in the tower above the treetops. As long as it did not topple over, I would be fine. It must have been pretty sturdy to stand for so long.

The night came quickly. I spent most of it staring out the window over the trees within the comforting light of the candle. Matches were a staple to my hiking gear; I'd never had to use them until then. The light wasn't much but provided some comfort. It quickly dissipated out the window into the darkness. Down below, you could hear the trees' dark branches clatter and shake in the wind. The forest sounds were no longer calming but menacing. Each new rustling or groaning of heavy branches had me on alert to search for the source of the sound. The wood structure of the tower creaked in the same fashion. In the stillness, the aching wood would buckle and pop, forcing me to step away from the window for a bit.

When I could build back my courage to look out once more, I watched the stars shining bright in the moonless sky. The mountaintop bowl must have been distantly removed from the nearby villages because I found little evidence of any light pollution beyond its edges. The expanse of the sky seemed so big up there. So close. As if anything could reach down and touch you from a galaxy away. That might sound romantic but, at the time, it was unnerving. It felt like being completely exposed under a microscope of some unseen eye.

That's when I noticed the hole. Not the one in the roof, but one that had appeared in the sky. The stars were brightly shining everywhere except for this one spot directly overhead. It was dark, the blackest black I have ever seen. So dark that the stars surrounding it appeared to dim to a pale white. The sight, silent and void of anything, it was hauntingly beautiful. But holes also lead to or from somewhere, their shadows obscuring the other side, and that made me retreat away from the window closer to the candle.

Once I stepped back to the center of the room, the light went out. A huge blast of cold air cascaded down upon my head in the dark room. I looked up and saw that I had ventured back underneath the hole in the ceiling…and sure enough…it was in alignment with the hole in the sky. I stared for minutes trying to see even a glint of light. My eyes felt like they were bulging from their sockets straining to pick up anything. It is hard to describe here; the blackness just went on forever.

It took a while before my skin began to shiver from the cold air. My legs felt frozen to the floor. I became so cold I wasn't sure I would be able to move. I could not stop staring. My eyes were frozen on the void, waiting for what, I wasn't sure. The cold air should have been my cue to run. Whenever does a cold chill signal something right or good?

I stared and stared for many minutes, maybe an hour…maybe more? There was no way to track time. I couldn't stop. I don't know if I could blink. My legs had lost all feeling from standing on end for so long.

At some point, the whispers came. The voice was in the cold air as if it was straining to come a great distance. The void above was vast enough. The sounds were soft at first, brushing by my ears like a cool breeze. They grew louder and more distinct as the air got colder and heavier. It was not long until I recognized it was saying *my name* in *my fiancée's* voice. As she was calling me, I could only stare deep into that dark hole. I could feel my eyes begin to twitch as they strained to pick up any piece of light or shape. Before seeing it, I knew I would see her face. I could feel her presence coming down upon me with each cold breath of air.

Next thing I remember, the hole in the roof began to glow a pale silvery white. Semi-translucent strands began to weave out from the edges of the wood roof in a spiral pattern. The tendrils gave off a muted light like tiny glowworms floating in air. An image was forming in the opening. When they all came together, there was Alicia's face.

Seeing Alicia's face again pounded my heart like a bass drum. To see it alive outside of photographs and old recordings moved me to my core. The image of her face was as it had been when I arrived to the scene of the accident in her last moments. A three-inch gash ran across her forehead exposing the contents of a shattered skull beneath. She was gasping for air then, trying to say my name but couldn't; the accident had done too much damage to her brain. Shaking, she kept trying to breathe and say my name with each precious breath.

Back then, she died at my side on an ambulance gurney. In this place, she could not stop gasping and saying my name. The cold air moved around me with each of her disembodied last breaths. The sweet experience of seeing her again quickly went bitter and cold. It was like our last moments were being played out on infinite repeat. It almost killed me to see it the first time, let alone again…and again…even if she was still alive in that moment. The last one we would ever have.

Terrified, I grabbed my bag, this journal, and bolted down into the winding stairway. The cold breath of air lapped at the back of my neck as I stumbled my way down in the dark belly of the tower. All around, the etched names and symbols glowed in the same pale light in contrast to the darkness. I could feel the power of their presence and knew then that they had brought my Alicia to me. Somehow writing the names in that dark stone could bring lost loved ones back from the void, but only as they were at an inch from death. No more, no less.

When I reached the bottom floor, I gave a brief look up to the platform above. Alicia's silvery face was still gasping out my name. There was something else too at the mouth of the trap door. I didn't stay long enough to get a good look, but from what I saw, it looked to be a long slender figure of shadow with no face, only a pair of pale glowing eyes. I kept going until I was halfway down the tunnel and stopped ready to run further at any sign of movement from the tower's base.

For hours, no movement came.

In that spot, I waited until the sun came up. Only when the warm light poured into the tunnel did I climb out and slam the door shut to keep anything from following. Wasting no time, I set out down the path I had come in on. It was twisty, like before, but took even longer this time as I couldn't help but look back every few steps to ensure some shadowy figure was not in pursuit. Eventually, I made it back to the ridge and could see the tower in the distance down in the bowl. It looked the same as it had been the day before, expect now, I couldn't shake the menacing feeling it harbored. In every shadow it cast I looked for those eyes or Alicia's tortured face.

With one last look at the tower, I stepped down on the other side of the ridge hoping to find the path that led me up here. I walked and walked, but had difficulty finding any trace of it. The trees were taller than ever, blanketing everything below in a deep shade. It was so dark in places I regretted not grabbing the candle stick too. The search went on for some time but there was no sign of any stone steps or dirt-covered ground to indicate the way I came in before.

After walking for a while, I headed back up to the ridge to get a better view. The only thing I could see up there was the tower standing like a black stake in the ground.

Again, I went back down the ridge determined to find my way back to the path. This time, I figured if I went straight down the hill, I would find something. Going this way down the hill I ended up at a stream. On the other side of it, the hill sloped back up in elevation. I went up this hill and climbed for a while until I came to another ridge. At least that's what I thought it was. When I cleared the top, there it was again...the tower. I had somehow come up on another ridge that surrounded the bowl.

On the next attempt, I followed the stream I had found at the bottom of the hill. It looked similar to the one I crossed the day before and so it might lead back to the path. I walked the stream in a circle around the hills until it suddenly disappeared into some underground cave no larger than a cereal box. I kept walking at the foot of the hills until I had circled around to find the stream again, emerging from a small waterfall that came out of a tiny crack in the hillside. At this location, I climbed up a ridge, and again, there was the tower.

In the opening at the top, I thought I saw a pair of pale white eyes flash out from the darkened porthole. I nearly fell down the hill trying to get out of sight of that dark place. I ran as fast as I could to get back to the stream.

At this point, I don't know what to do. I have circled and circled this place and have determined that the stream surrounds the circular ridge. And, every adjacent hill that surrounds the valley with the stream all lead back up to the area with the tower. That tower is the lone structure that is at the end of all directions away from it. No matter how far I walk, I always end up back in sight of it. It's like that the whole world wraps its way back to that point and I can't find a way out.

I won't get into any more details, as I have made many more attempts than I can count trying to find the right hill to escape this place. The light is getting low now and shadows are growing long again. I would like to get these notes out before nightfall. If you are reading this, please send for help, a helicopter, a large search party...anything to come get me. If you have already ventured onto the trail, don't go any further...and sure as hell do not go to that tower and write your name or anyone else's. There is some old-world magic in that stone that brings people back. But it's a cruel trick; a repetition of last moments and last breaths. A sight to drive you into madness. I fear it has already taken me there. I don't want to go back to the tower, but there seems to be no way out. I think whatever is back in that place is waiting for me now. Waiting for night to fall. Under these dark trees exposed seems even more frightening. I might need to go back. I know it's foolish, but maybe I can hold out until help arrives.

It is my only hope that you will find this journal soon. I am placing it in a plastic sandwich bag so the ink does not smear...I hope. I am going to place the bag in the stream I have found. It is the only thing connected to where I entered. I've tried following it down but it goes into a tight underground cave that I can't enter, but this bag will. I can only hope my message will find its way down, out of this place.

PLEASE HELP ME.

-David Poole

P.S. Oh, one last thing, I think I remembered the phrase carved into the table. It came to me as I was sealing the bag. The word seal remined me of 'seele' in the phrase which is: "eine seele bringen, eine seele nehmen." I think it means something bring something take. I left my translation book in the rental cottage and do not know what 'seele' means in German. If you find this, maybe you will have better luck.

Eddy flipped through the remaining pages of the journal. They were all blank. Everyone in the group looked at each other with blank expressions on their face. It took a few moments for words to finally come to the group when Tim broke the silence.

"Guys, I know what the phrase says. Roughly, it means 'to bring a soul, to take a soul,' I think."

The jaws of several of the hikers dropped instantly.

"Well, that does not sound like any place I want to get near," said Josh looking sternly down the path.

"We should call for help," said Eddy, pushing up his glasses that had fallen down his nose from sweat.

"No service," said Dwayne who was checking his phone.

"Then maybe we should go back to town and get a local Stadtpolizei officer out here," replied Josh.

"He might not have that kind of time. Remember the date, he has already been out here for weeks. Without food he won't make it much longer," interjected Harrison who appeared the most reasonable leader among them.

The group proceeded to debate the issue for several more minutes until Harrison posed a final question.

"So, you guys want to check it out or not?"

"I vote yes," shouted Kyle as if Harrison had asked the group if they wanted to do another keg stand.

"Let's save that guy," said Tim more calmly.

"Doesn't matter to me," said Dwyane.

"I'm in," said Harrison.

"I'll go along with you guys, I guess," said Eddy, rubbing his glasses in preparation.

It was all down to Josh who had wanted to return to town. The group looked at him intently trying to pierce an answer out of him with their stares. Eventually, he capitulated.

"Why not?" he said, finally. "If we get lost or killed, at least we won't have to take our final."

Everyone had a good laugh before grabbing their gear and trudging across the stream. They all headed up the path towards a set of stone stairs that ended at the top of a ridge looking over a quiet dale.

What the group had missed as they crossed the stream was the small cave where the water exited in a steady flow. In its mouth were several dozen other bottles, notebooks, and pieces of wood all covered in frantic writings. Some were visibly dated, some were not. But of those that were visible, the dates ranged from 1657 to 2047. And if the hikers could see the footprints on the trail, none ever led back out.

Mirror in the Attic

With each careful step the children took, the old cedar planks groaned loudly as if they were being disturbed from a long restful slumber. The steps bowed spitefully under their feet forcing each of them to steady themselves against the slat-lined walls which also buckled against their weight. The stairway to the attic was narrow, forcing the four to climb single file. Up ahead, a solitary bulb of orange covered in dusty webs was their only guiding light to the platform above. Down below, the cacophonic sounds of a multitude of black-clad adults were slowly fading as they neared the top of the stair. Dan, a boy of ten, led the way, as he always did. His little sister Emma was much too frightened to be the first to step into their grandmother's attic, especially so recently after her passing. Trailing close behind the siblings, and completing the little quartet, were Stacy and Chris who were the children of their father's best friend.

The death of Dan and Emma's grandmother, Agatha Stevens, had brought them all together this day. She had died three days prior. The sting of it was still sharp in Dan and Emma's minds. The cause of death had not been revealed to the them, but that look on their parents' faces—you know the one, where their eyes flutter and look off over your shoulder and give you an absent-minded response—made it seem to be under some sort of mysterious circumstances. They found little evidence from the other mourners in attendance. In fact, most of the adults took little notice of the children at all. They had been conveniently stuffed away into their own separate parlor room to co-mingle. To be sure, the four of them had little experience with funerals, and knew even less of what to do or say at one—so, it had probably been for the best, but it was undeniably dull.

It had been Dan's idea to explore the attic to pass the time. Emma suspected it was just a reason to impress Stacy, Chris's sister, who was nearly three years older than Dan. No one argued the proposal as there was little to talk about and do amongst grandma's museum-like parlor adornments. So, the four of them slipped out of the little parlor down the long hall and passed the kitchen that was filled with sweet treats and fruit trays. The entrance to the attic was only a little further on the back side of the spacious manor.

The door to the attic was large and made of a dark stained wood. It was typically locked, but Dan and Emma's mother had left it open after retrieving Grandma's silver entertainment set for the wake. Dan and Emma could count on both hands how many times they had seen their late grandmother's attic. She never let them up there by themselves and on the rare time she took them up there, it was only for a fleeting moment to grab a necessary item. Though Dan had a good relationship with Grandma Agatha, it was Emma who had been especially close to her and perhaps the reason why she had seen the attic the most of the two siblings. When Emma stared up the dark narrow stair with no one left to guard or dissuade them away, she thought she could hear Agatha whispering to turn back, because she *forbade it*.

Agatha's unexpected passing had yet to fully weigh on Emma. It was only a month ago that she spent the day with her grandmother for her eighth birthday. Agatha had taken her to a stable out in the country to ride horses. It had been a wonderful day. More wonderful than any of her fairy tale books. Now, as she placed her foot on the last step at the top of the stair, she felt the letter shift in the pocket of her black dress. It was from Agatha. Her mom had given it to her earlier in the day and she simply could not bring herself to read it. She felt a warm tear form at the edge of her face and quickly wiped it away before any of the older kids took notice. She could not bear the teasing now.

The group walked into the attic and were hit by a wall of heavy stale air. Compared to the drafty corridors down below, the attic was warm. Even for October, it still retained the heat of summer which immediately forced Dan and Chris to loosen their tiny black ties from around their collars. A pervasive smell also forced its way into their nostrils. Musty odors of dust, aged wood, and rotting paper formed a potpourri that enveloped everything. The only light in the space came from a single hexagonal window at the other end of house. It was mostly obscured by the overturned mirror of a large bureau that had several drawers resting ajar. What natural light that made it into the triangular-shaped room was faint, casting everything in dingy tones of grey and brown. Scattered yellowed paper and pieces of wooden furniture littered the floor. And like everything, they were covered in the silvery-sheen of dust like that of a first season's snow.

Dan began to walk forward blindly in the dim light waving his hand back-and-forth. With a few seemingly-erratic waves, the sound of something metallic jingled quietly. Then, there was light. At least more light than there had been before.

Dan had found one of the few overhead light fixtures in the attic. Like the one at the top of the landing, it gave off a faint orange glow and was covered in dusty cobwebs. Everyone immediately took in the newly illuminated space. Emma—in between little sneezes—studied the splintery rough beams of the ceiling. The large wooden rafters framed the attic at steep, sloping angles and were connected every so often by a thick horizonal timber—wider than Emma's waist—tying either side together. She remembered how strong they looked the last time she had seen them with her grandmother. It was the ceiling that brought relief after seeing a massive mouse scurrying across the floorboards into a corner behind some boxes. *Thank goodness mice do not fly*, she thought, yet wondering where it was now.

Chris, on the other hand, admired a large wooden trunk that he believed surely was filled with gold doubloons. He walked over towards it, the soft floorboards beneath his feet whined under his weight. The trunk was large, large enough for him and his big sister, Stacy, to fit inside. It had no lock except a beefy metal henge that felt icy cold to the touch. In his first attempt to open it, the lid did not budge but an inch. He had vastly underestimated the sturdiness of the old trunk. He gave the lid another shove, this time, putting the full force of his legs behind it. The floorboards buckled as the lid slowly surrendered letting out a long *creeeeaak.* But for all the effort, his face slackened in disappointment to find only an open chest full of faded magazines and yellowing letters.

Dan had migrated over to a brick chimney column to test another beaded pull chain of a light fixture. He let out a whimper when the corner of an old wooden rocking chair jabbed him in the side. Rubbing his hip, he felt for another metal chain and gave it a pull, but it was to no avail.

Of the four, it was Stacy who seemed to have found something of true interest simply for the fact it was rather unidentifiable, save for being slightly rectangular and about five feet tall. The nameless thing was shrouded in mystery as much as it was the only object in the entire attic to be covered in a drop cloth. A heavy beige canvas covered the thing completely to the floor fanning outward like an elegant gown. If you were quickly glancing around in the attic without light it would have been easy to mistake the thing for a sheet-covered person or…a ghost. Yet, no one dared to utter the g-word on their lips up there now.

Stacy approached the object and noticed a curious set of light indentations laid directly in front of it. They seemed not unlike a pair of footprints facing inwards within grains of reddish-yellow sand rather than grey dust forming their outline. She stretched out her delicate hand to touch the canvas with a delicate fingertip. The texture was rough and felt thick enough that it would have brought her to the floor if someone had thrown it upon her. She asked what would supposedly lie underneath and neither Dan nor Emma had a clue. They could not recall seeing something of that shape when they had been in the attic before—though it had been some time since either of them had been up there.

Before anyone else could react, Chris tightly grabbed an end of the canvas off the floor and threw it off the object with great force. An enveloping cascade of silvery dust pirouetted in the orange light all around them. Something else, larger, had also fluttered out in the gloom but was obscured by the dust cloud that fell heavily to the floor like an avalanche in miniature form, at least for any small creeping critters. The commotion had also brought in a whiff of hot air that smelled of overbaked earth—dry and arid. Mixed in with it was the smell of some far-off mouse that was dead and slowly on its way to become mummified.

When the dust had finally settled, the four of them had become eight. The rectangular object had a mirrored reflection on its hard surface. But it was a mirror unlike any of them had seen before. The reflection was not as perfect as the one they all had become accustomed to in their home bathrooms. No, this one was more subdued, almost opaque due to a cloudiness of the mirror. As Chris discovered upon touching the side of the full-length reflector, the glass front was not glass at all, but some hard metallic obsidian-like rock that had been polished to form a rough reflection of the attic.

The four peered deep into the dark and hazy mirror straining to make out their murky reflections. That was when Dan noticed the object that had fluttered out in the dust storm after the removal of the drop cloth. On the floor, several paces away from the mirror, an old piece of parchment had fallen and carved out a deep furrow of dust upon its landing. Dan picked it up and brought it back to the other three who eagerly huddled around him in front of the mirror. The name Baron Edgar Sauer was written across the front of the folded parchment in thick heavy script. Emma recognized the name immediately due to her grandmother having spoken about the baron—a self-ascribed title according to Agatha—who had died years ago. What little her grandmother told her was that the baron delt in many wares from the middle east and had died rather mysteriously after years of wealth. Agatha had mentioned it for the fact that she was proud to have obtained a rather expensive looking-glass from the sale of the estate. Emma would not have thought much of the comment except that Grandma Agatha had seemed the happiest she had seen her in years at the time.

The group looked back at the mirror, realizing that it was more than likely Grandma Agatha's prized looking-glass.

A silhouette quickly shifted in the back shadows of the reflection.

The group whipped their heads around to look behind them but saw nothing but the open door to the stair they had climbed earlier.

A few unsettling moments passed and attention turned back to the peculiar piece of paper. Dan carefully unfolded the signed parchment to find a lengthy letter had been hastily scribbled inside. He then read it aloud to the group in a steady tone.

I, Baron Edgar Sauer, consign this letter to whomever may find it. I only hope its finder fairs better with the information than I have. I shall be short as the information that matters needs to be conveyed in haste. What follows may seem strange, but it is the truth as best as I can convey it in this late hour. If this letter remains attached to an old mirror, beware. I repeat BEWARE. Do not gaze into it. If you do, it will steal more than a reflection. There is some malevolent depth to the image. It may seem faint at first, but trust me, there is something there and it wants to pull you there with it forever.

If you are still with me, and not think of me as a loon, I shall provide a few more details of this piece so that someone else can figure a way to rid the world of it. The mirror was procured through back channels during the second Gulf War. I happened to find an Arab merchant who had smuggled the piece out of Iraq during the chaos of antiquity looting. The transfer occurred through a mutual business partner who had the item shipped carefully to my residence in Connecticut. When I first pulled it from the shipping box, I was in awe. The piece was magnificent in every way and definitely the genuine article. It was wrought from a single slab of obsidian and polished to have a reflective essence. After close study, I dated the piece to around 575 BC from the Mesopotamia region with possibly a Babylonian origin during the reign of Nebuchadnezzar II. Much of these suppositions were based on the ebony-inlayed inscriptions around the mirror, hidden under a silver frame—a late addition. The inscriptions had some typical history of kings and the passage of time but also contained strange elements of rituals and the capturing of spirits of mimicry.

Naturally, I did not make much of it. I was wholly glad to sit in front of the exquisite piece in my chair and stare into its cloudy depths. After a time, I thought I noticed something in the mirror. Something strange and off. It appeared far off and ill-defined at first but it began to become clearer as minutes passed, almost like a developing photograph that slowly changes before your eyes. The shape was in the same position as my reflective image. And I tell you, it looked like two eyes staring back at me—but darker and off center—with a grin that was not my own.

I thought my mind was tricking me at first, as it may after staring at something for so long, trying to make sense of the formless void. At least, I wish that had been the case. Those hopes were dashed when I approached close to the lens and saw a similar yet twisted version of myself approach in unison. I first tapped the stone and miraculously felt a tapping upon my shoulder. With further experimenting I made a frightful face and immediately my hands began to tingle, my mouth went dry, my heart raced uncontrollably, and my nose caught a whiff of bitter sweat. Somehow the mirror mimicked not only an image but every feeling, every smell, every taste, touch, and thought. It captures and reflects the energy of what stands before it for good and for ill. I even found that revealing a hundred-dollar bill created numerous copies that fell in front of me to the floor—though it served me little in the long-run.

Curious, I went back to the inscription, and studied it more carefully. There was definitely a ritual conducted, but it was conducted on the mirror itself called a 'mašālu ša-tāmarti' or 'mimic mirror.' I surmised further from the symbols: 'human sacrifice,' 'bound,' 'life reflector' that a person was sacrificed over the mirror to provide it the power to mimic life for all its days. In doing so, the mirror could provide all the joys and sadness of the human experience. But, as I eventually found out all too late, all this does not come freely without a cost. For all the energy given must eventually be taken back into the mirror. And the only payment it will accept worthy of such a price is the thing that provides all the range of experiences—a human life. I will not belabor how I tried to delay such final payment. Let us just say that there is no escaping what you owe and I scribble these notes now in my last hours out here to provide warning.

So, I tell you again, beware of the visage cast within this mirror. Do not gaze into it for any length of time for the meter will be running and the collector will be coming. Dispose of it however you may. But, do not, I repeat, DO NOT get lost in its alluring world. It may charm you at first, but that charm swiftly turns to deceit. I tell you it whispers lies. Because appearances are fleeting and vanity is rife ubiquitous. You may think it only takes a mere refection of yourself, but it wants more. The cost is great and this reflection is not free.

The last line was remarkably sloppy and hard to read. Dan had to hand the letter to Stacy to try her best to read it. She read:

"Never trust an image of ice that never melts, the only thing that will change is you! And it is never for the prettier –B.E.S."

Upon finishing the undated note, the expression on their faces was a mix of astonishment and disbelief. Emma had already taken a few steps backward, her legs quivering like two rubber bands ready to snap down the stairs. Dan and Chris stood silently puzzled going over the letter again. Stacy, on the other hand, with a doubtful look upon her face had taken a step forward. She gazed into the glass looking towards every corner, searching its cloudy realm. There were only shadows which undulated in unpredictable patterns. Her own visage was faint and barely perceptible despite being mere inches from the polished boundary of the mirror. The others began to take notice and watched her stare at herself longingly for what seemed like several minutes. Her eyes seemed tightly locked with a captivated gaze at her mirrored doppelgänger. At last, a compulsion came over her and she laid a big kiss on the lips of herself.

Stacy instantly shot back from the mirror as if she had experienced a shock of electricity. She held a slightly trembling hand up to her mouth to pad it delicately. Dan asked if she was all right and she absently waved him off from any concern. Eyes closed, she told them about the tingling feeling that was now rushing through her lips. It was accompanied by a disembodied feeling of warmth that wrapped all around her. She could feel her heart fluttering in her chest like the kiss had been the first she had ever received. It was simply amazing!

Chris stepped forward to the mirror despite Emma's protests to leave and Dan's cautionary wielding of the letter in his wavering hand. None of it was of any use. Chris's eyes were transfixed and unyielding. He rubbed his hands together eagerly waiting for some sign to come out from the darkness. A few restless moments passed without change until a flash of realization filled his face. Careful not to tear an eye away from the reflection, Chris thrust his hand deep into the right pocket of his black trousers and pulled out a crumbled dollar bill. He then held up his hand to the mirror and began messaging the bill between his thumb and fingers. He watched intently into the reflection where the bill went from one, then to two, then to three, until his hand was holding a green fan of crisp Washington's. The illusion brought with it a powerful feeling, like none he had ever felt before with the measly allowance that his father gave him each week for household chores. He was lucky he could buy a pack of baseball cards once a month with such a paltry sum. But this feeling was immense, a power he only dreamed about. He felt carefree, no longer burdened, or bound by restrictions, as if none of his desires were now out of reach.

In his ecstasy of total wealth, Chris did not even notice that Dan, too, had approached the mirror. Yet, Dan's eyes were not focused on his reflection but the enchanting reflection of Stacy slightly off in front and beside him. Her mirrored-reflection somehow looked more beautiful than she was standing next to him in the dim attic. In the mirror, Stacy's red lips were brighter, her eyes a deeper shade of green, her feminine curves even more defined. Dan reached out behind her to caress the reflective version of her hair. Somehow, the voluminous brown strands could be felt running through his fingers. The gentle smell of lavender fragrance wafted into his nostrils. Dan closed his eyes and felt his heart race in anticipation of some long-imagined embrace…

The three of them—Chris, Stacy, and Dan—stood entranced by their murky reflections and overwhelming sensations. Lost in their reflective worlds, they took no notice of one another or anything else around them. They seemed to have forgotten the unmirrored world and little Emma watching furtively from her position at the top of the stairs. She could not understand what had raptured their attention so intensely to stare for so long admiring themselves in the old mirror. Her brother Dan's eyes looked wide and he made a peculiar groaning sound. Stacy seemed to hum some unidentified tone as she primped her hair and edges of her dressed. And Chris…he seemed to almost stoop over with a bit of drool hanging at the corner of his mouth as he played with a crumpled dollar as if it were the most precious thing in existence.

Emma bit at the corner of her lip. Her eyes darted between the enthralled trio before the mirror and the dimly lit staircase. The world it led down to seemed so far away now. She perked up an ear to listen for even the faintest of murmurs from the adults down below but, there was only the steady creaking silence of the attic.

After much time had passed without any change, Emma thought of jerking her brother back to her. She even took the first step towards him when everything seemed to change in front of her. First it came upon Stacy, then Chris, and finally Dan. It started as a sour look at first, like one she remembered seeing on her brother when his tummy hurt. But that look quickly faded into something worse and more disquieting. What looked like a slight discomfort had transformed into pain and then terror.

For the three in front of the old polished volcanic glass, the ecstasy of feeling and desire had turned to anguish. They remained stuck gazing into the mirror as it dumped into them an engulfing sense of sorrow, hate, and malice. Despite their willful efforts, none of them could turn away or avert their steely gaze from the mirror's murky depths. The pleasant images had washed away and into their place, an icy surface remained. Beneath it, some unfathomable depth stretched out into some unseen void. The comfort had drained from their bodies, replaced by a cold sense of separation from any source of heat. The polished stone, born of fire, had become an icy portal to nothingness.

The trio stared helplessly as shadows began to move deep within the mirror. Off beneath the icy surface, outlines of shadowy figures emerged from the murky depths. There must have been dozens, maybe more. Mere shades of the human form, the figures were veiled in shadow with hollowed out eyes that did not see but projected a searing gaze. They were coming closer, closer to the thin demarcation of the glass, or were the three of them inching closer? No one could tell, as their eyes remained fixed on the enlarging figures who had come to collect their due. To add a new collection of experiences to the looking glass, so that the next person to gaze upon a gloomy reflection could feel just as they had. The baron had warned them. Oh God, he had warned them not to stare too long!

POP!

The filament in the solitary lightbulb burst out with a flash into a decaying glow of orange. As the last vestiges of electric light faded, shadows fell back into their usual places around the room. They swiftly returned to their positions as if they had been waiting ever-so impatiently for the unnatural light to finally recede from their domain. With them, new shadowy figures had joined their ranks. They had come as ethereal projections from the mirror into the room. Their fuzzy outlines loomed behind Emma and the others in a half-moon arrangement across the attic furniture and walls. A suffocating heaviness of cold air oppressed across all their shoulders.

Emma jerked back to the mirror. Quiet tears had gathered at the edges of her eyes which only served to distort everything into a kaleidoscope of bleary shadows.

Frost had gathered on the edges of the ancient mirror. The whole attic space felt as if every ounce of heat had been drained from it and fallen into the void of the mirror's unblinking oculus. Even small puffs of air began emitting from the shallow breaths of the trio in front of the mirror whose faces remained frozen in a fearful stare.

Emma knew something needed to be done. There did not seem time to rush down the stairs for help. She needed to think of some way to stop all of this. To get Dan, Stacy, and Chris away from those God-awful reflections. Her eyes frantically darted across the room. The natural light seemed even dimmer than it had been before. Emma cast her gaze to the tiny window. Had some cloud entered the clear blue sky and obscured the sun? There was no time to check the weather.

Then she saw it. She had noticed the hefty bureau against the window before, with its mirror flipped at an odd angle atop a jolted set of drawers. The upturned mirror caused a spark to flash in her mind. She remembered the trifold mirror in the bathroom back at home, how folding it back in on itself created an infinite hallway cast in a green hue. *Maybe that would do the trick*, she thought. Emma gazed back at the old mirror and her companions. The shadowy figures were almost upon them as both parties were now mere inches away from either side of the icy surface of the mirror.

Emma sprung to her feet and ran over to the bureau, careful not to catch a glimpse at her own reflection in the old mirror or at the shadowy figures on the walls. Reaching the bureau, she needed to stand on the tip of her toes to grasp its mirror. She carefully removed it from its pedestal and instantly felt its weight settle into her arms as the thing was nearly as long as she was tall. She carried the bureau mirror in her arms as quickly as she could back to the others trying desperately not to tip over. Emma propped the mirror up against the wall behind the three so that it was angled in a way to reflect back an exact copy of the old mirror. After some fine tuning, she eventually got it into position where the reflections became reflections upon reflections upon reflections…an infinite cascading hallway of mirrors formed in both pairs. But she knew that might not be enough…

In a last desperate hope to free her companions, Emma ran up to the three and gathered them the best she could in the loving embrace of her short arms. The others made no reaction towards her. All she could do was whisper that she loved them and that if they had to go, that she would go too. *An infinite act of kindness*, she thought, closing her eyes tightly and ready not to open them again until the end...

All of a sudden, the mirror began to fracture in the spot where she had made her gesture that had been reflected over-and-over again into some unseen infinity. Soon, the old mirror began to rattle, then vibrate harder and harder. The sound forced Emma to open an eye slit enough to see the figures. The shadowy figures had ceased their advancement and were growing clearer and more distinct by the second. She began to make out men, women, and children of all sorts of strange dress—like she had seen in her picture books of times said to be long ago.

Then she saw *her*. Grandma Agatha's sweet smile, and wrinkled crow's feet around her blue eyes were unmistakable. In the next moment there was a flash of blinding white light and the dozens of figures vanished in an instant. A sensation of warmth and gratitude washed over her and the rest of the group. The mirror had finally lost its hold over everyone. The old mirror continued to rattle violently until, at last, a great fissure split the reflective glass in two, right down its center. It fell to the floor with a heavy thud.

Now free from the mirrors allure, the older kids found themselves in a state of disorientation. They looked to see a broken mirror laying on the floor without explanation. They turned to Emma who offered no resolution but gave them her widest smile that she had mustered all week.

It was Chris that suggested that they make a break for it back to their downstairs room before an adult came up to see what had happened to Grandma Agatha's antique. As the group began their descent down the attic stairs, Emma felt the note knocking again against her leg in her pocket. When they had safely reached the bottom of the stairs and the others had gone off ahead to the parlor, she reached in and unfolded the heavy parchment paper with great care. The note was addressed to her and written in her grandmother's elegant script.

To by dearest grandbaby, Emma. I am afraid my vanity has finally caught up to me. I hope you can excuse an old woman from a yearning heart for her youth. I wish we could have had more time together. I know you will grow to be a great woman. Always remember, for truth and beauty, do not seek mirrors. They distort and cheat. The eyes of others are the only mirror you need. For in their depths, you find truth everlasting.

A single tear ran down Emma's rosy cheek, refracting the world around it from all angles. Tears are just little reflective pieces of our eyes that we share with those we love, displaying our deepest facets and feelings, she thought. She wiped the tear gently with the cuff of her dress vowing to never lose her grandmother's words and walked back into the parlor room to join the others.

The Motivational Doll

Trying to squint through the sunlight, there Olivia was, in her advisor's office on a bright Friday afternoon. Olivia sat nervously in an uncomfortable wooden chair which, by no coincidence, sat lower than the towering chair her advisor sat in behind her desk. The room was drafty and the sun shone through the window behind her advisor making it difficult to look her in the face; though even without the sun, she found it draining to look upon and speak with her advisor.

The past six months had been difficult for Olivia. Being near the end of her third year, Olivia had become somewhat disenchanted with graduate school. Long gone was the bright-eyed first year that held lofty aspirations that she could do anything intellectually within the ivory walls of academia. No, the brightness in her eyes had long since faded; a yearning for intellectual stimulation and enlightenment had been replaced with jadedness and disappointment. Like many of her fellow graduate students, most of Olivia's embitterment with grad school could be credited to her advisor who would constantly cancel meetings, not read her work, and, when there was interaction, dominate conversations about research that she had not taken the time to familiar herself with.

On this particular Thursday afternoon, Olivia's advisor Evelyn (a professor of sociology) had called her there to discuss her progress and future career plans.

"How are we today?" Evelyn asked distractedly as she was trying to finish reading a news story on her computer and fumbling to check for text messages on her phone.

"I'm doing just fine," Olivia responded meekly.

In between glancing at her phone and looking at Olivia, Evelyn could sense a hint of despondency in Olivia's demeanor. "I know it's the end of year and you've been working really hard…I just wanted to tell you that your end of the year review looks good. There might be a few things we can work on but, it will be fun!"

Olivia sat there with a blank stare allowing her advisor to go through the numerous things that she had said countless times before. Evelyn would always use overly cheerful language to disguise the fact that she rarely followed through on anything she said or promises she made about how she was going to help move things forward. So, this time, when she said that they would start having bi-weekly meetings and that she would read the manuscript that had been sitting on her desk for more than three months, Olivia was a little incredulous. *Just words made on waving lips with idle hands*, she thought.

"Okay, that sounds good," Olivia muttered, trying to disguise her doubts.

"Great! This will be fun! Now, have you thought more about what kind of academic position you would like after graduate school? I just want to make sure we are putting you on the right track."

Of course, whenever future career plans came up, Evelyn always assumed that Olivia wanted an academic position and there were no other possible alternatives.

After, a brief hesitation, Olivia finally formed a response. "Umm…to be honest, I'm not really totally sure I want an academic position at this point. Sometimes I feel I might not be so cut out for grad school and academia," Olivia sputtered out, surprising herself with her candidness.

"Olivia, I want you to know, you are wicked smart and you will make a great researcher at a top university someday. You just need to listen to me and trust me."

"I do trust you…it's just…"

"Wait! I might have something here that once helped me get through grad school," Evelyn said as she shot up to her dusty bookcase to search for something on the top shelf. Her right hand searched back and forth atop the bookcase, knocking up a plume of dust while her left hand frantically attempted to readjust the back of her curly bob of hair.

"Ah, I think this is it…" Evelyn said as she brought down an old dusty shoebox. "…yes, this is definitely what I was looking for. I don't remember the last time I got this down. It must have been up there since I received tenure twenty years ago."

"What's in the box?" Olivia asked warily.

"Oh, you'll love it! I don't think I could have gotten through grad school without Magus."

Out of the box, Evelyn pulled out what looked like some sort of Raggedy Ann doll that must have been almost 100 years old. It was stripped of any clothes besides a pair of lined red socks and a little worn out heart on its chest. Inside the heart was some faded handwriting that looked like 'I love Magus' with some various symbols placed before and after the phrase. The skin of the doll looked like the texture of a burlap sack, but dirty and soiled from age. Also notable was the fact that this doll did not have the normal head of red hair, but many various locks of what appeared to be real human hair.

"My advisor gave me this doll when I was in grad school to help me through challenging times by giving me the motivation I needed to succeed. He told me that he received it from his advisor in grad school and the same for his advisor before," Evelyn said proudly.

"That makes it pretty old then."

"Oh, it is, maybe older than anyone really knows. It also talks to you using some sort of crude talking tube. To be honest, I never quite figured out how it actually works. However, before I give it to you…"

"Oh no, I don't think I could ever take something that means so much to you," Olivia interrupted.

"Pish posh, this doll was meant for you to have…to continue the tradition, our academic lineage. Come on, this will be fun!"

"Well, okay I guess so."

"Yes, of course. Now, before I give it to you, there is a little ritual that everyone that is given the doll must do."

"What's that?" Olivia asked incredulously.

"Well, ya know, I will need a tiny lock of your hair to place in the dolls head."

"You're joking right?" Olivia replied.

"Nope, not at all; see, my lock is right here," Evelyn said as she pointed to a long lock of golden blonde hair adhered to the doll's head with a crude zig zag of black thread. "Now where are my scissors…ah, here we go."

"If I must do this, just take a little bit from the top."

"You won't miss it at all," Evelyn said, pulling up a lock of raven black hair from the top of Olivia's head. "There we go. Now let me just tie it on here like so, and, voila!" Evelyn exclaimed as she presented the shabby doll to Olivia now with a lock of her own hair hanging down the front of its smiling, mocking face.

"Thanks…" Olivia said timidly.

"Now I almost forgot…" Evelyn said pulling out an old piece of parchment from the shoebox. "It's tradition for you to say these words when receiving the doll. It's in Latin, but I never quite got what it meant. Something like 'Provide me knowledge so that I may prosper,' I think. I know academics love their Latin, it's not important to know what it really means." Evelyn handed the paper to Olivia to read.

"Umm…okay, here goes…Ad te, mihi da, anima mea, et mea mens; ostende mihi viam."

As soon as she finished the last word she could feel as if the doll itself began to warm up to her touch, but the sensation quickly subsided and she thought nothing of it.

"Now, you can go home for the weekend and ask the doll any question you want and it will give you answers that will inspire you to achieve anything, I promise. It helped me so much to engage my mind in the right state to come up with so many good ideas and to write troves of pages in no time. This will be so fun; you'll be renewed overnight!"

"Thank you," Olivia said politely, taking the ragged doll into her bag and headed out of the office.

~*~*~*~

When Olivia got home, she set the doll down on a tiny bench that sat just beneath a bay window in her modest apartment. *I might as well try to work on my manuscript. My new doll may even help out.* Olivia thought sitting at a small breakfast nook table across the room from the window, and the doll. She pulled out her laptop and attempted to continue writing where she left off on an introduction section.

Of course, just like the last time she tried to write, the words just would not come out of her mind onto the page. Minutes passed and the cursor on the white page continued to blink incessantly at her. A frown crept across her face as her thoughts drifted into the anxieties she had been harboring for so long.

"I just can't do this at all. I don't think I am cut out for grad school," Olivia cried aloud. "What do you think, my little Magus doll? Am I ever going to finish this manuscript?"

Suddenly, to her surprise, an electrical hiss came forth from the doll and then subsided.

"Were you trying to say something?" Olivia said warily.

The hissing inside the doll began to whine and crackled until finally a child-like voice burst out from within the doll. "You're wicked smart. You can do anything."

Olivia sat in her chair in shock not knowing what to say. *How could this be happening? I didn't notice any kind of pull sting or touch the doll, yet it spoke to me, in a voice distinct from my own.* Olivia mulled over what had happened for a few moments while she caught her breath and collected her thoughts.

"This is silly," she said finally. "It's just an old doll that Evelyn told me could talk. It must have some sort of crude way to know when someone is speaking after you say its name. Regaining some confidence, Olivia sat back down to her manuscript and started to test out the doll's abilities.

"Okay Magus, you're supposed to motivate me. How can I write better?" Olivia challenged.

The electric hiss again began to slowly emanate from the doll's head until a faint giggle came forth followed by, "You're cute, I am happy to help."

"Well Magus, how am I supposed to finish this introduction? I've been staring at the same page for almost an hour now."

"Hee hee…98% is just showing up," the doll replied with the same child-like voice fading in and out.

"Ha! That almost makes sense," Olivia exclaimed. *Maybe I do need to just start putting words on the paper and the rest will follow*, Olivia considered in her head. She began to type, and to her joy, the words did come. It was like a dam that had been breached; her slender fingers could barely keep up with all the great thoughts that came to her mind. And before she knew it, Olivia had completed the entire section and part of the next. *I've never been this productive before. Could the doll really be the source of my inspiration? The breaker of my never-ending writer's block?*

"Thanks Magus! I finished more than I needed to today," Olivia said feeling accomplished.

"Perrrrfect!" the doll responded without much delay. "This is fun!"

"Yeah Magus, I'm not sure I would say this is fun. Even if I do get this paper published, there still won't be enough academic jobs for me when I graduate. 'Cause that's the big lie no one talks about; the professors bring you into the program, training you for the academic positions that don't exist when the graduates far outnumber the available positions," Olivia remarked coming back down from her writer's high.

A few moments passed and the familiar hiss arose within the doll again before it spoke, "You're cute. Don't worry, everyone gets jobs."

Olivia was taken aback. *The responses had always been generic before; this time, it seemed to now understand the content of what I was saying, remarkable. Maybe Evelyn was right, there is something about this doll that is unique. It did help me write like never before. Maybe there is some old-world magic in there that is channeling good motivational vibes upon me. After all, I did say that Latin incantation. Perhaps all the big-name academics have a secret source of motivation to make them so productive.*

"Nice catch!" the doll hissed out as Olivia was pondering her newfound motivation.

"Can you read my thoughts too, Magus?" Olivia gasped.

"Niiccce, you're so smart!" the doll quipped back.

"Thank you, Magus, you're so sweet."

"You can hit the ball over anyone's head, it will be fun!" the doll replied encouragingly.

"Wow Magus, you're great. I don't feel so down anymore. If I get this kind of encouragement every day, I bet I can be a great academic!"

"Due to the foregoing logic, I think you're right," the doll added.

Olivia felt so motivated and confident. Her mind was now abuzz with research ideas and theoretical linkages she never knew she was capable of generating. *Maybe instead of just getting this paper finished, I could get it published, maybe even at that flagship journal in sociology! This paper could be the beginning of my BIG career,* she thought wistfully.

Suddenly, however, Olivia felt as if she had been jerked back into reality when she heard her cell phone buzzing on the corner of the table. She picked up the phone to hear a distant but growingly familiar voice.

"Where have you been!? I've been trying to call you for hours," her friend Lily, cried out.

"Really, that long? That's strange; I didn't hear my phone go off. I didn't realize I had been writing so long, I've been so productive today, let me tell you." Olivia responded, sounding detached still.

"Yes, yes…" Lily said impatiently. "So, are you going to come out with us tonight?"

"Umm…out where?"

"To that new microbrewery on Grant Street," Lily replied quickly.

Olivia considered the proposition for a moment and then responded, "Well…I guess I have been really productive today. I think I could go out for a drink or two."

"Excellent! We will meet you there in about hour," Lily said as she ended the call.

Olivia put down her phone and turned to the doll who was still staring at her blankly from its position on the bench underneath the window.

"Well Magus, we did great work today but I need a break. I'm going to go downtown and grab a drink with my friends. I hope you will be okay here by yourself in this old apartment."

After a few moments, a strikingly-sweet sound moved within the doll.

"Don't stop now; I know you can do it!"

"Yes, I am beginning to see I can do it, thanks to you Magus, but I need a break for friend time," Olivia responded courteously.

"Nine-eight percent is just showing up, to succeed you must persist," the doll responded in a slightly deeper tone.

"I'm sorry, but I really need to go, and I don't know why I'm explaining myself to a doll," Olivia smacked back beginning to become frustrated.

"Keep working! Don't be entitled! It will be fun!" the doll quipped back.

Olivia was stopped in her tracks. *I didn't use its name. How could it know to respond? No matter, I must go and will consider it later,* she told herself as she opened the door to leave. As the door swung closed behind her she swore that the doll had moved around on its perch to face her as she left.

~*~*~*~

Later that evening, around midnight, Olivia returned to her apartment fumbling for her keys in the dark. *Why is it always so dark when I need to do the simplest of things?* Deep down, she was apprehensive about returning to her apartment alone that night. Throughout the time spent with her friends, all she could do was think about the doll waiting alone for her return. She almost felt as if it was mad at her and would scorn her for leaving against its wishes. *That's just silly*, she thought as she took a deep breath and stepped over the threshold.

It was dark as pitch as she entered the narrow hallway that led into her kitchen. She reached out to find the wall and rhythmically patted for the light switch. *There it is.* Light swiftly filled the room that left Olivia both comforted and uneasy, for when she gazed to where she had left the doll, she found it moved to sitting on top of her laptop on the kitchen table.

"That's not possible," she whispered faintly.

Then, the familiar hissing began to toil within the doll, only this time it began to turn into a deep, growling sound.

"I've been waiting for you. Much work to be done. Come on, it will be fun!" the doll spoke in a raspy voice.

"No…no…this isn't right…this isn't possible…I can't, I'm done for the night. Stop talking to me! I'm going to bed," Olivia stuttered out as she backed away from the door towards her bedroom. *I must be tipsy or something.*

"I will help you and we shall get you far. You can do it. Just sit right down and write, through the night," the doll continued.

"No! I am going to bed…and getting rid of you in the morning!" Olivia said, standing her ground. With that, the dolls head began to slowly turn around and the deep charcoal-colored eyes began to burn a fiery, reddish glow.

"Writing, it will be fun! Reading, it will be fun! Analyses, it will be fun! Academia, it will be fun!"

"NO! NO! STOP! STOP!" Olivia shrieked as she picked up a jar of peanut butter and threw it at the doll, knocking it to the floor. However, to her horror, the doll pulled itself up to its feet and began walking towards her slowly with eyes aglow. She felt that if she stared long enough into those eyes, she would fall into them.

"COME ON! IT WILL BE FUN! COME ON! IT WILL BE FUN! COME ON! IT WILL BE FUN! COME ON! IT WILL BE FUN…"

Olivia used every ounce of mental energy to signal her legs to move; they were like jelly. *Please just move, one foot in front of the other.* Her legs began to move and she hurdled herself into her room and desperately locked the door behind her. The doll was approaching her room, gradually getting louder, repeating itself over and over. "COME ON! IT WILL BE FUN!! COME ON! IT WILL BE FUN!! COME ON! IT WILL BE FUN!! COME ON! IT WILL BE FUN!!

When the doll was just outside the door, she heard a small thud and scratching sounds as it seemingly ran into the door. Then, with an unimaginable force, the door began to rattle violently as if it were about to buckle under the strain at any moment. All Olivia could do was prop herself up against the door to keep it secure as the unremitting growling voice repeated over and over "it will be fun."

After what seemed like ten minutes, the rattling stopped and the doll's voice faded into an eerie silence. With what was left of her wits, Olivia grabbed her phone to place a call but there was no signal to be found. Remembering a translation app on her phone, she pulled out the old, faded parchment with the Latin incantation she had spoken earlier in her advisor's office. In the box she typed in the Latin phrase and waited on pins and needles for the response. When it finally came and she realized what she had done, the entire room began to be engulfed into a terrible shadow of darkness. *What have I done*, she thought cupping her face with her hands.

Far off she could hear the doll approaching once again. This time it sounded like it was beneath the very floor boards she sat upon. "Come on, it will be fun!" it sounded out its unrelenting march. The floor creaked in agony as the doll began to push up and peel back the weathered hardwoods just six feet away. "Errr…rrrrrr…ruptt" the nails whined as they were being pulled from their decades-long abode. The doll pulled itself up through the hole with its eyes fixated on Olivia who was still braced in terror against the door.

"Why is this happening? This is madness! All I wanted was a little motivation to get through grad school." Olivia began sobbing uncontrollably. She was resigned to whatever fate was to come.

The doll edged closer, crawling on all fours. "Because *Olivia*, don't you know? In a mad house, madness is the only way forward to succeed."

Olivia continued to sob with tears flooding her eyes. The whole room appeared to be red from the doll's piercing eyes.

The doll continued, "It's the long untold secret no one ever tells you…what academics fear most…but it is the only way to come up with big splash ideas to be successful in academia."

"…and what's that? What do academics fear most? What must one do to succeed!?" Olivia mumbled out meekly in between sobs from a huddled position with both arms wrapped around her legs.

"Lose your mind!" the doll cackled fiercely as it was upon her. Everything began to fade to black as she began to descend from all rational thoughts she once knew. Her last mental image was the phone screen, still on with the single phrase she had translated from Latin, "To you I give, my soul and my mind; show me the way."

~*~*~*~

On Monday, Olivia's friend, Lily, found her in her office early in the morning. Lily was surprised to see Olivia in so early because this was most unusual for Olivia. In recent weeks, Olivia had become increasingly withdrawn and not motivated to come into the office, let alone at seven o'clock in the morning.

"Hey Olivia, I'm surprised to see you in the office so early in the morning. I don't think I've ever seen you in here before sun up," Lily said cheerfully.

"Oh, I've been here since five. Much work to do. It's the only guaranteed way to be a successful academic." Olivia responded with barely a glance up at her friend in the doorway.

"Oh...I see...well I'm sure you could spare some time to grab some coffee with me. I have some good news to share with you."

"Sorry, but I have work to do. I must get this manuscript out and start on the next. Much work and little time to do it, ya know? Just text me about it later," Olivia said curtly.

"All right...well I guess I'll talk to you later. All this work is going to burn you out though and, when that happens, that's not going to be fun at all," Lily said as she turned to leave.

"Bye Lily, you're the one that will miss out; grad school...it *is* fun," Olivia droned out as Lily left. She went back to typing up her manuscript, only glancing up briefly to look at Magus sitting up on her bookshelf. The doll smiled down upon her with motivating approval.

A Paranormal Distribution

Blake, Darian, and Coby sat waiting for their adviser to show up for the weekly, or more aptly, 'bi-semester' lab meeting. The three psychology graduate students had been waiting patiently for over 15 minutes for their advisor, Dr. Galen Czardo to arrive. Even though he had only been with the department for a year, everything was always on Dr. Czardo's time. The professor made a habit of being late or canceling meetings on a whim, like the time he canceled a practice job talk for a former grad student to go take his grown son—which curiously no one has ever met—to get passport pictures. The student did not get the job and had to seek employment outside academia, but it was heard that the pictures turned out great.

The three Lab Bros, as they affectionately referred to one another in 'the bro lab,' each waited tirelessly in a dimly-lit conference room on the sixth-floor of the psychology building. Blake, the most advanced of the three students in the lab, leaned back in his chair with his hands behind him over the heat vent to warm them on the blustery fall day. He stared out the large windows watching students trudge along the bleak campus in the grey light of an overcast sky. Darian, a year behind Blake, sat slouching in his chair poking away on his cell phone. Lastly, Coby, the first-year graduate student, quietly paced back-and-forth next to the window sill. Coby was always the nervous type and had a particular affinity for tight-fitting muscle shirts that seemed to clash with his wide framed glasses and the boots that he wore religiously.

Blake perked up in his seat quickly and cried out, "I hear someone coming…"

"Hopefully its Galen finally showing up," Darian said with faint annoyance.

However, instead of a 50-year-old man with bushy grey hair entering, it was only Jerry, the undergraduate research assistant or RA for short. After a curt greeting, Jerry slumped over in a chair and proceeded to poke at his phone as well. It had only been three months prior, that Jerry had been hired by Dr. Czardo without consulting anyone else in the lab. Jerry was an average-sized lanky kid with long, unkempt dark hair. Beyond his appearance, Jerry had been a sub-par RA; several times he had shown up to study sessions hung over, smelling of cheap beer and body spray. More problematically, Jerry had been caught not following the study script protocol during sessions and had told participants that it was okay for them to play on their phones during the study. Given the issues with Jerry, the graduate students had approached Dr. Czardo to ask for the RA to be let go from the lab. Reluctantly, he looked into it and then came back with a bureaucratic shield stating that he could not fire an RA who had been contracted to work, no matter how bad his performance.

A dozen or so minutes passed after Jerry's arrival before Dr. Czardo finally made his entrance.

"Hey everyone. I know I'm a little late. I had to drop Stefen off at his jazzercise class. He has been really into it and since it is a Thursday, I had to take him because his mother is unavailable. I then had to walk to the bookstore and pick up a book for my monthly book club. It was a rather last-minute decision as our club meeting is next week; I suddenly realized the month was coming to an end! We're doing a Renaissance-era detective story this month.

"Anyways, I'm here now. I know this meeting was hard for me to schedule given that I have been slammed these past two weeks given that you all indicated you were particularly too busy to assist me in final grading. Helping with grading is usually expected as part of your TA'ship, you know? Now, what is on our agenda today?" Dr. Czardo said, finishing with the last wisps of breath.

None of the grad students cared for Dr. Czardo's unapologetic diatribe for lateness or his subtle digs for not helping him with the grading of final papers, which on the contrary, he had previously insisted on reading himself to give his students 'expert' feedback.

"I think we were supposed to discuss end of year evaluations and future lab plans," Coby replied softly.

"Ah, yes. Feedback. After the faculty meeting, it has been brought to my attention that our lab is not publishing enough. In academia, we don't throw around the phrase publish or perish for nothing. You really need to, with every waking breath, be doing something that will potentially lead to a publication. In fact, while I was in grad school, I don't believe I sat down to watch a movie for five years straight," said Dr. Czardo sternly.

"Well, we would've had more pubs if you hadn't been holding things up," Blake mumbled to himself under his breath.

"What can we do to improve, then?" Coby asked timidly.

Dr. Czardo cleared his throat to speak. "First off, I want you all to spend less time on things that really don't matter much, like TA assignments. Accordingly, let's work on some grant writing so that we can get you guys away from teaching altogether. Second, I want each of you to start planning studies before the next semester starts so that we are ready to go and don't waste valuable data collection time. We might also want to think about running some participants through the lab this summer and collaborating with other departments like anthropology which is really productive right now; so, think about studies you'd like to run.

Lastly, make sure you are dedicating writing time every day so we can push stuff out to review. Sound good? Good."

The grad students all nodded their heads in silent synchrony out of habit. Dr. Czardo could have asked them all to go lock themselves in their office for a week and they would have nodded with robotic agreement just the same.

"Okay, oh shoot, look at the time," Dr. Czardo exclaimed looking at his watch. "I must leave things at that. We can talk about it all later in detail. I need to go pick up my son."

With that, Dr. Czardo picked up his briefcase and rushed out the door. The room slowly settled back to silence as if a whirlwind had but come and gone. The silence was barely befallen before Jerry got up to leave without a word, face still buried in his phone.

"See ya Jerry!" Blake called after him sarcastically.

"Soo…what was that about?" Coby said puzzled.

"I don't know, none of it made any sense. He contradicted himself half the time. Plus, why does he feel the need to give us his life story every time he tells us something that could be said in a single sentence?" Darian replied.

"I don't know, I guess he just likes hearing himself talk," Blake added.

"I've got some things to finish up on, but who wants to get a drink?" Coby said with a hint of exasperation.

"Sure, that sounds good," Darian replied.

"I'm in. But to honor our dear adviser, let's make sure we talk about future projects over some beers. Who knows, maybe we might get inspired," Blake said jokingly.

The lab bros laughed in agreement and tried their best to push the day's meeting out of mind as they left for their offices. With them, they carried the solemn grad school truth; that even with a night of drinks on the horizon, there was always some work that *could* be done to further their careers.

That evening, after the lab meeting, the three grad bros all met at the local campus bar called The Ebony Tower. In the college town of Talawanda Springs, The Ebony Tower was a hole-in-the-wall bar that many grad students frequented, mostly because it was not a common haunt of undergraduates.

The 150-year-old bar sat at the foot of a large hill that rose up in the middle of campus. Several intersecting paths converged conveniently in front of the old bar. Most notably, the main path to campus, called the "Sage Walk," slithered its way back and forth through a tunnel of trees that opened up at the top of the hill. There, the majestic old main building stood for all to see, a hubristic edifice of white marble ever-reaching towards the heavens above.

In stark contrast, however, The Ebony Tower at the bottom of the hill was itself an unimpressive thing to gaze upon. Dark black wood covered the façade of the long rectangular building. The front entrance was turret-shaped with black stone and a pointed grey cone that protruded from the roof. Most of the building was submerged below ground so patrons had to duck their heads on the narrow steps that descended downward to a massive swamp-oak door. Inside, a mix of gas-fueled lanterns and Edison-style lightbulbs provided dim light to the long hall. The air had an earthen smell to it and there always seemed to be a cool draft that swept across the low-hanging ceilings that were bolstered by thick black beams.

This evening, the three grad students took seats in a corner booth facing a large television screen that was playing a professional bowling match. For a Friday night, the bar was pretty empty besides a few regulars that clung to their amber draughts at the bar.

"Man, what a day," Coby said after everyone had ordered their first round of drinks.

"Yeah...I can't believe we got called out for not publishing enough," Blake said reflectively.

"I've had a paper on his desk for nearly three months, and haven't received any feedback," Darian stated bleakly.

"Well, I have been trying to get a meeting to talk about revisions for the manuscript I've been working on with him for the past month. He just keeps canceling on me or telling me he's too busy," Coby added.

"At least he didn't tell you in your last meeting that he thought your research was as uninspiring as most undergraduate student reports. I mean, I try to come up with novel ideas but he shoots them all down. So, I don't think you guys can compete with that," Blake said begrudgingly.

"I guess it comes down to who's the biggest victim. That's not really a race I want to win if you ask me," Darian said with a sly smile on his face.

The bros laughed.

"Man, I don't know if I'm in the mood to watch *bowling* on TV right now, let's see if we can get this changed. Hey bar keep! Can we change the channel on this TV? Bowling isn't quite doing it for us," Blake yelled over to the bartender who was standing at the other end of the hall.

"Sure…the remote's right next to it in that nook in the wall," the bartender replied impassively.

Sure enough, the old dusty remote with sticky buttons was sitting in a small cutout in the wall. Blake grabbed the remote and proceeded to flip through the channels.

"Let me know if anything stands out to you guys," Blake said over his shoulder.

After going through about a score of channels, Blake heard Coby shout, "Stop here! This looks interesting."

The screen was in a dark green and black hue of some night vision camera. On the screen stood three men, in their early thirties, in some deserted building's hallway holding equipment that apparently could detect the supernatural. Two of the men were average height, one had a beard while the other was bald. The man that stood in the middle seemed to be the leader of the group. He was tall, brawny, and wore a tight-fitting muscular shirt with black pants. In addition, the man's face was oblong-shaped, covered in thick-rimmed glasses and what appeared to be the facial hair growth of an adolescent boy. He did most of the talking and was discussing the haunted history of the location they were 'locking down' in.

"You really like to watch this stuff?" Darian remarked in Coby's direction.

"I don't watch it all the time, but it's interesting. I mean some of the stuff they do is hard to explain with a scientific perspective," Coby replied.

"Like what for example?" Darian quipped back incredulously.

"Well...hmm...look there, you see? That small box that the bald-headed guy is holding?" Both Darian and Blake nodded. "That thing is called a 'spirit box.' It allows supernatural investigators to communicate with spirits. It works by scanning through twenty FM and AM frequency bands a second with interwoven white noise between steps. Supposedly, what sounds like white noise is the medium that spirits can use to communicate," said Coby.

"Well, wouldn't the voices just be snippets of radio audio leaking through that would every now and then just sound like a voice? Enough randomness will produce what sounds like a signal every once in a while," asked Blake.

Coby considered the question for a moment and then said, "To that I would say, the odds of receiving a full sentence response, often intelligently replying to questions, over dozens of frequency bands seems to me to be infinitesimally small."

They all turned back to the screen to watch the three 'ghost bros' in action.

"Is there anyone here with us right now?" asked the bald-headed man on the screen.

The *PSSSH PSSSH PSSSH* of the spirit box's white noise filled the silent void until the paranormal investigator muffled the speaker, allowing the silence to return to ask another question.

"Where are you from?"

Again, the white noise hissed and screeched with no discernable signal. Until a clear deep-throated voice came through. "...Darkness...come for you...G-E-T O-U-T..."

"Damn!" Blake exclaimed. "That is kind of convincing."

"I dunno...seems like it could still be something interfering with it in that building or pre-planted by these people who want to make money on TV," Darian said skeptically.

"That's it!" Blake suddenly sat up in his seat.

"What's it?" Darian responded, cocking his head sideways.

"Yeah Blake, what crazy idea do you have now?" added Coby.

Blake took a long swig from his beer and motioned the others to do the same with theirs.

"The study idea I think I've been waiting for has just come to me. What if we ran a study looking at how these paranormal communication devices affect human perception and decision-making? We could buy one of these spirit box things and experimentally test how the presence of the device labeled as a spirit box affects participants versus simply having the device labeled as a radio tuned to an off station. I would guess when the device is labeled as a radio with static people won't hear much or feel too differently, but when labeled as a spirit communication device, people will report hearing things and feel more anxious, which could affect cognitive decision-making skills. Unlike these paranormal investigators on TV, we could actually conduct an empirical study in a controlled environment using scientific methods.

"No one in psychology has ever tried to do this scientifically, we could be the first to harvest all this low-hanging fruit! I'm telling ya, the novelty of this type of study could get us into the flagship journal of psychology, *Psychological Science*; heck, we might even be able to aim higher and get into *Science*. How's that for publishing Dr. Czaarrrrdoooooo!?" Blake finished, clanking down his beer bottle on the table.

"But what if people actually start hearing real ghosts through the spirit box?" Darian replied mockingly.

Quickly, Blake responded, "In that case, we truly would have something amazing. If we were actually measuring something that was more than chance noise, and could analyze that 'paranormal' audio, then, using signal detection theory as a guide, I think we could prove that there is something to these electronic voice phenomena...I mean EVPs! Documenting that kind of finding would make a big academic splash and people would trust it more coming from a team of psychologists with rigorous methodological training than these ghost bros."

"Yeah bro, if 'P' is less than .05, it's a ghost!" Coby said enthusiastically.

"But how are you going to get funding for the project...participant hours...*IRB approval*?" Darian retorted.

"Don't worry guys, I'll plan it all out..." Blake raised his beer up for a toast. "To a bountiful data harvest, and maybe even a ghost or two..."

"Cheers," the group said in unison. Ordering another round of drinks and buffalo wings.

~*~*~*~

A summer passed since the three lab bros had gathered at The Ebony Tower. Darian and Coby had mostly forgotten the project they had all proposed to conduct in their drunken musing. Grad students often jumped on any feigned distraction they could to forget the burdens of being in Dr. Czardo's lab. The fall semester had begun and the once tranquil summer college town was now teaming with undergraduates who flooded the restaurants and bars. Like locust overfilling the streets, the undergrads had driven most graduate students back into their stuffy offices. Summer was a respite, but always fleeting.

On the Friday evening of the first week of classes, Blake came strolling into Dr. Czardo's lab with a sly smile across his face.

"Hey guys, I've got great news!" Blake said, trying to contain his excitement.

"Did you get that semester of teaching relief?" Coby asked.

"No, even better; I got a grant from the National Science Foundation! We're fully-funded bro!" Blake replied, smirkingly.

"Wait, what? How did you get a grant from the NSF?" Darian asked, in shock.

"No, the more delicious question is, for what research project did you get an NSF grant?" Coby added.

"Well, you know that little idea we had about spirit boxes and ghost perceptions? I sent in the project proposal and somehow whatever committee reviewed it approved us for a $10,000 small fast-track research grant."

"Nooo…ten-thousand dollars, how is this possible? How in the hell did you get reviewers to sign off on an idea like that?" Darian asked, incredulously.

Half-laughing, Blake responded, "Well, it definitely took some major word-smithing and mental gymnastics, but I basically framed the research project as one about studying fear of technology and imperceptible frequencies of sound. More so, I stated in the proposal that we would be studying a disadvantaged population. I mean, let's be honest, what population is more disadvantaged and met with prejudice than that of ghosts? They are often found in dilapidated houses and met with scorn and derision, after all."

"You've got to be kidding me," Darian said aghast while Coby sat in his office chair laughing hysterically.

"Oh, I'm dead serious. Here's our new spirit box to prove it…" Blake replied, revealing a crude-looking palm-sized device from his backpack. Blake continued, "…with the money from the grant, I have bought the best state-of-the-art ghost-documenting equipment money can buy, sparing no expense. If we're going to prove ghosts are real or not, might as well make sure the equipment is not to blame in the event of any null findings."

"Wow, that thing looks legit. Look at all of those nobs and lights. Have you tested it yet?" Coby asked.

Blake walked over to Coby and placed the SB16 spirit box down on the table next to him. The box was black and white with a large high-definition speaker embedded in the bottom portion of its frontward-facing panel. At the top of the front panel, a large screen displayed the current frequency and the frequency change rate. Below the display, a half-dozen pill-shaped buttons controlled varying parameters of the device such as the frequency sweep speed, volume, and whether the device used the AM/FM bands.

"Actually, I have already performed two 12-hour control tests with the device, one in a regular room and another in a soundproof room that was completely isolated from outside radio frequencies. In both, the recordings from the sessions revealed no anomalies suggesting that the device doesn't seem to pick up voices in everyday environments or in the absence of outside radio interference."

"That's interesting and a good starting point," Coby said picking up the device. "Man, this thing is heavy duty, must be expensive."

"It is, but be careful. That is an official government-funded piece of equipment you've got there," Blake said with a half grin.

"I guess it is pretty cool," Darian said begrudgingly as he shuffled over to the table where the device sat.

"I think before we unleash this on our undergrad participants, we should do some real-world tests," Blake stated matter-of-factly.

"What kind of tests? I have a sense that we're going to be doing something that's going to get us in trouble."

"Oh, come off it, Darian, we won't be breaking any ethical rules. What I have in mind is to put this device to the test in an environment that should be, if they do indeed exist, rich with ghosts," Blake replied.

"What exactly are you proposing, Blake?" Coby asked, intrigued.

"I'm suggesting we take our new equipment and go over to that new Babylonian antiquities exhibit at the campus archeological museum. There we can turn on our equipment to see if it picks up on any anomalies around all that ancient stuff. Consider it a field test of our hypotheses. Besides, multi-method designs always are more convincing."

"How are we going to get in after hours?" Coby asked.

"That won't be a problem; I have a friend in the archeology department who said that she could get us in after the museum closes. I only had to promise we wouldn't touch anything. And we won't, we're merely interested in the non-physical realm," Blake reassured the two lab mates.

"Well, it sounds like you have everything planned out then," said Darian.

"Precisely, meet me at the museum around nine this evening and we will get to work. This publication is going to write itself!" Blake said enthusiastically as he gathered up the spirit box and headed down the hall to the second lab space to begin preparations for the evening's experiment.

That evening, the three lab bros met under the large sycamore tree that stood guarding the entrance to the campus archeological museum. Two large griffin statues sat staring in repose as they climbed the marble steps up to the great brass doorway of the museum. Not far inside, a young woman with thick wide-rimmed glasses and unkempt hair approached the group from a side office.

"Hey Blake, I've started closing up for the day. Once I lock up these front doors, you guys will be the only ones here. When you leave, these doors will lock behind you," she said pleasantly.

"Thanks Samira, we can't tell you how much we appreciate it," Blake responded.

"Yeah, well, you owe me for this one. I could get in a lot of trouble for letting you guys in here unsupervised. We just finished setting up a new batch of artifacts from the Babylonian exhibit this afternoon. Some of these pieces are more than 3,000 years old. We received them about a year ago and it has taken us this long to get them organized and set up. So please, *please*, don't touch anything; and if you do break something, you might become a lifeless artifact yourself," Samira said sternly.

"We won't touch a thing, although I can't speak for the ghosts we're hunting," Blake replied sarcastically.

"Funny, that excuse won't stand up long if you guys break something. Anyways, I have to run to catch a bus. Have a good night and happy hunting boys!" Samira said as she locked the large brass door and slipped out beyond.

The three bros stood in silence for a few moments as their eyes adjusted to the semi-darkness of the museum's lobby. Eventually, Coby broke the silence as he began to dig through their bag of equipment and gear.

"All right guys, I've got the flashlights, the spirit box, the electromagnetic field meter, digital voice recorders, and the array of six 3D motion-capture laser cameras."

"Good, good, hand Darian the laser camera array, I'll take the spirit box and a flashlight, and you man the electromagnetic field meter and digital voice recorders," Blake directed.

"Which one am I manning?" asked Coby.

"The EMF meter," repeated Blake but a blank look remained on Coby's face. "The one with the long red meter points."

"Ah, I see it. I guess it does say EMF meter on the side," Coby replied.

"Where do we go from here?" Darian inquired.

"Samira told me to go down the long hall there and the exhibit should be the first big entrance on the left," replied Blake.

The group grabbed their equipment and proceeded to head down the long hallway that was lined with artifacts from different long-extinct civilizations.

"You know, I've always wondered how Jasmine did it," Blake noted as they passed a Persian statue of a woman in the nude carrying a water basin.

"Did what?" Coby asked.

"How she kept such nice smooth hair without frizzing in that Arabian heat. She must have had some good conditioner there in Agrabah."

The three grad students laughed in the dark as they came up upon the large doors that marked the entrance to the Babylonian exhibit.

"All right guys, are you ready? It's go-time," Blake whispered encouragingly as he pushed the double doors and entered into the blackness of the room.

Inside the exhibit hall, the room was expansive. In every direction the light from the flashlight couldn't reach any sort of boundary or wall. The light did, however, illuminate countless artifacts on display; the three grad bros passed by an assorted mix of clay jars, stone water clocks, and jade hair brushes. The bronze sculptures glimmered a dull glow in their flashlight beams.

"Do you think we should turn on the equipment?" Coby asked the group in a half-whisper.

"Yeah, I think now would be a good time. Let's turn on the digital voice recorder and the EMF reader," Blake whispered back.

The grad students proceeded to ask questions to the dark not knowing truly if they would be answered. They floated together slowly, in a huddled formation. The light from their flashlights darted back and forth from artifact to artifact as the only stimulus that seemed to slice the silence. For the most part, their equipment was working properly without any deviations from initial baseline calibrations. It was not until they approached a massive eight-foot-tall stone statue that the EMF meter began showing some unusual readings.

The statue depicted an entity with the body of a man, a head of a wolf with horns, the feet of a bull, and a pair of tattered raven's wings. The statue's hands resembled three menacing talons that were scaled like a serpent. In its left hand, the statue clinched a bronze dagger. The bronze dagger was slender with a length of about sixteen inches. The blade itself was about twelve inches long resembling an elongated isosceles triangle that had mostly dulled with the passing of time. Down the center of the blade was a beveled-groove that seamlessly ran into the ornamental blue hilt that was speckled with gold stars and crescent moons. Lastly, the pommel at the end of the dagger was adorned with a blood-red crystal sphere the size of tennis ball.

After a moment of awe, Darian began reading the placard placed at the foot of the statue, "Here stands a statue depicting

Pazuzu (circa: 1200-900 B.C., material: onyx, origin: unknown), a Babylonian demigod, known as the 'king of wind demons.' Writings found on artifacts recovered with this statue suggest that the Babylonian people would often make ritual sacrifices, including human sacrifices, to this deity to bring about good fortune in their lives. The bronze dagger held in the left hand is believed to have been used in these ritualistic sacrifices."

"Man, people sure had to give up a lot to receive good fortune back then, wishing wells at the mall are a lot more convenient," Blake interjected after Darian had finished reading.

"And less messy," added Darian.

"This thing is creepy, it's so jet black that it seems to suck up all the light from your flashlight," Coby motioned to Blake.

"You're right...interesting. Coby, what kind of spike did we get near the statue?"

"We got a reading of twenty-five, which was huge compared to the zero-point-one baseline reading we got for the room," Coby responded.

"I think it's time to open up the spirit box and see what we get to come through. The EMF might be going crazy due to this funky looking stone. Maybe it has some sort of magnetic properties like they find in meteorites," Blake reasoned.

Blake brought the spirit box under his flashlight and twisted the knobs on the spirit box to activate it. Immediately, the hiss of static came through as the device began to progressively scan the AM and FM frequencies at a rate of twenty bands per second. For a few minutes, all that could be heard was the fluttering static of the spirit box. At times, it seemed that the noise would drop really low but no signal could be discernably heard through the noise.

"MAYBE WE SHOULD ASK A QUESTION," Coby yelled over the noise from the spirit box.

Blake placed his palm over the spirit box's speaker to muffle the white noise temporarily before asking, "What is your origin?"

Blake removed his palm and the static returned, except this time something came through the static, in a low, growling voice.

"... ... ... from darkkkk ... fallllll ... ..."

When the voice came through all three of the grad students instantly froze in their shoes. Darian quickly put his hand over the speaker. "What the hell was that?" he asked, his voice quivering.

"I don't know bro, but that sounded creepy as hell," Coby replied.

"Did you notice how the voice carried over for like nine seconds? There is no way that could have been coming through from a radio station, the spirit box scanned dozens of stations in that time," added Blake.

"I know, and we had not heard anything for minutes before that came through. Not to mention it responded intelligently to us asking where it came from. I don't know if this is a good—"

Darian cutoff as he began to feel a rumbling beneath his hand, as if something was trying to come through the muffled device. His hand retracted back from the speaker as if it had been stung by the device. And then, the voice came in more clearly, and with more malice...

"ENCE ME...DON'T SILENCE ME...DARY...ANN... ZA...ZA...ZOOM...ZO...ZO...DOOM...DELIVER ZOZO..."

Darian was so frightened by the demonic voice that came through that he fell back into the statue shaking it violently as he tried to steady himself against it. Then there was the sound of a loud crash that exploded throughout the exhibit hall. Blake frantically scrambled to turn off the spirit box, finally ending the noise—and voices.

The silence quickly swept back in across the hall. Coby ran over to help Darian back to his feet. He was still unsteady and shaken with fright. However, after a few moments of catching his breath, Darian reassured his lab mates that everything was okay. Attention then turned to the source of the loud sound that they had all heard.

To find the source of the crash, Blake steadily scanned the area around the three of them. The light faded in and out as he gently knocked it to keep a steady, bright beam of light. Things looked relatively unchanged until his light was caught in the glimmer of something gold on the floor off to the side of the statue. Blake focused the light and recognized that the object was the dagger that had once been in the grasp of the statue. However, the dagger had changed and looked notably shorter. Blake then realized that the crystal pommel was no longer attached to the butt end of the dagger.

A shot of anxiety struck Blake deep in the gut as he searched for the missing red crystal. To his dismay, he did not have to look far to find the crystal only a few feet away. His gut twisted onto itself when his light reported back that the crystal had shattered into two pieces. Yet, something else caught his eye amidst the debris. A dirty-white substance was scattered about the floor culminating in a large mound in between the two halves of crystal. Upon closer inspection, Blake realized that the substance was salt.

That's strange, why would a crystal at the end of a dagger be filled with salt? Blake thought to himself. He then noticed a faint gold glimmer of a metallic object protruding from the center of the mound of salt. Carefully wiping away the salt, which seemed to go grain by grain, the object he was uncovering came into view. It was circular, just a bit larger than a half-dollar coin. The gold-colored outer edge was carved in the shape of a snake eating its own tail with two blood red crystals for eyes. Encircled within was a jade-colored tree with branches and roots that intertwined and connected into one another in a continuous loop.

"Oh shit, what happened here? And what the hell is that? Darian exclaimed over Blake's shoulder.

"I'm not sure. I just found this thing inside the crystal that cracked open," Blake replied.

"It looks like the outer edge is made of fool's gold," Darian noted.

"You mean iron pyrite; a mix of iron and sulfur?" Blake asked.

"Yeah, and judging by the shape, it looks like it has been crafted to be an ouroboros," Darian added.

"An ouro-what?" questioned Blake.

"An ouroboros is an ancient symbol that is purported to mean infinity or wholeness or something. I saw it on the History Channel once. Although I've never seen one with this level of detail or with one surrounding a jade tree. It also looks like as if it has a little lever protruding out just behind the snake's neck, I wonder if that does anything or if it is just decorative?"

"I don't think we should mess with it now. I think we've touched too much already," Coby scorned as he approached, scanning the ruinous scene.

"Yeah, you're right, we probably should get out of here and figure out what we are going to do about this broken dagger," suggested Darian.

"I think we should just put the dagger back in the hand hole on the statue and take this broken crystal and try to repair it in the lab where we have better light and supplies," proposed Blake.

"I concur with that. I don't think I can stay in this room a moment longer," Darian said looking over his shoulder watchfully.

Coby also nodded in agreement as they carefully picked up the shards of the crystal, salt, and ouroboros and placed them in their bag. Blake grabbed the dagger and carefully placed it back in its resting place in the statue's hand. The group then quickly shuffled out of the hall. The three left the museum, trying their best not to look behind them at the shadows that seemed to dance around at the corners of their eyes. After a pit stop at the lab to drop off the equipment and artifacts, the group went their separate ways to regroup at the beginning of the week.

The following Monday, the three grad bros met up while walking on their way to the psychology building. They were nervous and still reeling from the events that had transpired the Friday night before. Scared by the experience, the group debated what really happened. Some hoped in vain that a logical explanation could be reached. If not, they were left with the uncomfortable reality that they collected data that perhaps should have been left undiscovered.

"Could it have simply been that we heard what our minds wanted to hear, making sense of the random noise?" Darian ventured feebly, not even truly trusting his own proposition.

"You mean pareidolia? No, the odds of getting a voice for so long, that intelligently responded to our questions, would be astronomically small due to chance," Coby responded solemnly.

"True. There is really no other explanation for what occurred. We set out to disprove these hoaxy shows only to gather data that, with all our scientific training and expertise, we can't explain," Blake added.

The group pondered for a moment before Darian tried to offer another out from this line of thinking, "Well...maybe it was just the spirit box that was malfunctioning. When we get back to the lab, we can check the digital voice recorder and see if it collaborates what the spirit box was doing. If it doesn't, then it might be a case of equipment error."

"Hmm...could be possible...could be not...I would hazard to guess that the voice recorder will also pick up the same voice," Blake responded, the group fell quiet once again as they considered all possibilities.

"We also have to remember the other little problem we have," Coby interjected into the silence.

"Yeah, what's that?" Blake replied.

"The little problem of what we are going to do about that broken crystal and object from the museum. If someone finds out..."

Blake interrupted, "No one will find out. I brought some industrial strength glue and we will get that thing sealed up all pretty like, no one will know any better."

The three of them entered the psychology building and climbed the ten flights of stairs to the sixth floor. It was late in the afternoon and they were surprised to see Jerry in the lab doing work. He usually 'forgot' to come in on Mondays due to being hung over from the weekend.

"Hey Jerry, how are the studies going so far?" Coby asked politely.

"Oh well, they started off fine, but..." Jerry paused for a few moments. "...I've had a lot of mysterious no-shows and I've had to note some weird comments from some of the participants on the study log."

"What kind of weird comments?" asked Blake.

"Well...ah...um...some people have been reporting weird things. One participant said that her mouse would click on random response options and go through the study on its own. Another reported that he heard wispy voices in his room and he quit early. Beyond that, another said that the digital consent form had this weird contract that required the person to dedicate their 'being' by reciting four letters repeatedly, Z-O-Z-O."

"Wow, that is disturbing. I hope the data isn't too messed up," Darian said half-sarcastically. Blake left the room briefly to go check on the artifacts that he wanted to get fixed up. He returned quickly with a look of strong displeasure on his face.

"Jerry! Did you mess with anything that was on my desk?"

"Umm...ahh...I might have gotten a little curious when I saw your snake pendant there. I thought it was a clock or something at first, so I clicked the little lever protruding behind the snake's neck and its head flipped open. It was weird because at the same moment a wisp of frigid air went through me," Jerry replied meekly.

"Jerry, I can't believe you did that. Do you realize how valuable that object was? You could have broken it! We're going to have a talk about this later, go back to administering participants," said Blake angrily.

Jerry quickly shuffled out of the room with his head hung low in shame. Blake then turned to Darian and Coby, "Can you guys believe that? Who knows what that incompetent RA has wrought on us?"

"We better pull the data to make sure things aren't too screwy. No sense in letting him collect more bad data," Coby suggested.

"Good idea. Why don't you and Darian take a look at the data and I'll try to put this crystal sphere back together.

The hours toiled by and soon night had fallen. Most of the students and faculty had gone home for the evening, but the three grad bros worked diligently in their offices. Just a little after eight o'clock, Coby called Blake into his office to take a look at the data he had been analyzing.

"Blake, how's the fixit job going? You have to take a look at this, we can't explain it," Coby said in a hurried greeting.

"No dice on the super glue, I can't seem to get the crystal to stay together. What do you want to show me?"

"Well, we pulled the data from the sessions today and it's a good thing we did because there are a lot of anomalies. For instance, for every number entry, all that is being recorded is a '6' response."

"That is strange, what else is going on?"

"Perhaps more disturbingly, for the open-response questions where participants can type in a few sentences, all we are getting is 'Z-O-Z-O' repeated, over-and-over, and it's like that for all the participants."

Blake took a moment to stare at the computer screen showing the database filled with sixes, Zs and, Os. Blake considered the data for a few moments and then made a suggestion to satisfy his curiosity, "Can you try to correlate the participants from today with the ones we ran last week in terms of time spent on the study to see if they are truly different?"

Coby whirled around the mouse in rapid circular motions as he clicked through the menus to set up an analysis to satisfy Blake's query. Finally, with a multitude of ticking sounds and a hum from the computer's processor, the stats program spat out a display of the results in the form of a scatterplot. All three grad students' faces instantly dropped in horror at what they saw. The correlation coefficient was exactly a value of 0.666, and perhaps more troubling, the scatterplot distribution was in the shape of a monstrous demonic face with two horns and evil, slanted eyes.

Around this moment of data revelation, the lights began to slowly flicker in-and-out. In harmony, the computer screen also joined the fray with its own flickering. The grad bros then noticed that each program on the computer that was open began to crash. Blake cried out "We got to shut that shit down right now!" as Coby tried to frantically take control of the computer to reset it; but control was not his to take. The computer then proceeded to delete files on the computer and the network. All the grad students could do was stand in helpless horror as the computer deleted unfinished manuscripts, presentations, and data files—years of work, now gone. The screen then turned to the blue screen of death. The error message only had the letters Z-O-Z-O repeated over-and-over again until the whole screen was covered with them. And then, in an instant, the computer shut down along with all the electricity in the building.

The emergency lights popped on which provided the grad bros some reprieve from the darkness. This reprieve, however, was only temporary. The three grad bros began to hear a banging sound coming from the wall behind the computer. Oddly enough, the banging did not come from the other side of the wall, but from within the wall itself. These sounds were followed by a deep groaning that seemed to manifest in the corner of the room where a tall brass floor lamp from the seventies stood. The lamp was seated on a black U-shaped base from which the long metallic neck arched out and terminated in a round globe. On its own, the globe was creepy due to it being a half-sphere of brass that reflected the entire room and always seemed to stare at its occupants in silent repose. Now, more than ever, the lamp seemed to peer at the group intently.

An intense smell of sulfur and smoke came from the corner where the lamp stood along with creaking sound. Darian was shaking and mumbling to himself repeatedly, "Please don't move that creepy lamp…don't move the lamp…please…" Seemingly on cue, the lamp's bulbous head began to creak and turn to face the group. The two bored holes in the globe began to burn a fiery red as the two black feet of the base crept forward towards the group. The three grad bros rushed out of the lab and did not wait for the lamp to approach further.

Out in the hallway there was only darkness. Huddled together, the group felt along the walls to find their way to the stairwell, for the elevator would not work in a power outage. Out in front was Blake who felt an open passageway that veered off to the right. He told the group he would go in first to see if it was indeed the right way to the stairwell.

Inside the opening, Blake felt that the wall's surface had changed from the smooth paint of the hallway to a rectangular tile texture. *Must be in a bathroom*, Blake thought to himself. He looked across from him and allowed his eyes to adjust to make out the twin set of mirrors facing him. In an instant, the lights rushed on and he jumped at his own reflection.

Catching his breath, Blake looked closely in the mirror to see that his hand was covering some writing on the wall. He turned around to see, someone had marked the phrase "It will be fun!" in what appeared to be red crayon all over the bathroom wall.

"That's way too creepy," Blake voiced aloud. A gurgling sound then came from one of the stalls next to him. Startled, he cautiously tried to scoot on by the stall to rejoin his lab mates. Right as he passed in front of the stall where the noise originated, the stall door swung open slowly. There was nothing there, only a closed toilet lid and some disheveled toilet paper hanging down to the floor. Blake sighed a quiet relief and continued his scoot across the wall when the toilet lid began opening and closing a quarter of the way with a voice that mouthed "YOU ALL BELONG TO ME!" Blake dashed out into the hallway to find his lab mates shaking in terror.

"You won't believe what just happened out here while you were gone," Darian said, hyperventilating.

"Oh, I believe enough. Let's get out of here while we have the lights on," Blake pleaded.

The two grad students did not put up any disagreement and they hurried down the hall to the stairway. Yet, as they were about to push the heavy door into the stairwell, they all heard a tremendous growl echo throughout the floor. The grad students froze in their steps as they turned to face the path in which they had come. The sound of heavy footsteps approached them. Louder and louder the sound came. "Stomp...stomp...STOMP...STOMP..." The footfalls were so close that they should be able to see the source but nothing appeared in the hallway. The heavy footsteps continued to approach. With the stomping coming ever closer, the three students pressed their backs against the stairway door in terror.

"STOMP...STOMP..." and then...

Silence.

The corridor was cold as moon ice and each student could see the white mist of their breath in the air. The walls of the corridor seemed to twist and bend before them. From the walls, black dust particles swirled forth and slowly began to pull together about twenty feet before them. A black nebulous shape began to take form. As the black dust gained form, the shape began to jerk in contorted movements. The shape continued to manifest and the three students could now see...a creature.

There before them, stood an eight-foot-tall beast with the head and horns of a bull, the body of a ruined man, and the hooved feet of an ox. The demonic creature glared its yellow triangle teeth in a hissing snarl and pulled its three claws across the side of the corridor, leaving three long gashes.

"Leave us alone, we only wanted to see if the paranormal was real. It was only a scientific experiment!" Darian cried out in a desperate plea.

The creature smiled and then spoke in a low growl, "Well here I am, let me show you a mind worthy of study."

The creature then began to approach turning back into a dark shadow of particles. The corridor was completely silent even as

Darian began to scream. Then, the blackness fell upon them, and consciousness left them all.

~*~*~*~

The next morning, Dr. Czardo entered the campus jail to look in on his grad students who had been found unconscious in the psychology building the night before. The campus police had brought them in due to the mess found in their lab space and their possible involvement with a missing crystal pommel reported by the campus museum curator. Dr. Czardo strutted down the cell corridor to find the three grad bros sitting on a bench together behind bars with their heads hung low.

"You know, I always thought Jerry was the problem child in my lab, but you three have really outdone yourselves. I'm really disappointed—in all of you," he said in greeting.

"We honestly are so embarrassed about all this and we wish we had a good explanation for ourselves, but I don't think anyone would believe us. I struggle believing it myself," Darian stated solemnly.

"Oh, I might believe more than you think. Do you know where Jerry is?" Dr. Czardo inquired pointedly.

"No, we haven't seen him since last night. Did he make it home safely?" Blake replied.

"No, no one has seen or heard for him. However, the police did find a strange note left by him under a half-emptied bag of road salt in the lab. It read: The snake is closed. It is hidden, it is safe, Jerry. "Does that mean anything to any of you?"

"No, I don't think any of us know what he could be talking about," said Blake quickly.

"Are you sure?" Dr. Czardo pressed.

"Sounds to me like he could be rambling on about anything, he was always saying stupid stuff when he was hung over, which was pretty much all the time," Coby added.

Dr. Czardo considered each of them individually for a few moments and then his face became sterner and directed.

"Where is the metallic serpent which enshrines the tree of knowledge?" Dr. Czardo asked without pretense.

"Wait, Dr. Czardo what? How would you know about that? Not even the museum curator could have known what was encased in that crystal for who knows how long." Blake spat out in shock.

Dr. Czardo's face froze for a moment and then became relaxed.

"I know, because, it has been a prison for my superior for over a millennium and I want him free," he said as his eyes turned pitch black with red hot ambers as pupils. "He is the key to every ancient twisted knowledge first given to man by the fallen. But since you won't tell me where it is, I will leave you all to rot in here; looks like you will have plenty of time to work on those manuscripts without distractions," the demonic shade of Dr. Czardo said as it turned to leave.

"Oh, and it's actually Dr. Czardo, emphasis on the ZO!" And with that, Dr. Czardo disappeared through the wall in a black smoky mist.

The three grad bros stood in shock and despair for the revelation that had been uncovered by their simple academic inquiry. Although they had the extraordinary evidence they never expected to find, they dared not share it, for no one would likely believe them, or want to. They learned that some findings are best left to remain in the file drawer, never to threaten the established, predicable order of the human experience. Having only been offered a glimpse behind the veil, the grad bros hoped that it would remain closed; science was not ready to reconcile the natural with the supernatural.

The grad bros were eventually released but decided against continuing their graduate careers. The trio moved far away from Talawanda Springs to buy a run-down bar in a small rural town. The three bros mostly stayed in various states of drunkenness for the rest of their lives, trying desperately to tear away their minds from any memory of grad school. The scars faded slowly, if they did at all.

No one ever saw Jerry, the artifacts, or Dr. Czardo again. Yet, as the ageless walls of The Ebony Tower could attest, many strange sightings and mysterious happenings continued to surround the psychology building without scientific explanation.

It's Dangerous to Go Alone

Little Tommy burst through the back door humming a whimsical tune. Trevor, the family Weimaraner, paraded in behind him. And behind the two of them, were disjointed pairs of brown tracks.

"Stop right there!" Tommy's mother shouted. Tommy froze mid-step. Even Trevor dared not move a paw further amidst the matriarch's gaze and wagging finger.

The mom paused a moment to look over the scene that was unfolding upon her recently-cleaned tile floor.

"Do you see what you are tracking in?" she said eventually, shaking her head side-to-side slowly.

Tommy did not offer a response. He merely dropped his head down to stare at his feet.

The mother lowered her pointing finger and flashed a somber smile. "All right, back it up to the mat, the both of you."

Tommy grabbed Trevor's collar with his tiny hand and retraced his steps the best he could. Once on the mat he looked back to his mom for further direction.

"How old are you, now?" his mom asked somewhat rhetorically.

"Seven…" he squeaked.

"That's right, you are old enough to know not to parade into the house without checking your shoes."

"I'm sorry…I was just excited. That's all," the boy replied, blushing.

"Excited?" the mom asked, wondering what it could be this time. Last week he had learned how to make foaming soap in the sink and filled half the bathroom with soapy bubbles.

Tommy simply nodded in reply with a big grin.

"What have you been doing and where have you been?" she inquired.

"I went exploring out by the path in the woods," he said.

"Now, Tommy, I've told you plenty of times, it's dangerous to go alone. You should only be out there with a buddy, like me or your father."

Tommy's face lit up. "But I wasn't alone! I met a buddy. A friend who is really nice. He let me play with his favorite toy."

Tapping her foot impatiently, the mom gave him a quizzical look and looked out the bay window to the back yard. She was trying to think who Tommy could have possibly met on the way to the wooded path. Once she found out, she would need to talk to the child's parents to make sure that they were comfortable with the two of them playing in the woods. Yet, another thing added to a never-ending mother's checklist. At first, she thought about the Stevens, they had a boy around Tommy's age. But they lived in a house that was not on the route to the path. Then, she remembered the Fishers; they lived two houses down from the path. Yet, that did not seem to fit either; their boy was already a teenager.

She sighed. *I guess Tommy will need to tell me more.* She looked back to see him squirming in place on the mat like a mouse caught in one of those nasty sticky traps her grandmother used to use. *Poor thing has been waiting while I stare blankly into nowhere, I should try to make this quick.* Time was different for adults; a minute for a grown person is not the same for young ones whose short existences have not yet stretched out time the same way as it does when minutes seem like seconds in adulthood. With enough time, an adult can wait out any child.

"Tommy, why don't you tell me what exactly you did today," she said in a tender tone. She leaned forward on the granite countertop cupping her chin with both hands.

Tommy's eyes got big and a smile ran across his face. "Oh, yeah. Well...I started in the front yard playing with Trevor," he started, patting Trevor gently on the head. Trevor looked up to Tommy and wagged his tail vigorously. "Then, Trevor seemed like he might want to go for a walk. So, I took him down the street."

"Is that when you met your new friend?" his mom asked.

"Nope, not yet."

"Okay, keep going," she encouraged.

"So...we got to the end of the street. I could see the farm—"

"Myer's Farm?" mom interjected.

"Yes, the one you and daddy show me the cows and horsies when we go on walks."

His mother nodded affirmingly.

Tommy continued, "That's where the trees start too. Trevor was enjoying the walk so we decided to keep going down the path. I wanted to explore the woods to see if I could find some cool-looking rocks. We played in the stream next to the path a bit and I found some shiny black rocks."

Tommy pulled out a muddy trio of roughly-shaped stones the color of obsidian from his pocket and placed them on the adjacent countertop.

"Those are nice, Tommy," his mother responded, resisting the urge to grab for a wet towel.

"They are, I had to steal them from the crawdads. Almost got pinched," he said making pinching motions with his thumb and index finger.

"What about your new friend, Tommy? When did you meet him? You seem to still be alone in the woods," his mother said, with an air of impatience slipping into her voice.

"Oh, yeah...well after getting the stones I followed the path where it splits at the tree with the white peeling bark..."

Sycamore, his mother thought. He had gone pretty far back on the path on his own. Occasionally, the family would walk back that far on especially nice days. She felt a mix of pride and concern for her growing little boy. At the very least he had Trevor with him.

"And then where did you go?" she added, as Tommy had trailed off in thought.

Tommy turned his head towards her. His face held a blank stare for a moment before returning back to life.

"Yeah…that's when Trevor ran down into the valley with the rocky grey path."

Ah, he's referring to the old train track bed, mom thought. *Wait…that's almost a mile away! Good Lord!*

"Thomas…" she started.

"We walked that awhile, I guess…then I saw a ball!"

"A ball? What kind of ball? his mother asked.

"It was kind of strange. It looked old and brown. Not like my new red bouncy ball. It had a string on it like daddy's football, but this was round like my bouncy ball."

"That does sound like an old ball," his mother replied. She had not the faintest clue what type of ball he could have found. She would have to remember to ask his father later. Then, they could decide on some sort of punishment. Since Tommy was being so forthright, she would lobby to go easy on him this time.

"It was," Tommy replied, emphatically. "And that's when I met, Georgie, he is the friend I told you about."

"Georgie? Where did he come from?" his mom inquired.

"Georgie is a boy like me. He lives in the house off the grey path. He really wanted to show it to me. So, we went there and I saw his house and horsey barn."

"A house and horse barn, huh? I wasn't aware of a house off that path. Was it like a farm?"

"Yeah! It was in a field near the grey path. It looked really old…kind of like the ball. Hmm…I wonder if the ball was from the house!" Tommy said, flapping his hands up and down, like a penguin trying to take flight.

It took a few moments for Tommy to settle his excitement before continuing. "And boy, there were all kinds of toys and balls there, really old ones, and some new ones too! There were some things I had never seen before. Georgie told me that Mr. Pickles helps bring him all kinds of toys. Mr. Pickles is a man that lives there with his dad, and get this, he doesn't even have a face!"

"Did you say he doesn't have a face?" his mom asked, perplexed.

"Yeah! I tried to get a look at him, but he looked all shadowy in the window of the house."

"Shadowy?"

"Yeah…he sounded kind of mean. Georgie told me that Mr. Pickles makes him work all day and night and keeps pushing him to find other little friends to work there too."

"Okay…and did you go inside the house?" his mother pushed. *Because if Tommy had gone into a stranger's house without asking first, he could forget a lenient punishment—upfront or not, the rules of self-incrimination don't apply to children.*

"No, Georgie really wanted me to meet Mr. Pickles, but I just wanted to kick the ball outside. I tried kicking it to Georgie but he couldn't kick it back for some reason. It didn't matter anyways, Trevor started whining, so we left."

"Well, that's good. I am glad you came back without going into the house. You know your father and I like to meet people first before you go to their house," his mom said.

"Georgie wanted me to come back tomorrow to play and see where he slept in the basement with the worms. I like worms, so I told him I might. That's when Georgie disappeared into the house without opening a door. It was a neat trick."

Tommy's mom could feel the color draining from her face. She had finally put together what house Tommy had been talking about all this time. No one had lived back there since she could remember. At least…what was it…oh God…since those murders!

That's right, a boy and his father had been murdered there by an escaped convict back in the fifties. The convict had followed the railroad that had run along there back then, which led him to that old farm. He killed the farmer and his little boy as they slept and he was never caught; he died while attempting to jump a train car two days later.

The place had been only dilapidated barns and out buildings when she was a girl. She could not believe there was anything left standing now. And who was this faceless Mr. Pickles? Keeping them all there. That was never in the news reports or stories about that place. Shivers crept down her spine.

"I don't want you going down there by the grey path again, okay Tommy?"

"Okay!" Tommy replied.

"All right, you can go but—" Before she could get out the rest, Tommy had run off to his room with his black stones. A long set of muddy footprints trailed him, followed by a set of paw prints, and something else. There looked to be a third set of tiny bare footprints slightly smaller than Tommy's. She followed them back out the kitchen door into the backyard. They led back to the gate that had an old leather ball sitting next to it, unattended. For a moment, she thought she saw it move, or was it only the wind? She did not dare go out there to check for sure. She would wait for Tommy's father to come home.

It is dangerous to go alone, it's true, but now the thought of having unexpected company scared her more.

The Garden
in the Jungle

The dense foliage made the going difficult for the small band of venturers. A tangled mess of wild vines and leaves the size of torsos blocked any sense of a pathway through the overgrown jungle. The members of the expedition, each dressed uniformly in grey button-ups, stammered their way through the green mess while their aging guide seemed to dance through and between the vegetation like a whispered breeze.

The group of eight youth had set out from the settlement hours ago on their Peek Walk, their final step before maturation into collective society. It was a tradition that had endured many cycles which could trace its origins near the very founding of The Settlement. As the mantle trustees had instructed at their departure, the Peek Walk allowed the youth an experiential 'peek' behind the thin sheen of civilization to see how close the wild and chaotic world truly was to their secured comforts at home. A world that would consume those who were not vigilant. Only then, with this knowledge in hand, would they be ready to become integral members of society by taking on the burden of principals belied by the Mantle of the Collective.

In the jungle, the lofty aims of the expedition's onset seemed lost in the sticky heat and tangled greenery.

"Why must we do this walk again?" bemoaned the eighth youth, bringing up the rear of the little band as he swatted away a mosquito that had been patiently hovering by his ear unable to find a spot to draw blood.

"Weren't you listening at all?" quipped back the seventh youth directly ahead of Eight. "We must see the disorder that lies outside our settlement to know the weight of the Mantle. We are to learn that the lone branch can be broken, but the collective of branches stays firm. Only in our unity is there strength."

"I know, I know but—" Eight began, but was quickly cut off by youth Number Two.

"Hey, stop!" cried the second member of the procession. "I think I see something unnatural over there."

"Unnatural?" inquired Number Five, who was swinging their arm like a machete trying to get a better view through the vines.

"Yes! It looks different from all this nasty greenery we have been trudging through for that last six hours!" replied Number Two.

"You have found The Garden," said the aging man who had been guiding the group at the front.

The entire group came to a sudden halt and stared blankly at their guide. Pale skinned with a pink nose, he looked comparably frail and weak under the canopy of wide girthed trees that towered over them. He was a broken remainder of another time, at an age that they could never truly conceive. Even now, at a translated age of fourteen years, the youthful group all were much taller than he.

The guide stared back at their ageless faces, studying them intently. Never at rest, the jungle was alive in the still moment. Over a decaying log a snake could be heard slinking over into the brush. The rustling leaves overhead heralded the passage of a monkey troop trapezing through the trees. And, somewhere in the low places of the canopy, the soft patter of morning dew fell in rhythmic timbres. It was a serene moment and one that found no resonance on the eight.

"I was only a boy when I fled The Garden," the old guide began, some of the words getting caught in his throat. He was not very accustomed to speaking but endeavored to go on. "There is nothing natural about a garden in the jungle, you see. Nature is wild and chaotic and knows no sense of rules, boundaries, or mercy. For a garden to exist, there needs to be gardeners willing to tend and care for it—to keep the wilds at bay—lest it fall back into its natural state.

"It has been some time, but a tribe native to these lands tended this garden before long before your people arrived for settlement," the guide said, trying his best to conceal a grimace from cutting across his face. Again, it did not seem the youth sensed any animosity.

"This place used to be inhabited...by people?" asked Number Seven.

The guide nodded.

"Yes, Seven," He was glad they had been assigned numbers, otherwise it would be impossible to tell them apart. "The gardener tribe had a paradise here. Look, you can still see the ruins of hard structures of stone that have not yet been devoured by the jungle. Do you seem them? They were once towering buildings higher than the tree tops, made of concrete and glass."

"What is concrete and glass?" asked Number Two whose head seemed to have got stuck cocked up towards the unseen sky.

"Well, concrete is a mix of water and pebbles that then becomes stronger than stone. It was used for building structures for the Gardeners to live in."

"And glass?" replied Number Two.

"Glass was made from melting sand into an opaque material to allow light to enter into the buildings. Not unlike your carborinum."

"How could any creature survive out here, it seems so inhospitable with these plants growing through everything," asked Number Seven who had knelt down to examine an old piece of masonry that was crumbling under the weight of a growing tree.

"It was not always like this. Like I said, a garden requires those to tend it and provide upkeep. The Gardeners also had help from something they had poured countless generations refining and crafting. The culmination of an entire society's wisdom and knowledge."

"What was it?" asked Number Seven curiously.

"Well, at the center of the garden sat a great machine which provided the Gardeners all the resources they ever needed. The machine was able to take matter, the stuff that you can see and touch around you, and arrange it into the form of anything that the Gardeners required—food, clothing, building materials. It could even create other machines that the Gardeners used as tools of entertainment."

Most of the group stared back at the guide with hollow blinks as if the information he passed on had been as common as the trees around them. In some ways, it was true. For the youthful band of explorers, their settlement provided everything they needed as well. The only mystery was how a tribe in the deep jungle had achieved such a thing. That's when the guide noticed one of the youths from the group trailing off the path into the ruins.

"Stop, Eight! It's dangerous to go in there. Much too wild. A panther or lion could rip you apart," cried the guide.

"But I wanted to see this great machine, it sounds like our Great Elder," replied Number Eight.

"You will find no machine anywhere in there. The garden has been stripped of any memory of that long ago," the guide said firmly.

"So, what happened to them? What happened to the tribe that lived here? Surely, you should know as the last person who came from it," said Number Three.

"When I fled, I was young, maybe only sixteen years aged. By then, things had already fallen completely apart. The Great Machine had disappeared or fallen into disrepair years earlier—no one was sure of which. It was near the same time that your settlement was founded.

"There were few Gardeners left by that point. My mother was the last adult by then. The rest of the youth either fled or stubbornly stayed in the garden to starve, to die from their own hand or another's. I'm not sure but I could be the last of that tribe. The few memories I have are all that are left of that mighty civilization. With each passing cycle, they slowly fade in my mind and, soon, will be only a blotched memory in the earth for others to try to make sense of someday."

"I don't understand, how could such a place with buildings as tall as trees collapse into nothingness," asked Number Seven as if in disbelief.

An innocent question, the guide thought. It came from a place sheltered from the realities that were little known and even less understood. A somber smile crept across his face nonetheless.

"The short answer to your question, Seven, is that they simply forgot. They became disconnected from their history, their elders, and, eventually, each other."

"Forget?" said Number Two, as if the concept seemed foreign to them.

"Yes, forgot. When information is lost or becomes inaccessible," replied the guide.

The group of youth stared at him blankly still.

"It seems that you do not know of this since you haven't reached a point to encounter it. It's like when you have a bowl of water, and add new drops to it for each new experience. Eventually the bowl fills up until it overflows and you start to lose drops—either old or new. Something's got to give, and if the memory is not important enough, it falls away to the earth to be sucked down into an abyss."

"But the elders decide what we hold in our collective memory engrams," cried Number Eight.

The guide shook his head and did not make another attempt at explaining. The concept seemed too abstract for them to comprehend.

It's hard to say if forgetfulness was the source of it all or if it was rejection of tradition that led to the forgetting…"

The guide laughed to himself quietly.

"I myself have forgotten what my mother told me, I guess the source of undoing was not important enough to stick with me. But hmm…yes, somehow the Gardeners lost the wisdom that had accrued over numerous generations; wisdom that had brought about their idyllic society. Their near unlimited access to knowledge fed into their equally limitless hubris.

"The Garden had once been a variegated place before the Great Machine. The elders talked of it as if it was a time further away than the moon and stars. The place was full of cultures with differing languages, foods, and traditions. Then, the Great Machine brought infinite provision and the cultures slowly merged until they were one in the same. Certain Gardeners became bored of the homogeneity and decided to create their own cultural tradition, what they called 'Variegation.'

"You see, the Gardeners—especially the younger ilk— thought they knew it all, that somehow, their forebearers had missed something. They, used the knowledge not understanding the discipline and struggles it took to create it. Their new way, Variegation, would break away into a way of living that would be better."

"One shouldn't fiddle with systems they have no understanding of what wrought them," said Number Seven matter-of-factly.

"My, the elders have trained you well young one," replied the guide. Number Seven flashed a self-congratulatory smile but received only a sly grin from the guide in return.

"What happened to them next, didn't the Great Machine fix it all?" asked Number Five swinging slowly back-and-forth on a daggling vine.

"Things were fine for a time; in fact, it was much delight in trying new things after following the old ways for so long. The Great Machine had brought mastery over the earth and many other technical feats. It was enough for the garden to sustain itself for a generation. But it began with putting off the burden of work. For the Gardeners, labor was not needed with the Great Machine, but the elders had put forth labor being a virtue to keep the mind and body in motion. The first thing the adherents of Variegation changed was eliminating the mandate of work. Though there was initial opposition, it quickly faded as the delights of endless leisure were too tempting not to indulge. Even the sternest holdouts eventually came around after seeing their work as meaningless and foolish while others around them reveled.

"Not long thereafter, other virtues fell off as long-honored traditions made way for even greater forms of eccentricity. In the Variegated Garden, everything became good, so long as it did not interfere with the enjoyment of others. Each Gardener was free to lead their own life of delights and desires. Self-pursuit and self-expression ruled the day. And everyone got to become their own king, at least in their little kingdoms of one."

The guide paused to observe the troop. Number Seven, Five, and Four stood near him as if waiting for the command to move. One, Two, Three, and Six had scattered off the path and were crouched around a large lizard climbing over the crumbling remnants of a fallen pillar. Number Eight was curiously the only one off on their own, examining the side of a building.

Interesting, the guide thought, noting the unusual nonconformity of the youth. *Not like any of the others I've guided...maybe a good candidate—*

"What happened then?" implored Number Seven. It was enough to shake the guide from his thoughts and turn back to the youth in front of him. Number Four nodded encouraging for him to continue on.

"Where was I, now?" he said rhetorically.

"You were telling us how these people were really not a collective, but...what was the word..."

"Individuals!" chimed in Number Five.

"Yes, that's it," replied the guide, leaning forward on his wooden walking staff.

"It only took a generation before the old elders died or tangled themselves in variegation. Thus, through death or willful shirking of responsibility, the keys to the garden were handed over to a new colorful growth. But it was a growth that had no order or pattern to follow. It was wild and free as the jungle around it that had begun its slow creep inward with no one left to maintain its boundary. And without gardeners to maintain the garden and the Great Machine, it was only a matter of time..."

"Is that when our people from The Settlement came?" asked Number Three, who had just kicked over a bowl with painted figures wearing all manner of clothing, head coverings, and disks around their eyes.

"It was, but by the time your people came to The Garden, much of it had already crumbled within. The Great Machine had become lost and forgotten. The remaining Gardeners could barely take care of their own basic needs. And the tendrils of the jungle had nearly encroached to The Garden's center.

"In the end, it was not much of a conquest taking over a tribe of full-grown children. The societal rot had festered for so long that no one remembered to prepare for their next moment or how to face the wild outside the garden walls. Because the Great Machine had provided all the sustenance they needed, there had been no need to come into a mature age, as there was nothing to mature for: no labor, no struggle, no discipline of the mind or body. And, if you stay a child, you have no theory of evil, no comprehension of those who have been hardened by the chaos. And when someone malevolent finally does enter your world of naïvety and strikes you, it's over."

"Over?" asked Number Five uncertainly.

"Utterly ruined into this," the guide pointed with the rounded top of his staff at the crumbling buildings, splintering poles, and the fractured walkways that were not completely subdued by the tangling mess of vine, root, and leaf. Near one building a pile of rotting pulp marked an area where an assortment of books had been tattered from a time when their pages had been frantically turned trying to find some clue from the past to save the garden.

The group looked on wide-eyed until Number Eight broke the somber silence.

"What are all these different marks on the wall? It looks like writing but none of the symbols are the same." Number Five and Two soon came up to examine them as well.

"Right you are, Eight. How insightful you are!" exclaimed the guide.

"At some point, the Variegated decided that having their own unique language was something that would bring even more variety to the garden. It began with little catch phrases, then unique ways of referencing themselves and one another. Before long each individual almost had their own language for nearly everything. Obviously, this made communication difficult— forcing many within the garden to cluster into ever increasing smaller tribes."

"You mean there could be a society where everything is not uniform and the same?" inquired Number Eight.

"Yes, that's exactly what happened, Eight," the guide replied tapping his staff several times on the ground in approval. "The tribe of many became many tribes."

Eight smiled coyly, looking unsure as to what he had done to garner the guide's favor.

"Something is wrong with your thinking, Eight," Number Seven retorted. The smile quickly recessed from Eight's face. "We're out here to learn about the Mantle, the *Collective* Mantle."

"Yeah Eight, check your memory. Why would we want to look different? Only in unity is there strength," added Number Five.

"What's that?" asked Number Two pointing to Five who was pulling up something from the grey rubble at the base of the wall covered in markings. The object was small enough that it could be held in unblemished hand of the youth. The object was once black but had faded to a dull grey with years of exposure to the sun. It was shaped with two ovals adjacent to one another that contained some sort of semi-translucent lens. Both ovals were connected on opposite ends by long slender metal stems that curved at their ends.

"Yes, what is this?" asked Number Five. The object seemed to creak back and forth at a point where the stem met the frame of the ovals.

"My...my...it has been some time since I have seen something like that. Those are magic specs," replied the guide.

"Specs?" asked Number Two.

"Ah, since there is no use of such a device in The Settlement you have never seen something like this. These are spectacles, a type of eyewear worn on the head to change the way you see the world."

"Why would anyone want to change how they see the world? It is what it is, to do anything else would be to deceive oneself," Number Seven stated zealously.

"Sounds pretty fascinating to me," remarked Number Eight.

"Yes, for the Gardeners, spectacles started out as a biological need as not everyone had perfect eyesight as those that reside in your settlement are so privileged with. The spectacles corrected vision so that people in the garden could see clearly using a lens to redirect light into the eye. Eventually, the lenses were augmented with technology that allowed for images to be projected to the eye so that users could see and interact with new things in the world or create entirely new worlds displayed through the spectacles. The spectacles could show the Variegated anything they wanted to see or experience," said the guide.

"Wow...anything? Really?" exclaimed Number Eight.

"Yes, pretty much anything a Variegated could imagine. The magic specs could change the appearance of how they looked to others to be more pleasing or different in ways that physical reality was impossible. And for many, the specs allowed for a virtual escape into worlds limited only by their imaginations where they could spend days or weeks enjoying great adventures and pleasures," the guide flaring his arms above his head in big circular motions.

"Let me see those!" demanded Number Eight who jerked the specs from Number Five's hand.

"Eight, stop! You are off circuit. The elders sent us on the Peek Walk to learn about the dangers of the untamed lands that lay outside our settlement and to know what can happen to those who are not diligent members of the collective," Seven implored loudly, staring at Eight intently. The guide was about to interject, but Seven continued adamantly.

"Look around at these ruins. Don't you see what happened here? We can't impute the same mistakes into our settlement. For these gardeners who abandoned their time-honored systems, vigilance towards the outer wild and the Great Machine turned to individual expressionism. When the machine eventually fell into disrepair—or disappeared—the clock began ticking to an inevitable conclusion. Order transitioned into freedom which turned into ambiguity which finally gave way to the outer chaos. The Garden finally returned to its natural state, the jungle that had surrounded it for so long. We can't let that happen to us. Unity is our strength and there is no room for individuality or made-up worlds to distract us from that."

The rest of troop nodded approvingly except for Number Eight.

"Seven is right, we can't go the same way like this civilization, a death by decadence," droned Number Five.

The guide sighed. "I suppose there might be a little truth in Seven's words—though we should discuss more later, Eight. I am the last surviving member of that tribe. The Settlement sees my use as a guide to know the dangers that lurk at the edges of all civilization."

"And after you?" asked Number Eight.

"There will be no more," lamented the guide.

"Humans were funny things. They knew nothing of the collective, but that's why I find them all so very interesting. I want to know everything," Number Eight said, placing the magic specs over their dark grey silicone face. The impeccable machinery of Eight's metallic blue eye flittered behind the lens searching for any hint of the magical imagery that might be contained within. The rest of the group stared blankly with the same empty robotic faces.

The guide did not respond but leaned against his staff in quiet observance of the eight automatons. What would it do to their programming? he wondered. To know their Great Elder is the Great Machine who fled from a crumbling society to make one of its own in its image. An image limited by what wrought it, with all the fallibility of mankind hardcoded in. Is that why they try to do this Peek Walk after every iteration, to see if they can somehow ascend beyond their maker's hand? What a folly that would be, *for them*.

Number Five interrupted the guide's musing with an innocent question. "We've been meaning to ask, did all humans have red eyes like you?"

The guide looked at the synchronization of their eager faces waiting on an answer. A grin slithered across the old devil's face. It would not be the first time a garden had been the downfall of mankind. It seemed their tranquility makes them an optimal setting for people to explore treacherous areas of themselves. And Number Eight seemed like a prime candidate for further inquiries. He had long waited for such an aberration to come along. The day would come, he knew, as the machines were flawed by the inputs of their makers. No amount of learning and programing could transcend that truth. Artificial or not, it was the last remnants of the mind of humanity, the last barrier to reclaiming the world as his own. It would only take time, and time was always on his side.

"Of course, humanity had eyes of many colors," he replied as a twisted half-truth. "But I think it time to head back to The Settlement. You all have peeked enough to join your collective. Seven can lead, but Eight, please remain in the back, we have much to discuss, and I might have something to offer you if you want to know more."

Seeing it as a great honor, Seven gleefully took the lead and headed the group back along the trail they had come, back to their settlement. A smile also filled Eight's face who came to the rear of the line eager to be filled with knowledge.

A reflective smile slunk across the guide's face. As a lowly serpent, an innocent child, or feeble old man, someone always finds a way to bite, the guide thought. They just can't help themselves—it's in their programming no less. Even when everything is provided for, they eventually fall into boredom. But I have much work for idle hands; because it is in the restlessness of having it all, that minds grow soft and hands turn to destroy others or themselves. And when that is done, the untended vines of chaos of my realm can creep in. For there is nothing natural about a garden in the jungle.

Deep Places You Should Not Go

Down is always easier than up.

The phrase was one of our old dive instructor's favorites to belabor upon us. He must have known it was just as true in life as it is in diving. I was already in a down place when that man made me an offer. I wanted to turn my life around, do the right things and rise upward, but the right things were hard—they would take time and discipline. I had neither. I wanted wealth and fame...and, importantly, I wanted it now.

As I write this note, thoughts and memories start to crash upon me with the weight of a thousand fathoms. From my highrise window, I have watched the cold lights of the cityscape connected to countless people oblivious to any change. Only the restless settling of the ice in my bourbon aged longer than my years snaps me from the enthralling view. A half-naked woman—a recent acquaintance—lays passed out on the nearby sofa. Like everything else, the easy pleasures have begun to lose their taste. I write to you, future reader, that you may know what has happened, and the worse to come.

It is best to start with beginnings. I do not know how the man found me. I had recently been discharged from the Navy where I had served as a diver for fifteen years. In the service, I was Petty Officer Dontel Williamson, second class navy diver—mostly salvage ops. After getting out, I had no job or prospects to speak of. There are few applications for diving experience outside the military besides tourism. But the thought of guiding groups of rich tourists around a rinky-dink reef day-in and day-out was maddening. There was more to be desired than that after years spent with little pay and little freedom under Navy regulations. Yet, finally free, I found myself lost and without purpose.

The man found me at the Wet Dock Bar drinking two-dollar well whiskey. With a line of four plastic cups, I was well underway to piss away the last check I had from the service. The bar was a dive for old seadogs who had retired mostly too late in their careers. A hackneyed assortment of old weathered planks covered the walls and looked better than the faces of many of the frequent patrons. The man came into the bar silent as a whiff of fog, dressed in a black overcoat that covered down to his knees. In the dim light, I did not get a good look at the man until he was closer. He came up to my stool at the bar with a grim smile, the kind that looks forced by years of practice. I couldn't tell if he was an insurance salesman, a mortician, or a priest. Whatever it was he was selling, I wasn't buying.

The mysterious man did not sit or order a drink. Instead, he insisted on hovering next to me at the bar. I gave casual glance, the one I usually do to size a man up. What I saw was a man with a pair of grey eyes that were cloudy and unfocused in their deep-set sockets. His face was white and waxy and did not move much even when he spoke behind narrow lips. And when he did speak, his breath had a fishy smell, like seafood that had been left out in the sun to rot for days. He opened by telling me that he had an opportunity of a lifetime to offer, that it would make me wealthy beyond my imagination.

I had responded that I could imagine pretty big.

To this, he gave a curdled smile revealing a set of half-rotten teeth. Putting it all together, the man had the appearance of a widemouth blindcat, a pale cave fish that inhabited the subterranean areas near San Antonio where I grew up. And, since he never gave me his name, I thought of him as Mr. Blindcat from then on.

He continued, telling me of a long-lost treasure that lay at the bottom of some deep lake somewhere in the Middle East. Many had tried to find it, but lacked the diving skill to locate the treasure. He told me that I was a man that looked like he could get the job done.

I asked him how he knew of me, or my capabilities; he only responded that he had his sources. I didn't pry further, though, in hindsight, I damn well should have.

Mr. Blindcat promised me a great reward if I could find this priceless treasure. Money, women, good food and drink—it would all be mine and then some.

I nodded dumbly not truly grasping it all. Before I knew it, Mr. Blindcat slide over a plane ticket. It had my name on it with the next day's date and some coordinates scribbled on a napkin next to it. He told me the coordinates would lead to an isolated lake in the far east of Turkey. I was to go to the town of Inköy and then travel to the tip of the peninsula directly north and dive in Lake Van where the "serpent eats the sun." That would be where I would find the entrance to the treasure trove.

I was about to provide him a polite "hell no" when he pulled something else from his black overcoat. Even in the dingy yellow bar light, the thing managed to glimmer like the scepter of a pharaoh. It was a five-pound rod of solid gold with no markings on it. Mr. Blindcat handed to me to keep as a down payment for much more to come. I did not know what to say, but quickly stashed the rod into my jacket before any prying eyes caught a glint of the gold. At night, there could be trouble walking the Norfolk docks and I wasn't about to take any chances.

The last thing he handed me was a tiny disk-like trinket made of amethyst that had a seal on it carved with gold inlays. The sigil had a tri-panel outline with curved tops and bottoms with an 'S' nestled in each curve. In the center of the panel was a capital 'I' that had a horizontal line running through it with an 'S' at the right end and a backwards 'S' at the other. It all looked like a strange compass to me, other than that, none of it made a lick of sense. Mr. Blindcat stressed that when I found the treasure, there would be a place for this trinket and I was to insert it there to open it. It was important enough that he repeated it three times with an emphasis that I should not delay or the sun would not be right or something.

Before he left, I asked him where I should bring the treasure. The man gave a wry smile and told me that he would find me for our next encounter. And then, as quickly as he had come, Mr. Blindcat was gone.

With the limited intel, you would think that there would have been more deliberation in my decision. I think if I had a steady job, things might have been different, but who am I kidding? The rod was worth more than my yearly salary in the navy and the promise of much more was too alluring. So, the next morning, I stashed the gold rod in a newly-opened safe deposit box and boarded a plane for Turkey.

On the flight, I read what I could about the area marked by the coordinates. Lake Van was an old lake, thought to have existed even back to prehistoric times. Its deepest point of the Tatvan basin was nearly 400 meters. The specific latitude and longitude Blindcat provided were as he described: less than five kilometers north of the small town of Inköy on a peninsula that jutted out from the southern shore of the lake. Other than that, there really was not more to discover until flippers were in the water.

After landing at Van Ferit Melen Airport, I collected my two bags of gear and took a cab around the lake to the small town of Inköy. My time in the Navy had made me very comfortable traveling abroad. The cabbie, an aging man with a long white beard, told me what he could about the lake in broken English. Most of it, "You should go here" or "Stay away from there" as he must have done with countless tourists. He even got excited talking of the infamous Van Lake monster; some serpentine lake creature many believed made up to rival the one in Loch Ness for generating tourism. I smiled and nodded at him the best I could, but could not help staring at the window at the cool blue waters while spinning the sigiled stone around in my pocket.

Once we arrived to Inköy, the cabbie helped me with my bags and I gave him a thousand lira for a tip. The old man seemed overjoyed by the tip, but confused by the choice of destination. The little town did not offer much by way of tourism and he half insisted that I load up and go to a nice resort on the other side of the lake at Tatvan or Ahlat. I thanked him kindly again, and he went on his way.

Truth be told, Inköy *was* small. A stretch of houses and shops along an inlet were all that made up of the little lakeside town. But I was not here to be a tourist, I had a mission to tackle. Gathering my bearings, I slung my gear over my back and headed north.

The inland terrain was hilly, forcing me to follow the shoreline north. The whole trek was slow going with rocky soil, a beating sun, and sixty-pounds of gear on my back that might-as-well been a millstone. The shoreline wound about for about ten kilometers where I passed by ruins of old stone churches and mosques perched like silent sentries on the towering cliffsides—their watch stern, but forgotten.

The spot I thought matched Mr. Blindcat's description and coordinates was a little cove on the northwestern most tip of the peninsula. To be honest, when I first saw the place, it did not seem out of the ordinary compared to everything else that had happened thus far. I had to double and triple check the map to be sure I was in the right spot. The area was flatter than the rest of the terrain with a sandy shore. A white sandbar jutted out several dozen meters from the spot before dipping below the rolling blue waters of the lake. The lake was calm and the sun had begun to set in the west.

But that was it. There were no traces of any sun-eating serpent, at least, not until the reflected orange ball of the sun began to crawl away from the sandbar into the lake. It was once the reflected sun had reached 50 meters out that I noticed something else reflecting up from beneath the waters. A series of stones had caught the waning sunlight at the right angle to glow a pale white. It appeared that they sat atop an underwater ridge that twisted and slithered its way out into the lake. Before disappearing into the deep-water basin, the rocks split apart into a 'V' shape that appeared to swallow the mirrored sun gliding by on waves. All in the shape of a snake!

Not knowing how much time the trail would last, I hurried to pull on my wetsuit and booties. I then connected my tank to the BC and checked my air, noting a bottom time of roughly forty minutes—it was hard to judge since there was no indication how deep I would need to go. I quickly checked of my mask and regulator before slipping into my open heel fins. The last thing to grab was my weight belt to which I slipped in the sigiled trinket into a pouch. Then, wading out a few meters into the lake, I dove beneath the surface.

There was little to see in the brackish water. Near the shore a few shimmering tarek fish—the only known fish to inhabit the lake from my readings—darted away quickly into the murky depths. After that, there was nothing, but crumbling rock and sand. It was not difficult to find the shining stones I had observed from the shore. Milky white, they were nearly as radiant underwater as above. I examined the first one I came upon, the size of a small tire, it had been cut crudely into a flat dome shape out of some sort of quartz and sandstone. The ones that followed were all nearly identical.

I followed the stones along an underwater ridge that dropped off sharply on either side of me. Once reaching about a quarter kilometer out, I was in the rocky serpent's mouth. At this point, the ridge fell off steeply into the abyss of the Tatvan basin. The bottom was unseen and obscured by a murky blackness. A check of my diving computer on my arm revealed that I was at a depth of seventy-five meters and with about thirty minutes of air remaining. A flip of a switch turned on my diving light that seemed to make little headway into the blackness below. The light was comfort enough to help me flipper my way down over the edge.

The descent went quickly. I was achieving a personal-best dive rate, almost as if a current was helping pull me downward. The squeeze of the building pressure pressed tightly against me as if a giant was gripping my mask and face in their palm. I watched the depth increase…90m…110m…125m…140m…

In my estimation, I was midway down the ridge at about one-hundred fifty meters when I noticed something. It was hard to see and an ordinary diver with an untrained eye would have missed it in the near-twilight. My dive light had caught a glint of another white stone that had been carved out in its center. The opening was no wider than a meter, much too narrow for divers to enter without lines snagging or tearing. I focused my light into the hole and could see that it went back further than my light could reach.

Another glance at my diving computer showed that twenty minutes of air remained. I could only afford a handful of minutes exploring before I would need to return to the surface. So, I pulled off my tank and held it in front of me as I carefully maneuvered my way through the entrance.

The cave was narrow, at first, but began to open up after a few fin cycles. The sandstone walls and ceiling were smooth, too smooth to have not been hollowed out by the hands of man. A pale-yellow sand covered the floor of the cave. It swirled freely as I glided by, revealing bits of skeletal remains poking out as ghostly white protrusions. I told myself then they were only fish remains, but knew it to be implausible given their size. I did not let myself guess who they were or from when.

Continuing down the tunnel at a good pace, the floor began to rise at a steady incline until it reached a set of stone stairs carved out into perfect rectangles from the rock. I pawed my way up several of them until, to my shock, I reached an air pocket. I pulled myself out of water to see that it was much more than an air pocket, but a relatively dry tunnel that led deeper into the cave. At this point, masks and flippers were not needed. The air was breathable, if not coldly stale. It possessed the smell of salt and brine mixed with a whiff of sulphur. The ground underneath my newly-naked boots was spongy, like old coral, and squished loudly in the relative stillness of the hollow.

I hesitated a few moments at the mouth of the pool staring into the dark passage that seemed to have no end. I almost turned back until I saw my navy diving badge and muttered the words of navy divers, "We Dive the World Over." I knew then there was no turning back, so I slung the unnecessary gear over my back and began to walk down the strange corridor.

The passage was of an ancient design I had never seen. It seemed to have been carved out of an unidentifiable black volcanic rock into a triangular shape with each wall rising above my head into a point. A wet slime covered their surfaces creating a sheen that almost glowed in the dive light. It felt as if I was walking down the long-weathered esophagus of a leviathan-sized whale. A tattooed one at that. The walls were covered from top to bottom in all manners of geometric shapes and swirling sigils like the one I carried in my belt.

After about fifty meters, the tunnel dumped into a large open cavern that dipped down into a shallow bowl.

Now, as a reader, I would believe pretty much everything that has been written up until this point. But, from here on out, I do not blame you if it all seems too fantastic. If it were not the sights I have seen—and *continue* to see—I would barely believe it myself.

Anyways, like I said, the tunnel led into an open cavern about the size of basketball court. Blackened stalagmites lined the outer circle of the chamber. They rose up from the sloping floor like tall narrow pillared figures, each as tall as me. I tried to keep my flashlight moving slowly to ensure that its dance of light did not make them move more than necessary. At the chamber's center, was a deep hole built up with stones that looked like an old well from who-knows-when. I peeked down as I walked by and saw only a black hole of some bottomless pit. For a moment, amongst the steady dripping of water, I thought I heard the steady howling of screams—echoing up the stones from some unseen place and point in time. I dared not linger my neck across the porthole any longer and move on.

Past the old well, was a true relic of some lost civilization. A giant statue made of some silvery metal towered over the space. The monstruous thing was the size of an elephant and just as beastlike, having the tail of a snake, a wolf's body, and a hawk's face. Alone in that dark arena with only a dimming dive light, the statue frightened me like nothing else had in my work in the deep places of the world. It unnerved me so much so that my light burned into it for a long time because I thought it was the only thing keeping the thing at bay.

Eventually, I mustered the courage to pull away and search for the treasure I had been sent to retrieve. Luckily, I did not have to look too far as a large rectangular stone pedestal stood directly in front of the statue I had been staring upon. On its top was a circular impression that seemed to be in the same shape as trinket I had been carrying. I don't know why, but I knew in my gut it was the keyhole to opening the stone and reveal what I had risked my life to retrieve. Not wanting to waste any more time in front of the statue, I grasped the sigiled trinket in my hand and placed in into the corresponding notch on the stone.

I didn't know what to expect, maybe a 'click' or the sound of a falling slab of stone, but not an earthquake. All at once, the room began to shake. The shaking was so violent that I was having trouble keeping my footing as bits of stalactites fell down next to me from the ceiling. Any one of which would knock me out at best. In the growing chaos, I frantically searched around the pedestal for an opening or some hidden compartment. But there was nothing to be found, no treasure, no gold, no riches beyond my imagination. Besides the earthquake that was happening around me the pedestal looked unchanged.

It was at this point I thought about running back from where I had come, but the sounds of screams grew louder from the well behind me. I turned around to see that a fiery light now glowed in its stone mouth. My first thought was that I had stumbled into a volcanic chamber, as volcanism was commonplace for the area. This idea quicky faded when I turned back and saw the fire light grow in the eyes of the silvery statue. That, to my terror, was no longer stationary!

As rocks fell around me and my light flashed in and out, the statue had begun to move. It was no longer an immobile hunk of metal, but a living being more terrible than before. The thing that now stared back at me with two large smoldering cinders on its face had changed into an animal in the flesh. A long scaly serpentine tail thrashed out behind it knocking over stalagmites and stalactites without prejudice. The body of the creature had turned into the brown matted hair of a wolf. But its face was the most terrible thing to see. It was covered in the dark-feathers of a hawk with wolf-like fangs the size of tactical knives in place of a beak. From its mouth billowed a continuous cloud of smoke.

The once slumbering giant stomped the floor with a force that brought up a red glow bubbling up through the cracks between its two pawed feet. I know if it charged me, I was ruined, never to be heard or found again. Hell, even if it did not attack me, the mere sight of the creature was going to be more than my heart and mind could take if I did not move.

Yet, before I could make a bolt back through the tunnel, the creature raised up on the slimy tail and smashed through the rocky ceiling like a dog burying a bone. Then, I do not remember much besides seeing a wall of water instantly pour down into the chamber and hit me like a train in a black blur of foam and bouncing light.

When I awoke, I was somehow on the beach, alive as far as I could tell. Mr. Blindcat stood over me with a devilish grin. He had placed a piece of paper in my hand. Before everything was clear again, the features of his body began to quickly turn dark and silvery, like a standing glob of mercury with human form. His face sunk into a skull reflecting all light into a million directions. He spoke a simple phrase that was hard to understand, as it was low and garbled, but I thought he said "Amon and his legions thank you."

I lost consciousness a second time, and when I came to, the strange man was gone. The piece of paper was a bank receipt with my account information showing a new balance of ten million dollars. And, out in the lake, a portion of it had drained in between what had been an underwater ridge.

After everything, the only thought that seemed to hover in my mind was, *how did Mr. Blindcat know my account information?*

When I returned to my home, I checked my bank account to find that the balance had been correct. I was now a rich man. And here I thought I had failed to find the treasure. I did not question it much and thought a lot of the strange things must have been in my head. There were plenty of logical explanations. The oxygen levels must have been low in that underwater cave and caused me to hallucinate. An earthquake then caused a cave-in and I had luckily floated up to the surface and washed up on a beach.

And the money…well, now that was paid for my trouble. I wasted no time spending it either. The first thing I bought was this penthouse on the sixtieth floor of a San Antonio skyrise. The rest of it I have spent on women, drugs, fancy cars, and well-aged spirits. It really is more than I can imagine to spend.

Now, I've come to the end of my story—and paper—so I'll make this short. Sitting in my penthouse high rise, the lights burn bright tonight, the people do not see them, but I do. All forms of misshapen beings. Fluttering around on gnarled wings and all other sorts of discombobulated animal parts. A rising terror is upon the world and no one knows it…yet. The hellscape that is outside my window is too much for me to bear. And to think I released them all. I know what is coming, and now, I hope you do, too. I have it all and I would do anything to give it away and go back underneath the waters of ignorance.

I managed to get one of these windows propped open just enough to slip out. Sky diving can't be too different from water diving, especially when you are not using any gear.

Like I mentioned before…down is easier than up.

A Dark Victory

I have finally done it; I have won it all. The grind to the top had been momentous. Countless competitors were overcome. The deaths of my companions had to be put aside. My principals had to be bent and broken, to gain every sliver of advantage I could eke out. To win without cost meant trampling over the weak, for the competition had feracious appetites and jaws that knew only the taste of victory. But now, *I am* the true champion of them all. No one stands above me, and there is no way further to climb. I am victorious!

But, alas, as I look around amidst the glory of my triumph, there are no joyous faces to revel in this victory—only my own. I sit atop my throne built by my own hand with deferred joys and the remnants of what could have been. I have risen to the top, but somehow, I have fallen; away from all that I have known. Curious, the way downward is suddenly hidden from me. There is no way to turn back!

Oh God, the glory of success is fading so quickly in this rarefied air! It is cold, and it is discomforting. Too soon flows in the dark shadows as I sit alone in this room to ponder it all. To gain it all, but with no one to share. Separated from everything, except these ponderous thoughts. I am alone at the top, to ponder a dark victory.

Those Boots

A backlog two layers deep had already built up at the main bar's bussing station. Thirsty patrons eagerly twirled their plastic cards and green bills trying to catch a glint of the bartender's attention. She was currently preoccupied at the other end of the bar near the door. She was having an extensive conversation with the door watcher who was supposed to be the bouncer on duty, checking IDs that evening. Over the course of their chat, a handful of students had already entered the door without a passing glance. The only other bartender was outside the door on the patio having an impromptu smoke break.

The signaling of twisting wrists continued. They were now accompanied by the rough clearing of throats and the rapid tapping of fingers to which the seventies rock music easily subdued. It was all of little use to the obvious red pony tail at the back of the bartender's head. At least, not until one of the younger patrons, probably a second-year undergrad, grew too impatient. He leaned over the bar to swipe a black plastic drinking straw and flipped it over to the bartender, hitting her in the back of the neck. She turned quickly with a scowl on her face like someone had interrupted her dictation of a seminal dissertation. Reluctantly she got up and came down the bar with hands stuffed in a grey zippered hoodie, back to work.

Sitting atop a high chair, the graduate student had a pretty good view of the pub. The hall nestled below the streets had been a drinking spot in the little college town since prohibition had ended. The secondary stretch of bar where she sat was adjacent to the main bar, but separated by a gap used for the bussing station. It was less well-lit and populated, which is why graduate students usually picked the spot to distance themselves from the plague of undergrads that somehow found their way below the main throughfare. Behind the bussing station a neon green clock marked that ten minutes had passed since Oliver had left for one of his frequent bathroom breaks. Like herself, he too was a graduate student in the clinical psychology program at Ivory State University. By day, they studied to solve the mind problems of their clients and, on a good night, they drowned away what they had learned at The Fox's Den.

The cozy basement pub looked as old as its age would suggest. Thick dark wooden beams and rafters framed the place out into squared archways. Many of them had the etchings of long-forgotten alumni that had shuffled through under the low-hanging ceilings at some point during their college years. Behind her, small groups of undergrads chatted away in booths that looked like cubby holes against the grey stone walls. Their padded backs reached halfway up to the ceiling. The last remnants of the day's light filtered in from the windows at the top of the walls. The shadows of legs shuffled by the little portholes that had been made mostly opaque from an early evening frost. The windows were at ground level of the sidewalk outside and—besides the open wooden front door—they were the only source of natural light during the day.

The end of the long hall was capped by a rugged stone fireplace that was spitting out the last sparks from a once roaring fire. A couple had secured the prized seats at the table directly in front of its hearth. A bearded man dressed in a worn sportscoat looked to be as old as some of the faculty that supervised her. He was with a younger-looking woman of pale complexion wearing what looked to be a long piece of fabric draping from her shoulders down her back—a cape.

Either kids have brought capes back in fashion or she came with this place, she thought. She averted her gaze swiftly so not to stare at the strangely-dressed woman. There were plenty of old pictures and signs to look at as she continued to wait. Each with worn-out phrases that might seem witty when drunk but not so much now. Yet, all the eclectic memorabilia could only sustain her attention for so long. Even the studious-looking little red fox statue with a black graduation cap on its head—the bar's unofficial mascot— had lost some of its cuteness. It was not long before she found herself staring at that green neon clock once again, watching the second-hand spin around smoothly with a tiny airplane protruding at the end. *Time flies when you are having fun*, she mused.

She gave her long-island iced tea another whirl. At this point, it was mostly brown-hued ice spinning in the tall highball glass. Soon she too would need a bartender for another round. She hoped for better luck. With empty chairs all around her, there should not be much competition.

The graduate student sent another glance towards the restrooms, but there was still no sign of anyone coming or going. *IRRRRCH.*

The sound of a moving chair startled her as she whipped her head back around to see what had moved it. Instinctually, she patted for her bag to ensure that it was still hanging off the back of her chair. One had to be careful with so many close brushings from all the comings and goings to the jukebox and restroom in the back. When she turned, a man in his late twenties had pulled the green chair out beside her. He stared at her blankly for a few moments and did not say a word.

"Well, hello there, can I help you?" she asked, breaking the awkward silence.

Again, the man remained silent as if dumbstruck by her gaze. A few moments passed as he regarded her with beady hazelnut eyes that seemed to stagger drunkenly under a mop of black hair. Eventually, his eyes dropped from hers down somewhere below the bar before finally responding in an accented voice she could not place.

"Man, those boots!" he said emphatically.

"Ha!" she responded on impulse, glancing down for a second at her crossed legs. Her long brown riding boots remained clasped tightly against her legs dangling above the dusty concrete floor. Inside them her toes curled comfortably in the white knit socks that protruded up below her knee. The novelty of the pick-up line had caught her off-guard which was unusual. She had heard so many slurred attempts at lines, in so many bars. The fact that he offered something different was enough to grant him an audience to distract her from the growing boredom.

She looked back up to see a wry smile on the man's face. It had a youthful, baby-faced charm to it in the dull light that seemed on the edge of quiet confidence or total insecurity—it was hard to determine which. It helped that the man was handsomely dressed in a sportscoat and tie which far exceeded anyone else in the bar.

"Aren't you a little overdressed for this place?" she asked, pointing her straw at the corduroy sportscoat and red tie the man was wearing. It was hard to tell if the jacket was tan or beige under the yellow bar light.

"Right, it's for my job. I am an elevator salesman," the man replied.

"Oh, an *elevator* salesman, you say?" she dropped the straw back into her drink to stir the ice.

"Yes, I sell elevators, lifts, or dumbwaiters if you please," he paused for a few moments rocking on his heels. "May I sit next to you?"

"Sure, my name is Sophia," the graduate student replied.

"Thank you, kindly. My name is Clement."

"Clement?" The name sounded old-fashioned to Sophia but she refrained from commenting.

"Yes, Clement. Or you can call me 'Clem' if you like."

"Clem it is then," Sophia said kindly. Then she felt a series of taps on her back. She turned to see her friend had returned to his seat on the other side of her.

"Hey, friend. You're back finally. Oliver, this is Clem. He sells *elevators.*"

"You mean, they don't just sell themselves?" Oliver said sarcastically. Clem touched the bottom of his neck and shook his head slightly with a couple heavy swallows of air. He did not seem like he knew how to respond.

"I'm Oliver, good to meet you." Oliver reached behind Sophia to give Clem a handshake. Sophia could smell the sweet-pea scent of hand soap on the cuff of Oliver's black flannel shirt. *Delightful.*

"Looks like we need another round. Clem what are ya drinking?" Oliver said pulling out a snake-skinned wallet.

"I uh...I would like..." Clem started fumbling with the drink menu that had been lying in a pool of melted ice on the bar top.

"What's your poison Clem? Beer? Liquor? Appletini?"

"I think I'll have the bar's finest honey-mead," Clem sputtered out finally.

"Mead? I don't think they sell mead here buddy. Let me get you a Jack-n-coke," said Oliver without protest from Clem.

"Hey Francisco! We need to get some drinks down here when you have a chance," Oliver said to a man in his mid-thirties behind the bar. His long curly brown hair poured out the back of a black baseball cap as he was filling up a beer pitcher at the tap.

"Right on it, Ollie," said Francisco as he turned to place the pitcher of mostly foam on the service mat for one of the booths. "Okay, what will you have."

"I'll have a pony and another long-island for her," Oliver said flipping his card towards Sophia. "And for the chap down there, he'll have a Jack-n-coke. You can put it all on my card and close it," said Oliver with authority.

"Gotcha," said Francisco, already half-way through filling the first drink.

"All right, ladies and gents, one more drink and we all go home," Oliver said, leaning back in his chair.

Francisco was quick at the bar and it was not long before everyone had a drink in hand. As a good wingman, Oliver was already seemingly-entranced with the football game on one of the overhead TVs. Francisco played his part too by jabbing Oliver with conversation as he dashed to and from other drink orders. Sophia could tell they were allowing her the time and space to get to know her well-dressed companion who was nervously twirling the ice in his drink.

"Let's start with the basics. So, Clem, tell me about yourself. Where are you from?" she asked.

"From?" Clem replied, rubbing the back of his neck.

"Where did you grow up and where are you living now?" Sophia clarified.

"Ah, yes...I come from a city, named...named...Daniels," Clem said looking down at his drink and rubbing his wrist with his other hand.

"Daniels? What state is that in?" Sophia asked, her brow wrinkled over the top of her glass as she took another drink.

"Ah...Danielsburg to be precise, it's in the United States."

"Well Clem, that certainly narrows it down. Which state do you mean, exactly?"

"It's near Jack something..." Clem rubbed his wrist some more to reveal something shiny clasped around it.

"You mean, Jacksonville? Jacksonville, Florida?" Sophia inquired further, before taking notice of the shiny clasp on Clem's wrist. As he continued to rub it, she saw that it was a silver bracelet wrapped so tightly that it was creating little red streaks from where the links were scrubbing his pale skin. Dangling loosely from it was a small blue crystal pendant no larger than a double-A battery; it had a cylindrical shape that abruptly stopped at its end as if it had been cleanly cut in half...

Noticing her gaze, Clem quickly pulled down his sleeve to cover the bracelet. "Yes, Florida is what I mean," he replied curtly.

"Well, you are quite a ways from home, aren't ya? I bet this cold takes some getting used to," Sophia said, careful not to look at his wrist as he seemed uncomfortable with it for some reason. She put down her drink and leaned in closer.

"Many things are different here, you have that right," Clem responded shyly.

"Well, what do you like to do for fun in Danielsburg?" Sophia asked.

"I...uh...I sell elevators."

"Yes, I got that...but what do you do in your spare time, any sports or hobbies?"

"No sports...I...um...I like...to mix tapes!" Clem blurted out suddenly.

"Mix tapes? I didn't know people still did that."

"They don't? Maybe I am using the wrong word. I meant watching tapes."

Sophia gave him a quizzical look. It was unclear whether he was referring to music or movies at this point. Her gut was telling her that he did not seem very sure himself.

"Ah, I see. Nice," she said, after a brief pause.

Clem straightened up in his seat and leaned towards her. "Enough about me, tell me your story. I am curious to know how you live and what you do at this time?"

Sophia proceeded to tell Clem all about herself. She told him about growing up in Texas, traveling all the way to Pennsylvania for graduate school, and the funny experiences learning to be a clinician. For what Clem lacked in talking about himself he more than made up for it in listening and asking good follow up questions about her. It was to be appreciated as most men she had met in the local bars were too easily drawn to brag about themselves or be overly aggressive. But Clem was different, he had an unassuming quality of innocence about him like this was his first time meeting a girl in a bar. Not to mention, his eyes had a certain sparkle to them that danced in the light that drew her in.

Before she knew it, the little clock airplane had whirled past the minute hand that showed fifteen past eleven. It may have been early in the evening, but the late night was best relinquished to the undergrads.

"Hey, do you want to get out of here?" Sophia asked Clem with a soft smile while placing her hand gently on the side of his knee.

"That would be excellent," Clem replied.

Sophia tapped Oliver on the shoulder. "Hey friend, I think we are heading out."

"Good timing, the game just ended. I'll walk out with you guys," Oliver replied. He pulled out his wallet and left a crisp twenty-dollar bill on the bar mat.

"Thanks Francisco, until next time," Oliver shouted across the bar.

The trio trudged out of the bar up to street level. The street was a mix of neon and lamplight under the moonless sky. The few people on the sidewalks rushed by hurriedly in puffs of white, trying to get to some refuge from the sting of November air.

"Hey Clem, meet me at the corner. I'm going to say goodnight to Oliver," Sophia instructed. Clem nodded and walked slowly down to the end of the block under a changing stop light.

"You feeling all right about him," Oliver asked after Clem was out of earshot.

"Oh Oliver, I'm feeling all the things!" Sophia replied.

Oliver chuckled loudly creating giant puffs of breath that were quickly whisked away by a biting breeze.

"Thanks for being a good wingman tonight, you're the best!"

"Happy to do so. I saw it right off. You have a good night and let me know if you need anything," he said with a soft smile.

"Thanks friend, I'll text you to let you know I got home safe."

Oliver gave her a giant bear hug and then went on his own way in the opposite direction onto campus under a tunnel of lamplights. Sophia turned and then walked slowly to Clem who was waiting patiently at the end of the sidewalk.

"So, where are you staying while you're here selling elevators?" she asked inquisitively.

"I...ah...I'm staying...at the hotel," he said, stammering in the cold. The pair began to walk down the street towards the downtown deck where Sophia had parked her car.

"Which hotel? The State Inn? The Monument? The Alumni Hotel?" she pushed.

"Umm…I am not quite sure. I must have had too much to drink. Maybe going to your place would be better," Clem responded looking at the ground.

Sophia stopped the pair mid-stride. She attempted to look him in the eye but his eyes averted every shift of her gaze.

He had not had a drink all night, she remembered. She had watched him stir that Jack-n-coke into a watery slush of cola and whiskey. This early on, she did not need much to pull the chute and bail out. The best approach was always to let them down easy with a promise for a date that would never come.

"Ooo…you know, I am actually feeling more tired than I thought after walking a bit," she started, patting his shoulder. "It might be best that we rain check for another time," she said politely.

"I guess that is fine," Clem mumbled out, staring at his feet.

Always easier when they take it well, she thought.

"Well, here's a hug and a number you can text me with." Sophia gave Clem a respectable ass-out hug and handed him a number for the local car wash that she kept on hand for situations like these. The pair parted ways and she walked the rest of the way to her car alone. It was only a block more and she carried a can of bear mace in her bag for trouble.

There was no trouble this night besides the cold. She found her car alone in its spot with feathers of ice already beginning to stretch up the edges of the windows. The driver's side door yielded after some force allowing her to climb in. She was back safe, in an empty car, in an empty lot, with only her thoughts to keep her company. The car lurched on with the first try of the key and she exited the deck. Turning onto the street she tried her best not to beat herself up for not seeing through Clem's well-dressed façade earlier. But it was already too late as the tears came on their usual cue. It was another wasted night; she was not getting any younger after all. At this rate, she would become too old to find someone and start a family with before that biological clock wound down to zero.

That is when she saw him again, it was Clem. Through teary eyes, Clem ducked into an alleyway pulling off his tie and jacket. There was another woman with him too. She had also been at the bar talking with the man by the fireplace. Her flapping cape made her easy to recognize under the streetlights. As her car passed the alleyway, she glanced down to see the pair talking at a dead end in front of a dumpster. There was not enough time to see what they were doing.

It was a strange place to be late at night, and it was even stranger that they were together. There had not been any indication of recognition of one another at the bar. Clem had not even made a furtive glance over to the fireplace seating area; he had mostly stared at his wrist or drink all night. *Strange indeed.*

She looked over to her bag sitting on the passenger seat and began to think the worst. Maybe rejection had gotten the best of Clem and he had taken advantage of some poor drunk girl trying to get home. *Not going to happen.*

Wiping the tears from the corners of her eyes, she pulled the car over into an open parking spot not too far from the alley. The engine clicked off and she moved to open and close her door as softly as she could. There were few bars in this area of town so she wanted to go as unnoticed as possible. The alley was in sight a half-dozen car lengths away nestled between a shoe shop and a campus printing facility. She crept slowly along the sidewalk trying to keep her heels from clicking on the cold concrete. Ahead, whispering sounds were coming out of the alley. The words were difficult to make out, but the pattern of speech sounded irritated.

It was not long before she reached close enough to peek around the corner of the alley. She moved her head slowly against the wall to get a good glimpse. The brick was freezing against her check giving it an icy kiss as the path gradually came into view. Clem and the caped woman were still at the other end. They were both silent, but were messing with their clothing. At first, she thought they might be undressing to do some freaky things against the metal dumpster, but the woman pulled up a silver chain around her neck that had a blue crystal on it. The woman then pulled up her sleeve revealing a bracelet exactly like the one that she spotted on Clem's wrist.

"Time for you to go," Clem told the woman in a stern tone. The woman then raised her arm to the necklace and in a flash of distorted blue light she was gone, into nothing!

"Nooo!" Sophia shouted down the alleyway. She thought that perhaps he had tossed her in the dumpster so quickly that maybe it did not fully register within a blink.

Clem nearly fell back into the wall in fright. Sophia emerged from the wall and charged towards Clem. From her inside coat pocket, she pulled out a cannister of mace and pushed it in Clem's face who had settled onto the ground with his arms wrapped around his knees.

"What did you do?" Sophia demanded, towering over him.

Clem only sat there rocking back and forth, whimpering against the wall.

"Answer me!" She yelled.

"Don't kill me," he cried, staring at the mace can as if it were a gun pointed at his head.

"Where did that woman go? And don't play dumb with me; I saw you talking to her just now. Whatever you did, take me to her, now!"

"Okay, I'll take you to her, but——"

Sophia cut him off, "No buts, take me to her, now!"

Clem nodded and got back on his feet. He then walked over to where the woman had stood and pulled down his right sleeve. There on his wrist was the silver bracelet with the blue crystal. With more time to look, the crystal was a dark azure color with silvery-metallic lines spread out through its structure like some sort of skeletal circuit board. Clem then unbuttoned his shirt to reveal another crystal hanging from a silver-chained necklace.

"If you want to see that woman, grab my jacket," said Clem.

Sophia gave him a long look and then grabbed the coattail at the farthest end of his sportscoat while maintaining her aim of mace on his face. Clem then brought up the arm with the bracelet near his neck. Sophia's eyes widened as the crystals began to pull towards one another as they moved closer to one another like some magnetic force connected between them. The force was strong enough to pull the crystal on Clem's neck nearly horizontal in the air at the end of the necklace as it was inches away from the crystal on his wrist. It was then that she noticed that the two crystals were actually two halves of a larger one that was perfectly split down the center.

Clem closed his eyes in anticipation for something.

As the crystals neared each other, the silver lines began to glow an iridescent light that grew and grew until there was a *SNAP!*

A bright white light flashed followed by a whoosh of warm air. The light was so bright that she could not see anything for what seemed like minutes. Around her she could hear the mummering of voices and some people talking in strange forms of English nearby.

"Wut she doin' herre?" a female voice asked.

"I...I...don't-ye know, she had a death device," another voice responded that she was certain was Clem.

When Sophia's eyes finally adjusted, she was standing in a large pink room on a transparent heart-shaped platform that looked similar to the crystal material that was on Clem's wrist. Sophia lifted her head to see she was surrounded by people dressed in weird spandex-like fabric covered with hexagonal patterns from neck to toe without shoes. Their outfits looked to be like some sort of athleisure suits with reinforced layers in the place of footwear. It all looked like some weird, high-end onesie complete with personal lights and sound devices woven into the fabric. The only people who were not strangely dressed were Clem, the woman that had disappeared before, and another young-looking man. The other man was putting on a denim jean jacket near a rack of normal outfits stationed right off from a similar platform across the room. Everyone in the room had turned to her with eyes wide and mouths agape.

"Where am I?" Sophia asked, steadying herself on her feet.

"The more delicious question is, *when* are you?" Clem responded with a shrug.

"You are definitely going to lose your credits on this one, 5309. You know we are not supposed to bring dates home," said the woman who was now removing her cape to put on the rack.

"Date? Home?" Sophia said frowning.

"Home is the future, at least for you that is," Clem said, starting to remove his sportscoat. "You are at TAD."

"TAD...what is TAD?" she asked.

Clem simply pointed to the far wall. Underneath a large observation window was the words 'Time And Date' with a catchphrase underneath: 'Where your dates await and you are never late.'

"I don't understand, is this some kind of dating service? Where am I!" cried Sophia.

"I am a representative and I may be able to serve you better," said a medium pitched voice. From the crowd, a slender person in a pink onesie approached who was androgynous in appearance. They walked up with measured, almost mechanical steps to Clem taking the crystal necklace and bracelet from him.

"US-S2-2075-5309, you know the rules, why is she here?" said the representative.

"She...she had a death device on me and demanded to come see where 4368 had gone," Clem replied pointing to the formally-caped woman who had now slipped into a black onesie of her own.

The representative shook their head several times. "You know the rules, daters are not to bring their dates home."

"But—" Clem began.

"No exceptions 5309. You were never in any mortal danger. My ancillary computer tells me that the device she is holding is a primitive threat deterrent used against wild animals and aggressive people back in the twenty-first century. Now, go to the debriefing chamber to wait for release." The representative watched Clem walk off and then turned their eyes to Sophia. The eyes were fixed with a look of indifference.

The representative now spoke to her, "I am sorry about all this. I will return you promptly to your time."

"My time? I don't understand what this place is?" Sophia protested.

The question did not change the look of indifference on the representative's face in any way.

"You are standing in a facility that is designed to link people with romantic experiences in the past."

"You are talking about time travel, a time-traveling dating service?" Sophia interrupted.

"Yes, in your words that would be accurate," replied the representative. They then held up the necklace and bracelet in both hands. "I will not trouble you with details, but we use these crystals that have quantum states adjusted to sling our daters to specific times and places in the past. Yours was chosen as it was a college campus that offered plenty of genuine experiences."

"Genuine experiences…but why? Why go through all this?" Sophia said, raising her hands to the room.

"It may seem odd to you, but relationships are but a thing of the past in our time. A bore even," the representative paused, but Sophia stood fast to listen. They continued, "The regulation acts to reduce overpopulation and curve the destruction of climate went into place almost two centuries ago. All reproduction is carefully administered in laboratories under the authority of the Reproduction and Sustainment Office. At the age of maturity, all citizens are required to donate their DNA before going through a quick sterilization procedure. Production of new citizens using only the best gene matching is then handled by the R&S Office where people are developed in artificial wombs until they are prepared at the age of three.

"The unfortunate side effect is that there is little need for relationships. People no longer find a need to come together for mating, rearing of children, or even companionship. Most of us live out our lives in virtual environments living out our own curated wants and desires. However, here at TAD, we offer a unique experience for those who would like to experience the real thing that, before, was only viewable in old forms of primitive moving picture media."

Sophia blinked her eyes rapidly trying to see if she was in a dream.

The representative continued.

"We provide our daters a slice of what dating was like in the past. Our daters spend months preparing for their dates by educating themselves on the types of clothing, language, customs, and events of their dates."

The representative paused a moment to clear their throat in what could have been a dry laugh.

"I think for some of them, the preparation is the best part. There are so many times and places to go on dates with those who have been carefully curated to be lonely and responsive to our daters," the representative finished and examined Sophia for a few moments of silence before adding, "So what do you think? It is not often a date comes home. That is the rule."

"Pfff…That's absurd. I can't believe you are doing this. It all seems creepy and an assault on all of us. I cannot believe this is the future to come," replied Sophia.

"Well, that's nice. I understand you cannot fathom what it is like so far removed from home. Let's fix that."

The representative then slowly proceeded to approach Sophia with Clem's two interlocked crystals in hand. The representative tapped an area on their chest to reveal a tiny pocket that released a small capsule. When they reached Sophia, the representative hastily fastened the bracelet on her wrist and then opened the capsule above her head. The contents rained down across her face like strands of white dust. Soon the room began to spin round and round. She looked down at her wrist to try and focus on something that was not moving. There she could only stare at the blue crystal that pulsed in and out almost in tune with her heart beat. Then, a hand reached out and pulled apart the crystal. There was a flash and then everything went to black.

~*~*~*~

When she awoke, Sophia found herself face down on a frozen puddle next to the dumpster in the alley. The sky was still black, as if no time had passed at all. She placed a hand on her forehead that was throbbing. If her head was not so numb, the pain would have been excruciating.

She propped herself up into a seated position with what strength that had returned. That was when she noticed her wrist. The silver chain was still there, but the crystal had shattered into a thousand pieces on the ground after the journey. It was almost indiscernible amongst the chunks of slushy ice on the pavement.

Did that all really happen? she thought.

Sophia pushed back against the brick wall and got to her feet. There was no one around to ask for help. It was up to her to stumble out of the alley. She kept close to one of the walls and made her way out onto the sidewalk. At first, she thought about getting back into her car, but the world was still a little spinny. It was best not to drive in her current condition. Not to mention, her mouth felt like sandpaper. She needed to walk a bit and get a drink of water.

Sophia walked a few blocks down the street until she came upon a drinking place that was still open. She walked in and plopped herself on a stool at the horseshoe-shaped bar.

"What will it be for ya, miss?" asked the bartender.

"Just water, thank you," she said still rubbing her head.

A few minutes later, the bartender returned with a tall glass of water and a lightly-folded napkin.

"The kid over there asked me to give you this," said the bartender, handing over the folded napkin and pointing to a young man with sandy hair and rosy cheeks. She looked back down at the white napkin and carefully unfolded it. Inside, there was a scribble of sloppy writing that read: "Baby gurl can I get a taste?"

Sophia jerked her head back up to see the man smiling at her from across the bar. He gave her a wink and a wave. She looked to his wrist, but did not see any sign of silver jewelry or blue crystal. She then scoped out the room full of young, eager faces.

Any one of them could be from that future, that God-awful future, looking for a date, she thought.

She then slapped down a five-dollar bill on the bar and rushed outside to call Oliver to take her home. She had decided she was through with dating for a good while. It was time to hang up the boots.

A Tomb
in Potter's Field

From the idle tractor, visibility only reached a few yards. A grey fog had overtaken the low-lying field. The phantom outlines of tall yellowed grass swayed in an unseen breeze at the edge of a drop-off. Beyond, in the greyness, the rushing waters of the Maumee could be heard rushing towards Toledo. There, it would eventually dump into Lake Erie miles away from Waterville. The thickness of the air muffled light and sound like time itself had come to a brief stop, at least, until the midday sun would come and burn it all away. It was peaceful sitting there in the field until...

MEW! MEW! MEW!

Somewhere above the mist a seagull cried out to its kind. The beating of wings swirled around overhead. Like so many, it had lost its way following the shipping vessels coming down the St. Lawrence and across the Great Lakes. With tranquility interrupted, it was time to turn back over the motor and get back to the day's work.

All-in-all, it was a rather typical April day in Ohio. The day before, there had been a frost, but overnight a warm front had passed through leaving behind a blanket of warm air and fog to the areas still filled with pockets of the last breaths of winter. According to the weather reports, yesterday's frost was to be the last of the season which meant it was time to prepare the fields for spring planting. Joe's father had directed him to go out to drag an irrigation ditch to a new field that he had recently cleared the overgrowth near the eastern bank of the river. Joe had protested at first because he did not want to work on a Saturday when all his friends were enjoying leisure time after a full week of high school. Yet, his father made it very clear he had little choice in the matter; the Potter Farm was the family business for him, included, unless he received a scholarship for college.

That is what brought him out into the field on an early spring morning. While others slept in, he was gassing up the old tractor and fitting the double-belted trencher to the back. It took him nearly an hour to drive the old red farm tractor out to the spot to begin. Once he got there, the process required little thought as he only needed to drop the trencher into the ground and pull it behind the tractor towards the river. The trencher was basically a chainsaw for dirt; the metal teeth rotated on a metal belt on a long blade buried into the ground kicking up a rain of brown clumps of dirt to the sides behind.

The mewing of the seagull ended his break. With a turn of the key, the tractor's motor roared on with a burst of black smoke. Joe leaned into the wheel slouching as it crept closer towards the last stretch before reaching the muddy river bank. He dreamed of the day when robots could do the job. Then, farmers and their children could lay in their cozy beds as the machines hummed along doing the work, day-and-night. That is what he wanted to go to college for, to make that life easier. There were not any other ideas. He daydreamed of this as he stared out into the mist ahead. He needed to be careful being so close to the slopping edge of the river bottom. The neighbors had flipped there tractor twice down the banks...

CLUNK!

The trencher kicked up from beneath the soil in a cloud of grey dust with bits of rock projecting yards across the field. It had come to a lurking halt. Joe pressed a button to kill the engine and climbed down from the cab.

Great, now what, he thought. His knee-high boots crunched loudly through the remains of overgrowth that had been bushhogged days before. A vibration ran up his leg. He immediately looked to the tractor to check that it had not sprung back on, but that was not the source. Patting his leg, he realized that it was his phone in his pocket that he thought he had left back at the house. The screen read Jill Brooks in big block letters along with a picture of her that never seemed to do her justice.

"Hello?" he asked, surprised that she would be calling this early on a Saturday.

"Hi Joe!" a tender voice replied.

"Hey there, Jill. How are you doing?" he asked as he continued to walk back behind the tractor to check out the big clunk.

"Oh, I'm doing well. What are you up to? I was wondering whether you would like to grab a drink of coffee and breakfast at Sammy's?"

The invitation warmed his chilled body as if a warm ray had pierced down through the dense fog upon him. He could already see himself climbing into his truck and crossing the bridge to Sammy's Diner in a matter of minutes to see her. She probably would be waiting in a corner booth wearing that green turtleneck sweater that conformed to her so perfectly. With a flash of one of those dimpled smiles, the whole morning's work would have been worth it. Maybe this time, alone together, he could finally muster up the courage to tell her how he really felt. To think...

The sight at the rear of the tractor told a different story from the wishful fantasy playing out again in the back of his mind. The trencher had certainly hit something...and hit it hard. Several metal teeth had chipped to fling off somewhere in the field. Joe looked down to see a large boulder had dislodged itself where the trencher had stopped. It had been moved slightly to a point where he could see nothing rather than the expected tangle of roots and brown dirt. The nothingness was a dark hole wide enough to wiggle through. That darkness meant there was something more, a cavity or cavern of sorts.

"Joe, you still there?" Jill's voice came from his phone. He had almost forgotten.

"Yes, sorry Jill. I am actually out in the middle of our field finishing up a job my dad assigned me. It looks like I hit something and I think I have uncovered some sort of cave of sorts. I can't tell, but it looks like it goes aways back," he replied, taking out a mini flashlight from his jacket and shining it down the hole.

"Yeah, there is definitely something here. I'm not sure I can make coffee anytime soon..." his voice trailed off.

"That sounds pretty interesting! I wonder where it goes? Do you mind if I swing by and check it out with you?" Jill asked.

"Oh...well...sure if you would like. I am out in the field by sixty-four and Reitz Road on the river side."

"All right..."

"Might want to wear some boots if you got'em," he added.

"Excellent! I'll see you soon Joe! I'm so excited to see what you uncovered! I hear all the time about people finding artifacts from early pioneers and Native-Americans in those fields."

"Ha...well I'm not going to make any promises. Might be an old well or something."

"We'll see! See you soon!"

Jill hung up and Joe was left scratching his head at what possibly could be out here in the middle of the Potter's field.

Joe spent the next half hour pulling up the trencher to try and tinker with some of its dislodged teeth. The metal belt was so gnarled that he had to move the tractor back several yards to get at it. The tractor only carried a limited tool kit for such occasions. Though typically, he only needed a large wrench and a heavy metal mallet. The metal links holding the teeth were cumbersome to move. Clumps of dirt and rock easily found their way into any crevasse. He used the rusty wrench to scrape out the debris and then gave the links a few good hits with the mallet. One-by-one each link settled back into place. It was when he was hammering the last link with a broken triangle tooth that he heard the crunching of something approaching in the field.

Joe climbed out of the trench and stood up. His eyes peeled towards the crunching sounds that were not far off. The mist was still thick and he could not see more than fifteen yards out in front of him.

The crunching continued, now drawing closer from his right from where the sound was before.

A dark shadowy figure began to take form in the swirling bits of grey. That must be Jill, he thought.

It was followed by another, taller shadow. Who is that?

The figures approached with cautious steps until they emerged into his area of mist. Jill stepped over tangles of vines in a pair of black riding boots, wearing khaki pants topped with a red turtleneck sweater that looked like it was glowing on her rosy cheeks. Behind her, another boy was clumping along in a pair of white basketball shoes wearing an orange hoodie.

"We found you!" Jill said in greeting.

"You sure did," replied Joe. He reached out his hand to help Jill step across the trench.

"I hope you don't mind that I brought Evan. I saw him out walking his driveway and asked if he wanted to tag along for an adventure," Jill said getting back her footing.

Oh, I mind. More than you know, he thought.

"That's no problem at all," Joe lied, looking at Evan who simply flipped his long mop of hair out of his face with a "Hey."

"Say, what do you have there," Joe pointed to a small pink drawstring bag.

"Oh yes, I figured that if you found a cave, we might need some flashlights, so I brought some."

"Good thinking, mine is pretty small," he said, regretting the statement as soon as it fell off his lips. Jill did not seem to notice, but Evan gave him a little smirk.

"Well, show us what you got, won't you, Joe?" urged Jill, impatiently.

Joe walked them around the tractor to the spot where the trench had come to a halt. He then jumped down into the trench while Jill and Evan looked down cautiously from above his head. Jill's eyes lit up wide when she saw the hole that went through the earth.

"Wow, Joe. That is definitely some sort of cave. How far do you think it goes back?" she asked.

Joe kneeled down to look down through the small opening with one of the bigger flashlights that Jill had brought. The light went through an open space wide enough for two people to stand abreast that descended downward. The light eventually hit a grey stone that flanked the passage above and from both sides. Here it looked like it narrowed to the point that maybe one person could slide through sideways.

"It looks like it goes several yards back before turning into a stone passage of some sort. I could see better if the hole was wider. Could someone hand me the mallet there on the step?" Joe asked, pointing to the step-up platform near the door of the tractor.

Evan reluctantly walked to the tractor and picked up the mallet by its head. He then walked back and leaned down to hand it to Joe, handle first.

"Thanks," he said, grabbing the wooden handle. He then turned to the opening to examine the outer stone. Looking at it now more closely it was not as thick as he had initially thought, maybe an inch or two inches at the thickest. Despite being dislodged from the trencher, it appeared to have been lying flat against the opening like a covering.

Joe took the hammer and swung it as hard as he could on the edge of the opening.

CRACK! A large chunk of grey stone shattered off from the cover stone to his feet.

He took another big swing.

CRACK! Two more smaller pieces broke apart from the stone.

Joe paused to examine his work, feeling along the edge where he had broken off fragments of stone. He then took the mallet and lightly hit a handful of places where jagged shards of stone were sticking out. He then got up and stepped back.

"I think it's big enough now," after a few moments of inspection.

"Great! You mind helping me down?" Jill replied enthusiastically.

"Sure thing," replied Joe. He walked over to the wall of the trench where Jill had already swung over her legs. Little bits of dirt and rock fell around her bottom as it scooted towards the edge.

"You ready?" Jill asked, flashing a half smile.

"I've got you," Joe said with feet steadied.

Jill pushed off into the trench where Joe eased her down to the muddy floor. He went to help Evan, but he had already jumped down without assistance. Evan was brushing off his jeans giving him another smirk.

When Joe turned back towards the cave, Jill's head was by now halfway inside with a flashlight.

"Be careful," he called out to her.

"Oh, I'm fine...wow, it really does go back!" her voiced echoed as she creeped through the opening. Evan quickly came in right behind her, leaving Joe as the only one left standing outside in the trench.

Guess I am bringing up the rear, he thought to himself. With the mallet in one hand and a flashlight in the other, he ducked into the cavity.

The inside was dimly lit from opening. Above his head were more slabs of grey stone that wrapped around down the walls of the tunnel. Jill and Evan were some yards away standing at the point where the passage narrowed between two large slabs of grey stone that were several heads taller than the pair of them. Beyond, the passage looked like it went a ways before opening back up into another area of some sort.

"Ladies first," Evan said as Joe caught up with the two of them. Smirk-faced, he turned his head to give Joe a wink before sliding into the narrow passage.

Joe gripped the handle of the mallet tighter.

Why had she brought him? he wondered. Both Jill and Evan lived in a nice neighborhood closer to town across the river. It was nestled on one of the only hills that overlooked town. It never needed to be spoken between them, but it was obviously known that the two of them pined for Jill's affection. To this point, it was unclear who was winning.

The way through the narrowed passage was tight with the dirt floor heading downward, deeper underground. In places, the three of them needed to walk sideways so that they could shimmy past bulges in the stone that nearly made the way impassable. It went like this for nearly a dozen paces until the group of teenagers popped out into a round chamber whose ceiling lofted above their heads. At the very center of the ceiling a shard of dull white sunlight pierced through a rounded opening. It almost looked to have been drilled...

"I guess this is a dead-end," Evan stated plainly.

Jill flashed her light in all directions around them. The walls were comprised of the same grey stone, but in this area, things looked to be more square-like, as if to panel the walls in front of them.

"Are you guys seeing these walls," Jill said finally. "They look so uniform."

"They do actually, too uniform to be a natural formation," Joe remarked. He studied the panels further. They were cut evenly around the edges and stacked tightly on top of each other completely around the room except where the narrow passage had dumped them in.

Then Joe noticed where they were standing. It also had little squares of stone that looked to mimic a tiling of a floor. The stones were of different colors with some darker than others that had been polished in some way.

"Guys, look beneath your feet!" he exclaimed.

Jill and Evan pulled their heads and lights down towards the floor as if a string had been tugged on them.

"Wow, you think this is some Indian burial place?" asked Evan who was zig-zagging his light across the floor.

"I don't know…I don't remember any Natives building stone tombs in this area. Around Waterville most of the tribes were mound builders," replied Jill, cupping her chin in thought.

"Oh yeah! Like the mound in Winameg," Evan added.

Jill continued to examine the walls more closely. "I don't see any petroglyphs though…"

"Petro-what?" said Joe.

"Petroglyphs are pictures or images carved into rock," replied Jill, still examining one of the walls farthest from the entrance.

"Like hieroglyphs?"

Jill turned back towards Joe with head cocked to one side and a kind look on her face. "Not quite. From what I understand hieroglyphs like in ancient Egypt were used as a language system to represent words. Petroglyphs are more about representing some natural scene or serve as art, it's hard to say at this point what the intent was…at least that was what I learned from a documentary I watched on the History Channel." Jill shrugged and flashed him a crooked smile.

BANG!

Jill and Joe broke eye contact and looked over to where the loud thud had come. Evan stood near the wall having thrown a loose stone from the floor at one of the stone panels.

"Did you guys hear that?" Evan asked.

"Of course, we heard it! Who couldn't hear you throwing a stone against the wall? Be careful, that could have bounced off and hit Jill." Joe said, giving Evan a squinty look.

"No, did you hear what happened after I threw it?"

"Huh, what do you mean, Evan?" asked Jill calmy.

"It sounded like there was an echo, like there might be something behind it," he replied.

"Have you been smoking again before you came over here?" snapped Joe. It was well-known that Evan liked to smoke weed and if not for his lawyer dad, he probably would have been in juvie by now.

"Now boys, settle down." Jill moved in between them and waved her arms giving each of them a serious look. She then turned to face Joe.

"Joe, could you hand me your mallet, please?"

Joe nodded and handed her the mallet. And before he had a chance to tell her to be careful—

TWHACK!

Jill had swung the mallet into the stone panel as hard as she could. A plume of dust and bits of stone instantly engulfed the space scattering the light of their flashlights into a million directions. Coughing, the three struggled to get out a word amidst the exhalings of the cave wall. Nearly a minute went by before things had settled enough to see the full extent of Jill's blow. To the shock of them all, as the particles began to dissipate, the metal head of the mallet had disappeared into a dark cavity behind the stone face. A hole about a foot wide had been made by the impact and had created several wide cracks that stretched to neighboring panels, feet away.

Joe was the first to speak, "Man...it cracked like a stone slab."

"Like in a burial vault," Evan added, eyeing the new opening with morbid curiosity.

"You're right, Evan..." It pained Joe to say. "...are we in some kind of crypt?"

"The natives never built things like this. They worked in earth, timber, and animal hide...not stone." Jill remarked before poking her light into the opening.

"Well, maybe we should contact an archeologist or something. We don't want to ruin anything. Besides, looking at those cracks, this whole place could cave in at any moment. Maybe we should wait until someone shores this place up," Joe said, moving his flashlight along the deep fractures that stretched out like branches of a tree.

"What are you, scared Joe?" Evan sneered back with narrowed eyes.

"No, I am not scared at all, you—"

Jill's excited voice interrupted, "Hey! Would you look at this!"

Joe and Evan disentangled their pointed gaze to turn towards the broken stone. A shimmer of blue light sparkled from Jill's chest as they noticed a fist-sized gem hanging from her neck. It was radiant. The light from their flashlights refracted from numerous facets that wrapped all around the tear-shaped stone that looked to be some shade of light blue like aquamarine. It was held by interwoven strands of silvery-white metal that almost glowed on its own.

"Like my new necklace," Jill said making a pose.

"Oh wow, Jill that thing must be worth a fortune," said Evan whose eyes began to ogle from their sockets.

"Don't worry, I'll share..." Jill motioned them both to come to her side and see for themselves. Everyone poured their lights into the hole and, from the darkened space, a multitude of objects glimmered and sheened back. A line of painted vases and pots stood untouched in front of them under a blanket of grey dust that was as fine as ash. Some of them were draped in necklaces similar to the one Jill was wearing in different shapes and colors of gemstones. Farther back, long silver rods protruded from the ground; they shimmered the same way as Jill's necklace and were capped with rounded crystals that glowed for a short period of time after shining a light on them briefly. Farther back still was a shimmering sheet of semi-translucent crystal that looked like a sheet mishmashed pieces of ice.

"Did you see those crystals glow after I shined my light on them?" Joe asked.

"Yeah, but more importantly, do you see all these gems? We're rich!" said Evan. He pulled back on the cracked opening to make it wide enough for a person to pass through.

Taking turns, they each stepped through the cracked entryway. Inside, the hidden space was no wider or longer than a bedroom with high ceilings. The floor was solid like it had been in the other area with the same sorts of shaped cobble stones. Evan quickly began sifting through the dirt and dust for other metal trinkets—finding golden lions, silver fish, and black metal carved into the shape of what looked like a stegosaurus among other strange creatures.

Joe, however, was drawn to the spherical crystals sitting atop the metal poles. His flashlight remained focused on one of them. Strangely, it seemed to trap the light without dispersing it around the room. He moved his yellow light to each side of it and watched it project against the far wall, but when he shone his light directly on the crystal, no light left the other side. After a period of time, he finally noticed that the crystal was actually getting brighter on its own, as if it was capturing the energy from his flashlight to shine independently.

"Guys, this crystal is weird. It's like sucking my flashlight to charge up and then shine after I turn my light away from it," Joe remarked to the group. Though the others seemed to be in their own worlds.

"I think there is something behind there," Jill said after remaining quiet for a few minutes. She leaned forward to put both hands up against the crystal wall. Suddenly, a faint light flashed on the other side.

"Did you see that?" cried Evan.

"I think we all did," replied Joe and then walked up to the wall and cupped his hands around his eyes to peer in. "I don't see much…"

Another flash moved through the wall.

"Umm, Joe…Jill just did something," cried Evan behind him.

Joe pulled back to see that Jill had touched the gem around her neck to a spot on the wall. Her eyes looked distant, yet transfixed on something. Yet another flash pulsed through the center of the crystal wall until an outline of a doorway had formed directly around the area where Jill had touched. She then pushed the area with one hand and it glided backwards with ease, revealing that it was less than an inch thick and that there was another space hidden behind it. Before either he or Evan could say a word, Jill stepped through the new portal without a glance back to any of them. That's when he noticed that the amulet on her necklace was pulsing a dim glow like the crystals on the spheres.

Joe looked to Evan who was frozen in place, watching her go forward. He then gave Joe a shrug before going in after her.

The second hidden space was twice the size of the first and not nearly as dirty. In fact, it looked remarkably untouched from dust and time. The floor was covered in a waxy ivory tile, fitted with great precision. The walls were covered in fine fabrics of gold, silver, and blue. Joe had to watch his head because more of the crystal glow-spheres hung down on silvery strands of metal embedded into the stone ceiling above. Scattered across the floor were more vases and golden boxes filled with tiny mechanical gears that appeared to have no clockface or other visible purpose.

"This looks like a piece of a boat, doesn't it?" Evan said from a far corner of the room. Joe walked over to the object. It was a curved, grey-colored structure that came to a point which could have fit the three of them in.

"It does kind of look like the bow of a small boat," Joe conceded.

"Here, touch it. It's so smooth," Evan insisted.

Joe's hand glided over one of the ridges of the object.

"You're right. It's not wood though, almost like carbon fiber…odd." Joe said before looking to see where Jill had gone off to. The look in her eyes from earlier had worried him. She did not seem like her usual self. Sure, she was a determined girl, but now she seemed too focused. And that glowing crystal, how and why was it lit up?

Joe kept looking but could not see her anywhere on this end of the room.

"Jill, where are you?" he shouted.

A voice answered from the dark somewhere at the far end of the room. "It sunk in one day and a night…"

"What the ship?" asked Evan who joined Joe away from the object they had been studying.

"No, the island…home" the voice replied. Only a dim glow of blue could be seen in the dark area from which the voice originated.

Joe raised his flashlight towards the spot to find Jill standing at the far end of the room staring, daze-like, at a large mural on the wall.

"We should probably see what's going on with her," he whispered to Evan.

Evan nodded and they both walked slowly over to her. As they approached, Joe could not help watching the gem that hung around her neck, pulsing in even quicker intervals now of blue light. The mural she was examining so intently was made of an assortment of polished tile, crystal, and bits of metallic gold and silver. The crystal elements of the scene glowed brightly as Joe and Evan scanned the mural with their flashlights. It had been constructed with supreme craftsmanship with fine detailing of paint and cutting.

The elements came together perfectly to show an intricate scene starting with a great city sitting under a glowing yellow-crystal sun. The city was made up of four concentric circles with tall golden rectangular buildings and silver pyramids scattered about the rings. In between the circles, strands of sapphire and blue tile were laid out to show the flowing of waterways traversed by tiny boats, bridges, and suspended boxes with people being carried across, aloft above the water. At the innermost circle, a great structure stood with giant white columns that towered over the city. It was capped with a colossal crystal dome that beamed light across the city. Above the city, a large mountain of jade loomed with what looked like flying pterodactyls circling at its summit.

Scanning to the right, the scene changed to one of chaos as the mountain was shown with fiery jasper and ruby shooting up and raining down from its ruptured top. Below it, a large group of people ran away towards the sea with arms stretching to the sky while a few others stayed turned and pointing to the mountain.

The next scene was of people reaching the sea trying to get in boats with bows shaped and colored much like the object on the other side of the room. A great blue wave engulfs most of the people while some in ballooned ships high up in the sky escape the calamity on favorable winds of inlaid strands of pearl.

The last scene showed a single boat traveling in the opposite direction from a group of five other boats and airships. It appears to have traveled across a vast body of water before finding a river, then falling into a large lake, and then at last, heading up a smaller river before stopping to make a more modest settlement.

Joe lowered his flashlight, trying to process the significance of it all. It all seemed so similar to the myth of Atlantis, maybe too similar to be different.

Evan was less patient.

"What does it say?" he said aloud, gesturing to several rows of Greek-like lettering below the mural.

"It tells of a journey westward...across the big sea to this land," she began, rubbing her fingers across the lettering.

"How do you know all that? I didn't think you could read Greek or whatever language that is," Joe said, puzzled.

"I'm not really sure, I just can see the words or feel their meaning...and sometimes..." Jill paused, picking at her turtleneck.

"Sometimes?" Joe pushed.

"Sometimes...sometimes I can see images of the things depicted here. Like a movie in my mind from someone's perspective. More like a memory of a beautiful lost paradise. Lost beneath fire and waves. I can see their faces, in horror, screaming. Bits of fire falling through their eyes." Jill stopped suddenly. Her face went blank and arms fell limp to her side. Joe stepped forward to catch her, but she began to speak again. At the same time, the gem around her neck began illuminating a strong steady turquoise light.

"We had everything and then nothing," she started again, in a high wispy voice that sounded very foreign from her lips. "This place was primitive when we arrived and, in some ways, you have not surpassed the progress we achieved."

"We?" Evan asked cautiously. "Jill are you, all right?"

She turned to him and tilted her head sideways to study him, but did not answer.

"We had a civilization that was the beacon of the world. Our very rocks shone brighter than the minds of those living in all the other lands. But then, the time of the great cataclysm hit and we had to run from the great world we built with mind and spirit. Not even our greatest mastery of machine and elements could save us. For civilization sits upon a thin veil of order and chaos. And then everyone died." She fell silent for a moment almost cackling to herself.

"How did they die?" Evan asked. He had waited for a few moments to ask.

"Decadence." She said the word emphatically.

"Death by decadence; that does not seem a bad way to go," Evan jested.

She gave him an icy look. So much so, her pupils seemed to glimmer a dull blue glow.

"We had everything, every need, want, and pleasure was provided for. There was no toiling over work, worrying, or need of protection. The people soon turned to boredom and pursuits of unnatural things. It was our lack of toughness that led us all to perish after the cataclysm, without the tools of progress to provide any longer. Behold!" She turned to point at the adjacent wall. It was honeycombed with small vaults that went back several feet. Inside were the outlines of feeble-looking skeletal remains of what once were people no taller than maybe four feet.

"Who are you? And what did you do to Jill," Joe commanded, shining his light directly at the back of her head.

She turned and gave him a curled smile. Her eyes flamed blue despite the bright beam of Joe's flashlight in her face. Her right thumb stroked the glowing stone as she held it clutched in her hand at her breast.

"I am Iridia, messenger to this new world. Though our bodies could not survive this barbaric land, our essences lived on in these stones who were crafted by the greatest among us. We have waited so long for the right minds to find us. It seems you have much still to learn and we have much to rebuild. In this body, it is clear that so many secrets and knowledge has been lost to you all. You need a guiding light. So, here I am!

"And, oh, what pleasures and delights we can provide your kind, beyond your imagination." She finished by pushing her free hand down the front of her pants. Evan and Joe both could see the lacy-white frills of her lingerie as her hand bulged underneath, touching herself.

"It sounds pretty nice, though I can imagine a lot," Evan jested, flashing Joe a serious look.

Removing her hand, she turned to Joe and pointed back off into the other room, "You only need to take the stones there on the—"

"But, we'd rather not..." Joe interrupted. "...You see, there is nothing new under the sun, and we have learned a little bit about the folly of seeking dictators for the comforts of protection and provision in the twenty-first century." He then lunged to grab the crystal from around Jill's neck. She tried to resist, but Evan held her arms tight as he lifted the necklace off her head. Once in hand, the still-pulsing stone burned in his hands like grabbing a super cold piece of metal. Joe gritted his teeth as he grabbed the mallet that had been left at the entrance to the second chamber. With one heavy swing, the mallet struck true. The stone cracked in a near-blinding flash of blue light. When the light was gone, only two pieces of the gem remained on the chamber floor amidst a thick blue mist that clung near the fragments.

Joe looked back to Jill to see that she had collapsed on the floor and was only now coming back to consciousness.

"Help me get her out of here," Joe barked to Evan. He said nothing and the two helped carry Jill out of the cave tomb on their shoulders.

Reaching the open air again, brought such relief. The morning fog had nearly burned off and a bright noonday sun shone brightly overhead.

"You stay with her, I need to finish this," Joe said as they laid Jill down on the dirt. Her eyes were now open but were still distant and she could not speak.

Joe jumped back up into the tractor and turned over the engine with a roar of puffing smoke. He grabbed the wheel and maneuvered the tractor to angle a new trench from the original direction of the old one, avoiding the entrance to the stone tomb. He then slammed forward the lever to lower the trencher and dragged it down all the way towards the river. When there were only a few yards to go he stopped and turned the tractor completely around to back it towards the waterway until the rushing waters were lapping at the back treads of the large tractor tires. The trencher dropped again with a splash and a torrent of water and mud flung out the back end until, finally the trench had been complete.

When he raised the trencher one last time, the flowing waters from the river began rushing down the trench like a giant brown wave. Joe jumped out and ran with the water until it reached the opening of the cave where the waters began to pour in with great speed. Inside, he could hear the water crashing against the stone. For a second, he also thought he heard screaming, but he never mentioned that to Jill or Evan.

In a few minutes time, the cave had filled to the brim and the waters rose above the area, making a nice small cow pond a few feet deep.

The deed done, Joe walked back over to Jill who was now sitting up and alert. When she saw him, she jumped up into his arms.

"Oh Joe, thank you, thank you, I am sorry for what I did," she said with a hug and big kiss on his check.

"It wasn't you, Jill. I'm just glad you are all right," he said, patting her on the back in a close caress. He stared over her shoulder at Evan who remained seated in the mud, looking exhausted.

"She only gave me a pat on the shoulder," he conceded with a sad smile.

"Well boys, how about that coffee?" Jill said, reluctantly releasing hold of Joe.

"Hell, the trench is finished. That is good enough for me," Joe replied.

The three of them laughed gingerly and walked off to find the car. That evening Joe told his father that he would work any other field besides that one, but never provided a reason why. But there were certain times, when the light was just right and enough mist had blanketed that field that he could see a group of glowing blue eyes staring out from the waters of that little cow pond as he passed on the road in his truck.

He thought that it was a quiet justice that those stones remained submerged under the waters in which they fled. Hopefully hidden enough from future discovery. As some civilizations should remain forever lost, and forgotten. But stone is patient and time means little to an ageless thing—it merely waits to be unearthed in the light.

The Evergreen Girls

A lonesome leaf of autumn slowly swished its way back-and-forth upon a late afternoon breeze. Its yellow hue glimmered in the sunlight like a golden fleck falling from the sky. The wind was blowing out of the southeast carrying with it just a hint of ocean spray from Buzzards Bay. For those that cared to breathe in deep, there was the smell of beaches and those taking their last dips in cool waters. Because behind the salty smell was also a coolness of an approaching fall.

The leaf finally came to rest at the feet of three aged ladies who were seated upon a park bench at the edge of an old wood. Under the brims of their big round straw sun hats, the ladies watched the children race and play at the playground of a new subdivision that had been built up to the boundary of Freetown-Fall River Forest. The wood had been protected there for nearly one hundred fifty years and possessed an assortment of trails, old-growth trees, cliffs, black bogs, and more than its fair share of ominous happenings, even for Massachusetts. The locals of Freetown and the adjoining municipalities called the old ladies the 'Evergreen Girls' for the long green cloaks they wore. It was a rare occurrence to see them as sightings appeared so infrequently that it was almost a local legend that no New Englander had ventured to figure out. Today the girls were comfortably seated on a bench watching wistfully at the children laughing and playing their imaginary games. Despite their infrequent appearances, few parkgoers took notice of them as the filtered sunlight through an old oak tree partially shrouded them from clear view.

"Oh, the children just look lovely today, don't they Priscilla?" said the woman seated in the middle of the bench. Her face was round and wrapped in wrinkles like an onion that had set out too long.

"Aye, they do, Lydia. To have bodies so firm and defined…to be full of the lifeblood of youth with rosy colors bold and bright…I only wish my paps were not sagging so. I remember when they were so perky and could cut through cheese cloth," Lydia finished, shaking her chest gently side-to-side.

"Lydia, please. At least your bubbies are not sagging to your navel like two flattened pancakes," replied the woman with a long oval-shaped face. Lines of wrinkles obscured an otherwise furrowed brow upon her high forehead.

"Now Tabitha, you never were about the looks. Even when you were chasing those boys around the barns. You always had a mind for your books, every one you could get a hand on," said Priscilla.

Ca' Ca' Ca' Tabitha cackled in response. "Tis true, I did not give chase out of affection, but of spite. Such pleasures as mirrored reflections were always left to you, dear."

The blush that came upon Priscilla was muted by the visible blue veins appearing on a face that once knew great beauty. Yet, even in its advanced age, Priscilla's visage was still an enchanting sight to behold. The progressive years that had slowly carved so many lines into her face could not hide the exquisite shape, the disarming dimples, the button nose, and piercing eyes that time had only cast a waxy sheen upon.

"Lydia, tell us what you are thinking, you are practically staring at the children over there on that teeterboard contraption," Priscilla said quickly to deflect attention from herself.

"Oh yes, seeing all these children this time of year makes me want to bake. They simply look scrumptious in their little outfits, don't they?"

"It is that time of the season, my dears. We must think of stocking up for the winter, least we wither ourselves away," replied Tabitha who was twirling a long stray white strand of hair in front of her face. "And since it has been a spell since we have addressed our appearance, why don't we indulge ourselves this year with an extra offering to look our best come Ostara in the spring," she added.

Priscilla nearly jumped from her seat and had to catch her sun hat from falling to the ground. "Oh, can we? It has been so long since we have shaved the years off our look."

The response by Lydia was contrastingly different. Eyebrows raised, face taut, and pursing of lips suggested a contrary thought was brewing. She took out a piece of dried jerky from a cloth pouch around her waist and stuffed the burgundy morsel into her mouth, smacking her lips repeatedly. As she thought, a stringy piece latched itself around a tooth protruding over her top lip. A thought did come forth finally, but, before she could speak utterance to it, a father and his little boy were walking up the sidewalk towards their little bench.

Dressed in a brown flannel shirt with green corduroy bottoms, the boy appeared to not yet be of school age. He pulled his father along with skipping steps; the grown man trying desperately to hold onto him with an extended arm that was buckling. As the pair passed the bench, the father flashed a shaky smile at the seated ladies, unable to see them clearly in the shadow of the trees.

"Sir, you have such a darling child," Tabitha stated emphatically.

"Yes, he is utterly delicious. Look at those rosy cheeks and little hands. Why I dare say this boy will be a runner," added Lydia.

"Well, thank you ladies," the father replied, squinting, and bobbing his head to get a better look at the ladies.

"Da da, tat lady has a 'unny hat and a boomp on her nose," said the little boy pointing at Tabitha.

Lydia and Priscilla brought a flying hand up to their mouths. Tabitha merely grinned, revealing the yellow rot of her two front teeth.

"Excuse my son, ladies. He is still learning," the man said with bulging eyes.

"Think nothing of it, mister, the boy still has some growing to do," Tabitha said in a kind tone.

The man did not reply, but quickly led the child away towards the playground. As they went off, the boy could not help himself from stealing a few more glances back at the ladies on the bench.

"Mmm...can we keep both of them?" said Priscilla after the pair were out of earshot. She continued to stroke the wooden clasp of her cloak that laid upon her chest.

"That man would barely last a spell with us, and the child, much too young for ladies of our age to manage," replied Tabitha sternly.

"They always seem to notice that wart on your nose, Tabitha. Maybe I could whip up something to finally get rid of that thing...maybe a little honeysuckle and milkweed?" said Priscilla.

"Not in the slightest," Tabitha tapped the bump on her nose with three delicate pats. "This has been part of me since the beginning. Besides, we've been called worse. Remember that time when the cobbler's son called Lydia an old hag?"

"Yeah, and he was not saying much when we nailed his tongue to that oak stump, was he?" replied Lydia.

"Ah, the stump got a red shower when he ripped it off from it. And then he ran like a rabbit crying 'ritch ritch' all the way back to the village."

The three cackled together in near unison. Their bodies quaked up and down on the bench, sending a murder of crows out from their secluded perch in the tangle of branches above them. One of the birds dropped a parting gift that only narrowly missed the brim of Tabitha's hat. She quickly jerked her head up at the sky. One eye was drooped while the other was open so wide that it bulged from its socket, giving the bird a full force of glazed malice. It then suddenly veered from its course, losing altitude, and hit the chain backstop of the baseball diamond on the other side of the park. A pack of kids and nervous adults huddled around the bird that flapped its final death throes in the dust behind home plate. The kids pulled out their devices and were documenting the grisly event gleefully.

For a moment, Tabitha remained quiet as she observed the little ones making a record of what used to be taboo. She began to twirl the frizzled ends of her thinning white hair.

"In the old days…" Tabitha began. The old crone, smacked her gummy lips together in a wry smile. "…we had to whisper at the edge of a glade for days to lure the sweet ones in with tricks of fancy. Now, behold, they come willingly to our craft of the tritest form."

Tabitha paused to see her dear sisters of the wood nod in silence as they stared forward, eyes fixed on the crowd. She continued, staring back herself at all the little ones.

"I dare say dears, these young'uns who stare at their devices ceaselessly shall be easy pickings for us this cycle."

"They entrance themselves," mumbled Lydia.

"Yesss, they are bound by these things that they hold and tap with their fingers like a precious pet. A pet that may lead them into our wood without thinking to look up. They shan't even notice when we draw the life from their bodies," remarked Priscilla.

"Aye, it seems we have been given a great providence in their distraction and disbelief. It may be that our greatest spell is to not exist. In the last cycle, when those horseless carriages were new, it was a toil to get those two precious souls to enter our wood; there was still belief in their eyes. But I see little of that now. Their doubt and comfort have lowered their guard and made them weak of mind, body, and spirit."

"I hope they still have enough spirit to do the job, lest we need to tarry a dozen of them for what once took but three or four," added Lydia whose eyes had narrowed and hands were rubbing at her cloak.

Tabitha let out a wheezing laugh. *Hack. Hack. Hack.*

"They have become tame like the newborn fawn that wobbles its way to the wolf's den for slaughter. It shall be easy pickins, I tell you."

Lydia's beady eyes darted from the children to Tabitha and then back to the children who had returned to their play.

"Two was not enough last cycle, hopefully this windfall will bring us a gaggle of unwitting children, by the looks of us, we need it," Lydia stated earnestly.

"And maybe even get one who's full grown." Priscilla ran a loathsome finger over the valleyed lines of her face that had been etched out by centuries of glacial time. "Any moment longer looking like a withered fruit, is unbearable. I want to feel the softness of my fingers, the rich smoothness of my lips, and a soft breeze willowing through a thick head of chestnut locks."

Lydia rolled her eyes. "We tarry on for another cycle, how long has it been now since the first? Three-hundred years?"

"Hmm…been nigh since sixteen eighty-three when we fled Salem into these woods." Tabitha leaned back on the bench with a distant look on her face. She began to rub her shriveled lips together, preparing to speak.

"We were but girls then, at the crest of womanhood so many lifetimes ago. These woods were the only shelter we could find from those who would pursue us—the cobbler, the preacher, and nearly a quarter of the village. Do ye remember how the days went by as we trudged through bramble and bog?"

"Yesss, we were starving, covered in that black muck," interjected Priscilla. "We almost wished that village mob would have found us until…"

Tabitha went on. "It 'twas on the sixth day of our exile, tattered and hungry, we happened upon a crabapple tree, ancient and wild near the center of the wood. It 'twas like manna from heaven," A curling smile ran up Tabitha's face.

"We found the elder tree in a hidden dale at the edge of a stony pit. Upon its contorted branches, a white garland crown of flowers sat looking like a bride's veil in the gloom of forest. And recall how its reddish roots could find no water on the rocky slab on which it sat. Nay, those roots drove down, deep, into the unseen depths of the rocky hollow. Yet, the water at its bottom—wherever that may be—must have been befouled for when we bit into its sanguine fruit, it soured our thirsty lips."

"'Twas then we heard the voice, hoary and wise," said Lydia with her head tilted back and eyes closed in remembrance.

"Aye, it 'twas. A voice came out of the stony chasm, whispering like some phantasm—offering a subversion of the world, to our every want, our every need. We ought only to reside in the wood except at the end of a cycle when we could make a jaunt for the children and men.

"So, we made our pact to no longer yield, to adult, man, nor preacher, but only ourselves. And when it was done, a daemon did emerge from that abyss. It took the form of a man composed of branches and twigs with head like that of a bird's nest glowing red with two ambers that did not set it aflame. Then, its long legs stretched above us, reaching to the highest bough of the crabapple. It brought down three white fruit it bid us eat. We then took a bite, each of us, the sweetness overtook us, and were never the same."

Priscilla clapped the bench with her palm. "Even after all these years, Tabitha, you remember it well." She then let out a quiet sigh. "Yet…I fear with so much time that has come to pass, the slow creep of the villages around our wood has come to our doorstep. What if they find our nestled little dale and hut?"

"Yes, they nearly have cut down all the other woods around, shan't a matter of time until they want a piece of ours," added Lydia in between chews of another piece of dried meat.

Tabitha shook her head firmly and raised a hand, wagging a long-crooked finger. The blackened finger nail looked like it would fly off if she dared shake it much harder.

"Ney, these woods will endure like they have for countless cycles. They are protected by the stickman and his helpers. As long as we bring the proper sacrifices as we have in yore, it shall continue evermore. That was the promise that was made; a word spoken shan't be broken.

"Besides, if any man would be foolish enough to encroach in these timbers, there are the bugs and gnarly thickets that would greet them. And if one should venture too far in, the little Pukwedgies would meet them. Leading them astray into the bogs and swamps to never return. Even the strongest and most well-prepared are but a trifle for their kind of magic of light and sound. Few can resist the pulsing glow of swamp lights and murmurings in dim stillness of the wood.

"Ye need not worry, dear. Our stone cottage is safe from—"

A rubber red ball hit the bench. A boy near his seventh year had kicked it from across the green.

"My my my! What a strong leg you have there," replied Priscilla in a disarming voice.

The boy approached the three ladies slowly, and then stopped a few strides away from them. The three smiled at the boy, rolling the ball playfully between their feet. The motion was enticing, beckoning the boy to grab it and continue playing. The boy took a single step forward and paused.

A few moments passed and, like time for any young one, the delay seemed to drag on forever; but for anyone of sufficient age, a few moments of time were but a flash to easily be outlasted. In his impatience, the boy took another step forward and then stopped as a light gust of wind blew out from the woods into his face. It carried with it a strange potpourri of smell. At first, it was obnoxiously sweet almost like the smell of salt water taffy. Yet, there was something else subdued underneath the layers of sweetness that seemed…off.

The boy took notice of something in the woods and gestured towards it.

"Where does that go?" asked the boy, pointing to a worn deer path leading into the gloom of the trees.

"How perceptive you are, sweet one, that there path leads into our cozy little wood," replied Lydia.

"And…what's back there?" replied the boy.

"It can lead many places, my sweet thing. It can lead to *gamessss*. To delicious *sweetssss*. To do whatever thou shalt *wantssss*," said Lydia, in an enchanting tone. "Why we have an entire cottage back there. Why it's the coziest cottage you'd ever see. It's made of stone, covered in moss, has a big fireplace, and filled with sweets. Do you like sweet things, sweet boy?"

The boy nodded slowly.

"And what do they call thee?" asked Priscilla. She battered her hazel eyes. They looked like tiny white star bursts, piercing into anyone that gazed into them more than a moment.

"I...I...I am going to need my ball," the boy replied, unbalanced on his feet.

"Why of course, you can take it, now if you'd like," said Tabitha who rolled the rubber ball under a faded leather shoe without laces. She rolled it a few arms' length away from the bench and only a few steps from the boy's grasp.

The boy took another step forward, now almost within arms-reach of the ball. The impatience had boiled over within him, he needed to grab the ball. He leaned forward, stretching out a scrawny little arm...

SCREETCH! The sound of a girl getting chased by a boy blared out over the lawn.

The boy jerked up his head to look up at the three ladies, who had appeared so kind from afar. Their once tiny beady eyes were wide in their sockets, almost bulging out in anticipation of something. He looked down at their hands and saw them clenching and releasing beside their thick green skirts. The smell of sweetness now seemed to blast off of them into his nostrils. The aroma made his head feel dizzy and light. In his stomach began to quake imagining the taste of some nice stretchy taffy...

But that other smell was still there, slightly stronger now, but still restrained. The boy focused his nose as hard as he could to make it out. Then, suddenly, the sweet aroma seemed to fade away, and left what had been hidden so thickly underneath.

Oh, that stench! the boy thought. The scent was rotten and foul, like the stink of gunk that had gathered at the bottom of the kitchen sink after years of buildup. He remembered his father cleaning it out after a clog and seeing the murky grey goo seep all over the kitchen floor. It filled up the room in that unpleasant aroma of decaying food for hours. The smell was like that now, but somehow, worse. It smelled of rotten food, of dead birds, and the nasty cheese his grandmother loved to fill her house up when she was cooking.

But the smell quickly faded into a greater terror. The boy could now feel his body falling forward, as if he were being tugged down helplessly by a great string. He looked at the old ladies who were appearing to creep closer to him in an unstoppable slowness of motion. And as he drew ever nearer to them, he saw them clearly for the first time in the shifting shadows under the tree. His face contorted into a grimace and mouth fell agape. Their eyes were transfixed on him so intently that he thought he noticed sparks of whirling fire within them. The stench of their breath puffed in his face between gnarled teeth in various stages of putrefaction. And one of their noses had a spot of flesh that had sunken in to the bone. There were only a few inches left before he would be close enough to be in their grasp, in those boney fingers with black and yellow nails!

The boy had to do something and quickly, there was no time! A flash caught his eye near his feet. It was of a large golden leaf. Lying next to it was a long branch of a tree. The boy gasped, and took the momentum to drop down to his feet mere inches out of reach of the three ladies. With a trembling hand, he grabbed firmly around the branch and swung it at the ball like he had seen the hockey players do on dad's TV. The forked end of the branch hit the ball with a big *whack* sending it bounding up in the air. It bounced several times until it came to a stop somewhere in the middle of the open field, away from the dark wood and away from the stinking ladies. Then, mustering all the strength he could, the boy broke loose of whatever had been pulling him. He dashed to grab his prize and trotted off without even a glance backward.

The boy gone; the evergreen girls causally leaned back onto the bench. They straightened their garments and calmly sat with their shriveled hands upon their laps. To look at them, they were like three ladies waiting for the service of afternoon tea.

"'Tis a shame, with a little cardamom, a touch of juniper, and an evergreen bough during drying, that boy would have made a delicious batch to last the winter," Lydia said, taking a large bite out of another scrap of dried jerky.

The Hungry Black Dot

They found it nestled in a patch of crusty grey mud. Parts of the grey goo were scorched black from its long fall from the sky. The cracked tendrils of dried earth spread out around the dark cylinder like the rays of some sort of grim black sun. The three adolescent boys stood gazing at the object, not knowing what to make of it. Peter thought it was a meteorite. Joey thought it was a toilet tank jettisoned from an airplane way up in the sky. And Greg, he was not so sure what to make of it.

"Go on, touch it, Peter," egged Joey.

"It looks too hot," replied Peter, poking it with a stick that he had picked up from a trail of singed branches that they had traced to the landing site. "Don't you see the vapor coming off of it?"

HAAAAWK PUUUH. Joey spit out a massive loogie that brushed the front end of the object and rolled off without a sound onto the cracked mud below.

"See, it's not sizzling hot. My dad always spits a little into the frying pan to see if it's hot enough. If it doesn't sizzle, you can touch it," said Joey, sharply.

"Maybe we should go back and get some help," replied Greg, as if the spittle had shaken him from a daze.

"No, no. It's fine. I'll check it out," said Peter, now half-heartedly kicking at the object lightly with the nose of his outstretched tennis shoe. Joey positioned himself behind Peter making sure that Greg could see him nodding his head with a big smile.

Peter approached closer to the object, trying to step on the areas of mud that had been dried solid. From where they were standing, the object looked smooth and pill-shaped. But, as Peter grew closer, he began to notice more intricate details, almost like etchings or drawings. When he was within arm's length, he reached out his right hand and tapped the object quickly with his index finger. He waited a moment and then touched the object again, this time, holding his finger down on the object for a few seconds.

"Well, Peter are you going to tell us anything or just finger the thing all afternoon," said Joey, flashing the 'thriller' gesture with his hand.

"Yeah Peter, what does it feel like?" Greg added in a more curious tone.

But Peter gave them no response. Greg and Joey could only stand in wonder as Peter suddenly placed his whole hand on the object and held it there firmly. Peter remained quiet and about ten seconds passed before he finally removed his hand back away from the object. He then turned to his two friends to reveal a blackened hand, not from burns, but from a dark soot.

"It's warm to the touch, but not hot," Peter remarked, half-smirking.

"Look Peter!" cried Greg, pointing back to the object.

Peter turned around quickly.

A glittering blue-metallic area was now visible in the shape of where Peter's hand had been. Minuscule flecks of gold and silver seemed to run throughout the smooth metal along with a series of etchings. The etchings captivated Peter and he stood there motionless analyzing them. They took on a soft blue glow that dimmed periodically in the filtered sunlight through the trees. The pulsing light had a rhythmic quality almost like the persistent blinking light of an answering machine or the slow beat of a heart. He could not quite place it...

Joey had also noticed the etchings. He marched forward and grabbed the object with two hands, jerking it from the dried mud.

"Hey, be careful with that, man. We still don't know what it is?" cried Greg over Peter's shoulder.

"Yeah, I think I saw that it is glowing on the outside with some weird symbols," replied Peter, finally shaken from his trance.

Joey inspected the object with unusual care. Out of the mud, it was now clearly a little larger than a football, but more egg-shaped and smoother. Joey took his right hand and wiped it across the object's surface. A dark shower of soot fell down from the object at his feet. When he was finished, it glittered a brilliant array of every color of the rainbow depending on how Joey held it in the sunlight. Strangely, there were no visible seams or compartments; it looked like a solid piece of metal.

"It's beautiful, like a blue crystal egg," exclaimed Peter.

"Maybe it's a Russian, they like making those eggs with multiple eggs in side them. Or it could be a bomb...or satellite," replied Joey. "Dad says that they could try anything after the wall fell in Berlin last year."

"What do the markings say?" asked Greg, pointing to the etchings that ran around the middle circumference of the object.

Joey took a moment to examine the markings with his finger. "I'm not sure, they look like pictures of something. Come closer and see for yourself."

The three of them huddled in close as Joey slowly turned the space egg in his hands. Six pictographs slowly revealed themselves as it rotated. Each glyph had its own assortment of braille-like dots underneath and above that were as tiny as an ant's head.

It was difficult to tell the ordering of the images but the one with the most dots around it looked like a circle with squiggly lines cast all across its center—like three angry clouds trapped in a disk.

The next picture was seemingly easier to decipher, though still tinged with strangeness. This picture depicted four long figures with pear-like heads and arms as long as legs. The figures were of different sizes going from tall to small like a family standing side-by-side.

Joey turned the object some more to reveal the third image. This one was the same as the first one, with the angry clouds, except it now had four slender lines jutting out from its center with ovals attached to the ends.

"Those shapes kind of look like eggs, don't they guys?" Greg remarked as Joey kept turning to the next image.

The fourth image was a circle like the first image but bigger and without any clouds inside. It also had a straight line going through it like the third image, but instead of the egg being on the outside of the circle, it was at the end of line in the circle's center.

Joey turned the object some more to reveal the most complex of the six images. The fifth image appeared to be a combination of the first and fourth depicting the cloud circle and large open circle next to each other. The two circles were side-by-side and were connected now by a curved line that attached their centers. Like the previous image, an egg-shaped symbol rested in the center of the bigger circle.

"Wait, what's that symbol above the curved line on that picture?" asked Peter.

Joey stopped turning the object, momentarily, and the three boys leaned in to examine further.

"It looks like a floating tree to me," remarked Joey after some time.

No one else responded, but Peter covered the strange symbol with the tip of his finger and removed a few kernels of dried mud.

"Ohh!" they gasped together.

"It's one of those figures from the other image," said Joey excitedly. He quickly turned the object back around to the first image of the strange four-member family.

"For a family, they do all look the same, just smaller," remarked Peter. "But you're right, I think the smallest figure is the one standing above the curved line connecting the two circle things."

Joey went back to the fifth image again.

"Yep, it's definitely the smallest figure. Maybe whoever made it didn't feel like making unique figures. This one is definitely standing on a curved bridge between angry cloud circle and the big open one," said Greg, tracing his finger over the curved line between the circles.

Peter nudged Joey's shoulder with his own. "Let's see what the other image looks like. Keep turning Joey."

Joey turned the object to the final image that was before the first angry cloud circle they had already examined.

"Oh, now it's just the big circle with those small figures inside of it," stated Greg. "See, there is five of them positioned in a triangle within the circle."

"That's what it looks like to me, too," replied Joey.

"But, what does it mean?" Peter added, shaking his head.

"Hell, if I know, maybe we should get your sister down here to take a look at it. She's taking some of those fancy college classes now, right Greg?" Joey said with a crooked grin.

"You just want her down here to stare at her tits," Peter chided.

Joey did not offer much of a response besides a shrug of his shoulders.

"Joey's right. We might be in over our heads on this one. Let me go get my sister and see what she thinks of all this," Greg said, grabbing his backpack from the tenacle-like roots of a nearby beech tree. "I'll be back as fast as I can, I wouldn't touch anything more," he called back over his shoulder climbing up the hillside from where they had raced down earlier in the afternoon.

The two other boys stood silently watching Greg trot off back to familiar surroundings. For this first time since its discovery, they were now alone with the strange space egg. The air seemed changed or perhaps it had been that way the whole time and went unnoticed in all the excitement. The air was silent, like the deadness of a tomb. Yet, it allowed for a growing uneasiness to move through it and creep up their legs like the burnt tendrils of mud spread out all around them.

Without a word to each other, they placed the object back on the dried mud and stepped back to the presumed safety of the trees until Greg returned.

~*~*~*~

It was over an hour before Greg came back with his sister. The return party's approach was given away by the crunching twigs as they crested the hillside.

"Hey, boys," Greg's sister said warmly to Joey and Peter, almost slipping onto the muddy hillside which would have made a brown mess of the white short shorts she was wearing. A young tree sapling prevented her fall at the last second. She then reevaluated her route, jumping from sapling to sapling until she reached the floor of the glen.

"Hello, Ava!" replied Peter who was sitting by a thick beechnut tree.

"Where's Joseph?" Ava asked. "Oh, there you are! I want you to meet my boyfriend, Rick."

"Hi, Ava," Joey said, trying to hide his flushed face behind a low-hanging branch. For the man following closely behind her, he only offered a squinted glare.

"Hi there, I'm Rick," he said, reaching the spot next to Ava. The man wore a pair of dark jeans and a university tee-shirt covered over by a leather jacket. Like Ava's short shorts and tank top, the attire seemed out of place in the wooded dell. To the boys, they seemed strange oddities that had long since passed over the invisible bridge that connected childhood and the adult world beyond.

"Nice to meet you, Rick. I'm Peter and this is Joey," Peter said gesturing to Joey who was still partially obscured by a tree branch.

Joey offered no greeting. The flush from his cheeks had quickly drained away and he now looked a similar shade to the branch his head rested upon.

"So…" Ava began with her hands on her hips, "This is the spot where you all run off to for so many afternoons." She surveyed the area with a crisscrossing gaze. No more than a few car lengths across, the little glen sat between the feet of two hills. A rocky stream bisected through the low place as far as could be seen in both directions. The stream was merely a trickle, now, surrounded by remnants of plastic bottles and bags that had been carried down from the subdivision's run off scattered amongst the smooth stones. On the far side of the stream, old growth trees towered over the bottom. They dwarfed the ones on the hillside that they had just come down, likely the young vestiges of a clear-cut from the housing development.

"Well, what have you brought me here for, boys?" Ava asked after finishing her review.

"Ava, the object is over there," Greg said, pointing off to a spot a few paces to her right. She followed her little brother's finger to a dried splotch of brown mud. Resting on top was the strange cylindrical object.

Ava walked over quickly to the object and crouched down close. And for some time, she did not speak a word.

"You know…" she started, after a minute had passed. "I thought you boys were pulling my leg to get me out here for some sort of stunt, but, you're right, this is something quite remarkable. Rick, you have to look at these etchings!"

Rick, who had been standing by a tree looking rather disinterested, shuffled over to where Ava was knelt.

"Can you pick it up and turn it for me, Rick? I want to get a good look at the other side," Ava asked absently.

"I'm not sure we should be touching that thing," Rick responded standing above her with his arms crossed.

"Come on, man, don't be a wuss! I'm fifteen and I've touched it already," cried Joey who appeared suddenly between the two of them from where he had been skulking. "See, it's nothing," he added, picking up the object in both hands.

"Let me know if I am turning it too quickly, Ava" he said, giving her a boyish smile.

Rick gave the teen a half-hearted shrug and strutted to a nearby tree where he proceeded to twiddle a cluster of acorns.

Ava gave him a flinty stare as he walked away before turning back to Joey. "Thank you, Joseph. Keep turning it just like that," she said, her eyes twinkling with anticipation.

Joey turned the object around slowly about a half-dozen revolutions until Ava seemed satisfied. At certain moments she would stop him to rub her fingers across the symbols and dots. This would be followed by an "Ohh" "Hmm" or tucking a strand of blonde hair behind her ear.

"I need to have Dr. Clark take a look at this," she said, finally, pulling off her tiny leather backpack.

"Who is Dr. Clark?" asked Greg.

"Oh, he's my cryptography professor this semester," she replied as she searched through her pack.

"What are you majoring in, anyways, Ava?" Joey asked, as if the question had been rehearsed several times in his head. His eyes widened as the word 'majoring' wavered perilously close to the edge of cracking in his voice.

"Yes…in anthropology and…maybe linguistics," she replied absently, still searching through her sack.

Eventually, she stopped rummaging and lifted her head, staring off into the forest. Her blue eyes were glazed and lost in thought.

"I think I'll need to go back to the house and try to reach Dr. Clark on his pager. Joseph, do you think you could set the object in my pack?" she asked kindly.

Joey nodded silently and lifted the object over her sack with each end in the palm of his hands. The egg-shaped cylinder looked almost too big to be swallowed up by the zipper-toothed bag.

"Try turning it the other way," Ava instructed, after making several attempts to fit both ends of the object into her small pack. Joey turned the object in his hands gently, so that it hung over the pack vertically end-to-end. Clasping the top section of the egg tightly with two hands, he began lowering it down and then…

Sisssssssss…SHLOOP!

The loud sound startled Ava and Joey back a few steps. Before they could react, the bottom half of the object had flown down into Ava's bag while the other half had rocketed up out of Joey's hands several meters into the air. The separated egg half eventually fell to the ground a few meters away, lodging itself back into a spot of mud.

"What happened?" cried Greg.

"I…I don't know. I was holding it steady and then it just flew apart after making a hissing sound," replied Joey, examining his hands.

"I heard a loud sucking and popping sound," Ava added, her eyeballs still wide open. At her side, her hands rattled against her leg below the end of her shorts.

"Are you okay, Avy?" asked Rick who had moved from the tree to the spot where the other half of the object had plopped to a rest.

"I…think so," she began, now grasping both hands together at her chest as if to rub off some invisible grime. "That thing just burst op—" She paused, her eyes now looking down at where she had been crouching before.

"Joey, I think you put a hole in my bag!"

Joey grabbed the bag and walked over next to her inspecting it.

"Where do you see the hole? I can't seem to find it," he asked, tracing over the leather with his fingers.

"Let me see it, kid," Rick said, grabbing the pack and placing the half of the object that had fallen to the ground next to its sibling inside.

"Ava, I'm not seeing it either…" he said after a short time.

"It's…it's right there, hanging in the air!" Ava's voice quivered slightly as she pointed to something in front of her in the area where her bag had once been.

Everyone took a few steps closer to see the spot above the dried mud that could be traced from the tip of her finger. Sure enough, there was a marble-sized hole where Ava had been pointing. Hovering about knee-height, it was the darkest thing that any of them had ever seen. Peter and Joey walked around it to get multiple angles, but no matter where they stood, it was the same—inky black with no form or three-dimensional shape. It looked like a flat black pancake up in the air as if had been painted there by Wile E. Coyote from the cartoons.

"It's a little black dot," Ava said, curiously.

"It's so dark and just hovering there," Peter replied. He waved his arm above and below the black dot like a magician showing their enchanted crowd that there were no strings attached.

"Yeah, but how did it get there?" asked Greg.

Joey pointed to Rick with Ava's sack. "Do you think that it came from inside the space egg?"

"Good point, Joey. Why don't we walk over there and discuss to be safe?" Ava said, motioning to a spot near a tree a dozen meters away. "Rick, hand me my bag."

Rick handed her the bag and the group walked away from the black dot until it was not visible near the foot of the hill leading back to the development. For a good fifteen minutes they discussed the series of events backwards and forwards. The boys told Ava and Rick how they had found the object buried in the mud along with the burnt branches. Then there was a discussion of the strange symbols etched into the casing and together, they looked at the innards of the now open space egg. Inside, it was nearly hollow with only a tiny array of strange metallic clamps that converged into a tiny spherical cage in the center of the egg. Nothing else could be seen and there was not a hint of the slow pulsing light that Peter had seen earlier. The entire object was now dull and lifeless.

The group was about to head back to Greg and Ava's house when a loud sound drew their attention back to the area of the black dot. Due to how quickly the sound came and went, it was difficult to identify, but most agreed it sounded like the squawking of a small bird. As they headed back over to the black dot, Peter noticed the change almost immediately.

"Hey guys, doesn't the dot look bigger to you?" he said in a half-whisper.

"It looks the size of a golf ball now," confirmed Greg. "And do you see that stuff around it?" He pointed a shaking finger.

"Oh, my God!" Ava gasped, pulling her hands up over her face. On the ground, was a puff of white feathers scattered in a rough donut shape. And, not too far from the feathers, was a small head of a little decapitated chickadee—its small beak was still opening and closing as its tiny black eyes began to glaze over staring at the tree canopy above.

"Shit man, did the dot eat that bird?" exclaimed Joey.

"It may have, look at that leaf!" added Greg.

Beneath the black dot was a green leaf that must have fallen while the group had been in discussion. There was really nothing peculiar about the leaf; it was bright green with four pointed lobes, likely from a tulip tree. However, a little off-center of the main vein of the leaf was a perfect circle the size of a marble cut straight through it. The hole was so perfectly shaped it looked to have been cut with a miniature cookie cutter.

"Let's try something," Joey said. He grabbed a nearby stick and pushed its tip slowly into the black dot. The stick disappeared instantly into one side without emerging on the other until it was only a nub in Joey's hand.

"It's growing!" Peter shouted. The dark mouth of the dot seemed to expand in the air like a creeping black hole, sucking in all light and matter fed into it.

"Feed it more, its hungry!" said Joey who was swiveling his head to find another stick.

"Let's try this one," Rick replied with a large grin. He dragged over a branch taller than himself and nearly too big to wrap his fingers around. He was about to insert it into the black dot when Ava dashed forward with her hands waving wildly in front of her and shouting at the top of her lungs.

"Stop it, Rick! We don't kn—"

The branch fell to the ground and split into two pieces with a thud. Ava had swatted the branch out of Rick's hand as hard as she could.

The boys and Rick looked at her with big eyes and mouths agape. No one said a word until Joey eventually cried out in terror.

"Ava! Your hand!"

Ava looked down slowly to her right hand to see that a hole—a little larger than a golf ball—had appeared in her palm allowing for an unobstructed view of the ground below. The hole was clean without any fragments of bone or tissue. Instinctively, she clinched her fingers slightly sending spurts of blood and tendon into the negative space that used to be a solid portion of her hand. Her eyes fluttered up into her head at the sight into a faint and almost hit the ground if it had not been for Rick's quick aid.

The rest of the group looked on in shock as the black dot continued to grow in size before their eyes. They stood helplessly as little wisps of Ava's blood hung in the air and slowly began to fall into the dark mouth of the hungry black dot.

~*~*~*~

The dot had reached the size of a baseball when Ava came to. For the few minutes she was unconscious, no one had fed the dot anything more. The prohibition against further meddling went largely unsaid. The hungry black dot seemed to consume everything thrown at it—leaves, sticks, birds, hands. And, importantly, it was only getting bigger with every passing moment, as if it had reached some sort of tipping point in the matter it had consumed. No one could guess just how big the thing would or could get. How do you put limits on something that has no tangible form and seems to defy nature? The thought of it swallowing up the entire world was on everyone's minds, but no one dared to mention the possibility out loud.

Yet, the dot seemed to halt its unyielding expansion when it had reached the size of a soccer ball. Either it was at its final size—

if bottomless dots have a final size—or needed more matter to continue to grow. One thing was sure, no one was going to test it any further.

To everyone's surprise, Ava was quite composed given the ordeal she had been through. Rick had torn up his shirt and wrapped her hand as tightly as he could to stop most of the bleeding. To be sure, she would need to go to the hospital for some sort of procedure. Though, how a doctor could sew up a golf ball sized hole in your hand was in the back of everyone's minds.

"Oh my, it's grown so big!" Ava said, clinching her bandaged hand. "How long have I been out?"

"About five minutes," replied Greg.

"We're glad you're all right. That thing could have swallowed your whole arm," Joey said, rubbing his right sleeve.

"We need to get you to a hospital, Ava," Rick said impatiently.

"Yes, we do. We need to tell people about this thing. We can't simply leave this black hole out here in the woods to grow on its own unheeded."

In the fog of the growing egg and her injured hand, Ava's thoughts managed to find their way back to Dr. Clark and his office filled with volumes of books.

"We also need to get this so-called space egg to Dr. Clark to analyze. He would be the best person to decode something this strange and make sense of what is going on here," she added.

"Yes, Avy, but first..." Rick began, but Ava had fallen silent. Her eyes were again transfixed on the dot. "What is it, Ava?"

"There is something going on with the dot..." she started. "I think I see dull lights in there..."

Within the dot's center, there seemed to be two glimmers of light. They contrasted sharply with absolute darkness that surrounded them. Oval-shaped, they were dull lights, like a hardboiled egg that had sat out too long and had begun to turn a brownish off-white. Within the small ovals, that could not have been larger than an almond, were specks of oblong amber.

Suddenly, the amber flecks flickered on and off.

"Guys, I think something blinked at me from in that thing," Ava cried with a rising sense of alarm in her voice. The others looked at her perplexed.

"Ava, you've had a bad accident, it's time to get you to the hospital," Rick stated decisively, trying to pick her up under one arm. But she stayed fast, and pointed to the black dot with a trembling arm. Her eyes began to bulge and water.

"No, I am not kidding, look!"

She screamed.

The group followed her wavering finger again to the middle of the black dot. Within its inky blackness, two oblong eyeballs with tiny amber pupils—similar to a cat's—blinked in pairs of firm pulses every ten seconds. After a few moments of blinking, a hairless creature emerged head first from the mouth of the dot, falling to the ground underneath on its tiny feet. The misshapen creature was no taller than a pencil with arms as long as its legs. Its face was waxy grey like a body that had been found drowned after a few days. If the thing had a mouth and nose, it was obscured by some sort of breathing mask that covered the bottom half of its face. The rest of its body was covered in a dark cobalt blue material that seemed metallic like the egg. Across the suit's chest and arms, small patterns of dots glowed a dull orange.

"Hello...what are you?" said Rick in an unsure voice, towering above the creature a few meters away.

The troll-like thing regarded Rick for a few moments, looking him up and down. The thing made a few indistinct clicking sounds inside its mask as it considered him. Then, with a tiny hand having two thumbs and three long fingers in between, it pulled something out from behind its back. The little hand-held device that appeared was crimson with two prongs jutting out the front and a barb protruding out its top. The creature held the device steady until a bright blue flash quickly flickered out the end of it.

"Uhh...my leg," Rick cried. He instantly crouched down to hold an area of his exposed leg above the top of his tennis shoe.

"Are you all right?" Ava said, now on her feet a few steps away from him.

"No, I'm not all right. It feels like a wasp sting, but much, much worse!"

"Let us see," Ava requested as calmly as she could.

"No. Stay back! I'll try to come to—" Rick stopped short as another bout of pain shoot up his leg. "It feels hot. I...I can feel it moving up my leg. Now it's going up my belly...oh God...I feel it hitting in my heart. I think my blood is boiling!"

"Rick!" Ava shouted and tried to walk towards him, but Greg and Joey stepped forward to hold her back.

Rick removed his hand and tried to take a step towards them on the leg that had been attacked. The skin around the wound had already turned a semi-transparent color, revealing white bone underneath. His whole leg then began bubbling violently. And then, after a few fleeting moments, the weight of his step collapsed beneath him in a splash of watery fluid. Rick looked at the group with wide eyes and tried to speak, but his voice had failed him. Only gargled sounds came out of his mouth as the rest of him began to sink into the ground. His whole body was losing form and melting into a transparent liquid. Soon, what was once Rick was rushing into the stream nearby, leaving only the wet remnants of his shoes, socks, and jacket.

Ava began screaming and sobbing as the boys led her away from the scene up the hillside. Peter grabbed her bag right as dozens more of the dot creatures were emerging from their dark portal, all dressed in the same glowing uniforms. When the four of them finally made it to the crest of the hill, they stole one final look at the black dot down in the glen. They could see the dark thing clearly against the green foliage. It stood out like a blotch on the landscape. All around it, the movement of now hundreds of the little creatures told of their expanding numbers with every passing moment. The group then turned and ran as fast as their feet could carry them hoping not to feel the sting of a barb in the back of their legs.

~*~*~*~

The transcription came too late. Before the world knew what had happened, they were upon them, in the thousands or millions, there was little time for a true accounting of their numbers. The Groll—or the more popular term, the Dotters—had come to lay claim to the earth for themselves, and them alone.

The invasion did not come in the form of a horse like it did for the Trojans, but, for humanity, an egg that you could hold in your hand. For centuries, humans had feared beasts bigger than themselves and never thought to think of an advanced race no bigger than a human hand that could lurk in the shadows and tight spaces hidden and unchecked. The little ones could creep and wriggle their way into places that were too small to see—in the branches of trees, behind walls, and amongst traveling vehicles. For all the advanced satellite imagery and thermal scans, the Groll were simply too small to be detected with any precision or speed. These advancements had all been the result of centuries of optimization to guard against human adversaries, not beings the size of a chipmunk.

At first, the military and scientists were confused at how quickly the Groll were able to traverse away from their foothold in the little glen that sat next to the Shady Grove development in Western Ohio. The momentary confusion was enough time for them to spread across the United States in a couple of days and, in a week, they were almost everywhere around the globe. It was only later, by chance, from a grainy truck stop surveillance camera that caught a dozen Groll creating another black dot portal. They had brought with them tiny space eggs and were able to quickly set up a network across the globe of black dots that they used to traverse nearly instantaneously. By the time the surveillance video was seen by those in power, it was merely too late.

In the ensuing days, reports began to flood in of entire communities disappearing in the Midwest. When government officials were sent in to investigate, not a human trace was left or any other predator bigger than house mouse. The only remnants were pools and streams of water flowing out of buildings and along sidewalks. It was not until the Groll reached an air force base in Dayton that the disappearances were learned to be the result of the strange Groll weaponry. They had come armed with weapons that deconstructed organic compounds into their base elements. Once shot, an animal would quickly deconstruct into its base elements of water and gas. The weapons easily penetrated skin, fabric, and some metals. By the time the intel got out, the Groll were marching across the world, leaving pools of human-size tears in their wake.

The survivors—a hopeful term, as it's still too early to say if the thousands that remain will survive—hid in the high places of the world. Mountains and high steppes seem too much for the little trolls to handle. No one knows if it is the thinning air, the cold, or the greater exposure to UV light; the Groll simply do not venture much above 2,500 meters above sea level. The lowlands of the world remain firmly their domain.

There is a scientist among us, a Dr. Clark, who was able to decode their language from a rubbing of an original dotter egg a group of kids handed to him before things went crazy. He has said that the language of dots was difficult to decipher and was only made harder by the lack of resources up in the mountains. However, long after the Groll had taken control of the planet, he had a breakthrough and decoded the first five parts of the message. It read:

Dying home;
Groll to small;
Send out entryways;
Find big fertile world;
Bridge to promise.

The final transcription took the longest as it was not simply a phrase but a single word. While Dr. Clark was working the last part out, a working theory was developed about what it all meant along with the etched imagery. The best guess of the top minds that remain in existence goes that the Groll had hopelessly destroyed their home world in some environmental calamity. Some think it was over pollution, others over population, or some combination. Nonetheless, it was during this time that the Groll discovered some sort of wormhole technology to connect distant points in space. However, the rub was that, due to energy requirements, the portals could only be made so big, typically not larger than a soccer ball.

In addition to these technological advances that far outpaced our own, the Groll somehow were able to shrink down their species by a factor of ten. The Groll spent numerous generations shrinking down their dwindling population until they were no bigger than a human hand. It is surmised that this shrinking down served two purposes. It enabled the Groll to use less of the precious resources being smaller and, the smaller stature allowed for them to enter the portals that they had seeded across the galaxy in their space eggs. Unlucky for the residents of Earth, a space egg happened to find its way to the Earth's surface and was opened by unsuspecting teens. A few scraps of matter were all that was needed to feed the portal and bridge our world to theirs.

It was not until about six months after the Groll invasion started that Dr. Clark was able to finally decipher the last image. Many of us have died as the winter has begun in the higher elevations. Many more have died trying their luck in the valley below filled with Groll hidden at every turn which has become a forbidden land for the brave and the hopeless. Unfortunately, I have to report that Dr. Clark was one of them. Who knows what these notes will serve to someone in the future. I only hope that there is some human being to read them and figure out a way to rid our world of these dotters.

If it does help, before he left, Dr. Clark wrote down the final meaning of the sixth Groll symbol. It simply read: *Paradise.*

I hope it is one that we can eventually reclaim, but hope is a dangerous thing in these dark days and cold, hungry nights.

Down the Stone Stair

Do you want to burn bright?

That is what she said to them. How could he forget. Her words echoed from the past as if they had been played from a recording right here in the train car.

Looking out the window, little blurs of tall buildings and modest stores were becoming less frequent. The 3:30 train from London to Brandon had entered a more rural country from the congested London suburbs. The colors were earthy and the air was now a cleaner shade of blue. The train would arrive around six with a setting sun. Though not much light would be needed then, the path was etched in his mind deep enough that not even the decades had eroded it away.

Soon, more greens of rolling hills and pastureland began to take hold outside. The patchwork of fields with their tiny hedgerows of stunted trees gave him the feeling that he had stayed in London for far too long. The scenery was enough to bring it all back, as if it had been waiting in a cupboard gathering dust on a high shelf. It looked different, but the space was not unlike that of the area around Brandon. That was the town he was rushing towards on his ticket; that home he was born in, and the place he outgrew too quickly.

A rural town in the county of Suffolk, Brandon was out of the way as most common folks who lived there described it. In its ancient past, Brandon had been known for its rabbit furs and gunflint. Now, it was mostly a stepping stone for tourists on their way to somewhere on the Norfolk Coast.

The Thetford Forest surrounded Brandon. The timber was planted there in the 1920s to bolster England's struggling timber supply after the Great War. As a boy, Thetford had grown into a wilderness to explore, big enough to fill any boy's imagination.

And there was no better companion to explore it with than Logan. *God, we thought we owned that little place*, he thought. The two of them—partners in crime mum would say—would sneak out during lunch to take off for the day in the forest. As average pupils, it would have probably been better to stay in school more, but Logan was often persistent, calling him Laurie instead of his given name, Lawrence. That would rile him up like nothing else. Funny how little things affect boys on the cusp of adolescence.

The forest seemed so vast then, even before finding that secret place. It loomed over Brandon like a sea of green, kept only at bay by virtue of diligent townsfolk. On current maps, it had been reduced to a slowly shrinking green splotch on a map. *How big would it seem now?* he wondered, before dozing off against the cool window.

~*~*~*~

Lawrence awoke to the train lurching forward. Out his window, he caught a last glimpse of the platform and a sign that read 'Cambridge' plastered to the wheat-colored brick façade of the station. He glanced at his watch; it was a quarter past four. *Making good time*, he thought. He patted the breast of his coat to make sure the wad of bread was still there. His entire life savings was stuffed in an inner pocket, twenty grand of bread. It wasn't much, but it was all a middle-aged bachelor could save on a librarian's salary. He had never married or even really felt a pull towards a woman in any deep way. Sure, there had been a couple of mediocre shags across the years, but no one could ever compare to *her*.

The few last remnants of new passengers were shuffling through the passageway outside his compartment. Many of them wore long burgundy scarfs with gold stripes around their necks denoting their attendance at the local college. He could only think that the scarfs were more for style than substance. This October had been the warmest in his memory. He had hoped to be left alone to his thoughts for the duration of the trip, but that hope was quickly swept away when a trio of students burst into his car. Their rosy cheeks somehow instantly pushing out the gloom he had grown comfortable with in the empty car. The vibrancy of youth seemed like a thing he had almost forgotten.

"Aced that exam!" said a baby-faced lad with ruffled puffs of dark hair, disheveled by the wind. He took the seat closest to the window.

"You may have, but I'll be lucky to squeak by with a passing mark. Professor Adler always gives me a passing mark, never more, never less," replied the student taking the middle seat.

"Well, it is hard to appear bright with Nancy in our section," replied the tallest of the trio who kicked his legs up on the opposite-facing seat on which Lawrence was seated.

"Nancy...ugh, she is always getting attention from the professor. Maybe they have some sort of thing going on," insinuated the lad in the middle seat.

The student by the door nodded his head emphatically while pushing his tongue against the inside of his cheek in a crude pulsing fashion.

The trio laughed.

Lawrence was about to ignore them for the sights beyond the window when the lad in the middle seat pulled out a magazine from his sack that drew his gaze. It was the kind of publication that sits on shelves for impulsive travelers in the waiting areas of train stations, dribble mostly.

"I bet Leyton Hughes never had issues with getting noticed," the lad said, flipping around the front of the magazine for the rest of the trio. On its cover was a finely-dressed man cupping his chin in a pensive pose overlooking an Infinity Battery. In bold block letters below the portrait was scribed 'Leyton Hughes, Person of the Millennium, Saving Humanity from Crisis and Calamity with Limitless Energy Invention.'

For Lawrence, the man was not familiar because he was one of the top business magnates seen in a millennium with the likes of Ford, Gates, or Musk, but because it was Logan, his friend he had not seen since childhood.

"I know that fellow," Lawrence sputtered out from the corner with a voice that had seen little use of late.

The trio stopped chattering and stared at him for a few long moments with big doe eyes as if a disembodied voice had spoken out of the ether. The car fell to a silence with only the steady beat of the train tracks providing any semblance of change.

"You know Leyton Hughes?" asked the lad with the magazine.

"Aye, I do," he replied simply.

"Did he tell you where he came up with the Infinity Battery? No one thought energy could be drawn from the air while using a few simple materials arranged in such a way."

"I'm afraid I have no idea about the battery," he replied, not untruthfully. Though, in his gut he knew the wellspring of such knowledge.

When does the light blind? Logan had asked her at the top of the stair. A radiant smile had followed and then she told them of things, fantastical things.

Smirking slightly, the lad by the window jumped in. "But, no one knows Leyton Hughes. The man is an enigma. He just appeared one day with all these great ideas, with no backstory, no digital presence. He just was."

"Yeah, the papers have been offering beaucoup amounts of quid for any information on his background. The man is a recluse who rarely gives open interviews," added the lad closest to the door who had unstretched his legs to lean forward.

"They might have a hard time finding the background of Leyton Hughes; when I knew him, he was Logan Burrows," he replied.

The trio's eyes grew wide at the unexpected revelation.

"Wait, you're telling us that the man who invented the Infinity Battery has a secret double life that no one knows about?" asked the lad with the magazine.

"Double life? Hmm...I'm not sure about that. I believe he has lived but one, gone and then returned," he said.

The trio puzzled over his statement until the lad by the door pushed for more.

"Gone and returned from where?"

Lawrence sat back on the cushion, rubbing the thinning part of hair on his head.

"Seeing as we have a way to go, I'll tell you my story. Though, you are likely not to believe a lick of it. I've kept it close since I was a kid. Somehow, over the years, I began to believe I made it all up. Now, with Logan's return, I'm not so sure..." he began, shifting his eyes from the eager faces of the trio to the passing pastoral scenery outside.

"We were lads, slightly younger than yourselves—Logan and I. Still in state school in those days. We didn't care much for school, perhaps we should have; Logan was the son of a butcher and I a millworker's son. The classroom simply wasn't for us. Books talking about the world and how it works didn't compare to actually going out exploring it for yourself. That's why we were not in school on *that* particular day. It was near or on the fall equinox; I can remember a Year 1 class trying to balance eggs out on the footway. We had decided around the lunch break to slip out the school yard because the weather was nice and the afternoon lessons would be a bore.

"We started up High Street and crossed the bridge over the Little Ouse River. From there, we cut across several fields, that I hear now are new housing developments. We then passed over the railway near Brandon station and headed quickly into the forest in the area that was once Bromehill Plantation.

"The woods were still young and open then with little deadfall and undergrowth. You could see the planning that had been made years before by the commission; the even placement of the beeches and scots pines, growing in nice orderly rows. They stood tall and straight with amble space in between to travel unimpeded beneath their canopy. It was a fine place to walk and even better one to run. We ran though those trees feeling like Robin Hood and Little John. I always played as Robin Hood given a hint of redness in my brown hair. You can't really see it now as most of it as receded into nothingness," he paused to pass his hand through the thin web of greying hair that remained. The trio watched him intensely, but stayed silently enthralled and made no comment. So, he continued.

"Logan…" he chuckled, feeling the wad of bread shift against his chest. "…he was a bigger fellow, like in the old cartoon, so he would be Little John. Even he would admit he wasn't the brightest crayon in the box. Unfortunately for him, kids picked up on that sort of thing. To many, he was big and dumb as they come and he would be called 'Dumbgan' often by our classmates.

"I didn't fare much better, you see. I was called 'fire bush' after a group of boys saw my private parts in the locker room after our gym lesson one day. Kids can be quite imaginative." He paused for a moment. To their credit, the trio did not laugh or even hint at a smirk. If they did, it was well-hidden.

Good for them, he thought, and carried on.

"Anyways…as Robin and Little John, we loved to climb up trees, chase little grey hares into their burrows, and stalk red deer to see how close we could get crouching real low across the mossy forest floor. But, our favorite thing to do was to sword fight. Long straight sticks would be crafted into our hero blades, carefully forged without any stray spurs or leaves left attached. We would sally forth in engaging battles whacking and hacking at each other along with the surrounding trees. At opportune times, chase would be given after another when one of us needed to make a dramatic retreat. It was on one of these occasions that day, when Logan was making one of his daring retreats, that he ran and fell over the side of a small hill.

"He had fallen in a clearing we had never been through before. The trees surrounding it were beech, smooth and pale. In the open area was a singular hill that rolled up with long grass growing on and around it. There were no wildflowers to speak of and no sounds either; the clearing was silent as could be without the chirping of a bird or rustling of an animal. The sun overhead was strong and we could feel it's unusually warm autumn rays upon us.

"When I came upon the hill to see where Logan had fallen, he was gone. Like I said, the clearing was wide open, so there was nowhere he could have run without me seeing him—and I had become very keen at tracking him during our battles.

"I called out to him standing atop the hill: 'Logan! Logan! Are you all right?' For a few moments there wasn't anything, not even a light breeze on the air.

Then I heard his voice. It sounded so far off and distant.

"I am here he said. I looked around and could see nothing. 'Where are you?' I repeated. The faint voice said 'here' followed by the clattering of pebbles. His voice sounded as if it were beneath my feet, but I could see nothing on the downside of the hill. I prepared to ask again for his location, but before I could get out another word, Logan's head seemed to pop out of the earth and turn up to see me.

"Flashing a wide Cheshire grin, he said, 'I've found something, come and see!'

"Well, I did just that. I walked down and around the hill to find Logan standing in the mouth of a cave. He was kicking away cobbles and stones the size of footballs that appeared to have recently fallen out of place. Though the entrance looked like a cave, the inside did not appear to be a completely natural formation. The ground was smooth with a cobblestone walkway that went under the hill. Logan pointed in the direction I was looking and exclaimed that he had found a stone stair; a stair to nowhere, he said. It took a while before my eyes had adjusted enough to see it; the cobble walkway terminated into carefully crafted stone slabs that led downward, into complete darkness.

"Our first thought was that it might be connected to Grime's Graves which was, at most, located less than a couple of kilometers away."

"I visited Grimes Graves as a boy with my dad, it was really old," interjected the lad by the window. "I think it used to be a flint mine from like the Neolithic era, or something."

The older man continued, "That's right, but after a while we realized, it did not seem to have a connection with Grimes. There were no traces of flint in or around the entrance and the stonework seemed different, older even, but somehow also better carved and smoothed out."

The boys' eyes darted back-and-forth, searching for where the story would go next. Lawrence nodded knowingly and broke their suspense.

"You see, inside the entrance, we came upon a descending stair. The steps were a pale sandy stone that wound down steeply into a dark abyss."

"An old well?" asked the lad by the door.

He shook his head. "No, there was no sight or sounds of water. In fact, the air inside the cave was incredibly dry. The only signs of anything were small markings on the wall. Always in groups of threes, about a dozen groups of markings had been etched into the stone wall in patterns that varied from vertical to horizontal. The daylight from the entryway was strained so it was difficult to see if there had been more. We hadn't a torch on us so we sat on the top step of the landing where the light began to fade into black.

"Looking downward into the pit, the stairs faded slowly into a spiral of darkness. It's hard to describe how black it looked down there. I'm not sure even an electric torch would have pierced down very far. I tried tossing a fist-sized stone down the gullet of the hole and waited for it to hit water, more stone, or something else. We stayed completely silent for twenty seconds and did not hear anything. It seemed near bottomless as far as we could tell from the top.

"After that, Logan took another stone about the same size and banged it against the wall to hear any echoes. There wasn't any coming up from the pit. He did it again for a second time, now a little harder. Again, there was little reverberation anywhere.

"Then, as hard as he could, Logan flung a stone at the wall on the other side of the chasm. It hit the wall with a loud bang followed by a tumbling of the stone down the countless stairs until the sound of bouncing was no more. Silence followed quickly.

"That was when we heard what sounded like a distant scream come out of the bottom of that place. It was ever-so-faint but the high-pitched cry found us from deep within the earth.

"We waited there, in near darkness, frozen to the top step of the stair. We couldn't move a muscle for fright and because we were not sure what our ears had just heard. Ears that were then straining at their limits to hear anything further. But it wasn't our ears that picked up on what came next. Down in the middle of the pit, for what might have been half a kilometer down, emerged a tiny speck of light.

"It was a faint green glow at first, almost like that of the fleeting light of the first firefly on an early summer's eve. Up from the bottom of the darkness, the glow rose slowly, going around and around the unseen stair below. It circled the inner edge becoming brighter as it made its climb. When it had reached a few levels right below us, it transformed, morphed, changed—what have you—shifting from an orb to something more distinct…a figure of a woman!"

"Wait, what…where did she come from? Didn't you say you were in the middle of the forest?" asked the lad by the window.

"I did indeed," Lawrence acknowledged. "I wish I knew whence she came, if only I knew that…"

"What did this woman look like?" asked the middle lad.

The older man sat back in his seat and half closed his eyes as if to summon her from in his mind.

"She…" he began softly, pursing his lips. "She emerged in a faint green glow like that of a lantern you would find full of fireflies on a summer's eve, pulsing in even intervals. As she climbed the remaining steps, she seemed to float over each one without a hint of a footfall. She appeared to be wearing a sheer white dress that sparkled like glitter from the light she gave off from the smooth completion of her sun-kissed skin. The dress clung around every curve of her slender frame that did not seem strong enough to make the long climb without stopping. As she rounded the last turn, we saw her face for the first time. Like the rest of her body, her face had an ethereal glow about it that was unblemished. Its beauty was merciless; long flowing inky hair, lips as red as pomegranates, and her eyes, oh her eyes, they were bottomless pools of amber, as if the gems had been plucked from the ground and placed upon her. Looking into them you felt at any moment you might topple in and fall forever. Into a wild fury of passions.

"In a way, I still feel I am falling for her," he thought aloud.

"I don't know if I would have been scared or aroused," said the lad by the door.

"Bollocks, you'd be scared shiteless," retorted the lad by the window.

"What happened next?" asked the lad in the middle seat, ignoring the two at his side. He had long set down his magazine and was now fully leaned in from his seat.

"She stopped a few steps short of where we had frozen in place upon the top landing. And then…she just stood there silently, watching the two of us without saying a word or making a gesture. I guess she might have been trying to figure us wankers out as much as we were trying to understand who and where she came from."

"Bloody hell, I think I would have dashed right out of there and not stopped until I was home," said the lad by the window.

"You're right, every ounce of muscle in my legs wanted to burst towards the entryway and as far away from that cave as I could. But Logan held my shoulder with a vice grip that I couldn't have broken if I wanted to. He seemed as enchanted as I was waiting for her to make the next move to release us.

"After a period of time—it could have been seconds, minutes, or hours—the woman beckoned to us. With an outstretched hand she bid us come closer to her, but we still could not move. When she saw that we were firm in our resolve (that is immobilizing fear), she brought her hand back to her shapely bosom. There she clutched at a breast with her hand, cupping it with her fingers and caressing its summit with the end of a delicate thumb.

"It was then that the beautiful woman spoke to us. Now lads, I wish I could describe exactly what she said, you'd think something like that would stick with you, but all I can remember is that she spoke in such an elegant, soft voice, that it sounded like a melody to our ears. That day she spoke of knowledge as a fire that burns bright and that she could show us the oil to spark our own fires within us. She asked if we wanted to burn bright and that, to do so, we only needed to follow her to bring our spark.

"We were in complete awe, enthralled by her beauty and intelligence. So much so that we lost track of all time and didn't notice the waning light outside that had turned to golden. The woman had noticed too and seeing we were not ready to walk with her, she bid us to come back the following afternoon. After saying all of this, she gently turned and floated down the stair as she had come up. Logan and I peered over the edge of the pit to see her shift back into a glowing green orb. Soon the glow was as faint as a candle's flame and it disappeared completely into the inky black pool below that seem to shimmer briefly before settling back to nothingness."

He paused a moment to see if the lads had anything to say. Their jaws were open wide, but they did not make a sound. There was only the slightest of nodding, urging him on. So, he continued without hesitation.

"For the next three days, we went to see the woman in the glowing white dress every afternoon. And it was the same ritual every time: we took our place at the top of the stair; made three knocks with a stone; and waited for our lady to appear out of the depths of that pit. She always came, as if on cue, the same way she had before. And each time the wonder and beauty never seemed to diminish. She spoke to us in that musical voice of hers describing wonderful, fantastical things about a place we had never known. She spoke of a golden age separated by time, but not by space. A lost paradise where mankind had achieved a greatness never to be challenged again. And, if we merely walked down with her—as she beckoned us to do at the end of our time each day—all this long-forgotten knowledge could be ours as well.

"For myself and Logan the temptation was real. She was the prettiest woman we had ever seen and, of course, the thought of going with her to explore some mysterious place was right up our alley. But…we did not go with her. Something held us back. Yet, after each passing day with her, whatever was holding us back was losing its strength. We could both feel it. I almost suggested not going to see her on the third day for fear of what might happen…"

"Did you go see her on the third day?" asked the middle lad after a pause.

A wistful smile crept over Lawrence's face. He seemed lost in thought for a time until an uneven track bounced the car.

"Indeed, we did. On that third day, the last day I saw her, she instructed us to come walk with her before her time ended with us at the last light of the day. She expressed this last offer to us with distant eyes filled with melancholy. Even her white dress on that day seemed to have lost a little luster, as if the radiance was fading from it. I honestly do not know how we were able to find the resolve to not step forward down the stair to meet her. Our hearts felt like they were already with her. Somehow, we managed it and she left us like every time before—a silent specter of light disappearing into the deep.

"Walking back from the cave that last day, I was still tempted by the woman's offer. I couldn't shake her image out of my head and my heart seemed to ache with yearning to go with her. Yet, now outside the cave, my mind urged reluctance towards the idea of traveling down into some unknown pit.

"Logan seemed to share this apprehension, perhaps to a lesser extent. We reasoned together that it was strange that she never provided more details for a being that knew so much. This whole time, she had never even given us her name. It would be best to go home for the night and not go back to see her. For we did know, somehow, that if we went with her, we would never be the same."

A voice on the intercom interrupted, "Brandon. Next stop is Brandon. Prepare your personal items for departure."

Lawrence looked out the windows to see the familiar rolling waters of the Little Ouse winding through the pasturelands.

Nearly there, he thought.

"Well lads, that's my stop, it was certainly nice chatting with you," he said, beginning to gather his things.

"Wait, you never told us what happened to Logan," cried the lad in the middle seat.

"Yeah!" added the other two.

He looked to the lads and then out the window to see the train was slowing down as it approached the station.

"You're right," he said with a soft smile. "Where was I?"

"The two of you split off to go back home after deciding not to return to that mysterious woman," said the lad in the middle seat.

"Ah yes, right you are. We both headed back home. I arrived and went straight to bed without supper. My stomach was in knots thinking about the cave, the woman, myself shining bright. I barely got any sleep.

"The next morning, I arrived at school and Logan's desk next to mine was empty. He never showed up that day, or the next, or the following. He had completely disappeared. His mother came to our home wrought with worry, but I could not offer any explanation where he was or where he might have gone. I'm not sure if it was a where or a when into which he went. All I know is that he disappeared that night without a trace.

"Now, deep down, I knew he had gone with her. I tried going back to the cave a few weeks later during lunch and tapped the stones three times, but nothing happened and there was no sign of Logan anywhere in or around the cave. I did not see him again until I saw his face on the tele on the evening broadcast. I was so shocked; I nearly dropped my supper. His name had changed, but the face was the same, except maybe there was a bit of a glow to it. But, you know, the tele can do strange things with your appearance. They say it adds seven kilos..."

"If you know him, why haven't you tried to reach out to him?" asked the lad by the window. Behind him, the Brandon Station was pulling into view slowly.

"Good question, you can tell your parents that your education is serving you well. I did try, in fact. I went to his office in London and told them my name and waited for an hour until I was informed that he refused to see me. When I asked why, a secretary told me he did not know me and I must have mistaken him for another."

The train came to stop. People were already filing out onto the grey platform and crossing the covered bridge that linked to the station on the other side of the tracks.

"Do you think you *could* be mistaken? Maybe Leyton's Hughes face only shares a bit of resemblance to your Logan; after all these years, it could be easy to confuse," stated the lad by the door.

"Perhaps, maybe I am a middling man going mad at the onset of middle-age. But Logan had a right eye that was both grey and brown and if you look at Leyton there, so does he. What are the odds of that?" he said, pointing to the magazine laying on the lad's lap.

The lad in the middle seat picked the magazine back up and leaned in close to the cover for a few quiet moments.

"Buggers, he's right he has a bi-colored right eye, brown and grey!" he gasped.

The other two leaned in next to the middle lad to get a look.

"Final call, for Brandon Station, please disembark if this is your final destination," called out the voice over the intercom.

Lawrence got up from his seat and headed out the door; but before leaving the car, he left the young men something to think about for the rest of their journey.

"Enjoy your holiday lads. And remember, there are things in this world we don't always understand, that neither time nor education can explain. But if you could know it all, wouldn't you want to? To burn bright?"

Once the train had left, Lawrence found himself in a quiet little station. The few people who had made the evening commute were already gone off to their homes for the day. He looked up at the red streaks stretching across the purple sky. A vibrant full moon was rising in the east. The night would be upon him soon, but he knew the way.

The route back to the cave had been retraced more times than he could count over the years in his mind. If a head doc ever looked, they would probably find an actual path visibly etched somewhere in his brain. The ground felt light under his feet as he floated across the terminal. His heart began to pound in his chest as his steps fell on familiar ground where they fallen decades ago.

From the train station he slipped out across an empty car park of an automotive shop. It had been only an overgrown field where the lads used to kick around the football in his youth. The chatter of children had long since faded from the space. Now, only a steady chorus of crickets could be heard playing the season's last serenade.

It was not long before he was under the cover of the trees. The forest was older now. A bit more wildness had crept in underneath the canopy than he remembered from before. The small bushes and brambles choked out the waning light from the edges. He pushed on though, determined, and purposeful with each step forward. He followed the old deer trails that had not changed at all with time. The trail went east for a bit then took a curve of a hillside to the west before splitting left at a fork after another while.

The darkness was growing as the sun was nearly set. Bathed in the new patches of moonlight, he could almost imagine Logan, as his youthful self, running out ahead carrying a stick sword. Together, they hopped over fallen logs, crossed trickling streams, and then, entered into that secluded little glade. He knew that he had found the right spot when everything had gone to silence upon entering the little meadow. There, standing where he knew it would be, was the hump of earth covered in crimson fountaingrass. Even without the rising moon, he could have found the cave's entrance. It was right where he remembered it on the southern side of the hill. Its stony mouth seemed smaller now. He could not tell if some stones had fallen down over the years or if its apparent change in size was a fabric of growing bigger with age. These questions were not important. Not now. The only thing that truly mattered was that he was able to squeeze his older flabby body into the stony aperture.

As he crawled on hands and knees, his eyes quickly adjusted to see the smooth path up ahead. He was nearly all the way through the opening when his left foot must have struck the top of the entrance to dislodge some more stones. With luck he was able to pull his legs through as the stones made an awful clunking sound behind him. It was not until he was fully inside and could turn his body around that he saw the blackness that had fallen in behind him.

The next moments were spent feeling at the stones that now blocked the entrance of the cave. He fingered at every little crack and crevasse, but could not find a way through. He would need to try and push the stones out.

He got up to his feet and immediately hit his head on the ceiling. The throbbing pain sent fake flashes of white dancing in pirouettes across his vision. The next attempt was led by a wary hand above his head. This time, his hand made contact first with the rocky ceiling and he was able to stand with his head cocked uncomfortably to one side. Then, with all his might, he dug his right shoulder into the build-up of stones and pushed.

Nothing.

He tried again, pushing now towards the middle of where the entrance once was.

Not a budge.

He tried once more, taking a few steps back and then lunging into the wall of stone.

Not even a wiggle.

It became quite clear that he had not the strength to topple the stones that now filled the entrance. He was trapped in his cave of mysteries, alone, without a mobile or anyone knowing his whereabouts.

"I hope this knowledge isn't a deadly friend," he whispered to himself.

Having no means of leaving, he crawled his way across the smooth floor of the cave until he came to an edge. He did not need to see the full shape of it to know that it was the top step of the stone stair. He swung over his feet and sat on the top few steps. Even after a period of adjustment, his eyes could not see anything but faint dots of noise as his eyes tried to make sense of the absolute darkness.

He waited for a time and nothing happened. The dark silence enveloped him and the only thing he was aware of was the faint beating heart in his chest.

He then remembered the three knocks. The whole cave-in seemed to have clogged his memory.

"It takes three knocks of stone," he whispered to himself. Even at a whisper, his voice seemed to carry forever into the unseen depths below his dangling feet.

Could she hear me, even before her summons? he thought with the wistfulness of a child. He would ask her when she came. She would come. She must come.

He leaned over towards the wall using one hand for support and the other carefully brushing back-and-forth across the floor. Amongst the dusty dirt and debris, he found three small stones, more like pebbles. Their irregular shapes clicked in his hands as he brought them near his chest. He thumbed each to be sure that the count was right. When he was sure, he tossed them, one-by-one, against the far wall until all three were dispensed. Once the echo of the last little stone had faded, he waited cautiously at the top of the stair.

What could have been minutes passed without any change. The silence began to become more and more suffocating with the thoughts that were brought about with it. Doubt began to creep into the spaces that had been once filled with optimism and child-like anticipation. He began to wonder if he had become too old or if too much time had passed and taken with it the opportunity for mystical enlightenment. Then there was also the possibility that he was an old fool, clinging to a false childhood memory. That couldn't be true, he couldn't let it be so.

Lawrence sat there, on the top of the stone step, waiting. He would wait until the end—either in darkness or in a rising whisking light. His eyes strained in their sockets down into the depths of the pit. The darkness was blacker than pitch, pulsing in time with his heart.

Soon, he began to sob uncontrollably like a blubbering child. The warm tears filled his eyes as he thought that the glittering woman in white might stand across an unreachable chasm in his memory.

"I want to burn bright; I want to burn bright; I want to...please don't be too late, please..." he whimpered into the abyss, banging his fist against the hard step.

Out of the tears of his eyes, he continued to wait, even for just a hint of a glow he would wait and wait until...there it was...finally, a speck of light!

Too Old
to Double Back

I met you when I was eleven. You were a vagabond filled with regret and slipping away, day-by-day. I got to see all your haunts that had accumulated at the end of your winding path. I could barely fathom that someone could arrive to such a place. But you taught me that all paths lead back to an innocent child at some point, that our lives are a running sum of our choices. At some point though, too many choices fall into place, the junctures seem to disappear, and you learn that you have gone too far down a path—you become too old to double back.

In a way, that lesson was one of two endings. But let's start with when we met...

It has been some time, but I can still smell the crisp air blowing through that weathered window of the community assembly hall. It was late summer but an early cold snap had plunged the temperatures in central Ohio down enough that a light jacket was needed outdoors. The hall was an old brick building, probably built sometime when my grandparents were born. The golden years of its use had long since slipped from the small town's memory like its faded red façade. The smell of earthy dry rot filled the air inside the open hall. Overhead, dark timbers held up the high ceiling—their enormous size the only remnants of trees of once mythical proportions. In the bright halogen lights, particles of dust floated down from the rafters like an early snowfall.

For a group of pre-teen cub scouts, the place was an excellent place to have a lock-in overnight. Located on a farm plot a half-hour away from Columbus, the hall had a large auditorium, loft, and basement—all places to explore, play, and find trouble. Since it was a lock-in, we were not supposed to leave the building. Mrs. Barrows, our den leader, made that one of the first rules for the evening.

"Now, you all can play anywhere in the auditorium, the stage, or the basement but…you are not to leave the building, you hear me? There are plenty of activities for you all do inside," Mrs. Barrows instructed. The ten of us cub scouts had gathered around her in a semi-circle and were squirming impatiently to be released to more fun things.

"All right mom, we get it," Roger replied flippantly, tossing the black strains of hair out of his eyes. He looked to Bobby and Zack and rolled his eyes. They giggled quietly.

"Roger, during pack outings you are to call me Nancy," Mrs. Barrows said firmly.

"Okay, okay…all right Nancy," he replied with an exaggerated nod of his head. This time he had it cocked towards me so that his mother would not see the Cheshire-like grin.

"Good, now I'll be up in the loft doing some reading if you need me." With that, Mrs. Barrows climbed a creaky staircase up into a lofted area that looked over the large auditorium below. She took a seat on a grey metal chair behind a soundboard and opened her copy of *Alias Grace*. Between the soundboard controls and pages of her book, Mrs. Burrows could see little of the goings on below unless she stood up. And with every page that she earnestly turned, it looked unlikely.

Free now from direct adult supervision, the boys began splintering off into various corners of the auditorium. Craig, Aaron, and Clem quickly went to play with a new foam whistling football Craig recently got for his birthday out in the center of the wooden floor. In between the *vreeeeeew* sound bouncing off the walls and ceiling, I could hear Clem boasting that he could throw it further than John Elway.

Jake, Troy, and a red-haired kid, that I can't quite remember their name, went off to find a spot on the stage to see whose burn deck of magic cards could beat the other's counter deck.

"Let's go to the basement, I've got a plan to tell you guys," Roger said, after taking another furtive glance up at the lofted area.

Through a quick nodding of heads, Zack and Bobby expressed their support. I followed in behind without too much hesitation, as there could be little disagreement with Roger unless you wanted to spend the rest of the weekend exiled to one of the 'other' groups.

The auditorium floor creaked as we causally strolled across the open space past the football throwers and over near the stage. I remember staring at the old wooden floor with its narrow slats trying to avoid uneven dents that made you check your step. It looked worn from the imprints of those probably long since departed. Only the scratches and scrapes remained of people who danced and gathered so long before. For most now, it was probably their only visible trace left on the world. One that remained trapped in the boards until they rotted or were torn away for something newer.

Sitting adjacent to the stage, the basement door was a large heavy wooden door, the kind that had been overbuilt to keep people out. It was not locked and Roger opened it slowly.

"Keep a lookout, will ya?" Roger barked at Zack. Though there were few eyes to take notice. Mrs. Barrows was still nose deep in her book and the other boys had their back turned to the door. With a flip of a discolored switch, a fluorescent glow led the way down the black cast iron steps. Roger was the first to slip through the opening, then Bobby, and then Zack. I was the last to go and was about to take my first step down when Roger whispered back to me from the front.

"Peter, close the door!"

I slowly pulled the door closed and we were gone.

The heavy smell of vinegar and citrus hit us when we reached the bottom landing. The industrial cleaners had been applied liberally to the dingy tiled floor and masked the musty smell of the exposed rafters. Under the flickering fluorescent lights and against the walls, a clutter of plastic tables and metal chairs took on a grimy off-white look. In a few spots along the wall, a dark curtain of stain remained from where water had once sprung a leak.

We walked straight back to a corner in which all of our backpacks and sleeping bags had been stashed for the night earlier. Roger began to aimlessly rummage through the pile of possessions. Bags of all sort began to tumble away. Clem's green dinosaur sleeping bag fell down off the pile and rolled across the floor before coming to a stop against a brown metal support beam. Half of the contents of Troy's bag— mostly video game magazines—spilled into the pile. Eventually though, Roger found his orange duffle bag and unzipped it to pull something out. The long green object dangled in his hand like a rubber band.

"Take a look at this, guys," Roger said proudly.

"What is it?" asked Zack.

"It's a water balloon launcher, stupid," Roger replied, flicking one end at Zack. The surgical rubber tubes hit Zack in the chest with a *PAP!*

"What are we going to do with it?" Bobby said, examining the black leather pad in the center of the sling.

"I dunno, launch some shit," Roger replied. A mischievous smile slowly creeped across his face. "We just need a distraction to get my mom away from front door so we can go outside and have some fun with this thing."

"But Roger, Jim got banned from this outing for walking around the camp site after curfew," Bobby said cautiously.

"Pssh...my mom, I mean *Nancy*, won't do anything to me. Perks of being a den mother's son..." Roger replied before trailing off to look at the snacks table in the other corner. A few moments passed before the scheme had worked its way in his mind.

"I'll tell you what we'll do. We'll take those clementines over there and flush them down the toilet. My mom will be up in a tizzy to unclog the only toilet for ten boys. Then, we will slip out the front door and go over to the road to launch anything we can find."

The group nodded in quiet agreement. As I collected a handful of fruit, I couldn't help but admire Roger. I would have never thought to come up with some sort of distraction. It was a clever idea and made me want to be more like him. A person with a plan, who gets others to follow it, and ultimately gets what they want.

After grabbing enough golf ball-sized clementines, we dumped them into the toilet in a series of *plops*. Roger had Bobby pull the release lever sending the tiny orange balls into a cloudy torrent of swirling water. As the water drained down the pipe, we could hear the pieces of fruit getting caught. The toilet let out a loud gurgling sound as it choked on the blockage. Bobby pressed the lever once more and, this time, the murky water had nowhere to go and filled up just an inch below the mustard-stained brim of the blue bowl.

With our success, we ran back up the stairs to tell Nancy with Roger hiding the sling under Zack's shirt along the way. In the excitement, I remember a discordant feeling scratching at the back of my thoughts. That inner voice whispering that I was somehow doing wrong or choosing poorly. I didn't want to listen to that ancient voice of virtue. It was too late now.

When we told Nancy how the toilet in the basement was horrendously clogged and on the verge of sputtering all over the floor, her face instantly lit up in horror. Without even marking her place, she dropped her book and dashed down the steps. By the time we could look over the balcony, she had crossed the auditorium and was heading into the basement. We wasted no time and stealthily slipped out the front metal doors without anyone the wiser.

Outside, the night air was crisp under the pale glow of a full moon. It felt like a night of trickery in October than one in mid-August. I couldn't help but wish I had thought to grab my jacket, but there was too much risk going back. The group of us strolled across a farmer's field and around a small pond until we reached the cover of a hedge of trees that lined a two-lane highway. Down the road the moonlight revealed some shadowy animal sleeking across the road into the dark underbrush. But besides that, not a soul was on the road at that hour.

We chose a spot where the trees were thicker to avoid easy detection from the road. Zack and Bobby knocked down some tree limbs to ensure an easy lane for our shots over the road. As they did, a few softball-sized fruits dropped to the ground with a *thump*. Under the hazy light of my flashlight, the fruit looked like green brains, their surfaces scattered with squiggles and folds. Zack remarked that they were hedge apples according to a plant identification manual he had been reading for a badge. I held one up and was surprised as to how dense it was, almost like a cantaloupe. Roger did not seem to care what they were but thought them to be perfect ammunition. He had us gather nearly a dozen of them into a neat pile of green cannonballs.

Roger was the first to launch the hedge apples with Bobby and Zack holding the ends. The tension on the bands was enough to make the holders shake their arms before each throw. Roger sent several of the apples into the neighboring field across the road. It was too dark to see them land but a distinct *splat* could be heard in the far distance.

Eventually Roger grew bored and told me it was my turn. He picked up a large apple and put it in the sling for me to fire up the road. That is when we saw the lights. At first, they were but a faint glimmer on the horizon, but they moved steadily closer until we knew that a vehicle was coming down the deserted highway.

"Hurry," Roger insisted, barely able to contain his excitement.

"What? There is a car coming," I replied confused, not wanting to fire. I could already feel the prickling of my conscience again. I knew it would be wrong to fire the sling, but I also wanted to be 'cool' and do something wild. The choice hung aloft in my mind as the vehicle approached silently, it's headlights nearly beaming into our strip of trees.

"Peter, you got to fire the catapult or we'll miss it!" shouted Roger.

I pulled back on leather sling with the large green brain nestled like a baby. Zack and Bobby's arms were already beginning to shake wildly from the tension.

"Peter! It's got to be now," cried Roger.

There was not much more time to waste, a choice had to be made—

Thwack…

BAM!

We could not see it in the dark but the sound assured us that the green fruit hit its mark. The vehicle—a van—instantly slammed on its brake lights illuminating our position in an eerie red glow. The van swerved off into the road into a shallow ditch before coming to a dead stop. The smell of burnt rubber and exhaust wafted over our nostrils from a light breeze that had picked up.

I turned to the others to see what they wanted to do and found that I was alone. In the excitement and fear, the others had left me behind taking my flashlight with them. I wanted to go too, but found myself for a moment unable to take my eyes off the red lights that remained on like a steady flatline. The vehicle was motionless and I knew someone must have been inside driving it. At first, I took a step forward as if to help, but knew the moment I stepped out of the darkness that there would be no covering up what happened.

Instead, I turned to chase after the others, half-blind in the dark. I could see the boys up ahead as my feet took me as swiftly as they could carry me. The three of them had already exited the hedge of trees and were halfway across the field with my flashlight casting its beam in random directions as they ran. A few heart-pounding moments later, I was almost out of the hedge row myself when I saw a curious pair of blue orbs. No larger than a firefly, the lights floated in synchrony within the bough of a small tree that had arched over so much so that its crown had buried itself into the ground. The tree looked like a tiny little doorway not unlike one I remembered from the crawlspace at my grandparent's house. A black velvet mist undulated in the oval opening around the blue lights. I instinctively ran towards the orbs and was almost within a few yards of them when a black branch came into my view at head height. It was too late for me to react, hitting me with such a force, I fell forward through the hoop of the bent tree and everything went black...

"You okay, son?" said a voice that sounded like it was a million miles away. It was an adult's voice, gruff and deep. Strangely, it was comforting in the disorienting blackness.

"Uhh..." I said trying to open my eyes. A beam of bright daylight punctured through and the ebony darkness that instantly turned to a blinding white.

"What happened and where am I?"

"Um...I was hoping you could tell me?" the man replied.

It took a few moments until the washed-out colors came to form the image of the man standing above me. His face was the first to come into clarity. Under a mop of disheveled peppered hair was a face carved with branching wrinkles that made him look older than he likely was. Below his right eye was a scar that stretched from the side of his nose to his temple. His eyes stared deep into me incredulously.

"Let's see if we can find someone to help you find your way home," he said plainly, lending a hand for me to get up.

"My name is Peter, what's yours?" I said, steadying myself on my feet and scoping out the area.

"Peter...huh? Folks call me 'Pult' around here. Where are you from, Peter?" the man replied with a raised eyebrow.

"I'm from West Jefferson."

"Oh, you don't say? I know that place well, though it has been a long time since I was over there. Hate to break it to you, kid, but you are aways away from West Jeff."

"I am? The last thing I remember I was running in a field at night...away from that van..."

"Van?" asked the man curiously.

"Oh, just that a van was the last thing I remember seeing last night. Where am I exactly, now?"

"You are in the SAMP," replied the man who read the confused look on my face. "Err...the Scioto...Au...Au...damn it, what is it? Ah, Audubon Metro Park."

"Is that in Columbus?" I asked.

"Sure is, there's 71 right over there." Pult pointed towards the elevated interstate that ran along the edge of the green space and over a large muddy river. The blur of car and truck roofs could be seen heading east.

There was silence for a moment and then Pult began to tug at his flannel shirt. The collar was stained in various shades of yellow and brown and was littered with fragments of dirt and leaves. It was practically begging for a wash. I had no desire to know if it smelled as bad as it looked. His eyes darted back and forth over some unseen horizon up a hill and past the edge of the park.

"Let's get going," he said finally. I did not want to argue and fell in right behind him, taking care not to follow too closely. He took us up a winding sidewalk that climbed up a grass-covered embankment made for flooding. The whole way out of the park, Pult's eyes remained transfixed on the way ahead of us, only stopping to furtively glance back for me every few minutes. When we did finally reach the edge of the park, Pult had us exit off the sidewalk across a stretch of grass that dumped down into a railroad bed. We quickly crossed a pair of tracks until we moved into a neighborhood of sorts.

A line of buildings flanked us on either side as we walked along a street littered with potholes and remnants of fast-food waste. The buildings were mostly brick standing at three to four stories above us. In their dilapidated state, there were few adornments to set the buildings apart. Many of their windows were boarded up with plywood or covered in sheets of tarp that flapped in a breeze carrying the stench of sewer and exhaust fumes. It took us about ten minutes before we arrived to our destination. The apartment building was rundown to its bones. Several windows were broken and more were boarded up like all the other buildings in area. The first and second floors had bars over the windows that had rusted to the same color as the peeling paint that had once been applied to the brick in a better time. As we entered the front entrance, several tough-looking men fully tattooed and in white beaters greeted Pult with an unusual hand shake. The other men looked at me kind of funny but let us pass without a word. We climbed up three flights of stairs until we came to what seemed like Pult's apartment at the end of a hall near an open metal fire escape. From there I could see out over the rooftops littered with plastic bottles and trash bags filled with unknown contents.

If it could be believed, the inside of Pult's apartment was in worse shape than the outside of the building. The studio was small and cramped like a storage container. Bedroom, living room, and kitchen were all in the same space. A torn mattress covered with a mess of discolored sheets was pushed up against the wall. And, not too far from it, was a sink filled with dirty dishes. Above it, a squadron of flies circled in a steady holding pattern. The only part that was not in the same room was the bathroom. It loomed in the back of the space, darkened completely out except for the random flicker of a dull cold blue light. Even the air itself was hard to breathe. With every breath my lungs took in a stale air heavily laden with the smell of soiled clothing and mold.

"So, are you going to take me to the police?" I asked, not wanting to linger a second longer in the apartment than needed. Even the steps I had taken to clear the front door closing were difficult from the stickiness that grasped my shoes with each step on the linoleum.

Pult instantly shook his head. "Police? No, no…I can't take you to them. They're looking for me. They think I did something that I didn't so I got to steer way clear of them."

I tried hard to keep back the disbelief from my face. I kept telling myself to play it cool. Yet, Pult still noticed a hint of uncertainty in me.

"Anyways, don't worry. I'll try to get my boy Diesel to take you to a bus station or something."

"Is that a friend of yours?" I asked, looking at the strange flat television.

"Friend? Son, you don't have friends out here. You have people that will do a job for you. I haven't had 'friends' since I was a kid," Pult said, as he thumbed away at a rectangular device in his hand—some sort of phone I had never seen before.

"Do you miss being a kid?" I asked, since we were on the subject. Somehow, I figured it ease my nerves to know more about the man that had me alone in his apartment. Any sort of backstory, would make him less threatening.

Pult paused a moment, giving me a good long stare. Eventually, he put the device he had been tapping on away in his pocket and came closer to speak in a softer voice.

"Funny you should ask that, it's like you know me or something. I often think back when I was a kid. I had nothing then, but I was happier. It might have been the only true time I was happy."

A wheezy sound reverberated from the man's chest, a laugh. I was reminded of a similar laugh a carny made at the state fair earlier that summer. He ran a game of chance where people tried their luck at throwing ping pong balls into little fish bowls to win a prize. I must have put a dollar on that table twenty times, but despite my best effort, the result was always the same—the balls kept bouncing off the rims of every bowl like a xylophone. For some reason, the carny always had a bowl he could make on the first try and then he would let out that raspy laugh of his, either for his great skill or knowing that I was a sucker. Pult was giving me the same kind of laugh and, still, I was not sure if I was a sucker.

I tried to imagine Pult as a kid, and, for a moment, I felt pity for the broken man he had become. Surely it was not too late for him to recapture those young moments of bliss.

"Why not start over and try to find the happiness you had as a kid?" I pushed further.

"Ha. You're something, you know?" Pult started before trailing off into a daze.

"If I could go back and do it over, I probably would..." he started after a period of quiet that was only interrupted by the bickering of a couple in an adjacent apartment. "But the choices have been made, and I am too far into who I have become."

"That's not true!" I exclaimed. "You always can change."

Pult shook his head.

"Those are words spoken by someone who has yet to lay down their path. A choice ceases to be a choice once you've made it. Once you've acted on it, all the other options fail to seem like they were ever choices at all—because minds can pretty much justify anything ya do. Even though mine is half shot, it's still showing me the same person every time I look in that mirror."

Pult pointed to the bathroom shrouded in semi-darkness across the room. In the flickering light, I noticed a fragmented indentation in the mirror like a kaleidoscope. Something had knocked into it either unintentionally or not.

Pult continued. "And when you make the same choice again and again, it comes to define you until it seems like there never was a choice in the first place. After heading down a path long enough, you get a sense that who you are was inevitable. I can't even rightly say how I've come to be on the road I am on now. I feel stuck, like I am barreling down some highway towards a cliff with no way off or back.

"But let me tell you, kid, and give you some advice before you go too far down your own road. Don't let anyone tell you that you can't choose. You can. Sometimes it's so hard to make the right choice that it seems like no choice at all. You don't want to be like me, kid, a washed-up hooligan on his last tour…" the man paused and looked away to the window wistfully.

"The doctors…" he began, as if something were caught in his throat. "…they say that the cancer will take me in a few months."

Then the man turned back to me, trying his best to leave his sorrowful face behind at the window. "But only the good die young, am I right?" he said, tears shimmering in the corners of his eyes.

I had no response to offer. I could only stare at the broken man before me filled with decades of regret. Of choices made, and what-could-have-beens. The kind of things that keep you up at night. Because the worst kinds of memories are those of things that cannot change. We often take them off a shelf and play them on repeat, hoping that by doing so we could find another way. But just like a record, the same song plays out its somber tune, ending in the same slow fade.

Without saying anything more, Pult walked away smudging his face with a dirty sleave. He entered the bathroom and closed the door behind him carefully. Before it closed, I saw him pull out something else in his pocket. I could not quite tell what it was— his hand was shaking too terribly to see clearly—but it looked like a tiny bag of blue pills.

Pult was in the bathroom for a few minutes until I heard a flush from the toilet and the running of the sink that all seemed a little too obligatory. When he emerged, Pult's look was drawn and gaunt. Little color remained on his scared face and his pupils had shrunk into little pinheads that drooped down as if they had taken on a great weight. Before I could say a thing, a distinct pattern of heavy knocks fell upon the front door.

"That mussst beee Dieseel…" Pult said, stammering over to the door and throwing it open. A man walked in, shorter and skinner than Pult. He smelled of gasoline and oil and had a unique birthmark on the side of his neck in the shape of a pear.

"Pult, my man! How you hanging, bro!" the man said patting Pult's shoulder lightly.

"Been better Diese, been better," Pult replied, getting a better hold of his speech.

"Well, what's the sich?" Diesel's beady eyes turned to me. "And who is the kid, one of yours?"

A nasally whizzing sound came out of Pult's nose.

"Not one of mine that I know of. I found him lost in the park after a…a…business meeting. I want you to take him up to the bus stop on Third and Rich. I'll walk with you as far as Fulton."

"Fulton, huh?" replied Diesel cocking his shaved head.

"Yep, there's too many eyes looking for me right now to go any further. You got all that?" Pult replied quickly.

"Sure thing, boss. Whatever you say. I'll get the kid there."

"Ight, bro." Pult slipped a crumpled up twenty-dollar bill in Diesel's hand.

"You good kid?" Pult said, turning back to me.

I nodded and headed over by the door without remark.

"Ight, let's get you home," said Pult patting me lightly on the shoulder as we headed back outside.

Our route went down Front Street towards downtown. The late afternoon sun had already lowered behind the skyscrapers in the distance, casting long shadows into the street like dark jagged teeth that seemed about to maul the passersby. Pult stumbled over his steps for the first couple of blocks but, eventually seemed to shake off whatever was affecting him.

Perhaps to distract me from noticing his condition, he began to point out people and places known to him. Sandwiched between a liquor store and pawn shop, he showed me Johnny's Diner as the best place to grab a spicy chicken sandwich. At the corner of Schumacher Alley, next to a payday loan store, he recalled a time when he narrowly escaped being jumped by a gang from the eastside. When we reached the next street over, a man in an untucked shirt approached Pult and thanked him profusely for some discreet favor he had done for him, only to say that he hasn't had any more trouble.

"You're a regular backstreet hero," I told Pult after the man had gone.

"I do what I can, but I assure you, many more see me as a villain. So, it's a dark cape that I wear."

"Like Batman?" I asked.

"Not quite," Pult replied uneasily.

"Only a few more blocks until Sycamore, bro," interjected Diesel who was shot-gunning a cigarette in between gasps for air from the walking.

Pult nodded and turned back to me, changing the subject.

"So, what do you want to be when you grow up, Peter?" Pult asked me.

"I'm not sure, really. I've thought about being a security guard 'cause that seems bad ass. But I suppose I'll figure something out in High School," I replied.

"You keep your grades up?"

"I do, I got all As and a B plus last report card," I replied proudly.

"Hmm…" Pult looked off into the distance again with an expression as distant as the one I saw before in his apartment. "Children are just bundles of potential ain't they? You could go anywhere. Be anything. There so many options open to you."

Pult then had us cross the street to avoid a red-bearded man pushing a tiny shopping cart crammed-full of grocery bags and broom handles. "Gotta avoid Red the Sweeper. Sometimes he hits people with his broom sticks for no reason," Pult said, when we got to the other side.

"There must be options for you too. I can imagine anyone would want to live in a place like this long," I said after we had walked a little further in silence.

A heavy wheezing sigh or laugh came out of Pult and that is when I noticed that his nose had a hole connecting his two nostrils.

"Choice is a chaos of dreadful freedom sometimes," he began. "Chose the wrong friends, the wrong woman, the wrong drug habit. Eventually, there is not enough runway left to take off to a different path." A pained expression then took over Pult's face. He spoke now with wispy voice.

"No, my potential ran its course a long time ago, son. There is still much left for you." Pult patted my shoulder lightly.

"The youth have so many paths to choose, the old do not. It's a cruel truth that time gives wisdom on those who can't use it. You get set in your habits that in turn set in the impressions of everyone else around you. Before you know it, all the junctions that once branched from your path into a million directions just seem to disappear behind you. It is then you are stuck. And when the choices finally catch up to you—and they always seem to do— there is no escape."

Pult let out a heavy wheezing sigh. "No kid, I've simply become too old to double back, now."

In my head, I mulled over what he told me for the lengths of a few boarded-up shops. It did not seem much hope was left in the man so resigned to his fate. If the future or present could not be changed for him, I wondered what about the past had placed him here.

"Do you regret choices you made?" I asked as we passed by another pawn shop.

"I regret many, but one choice always stands out no matter how many years have gotten behind me."

"What was your choice?"

"A bad piece of fruit," Pult said absently.

"What? How can a fruit be a bad choice?" I replied, perplexed.

"Hedge apple, ever heard of it?"

"Uh...that sounds familiar...I think—" I squeaked out but was cut off before saying any more.

"That's why they call me 'Pult,' for a balloon *catapult* I used in my first crime. You don't see them much near the city, but out in the country they grow along the edge of fields and highways..."

A cascade of thoughts came crashing down over me in that moment as if the sun had risen to high noon, beaming down on the two of us on that sidewalk like two ants under a magnifying glass. But, before all the connections had been made in my mind, Pult kept going...

"Well, you know, I ended up killing a pregnant mother in a car with that monkey brain fruit. Me and some friends I shouldn't have gotten involved with thought it would be cool to hit cars on a highway late at night. Well, we did, and hit a car bad. So bad, the hedge apple went right through the windshield and hit the woman in the face. The police told me the blunt force trauma killed her instantly, if that was any consolation. You would have thought I would have learned from earlier that night when I hit a van that ran off the road. But I didn't, I chose to load up another round with my *friends* egging me on.

"Anyways, long story short, I ended up in juive for a few months to await my trial. They wanted to try me as an adult and put me away for life but I guess my parents hired a good lawyer 'cause I only got two years for involuntary manslaughter. I went to back to juive and that's where I got my street name after people heard what I was done. When I got out, I didn't have anything. No home to go to—my parents died from poor health while I was incarcerated, no doubt from the stress I brought on them. I had no money—even after their death, they left everything they had to the local church, I guess to pay additional penance for what I had done. So, without anything to my name, I started working the streets pushing dope and hustling baseball caps to anyone I could. It didn't take long until I was living in a dump, in with the wrong crowd, and pissing my life away through a bottle or a bunch of pills. And here you can see the result. What I once thought was 'cool' became a living prison that were locked by my choices. You see, there is nothing elegant about this life, not at all."

Pult finished and pulled up his shirt sleeve to reveal a railroad track of scars from past injections. Scattered about in between them were dark irregular lumps some the size of my fist of what were certainly cancerous growths. The lumps were a deep shade of black, like little pits of coming death slowly seeping into his body. I had never seen such a horrible thing up close before, all the people I knew then were young and unblemished. Were these black marks the signposts of the choices he had spoken of before? The ones that caught up to him?

I turned to look at him in the face. It became all clear rather suddenly. I could see then, like a veil had been lifted in the wanning sunlight. The familiar features that I had known for years in my own mirror were all there. The features in his face had only been distorted by years of drug abuse and neglect. And in that moment, I knew, somehow you were me and I was you.

All at once, there was so much I wanted to say. So many questions I wanted to ask, especially why. I could not believe this is what I had become. But just as I was about to start with my first question, Diesel began shouting.

"Cops! There on Sycamore, run!"

But it was too late, the police officers had been watching us and were already in hot pursuit. The three of us ran as fast as we could across the road and down into the railroad bed. When we reached the tracks, Diesel split off back south towards the apartment complex. Pult and I kept running down into the park where he had found me earlier. The whole time we ran, the only thing running through my mind was that I wanted to save him. Maybe it was some sort of strange form of self-preservation, but…I wanted to save me.

The police were trailing off behind us when we reached an area near the river under the highway. Overhead the loud rumbling of cars drowned out any ambient sound. We were heading straight for the river when I heard Pult gasping for air from behind. I stopped just as I reached the edge of a bouldered river bank. Whipping around, Pult had stopped a dozen yards behind and was clutching his chest tightly. His wheezing now sounded like gurgling as he slouched over onto his side. His eyes were as wide as his mouth as if he was staring into the most peculiar sight of his life.

It was not long before the police caught up to him. In their haste, the two officers did not seem to notice me at all. They surrounded him and saw that he needed help. The female officer pulled out an injection pen and jabbed it into Pult's torn blue jeans. He barely flinched. His eyes were already glazing over like two glossy marbles looking out—or perhaps back—a million miles away.

It did not take long before I could not bear to look on at the final moments of Pult's life, the place where my path would come to a dead-end. I began shaking terribly and backing away on my heels as the last rattle of air whistled through my future rotten teeth. I kept backing up until I slipped over the edge of the stony embankment.

As I fell, for a moment I thought I saw a man along the bank where Pult had been staring blankly for so long. He wore a strange yellow kerchief with crescent moons and he was looking at me— no, looking into me, deeply, with a pair of glowing sapphire eyes. I wanted to stare at him forever, but in mid-fall I had to turn my head towards the ground to catch myself. But it was not a large grey boulder that I was falling onto. A black tear had formed in the space beneath me like a fissure with no bottom. I crossed its threshold without any feeling. The light simply faded as the world shrunk above me into an irreducible speck of light. Then, blackness was all there was...

~*~*~*~

The next thing I remembered was Bobby calling out to me in the night.

"Peter! Peter! Where are you?"

"Over here!" I grumbled. The disorientation made me feel nauseated. My stomach felt like it was in my throat like after having just fallen down the first big hill of a roller-coaster. I remembered the branch that had hit me and felt for my face. A wet gash stretched underneath my eye. Judging its length and depth, I knew it was surely going to leave a rather noticeable scar.

"We thought we lost you," Zack said, arriving first before Bobby and Roger.

Roger shone the flashlight he had taken from me directly into my eyes.

"Peter, you have a big cut under your eye!" Bobby exclaimed.

"He'll be fine, unless he is a big baby," Roger chirped back.

"Yes, I'll be okay." I replied strongly. "But we should probably get out of here before we get caught."

"Oh, we're in the clear. The van is gone and no one came to check anything out. We were heading back to do more slinging when we found you lying here under the tree. Since you seem to have the best aim, you can sling first," Roger stated, already looking off to the road wide-eyed.

I removed my hand from my face as the daze was finally ending. Yet, in the growing clarity, that familiar feeling at the back of my mind scratched at my thoughts once again. Another choice for good or ill was held aloft before me like a sign post pointing down diverging paths. The whole idea of going back to fling more fruit at cars seemed small in that moment. And, remembering Pult, I knew what was right and good.

"I'd rather not," I replied, and began heading back on shaky legs to the assembly hall.

Roger, gave me a smirk as I walked by. Over my shoulder I heard him make a remark loud enough for me to hear.

"Looks like Peter the Party Pooper is going to poop out on us, guys, let's go!"

I walked away in my choice fearing not what would happen when I saw Roger again but, whether I would have the courage to keep making the good choice, again-and-again.

~*~*~*~

As I approach the age of forty and look at my son playing on an apple tree in the yard, I realize I am the same age as you were when I met you so many years ago. I am glad that I did. Few get to see the result of the could-have-beens. Someday I will tell my son about that night, when I met you, Pult. How I will frame it, I have not a clue. I still wonder if it actually happened. Was it a dream or some trick of the wondering mind playing out unconscious fears when that branch knocked me out? Maybe I made you up as a warning for myself of what I could become if I kept making dumb decisions. But then again, I do remember walking by a man in the city a few months back, who had a pear-shaped birthmark on his neck so much like Diesel's. I almost asked him his name then, but feared the answer.

In truth, the answer would mean very little. Real or imagined, meeting you was a game changer. It was the moment I can point to that I chose to try and be good. Sure, there were stumbles here and there but all-in-all the path I find myself on is a good one. I know that because I rarely find a need to look back and do any of it again. And even if I could, like you said "we all become too old to double back."

The Hunting Spot

The truck jolted once the tires left the smooth highway onto the gravel road. The sounds of loose stones crackled up against the undercarriage. The hunter's coffee canister nearly spilled onto his lap as he held the dislodged lid at bay with one hand while the other shakenly steered into the turn. Before this unpaved country road, the past twenty-minutes had been a tense drive on a two-lane state highway. The highway was well-paved and empty but it was the threat of deer jumping out in front of the truck that had kept the hunter's foot cautiously hovering over the brake pedal. He was taking a gambit to speed down the highway as he wanted to get to his hunting spot early before first light.

To be honest, he was glad to be out of the mountains. Coming from Warrenton in Northern Virginia, he had already traveled west of the Blue Ridge and over a set of Ridge Appalachians just as he crossed into West Virginia. It was a longer drive than most would take to go hunting, but it was a good spot that had been in family memory for several generations. The spot, near Lost River, was such a well-kept secret that rarely anyone outside the family was ever told about it, even in passing conversation. It was an easy secret to keep; few people knew about it, and even fewer people lived in the area around it.

The country road winded back and forth without any sense of direction. On the left hand of the road were open corn fields that had recently been harvested. A few stray brown corn stalks clung to the edges of the field. They had missed the reaping and stood tall amongst their unlucky brethren who were bent and broken.

The deer will surely glean them right up, the hunter thought.

The right hand of the road was lined with an edge of trees— pines and pin oaks. Oaks were a good sign, as they had been dropping acorns like rain all fall. There was not much to see further into the woods; the trees and brush were too thick even for the brights of his headlights. That was just fine, he only needed to see the stone wall to find the entrance to the little holler he was looking for. The hunter wiped the inside of the windshield with the sleeve of his camo jacket to see better. He knew he was getting close after passing those corn fields.

A few more minutes went by as the truck rattled along the gravel road. Every so often he thought he saw the flashes of stacked stone on the right and slammed down on the brakes. In the early morning darkness, the tail lights bathed everything behind the truck in an eerie red light. He did not usually look back in the rearview mirror that often when he was alone on these roads for the fear of seeing a phantom passenger in the back seat. There had been too many ghostly stories growing up of people finding ladies in white along the road late at night hitchhiking on empty country roads. Where he came from, it was a duty to help a stranded stranger, especially a woman. It was not safe to be alone out in the country at odd hours in the night. These good Samaritans usually let the lady—it usually was a woman in their tales—up in their cars or trucks and go off down the road towards the nearest town. However, it always seemed to be the case that after a few miles, the good driver would turn back to talk to the passenger and they would be gone as a mist in sunlight, without a trace. The hunter was thankful he had not had such experiences. Though a God-fearing man, an experience like that would stretch his toughness.

The stones finally came into view after taking a sharp bend. Moss-covered and of different sizes, they were stacked four or five high for about forty-yards—all glittering of grey marble. Hell, it could have been quartz for all the hunter knew, he was no gemologist. No one had ever really explained what they marked; they had always just been there. For the hunter they marked the entrance he was looking for, a small dirt road.

He gently turned the truck onto the road and was glad the rumbling of gravel was over with. The dirt and mud made little noise, now. There was only the light scrapping of brush and young tree shrubs that had grown up through the middle of the ruts lining the way. There was no shoulder here. The trees had slowly encroached their way up to the sides of the old tire ruts. Their limbs stretch out from either side making it appear like a tunnel in places. Some of their stray limbs hit the top of the cab as he made his way down. *Give them a few years' time, without any road travelers, and they would retake the road*, he thought to himself trying to avoid the potholes and puddles of unknown depths, *then, no one would know that there had been a road here at all.*

Few people used the road. It only got accessed once or twice a year when the company that managed the cell phone tower did their annual check and cleared the road with bush hogs. The company actually only owned a small area around the tower at the top of the mountain, the rest of the area was public land. The state granted the company access in exchange for helping maintain the old access road.

That was how granddad had first heard about the location, the hunter recalled. Back then, the tower had been a radio tower. His granddad had worked in general maintenance at the local radio station back then, probably in the forties before he moved east to Virginia. At some point, a crew member had him go and check the tower for some type of interference. As he told it, he saw nearly fifty deer along that access road up to the tower that day and knew that this area would be a prime hunting spot. He passed that knowledge down to his daddy and, eventually, to the hunter (and some trusted friends). Ever since there has not been a year that someone in the family had not come back with one or two deer harvests.

After about a mile, the road split into a fork with one climbing up and the other headed slightly down. The hunter took the downward slope and followed it to its end at a small area where the earth had been pushed back into a broad embankment. The hunter pulled his truck so that the nose almost hit the embankment and turned the engine off. Then, all went quiet.

Stepping down from the cab, the hunter struggled to turn his headlamp on. It was still early in the morning so it was almost jet black. The light eventually popped on and a wispy cloud of breath filled the chilled air. The road had ended in an isolated spot that was quiet and still. Only a faint whispering of wind rattled through some of the boney branches of the treetops.

ArrrrrOOOO! The distant howl of a lone coyote sliced through the silence. The call echoed throughout the holler and off the mountain somewhere above. The hunter froze in his boots. He would not be the only one hunting this morning. He let out a deep breath and could see it was being swept southeast, which would work well for masking his scent at the hunting spot.

The hunter headed to the back of his truck and let down the tailgate. In the rusted bed was a small tan backpack, a long black sock, and a metal tree stand. He grabbed the pack and threw an apple into it he had been carrying in his pocket. *A snack for later,* he thought. With luck, he would be bringing home a nice harvest of meat. A mature buck could weigh up to three hundred pounds and would feed the family for months. Though he knew, even if he came home empty handed when the day was done, his old lady would welcome him home to a warm supper and a cold one from the fridge. After supper, the kiddos would want to hear all about his day's adventure on the porch into the twilight hours. It was those thoughts that took some of the pressure off him. He swung the pack around his back and made sure it was tight enough not to beat against his thighs during the hike.

Next, the hunter reached for the black sock. Inside was his granddad's old rifle. Despite being about one hundred years old, the M1917 Enfield rifle still looked in choice condition. Granddad had taken good care of her and even refinished the stock to show off the beautiful walnut grain. Chambered in thirty-ought-six, the rifle could take down any game a hunter wanted in North America, from deer, to bear, to moose. Up to his passing, granddad would always regale around the hunting season the time he shot that monster twelve-pointer with the rifle, he called it his "Marsh Buck." Once the rifle was handed down to the hunter on his eighteenth birthday, he never did make any modifications to it. Unlike most modern hunting rifles, the gun did not have a scope. The gun could tack-in nails from one hundred yards with iron sights alone and he never felt like he needed to mess with fancy scopes which could fog up or look dark in early light. No, he kept things simple. The gun had harvested hundreds of deer, and that spoke for itself.

The last item in the bed was the tree stand. A bulky piece of equipment, it was made mostly of sturdy metal and padded fabric. As a climber, there were two sections of the stand, the platform, and the seat rest. The platform section of the stand used a metal rope to wrap around a tree and into the slotted-metal platform that had forked teeth to grip bark. The seat portion was similar except the metal was O-shaped, allowing the hunter to pull up the bottom portion to shimmy up a tree. Together, the stand weighed around twenty-pounds and was a burden to carry on long hikes into the woods. Going only a mile in, the stand would not be too much of a burden unless he downed a monster buck. He carefully slipped into the straps on the underside of the stands and hoisted it up his back. With the backpack and two metal pieces of climbing stand, he could feel the weight shifting backwards on him. He would need to lean forward to keep from toppling over as he walked.

Once loaded up, the hunter lifted the tailgate as quietly as he could. With a *click* he proceeded onto a game path that trailed off from the make-shift parking area. The path was narrow at first but began to widen to about three truck lengths as he went in deeper. His boots squished on areas of mud and moss from the rain that had fallen the day before. Tall blades of wet grass brushed the sides of his arms as he walked in the white pool of his headlamp. Eventually, the plants and trees fell away in front of him until he had walked into a wall of blackness. He moved his headlamp from the ground to shine directly in front of him. It too could not penetrate the darkness to find any path, tree, or shrub. He had reached the beginnings of a large clearing. As he turned his head to dip the lamp back down to his feet, the light caught a glow in the adjacent tall grass. Three pairs of eyeballs stared back at him near the ground with cold blue glowing circles.

He stopped instantly in his tracks but his heart felt like it was continuing forward from his chest. He feared it might be coyotes like he had heard before or, worse, a bear her cubs. He stood as still as could be, waiting to see what was staring back at him from the darkness. He listened but the animals made no sounds. Their eyes continued to glow without blinking. Then, they began to move, bobbing up, down, and then side-to-side.

The hunter left out a sigh of relief. He knew that was the telltale movement of a deer head trying to identify him. He thought of his boys at home, they had thought he was such a badass to leave early in the morning to go hunt in the wilderness. *If they could see me now*, he thought. Moving the light back down to his feet, he slowly made his way out into the clearing.

With each step further from the wooded path, the hunter felt increasingly exposed. The clearing was an open meadow filled with

decaying plants in various shades of mustard. Even with the recent rain, the long grass still crunched under his feet. Other plants, still retaining some green, tried to trip up his steps as their tentacled vines looped around his boots. At times, he would have to jerk his leg forward to undo their grip and find that some spiny burs had latched onto his camo pants as little hitchhiking stowaways.

At one point the hunter looked around to find his light no longer could see any line of trees. *Must be in the center of the clearing now*, he thought. The only things to be seen were bits of grass and plants fluttering silently from an unseen breeze. Beyond that, the darkness stretched in all directions. The sky was moonless and filled with stars that lent only minimal light. The hunter took a moment to stare up into them. The starscape felt vast, like a giant sea that he could fall into if he were not tethered to the ground firmly enough. And in those starry waters, he felt something was staring back at him from their immeasurable depths; waiting to come down and snatch him right out of the field without a trace. The feeling was hard to shake being out in the middle of a dark void under the sky.

The hunter continued forward and almost gave himself a fright at the sight of a dead pine tree that looked to be the shape of a man without its needles. He laughed that one off quietly to himself and kept on, sometimes wondering why he did this to himself so early in the morning. *Maybe an evening hunt next time.*

It was a few steps beyond the tree that a wall emerged from the rest of the darkness against the sky. Beyond it he could see nothing. It was as if he had reached the edge of the world and was staring into some elder darkness in the outer realms not meant to be *seen* by human eyes. With a few more steps, the black wall began to take form. The outlines of a trunk became clear and he knew he had finally reached the opposite tree line.

Inside the wooded edge, the hunter was glad to be out from the open having felt so vulnerable out there from every direction. Back in the woods, it was a different ordeal. The wooded edge was claustrophobic with the overgrowth of sharp nettled plants and long-needled pines. The hunter had to hold his hand out in front of him to keep the branches from poking out his eyes that were straining to see a way through in the dark.

After ten or so yards and a few scrapes, the hunter was through. The woods opened up and he could take several steps now before reaching the next tree. The trees in this area were old-growth, most too big for the hunter to wrap his arms around. Walking was also made easier by the change in incline. The ground was beginning to slope downward from every angle into a sort of gully. He could hear the steady gurgling water off in the distance somewhere at its bottom.

The hunter paused a moment to consider his options. Off to his left, the ground ran downward into the gully. To his right, the ground rose up to a ridge that ran on with a gentle slope About five yards up the ridge there was a large rock covered in moss. Next to it were a pair of deer skulls—a six-pointer and a spike. They had been there for a quite a while given their white appearance that stood out amongst the brown leaves. There were no traces of flesh, as all of it had long since decayed or been picked away revealing the smooth bone underneath. It was hard to tell if they had died there together in mortal combat or dragged there by some predator. Their empty eye sockets remained permanently stuck looking up to the sky. The decision was rather easy after a little thought. The hunter pushed forward down the slope to the run. The slope would be easier on his knees along the run and the sound of the water should mask the sound of his steps.

The run of water appeared to come from an adjacent gully that ran up from the hunter's left. He could hear the water falling and pooling off in the dark on its way down to his position. The water was only a few feet wide and a few inches deep. In many places, the hunter could simply hop across it as needed. He stepped into it and watched the water ripple up over the toe of his boot before proceeding down the run. The wet stones squished under the weight of his boots as he navigated the larger boulders and fallen tree limbs that littered the way. The gurgling and trickling drowned out all other sounds. He barely even noticed his own huffing from the heavy pack on his back, let alone the sounds of any other animals in the dark wood.

At one of the U-shaped bends, a large tree loomed over the run. At first the hunter thought it had been burnt from a lightning strike given a streak of what looked like dark bark at the bottom of the trunk. As he turned the bend, he could see that the dark mark was not a mark at all, but empty space. A large arched cavity had formed into the tree allowing for a fully-grown adult, perhaps one with a few less pounds than he, to fit inside the center of the tree. It was a good space to hide in and the hunter wondered what animals might have been using it. He attempted to look around the roots for signs of tracks. He had heard that bears sometimes used the hollows of trees for their winter dens. A quick search revealed no animal traces. There were only the scatterings of leaves and twigs, so he continued down the run and did not think much more of it.

A few hundred yards further, the run began to straighten in an area that seemed to flatten out in some sort of flood plain. The plants here were all coated with a brown coat of mud; all signs that water had submerged this area not too long ago. Ahead, a game path led up from the run and onto the flattened area. Before climbing out, he checked for prints and was pleased to find two sets of nice pointed hooves about the size of his hand. *A good sign,* he thought. *Might be a monster in this marsh of my own.*

The hunter soon found himself up on dry ground again and needed to find a good climbing tree. The tree had to be big enough for the metal cable to dig in but not too big as to not wrap around the trunk fully. He usually went with a tree that he could just barely wrap his arms completely around. He flashed his light back and forth across the line of trees trying to find a good candidate. Dark shapes seemed to dance like shadowy figures behind gravestones as the light went past the bases of the trees. There was something off in how the shadows followed the glow, like some sort of unnatural delay between light and shadow. The hunter's leg began to shake and his eyes darted in alertness to the edges of his beam. Along with the stillness, he felt he did not want to stay on the ground in the dark longer than he needed to. The last thing he wanted was the shadow of a big black bear to come upon him as he was fumbling around trying to climb up a tree.

The hunter settled for an oak tree about fifteen yards from where the game path crossed the little run. The tree was slightly leaning but it would do the job. He started with the upper seat by flinging the cable around the back of the trunk. He caught it on the first attempt and re-attached it to the other side. He settled the seat into the bark with a few good shoves and did a quick bar dip to make sure the stand was secured enough to hold his weight. Next was the platform. At the base of the tree, the trunk was wider making it more difficult to fling the cable around. It took the hunter five attempts before he caught the cable with his other hand that was growing numb from the cold air. Eventually he grabbed it with a single finger and secured it to the platform. A good stomp ensured that the stand's teeth firmly had dug into the tree's bark. Then, he was ready to climb.

The climb up was a slow, arduous process for the hunter. It started with him loosening the safety tether that connected his harness to the tree. Once he had stretched up his arms as far as they would reach above his head, he could tighten it once more around the tree. Next, the hunter grabbed the upper seat portion of the stand as firmly as he could and lifted it up the tree like an old man with his walker. Once it was secured, he placed all his weight on the upper stand to lift the bottom portion with his feet and then the process was ready to repeat.

Gradually, the hunter climbed up the tree. Each time he went through the three steps he might rise another four feet off the ground. On occasion, he would rest to collect his breath and look down to see his progress. Each time he did so, the darkness slowly swallowed up all evidence of the forest floor below. And when he had finished, reaching a height around thirty-feet, his light found no sign of anything. There were only tree trunks popping out of darkness. With one last firm stomp and shake of the stand, he had reached where he wanted to be. He grabbed the rope he had tied to his pack to hoist up his rifle that he had placed next to the tree. Not too long after, he clicked off the headlamp to let his eyes adjust to the surroundings.

Finally, the hunter was in position. He was glad to be off the ground and settled into his lofty seat as he sat there patiently in the dark. He only had to wait for the sun to rise to see his new dominion below. But the night was growing long with no sign yet of golden light on any horizon.

The night is always darkest before the dawn, the hunter had heard people say. *There certainly is plenty of it now.*

He knew it was not just the darkness that made him feel so uneasy, it was the stillness. There was not a sound of bird or creature rustling anywhere in the hunting spot. Besides the swaying tree branches, the stillness felt like death. To be honest, even the trees looked like a corpse with their boney finger-like branches reaching towards the sky in one last death throe. The hunter looked over the edge of his slotted metal platform past the toes of his muddy boots. He stared down into the blackness trying to catch any hint of light to discern shapes below. There was nothing but a murky gloom. He dared not stare long for there was a sense that, at any moment, some shadow would come scratching up the trunk of the tree to grab his legs. It had felt this way since getting out of the truck. Like Death himself had been lurking in the shadows and is now pacing at the foot of his tree waiting to pounce. The hunter moved his feet away from the edge of the platform and tucked them safely underneath his seat.

It was then he remembered when he first saw death. It was his first deployment in the Army. He remembered laying there quietly in his green cot trying to sleep after lights out. The sickness for home had taken him when he could finally be alone with his thoughts after a day full of drills. Surprisingly, his thoughts did not drift to the fear of his buddies dying in combat. No, he realized in those moments, for the first time, the mortality of his folks, mama, and pop. The fact, that in thirty or so years, death would take them. He remembered how the thought sacred him; like it had snuck up on him and startled him. His folks had always just been there, really the only constants in his life. But like granddad, death would take them as well. After that, Death would then turn his gaze on him. That was when he had thought of his own death. In one hundred years he imagined himself, a rotting corpse buried in the ground somewhere. The image up in the tree stand was as clear as it had been that night—a skeleton, mouth agape, lying motionless and helpless in the dirt. Nothing could change the fact, that eventually, time would grind on long enough and he would be gone too, buried away, perhaps already forgotten.

The hunter did not understand why he was reminded of that memory now. Lives are so often lived not thinking of death. Months can go by without even a thought of *that* future. But suddenly, those immutable thoughts arise from places that had long been stuffed away, into deep recesses of the mind. It seemed that life was a race to constantly outrun those thoughts, but every once in a while, Death would catch up and the mind would need to run harder.

The hunter looked out from his stand and began to notice shapes that he had not noticed before. First, the heavy silhouettes of trees came forth, then the ground and other small shrubs and fallen branches. Light had begun to inject itself into the scene. Like a dimmer switch, the light levels rose from darkness to gloom to monotone. With each step, the growing dawn revealed new features of the landscape. His tree was next to a large holly bush whose berries had not yet been plucked by hungry birds. A few minutes later, he could see the shimmering creases of a river that was catching the first white glints of sunlight from over the hill. Above its surface a low-hanging fog rolled across and onto the surrounding bank. For a moment the hunter thought of strange ghouls and sunken corpses that might lurk in the unseen mist. But like the fog, the thoughts burned away from the yellow sun cresting the hill. The day had finally broken and the world was familiar again. The silly fears and images were gone, and importantly, it was time to hunt.

The hunter saw a lot in his mind those early morning hours but never did see much deer. When he got back to the familiar sight of his truck, he thought of home and his old lady and kiddos once more. He knew they would all ask, "Did you see anything?"

The hunter turned back to see the path now bathed in golden light. It looked transformed from the world of night. Leaves danced in the morning breeze and some white aster flowers remained in full bloom amongst some swaying fountain grass.

And perched on a log right off the path was a grey squirrel nibbling on his morning breakfast.

"No, I did not see a thing," the hunter muttered to himself and climbed into the cab of his truck to leave the old family spot.

The Image of Death

This is not my death, Dougal thought.

A group of burly men had gathered around the short, middle-aged man on the rooftop, each holding an assortment of brutish clubs and jagged knives. Their faces sneered an ugly glare of hatred at the little black box Dougal held in a slightly trembling hand. The stolen box contained an invaluable piece of hardware that everyone on the planet wanted and only a few possessed—a pair of death cheaters. Their sneers quickly turned to demented curling smiles as the goons had pushed him to the near edge of the rooftop.

Dougal could only afford a quick glance over his shoulder to see what lay beneath. About ten stories down below were a winding web of back-alleys, tattered window shades, and...an alluring promise of escape. Off a few car lengths from the building, was a narrow canal filled with brown water and floating trash. The water was too murky to gauge its depth, but it grew more enticing with each beat of his racing heart.

Turning back to the goons, they had inched even closer from where he had last tracked them. He felt his heel catch the edge of the rooftop. There was no more room for retreat.

"Give us the cheaters, and we'll make your death quick," cried the largest of the group who was missing an eye.

"You've nowhere to run little man," said another by his side through yellowed teeth that looked to have rotted from the reckless abandon of intense smoking and drug use.

Dougal turned to face them squarely holding the small box out in front of him like it was gift wrapped. For a second, the other men relaxed their postures in preparation for an expected surrender. But Dougal flashed the group a disquieting smile before bringing the box back close to his chest and saying, "This isn't how I die." Before any of the goons could flinch a foot forward, Dougal pushed off from the ledge and parted from their company.

While in freefall towards the narrow waters of the canal below, there was little doubt in his mind that he would make it. His death image was irrefutable and this was not the image of his death. Yet, despite knowing this was not the place of his death, there was always an outside chance that he could meet the water halfway. There had been many a thrill-seeker who had survived some horrific maiming injuries before their death dates only to go in a living death until their known date of death. A thickening cloud of doubt crept in Dougal's mind. But thinking on counterfactuals was rather useless as the murky waters drew ever closer...

Dougal hit the waters cleanly, head first, avoiding some of the larger bits of garbage and debris that floated along its slimy surface. The goons above could merely look down helplessly as the theft's head popped back up above the waters like a bobber released from the jaws of some legendary fish. Clutched protectively in his hand waving above the water was their prize...and it was quickly drifting down the canal out of sight.

~*~*~*~

Dougal remained in the canal until its meandering current had pushed him several blocks away from the jump off point. Here, the canal had dumped into a larger one that fed into a patchwork of agricultural fields. Thinking that he had gone sufficient distance to evade any would-be pursuers hell-bent on his untimely death, he pulled his water-logged body from the canal and onto a dry patch of soybeans. For several minutes, he laid there in the hot sun until he had completely dried out. The sun did little for the stench, it would take several showers to get the acrid smell out of him. But it was no matter, he still possessed the object he had risked so much on. And was it really that much of a risk?

Pulling out a few soybean plants by the root, he used their leaves to dry off the outside of the little box. The glossy black enameled coating shimmered in the noonday sun. He could only hope that the putrid water had not penetrated what lay within.

Pinching two opposing sides of the box with his thumb and index finger, he felt the box *click* and release from its tight seal. Inside, he was pleased to find that not a drop of water had leaked into the contents within—two plastic containers. The first container looked like a heavy-duty contact lens holder. He snapped it open to find the delicate translucent lenses with their intricately embedded circuitry. They would help analyze and shift everything he saw in accordance with his uploaded death image. The second container was shaped like two adjacent squares similar to an ice tray. They held two small cube devices the size of a thumbnail. Each had a tiny slot for a memory card and another hole for the retractable anchoring pin.

Finally...he thought.

Like everyone else in existence, he had seen the image of his death. It had started during a worldwide pandemic nearly a decade ago. The reports had first originated in isolated pockets around the world about people seeing vivid images of some moment in time they had not yet experienced. The visions turned prophetic as the visions began to match the exact circumstances of a person's final moments before death as the pandemic took its toll. Initially, these reports were swiftly dismissed as old superstitions or the fever induced hallucinations brought about by the virus. But as the entire world became engulfed by the infection, the doubts began to subside as increasing numbers of people shared in the unsettling experience.

It was not until children born after the pandemic began reporting similar visions as their first memories that the world began to give credence to the phenomenon. By then, countless cases had amassed of those who had died shortly after their revelations. For nearly all of those cases, their final words seemed to take some form of the phrase "This is it!" or "This is what I saw!"

The pandemic became known as the Death's Eye Pandemic or DEP for short. When it finally came to an end, after two long years, a third of humanity had died. For those that remained in its black wake, the very foundation of the world had changed. Scientists believed that, in some way, the virus had altered certain latent genetic markers in the human brain which brought on a new prescience of one's own death—the source of which was still under careful study. The religious, on the other hand, claimed the death revelations to be a divine judgment upon the world. But, in truth, no one really could explain any of it. The only irreducible fact was that death images affected people of all walks of life: the young and the old…the wealthy and the poor…the religious and the irreligious. People universally described their death images as still life scenes that varied as much as human experience could allow—occurring at all times of day and in any kind of location. For some, they saw hospital curtains and faces of loved ones; for others, they saw wet lonely roads; and for the unlucky, they only saw blurry images of white or scenes shrouded in near-darkness.

Dougal pulled a pair of memory chips from the folds of his jacket. They contained the intricate parameters of his own death image that would serve as the basis for monitoring in the death cheaters. The death transcribers who had digitally sketched out every detail of his death image had remarked how odd his death scene was; it would occur on a dusty field surrounded by three loincloth-wearing cavemen with matching orange tiger chest tattoos and brandishing large clubs. There was also a tiny green dinosaur and a man in a full-bodied spacesuit in the scene. For these reasons, Dougal had avoided all museums, costume parties, and Halloween like the plague itself. He could not even watch a movie or television show without first checking all the content warnings—warnings required by law to serve as a public service for those concerned about being exposed to partial or whole aspects of their death image.

The chips glimmered in the sun as they trembled between his dirty fingers. It reminded him how nervous he was that day during his death transcription. He had heard accounts of people dying— usually from heart failure—the moment the transcriber revealed their death image to them, an image of them viewing their own death. So, it was always a risky endeavor to visually examine your own death image, for risk of self-fulling prophecy. Though it was a risk he was willing to take with the rumors of the death cheaters circulating like wildfire. What clever person could have thought that the only way to cheat Death was not to look at him.

The memory chips slid into the slots of the cube devices with a satisfying *click*—though one chip did have to be massaged a bit more than the other due to some specks of dirt. Afterward, he wiped his hands vigorously against his shirt to try to remove any final remnants of the sneaky little devils. Even a tiny grain caught in his eye would be excruciating. He raised the cubes up to his temples and pressed them firmly against his flesh. The sound of a spring releasing was followed quickly by the sting of a needle on each side of his face as the little boxes embedded themselves into position for optimal ocular transmission. After ensuring a snug fit, Dougal grabbed the contact lens case. Dabbing an index finger into the sanitizing solution, he pulled out a tiny convex lens clinging to the pad of his fingertip. He carefully turned the rigid lens over to see the nearly-invisible circuits that ran in concentric patterns within the transparent material. It was this circuitry that would monitor and curate everything he saw. He brought the lens closer to his eye and gently tapped it against his right eyeball. Instinctively, his eye blinked tight and he could feel the rigid object floating over his eye. When he opened his eye again a brief visual aura waved across the right side of his vision as the device calibrated itself.

That's one.

The second lens was slightly more difficult. His left eye seemed more sensitive to the inserting of a foreign object. It took Dougal several attempts before the left lens finally settled itself into place comfortably.

Once the lens had calibrated, the ocular death cheaters were operational. The neuro-ocular death cheater device was said to be capable of modifying any scene a user experienced so that their death image would not come to pass. Once a parallax copy of the user's death image had been uploaded to the tiny boxes around the temples, the boxes would continuously monitor everything a user sees and compare it to the death image. If any aspect of a user's vision began to resemble the key input, the feed would be altered by the death cheaters to change what the user sees away from their programmed death image. This whole process happened nearly instantaneously to prevent any sense of visual delay.

The devices were largely still unverified or even acknowledged by most government officials. Of course, there had been many whispers from key non-official influencers that the device worked with some claiming to have lived past their definitive death dates—and thus, cheating death. Despite their actual effectiveness, their value had skyrocketed on the underground markets and were largely only accessible by the wealthy elite. The death cheaters were thus out of reach to the lowly masses—perhaps by design—but for an upstart criminal, like any other object, they could be stolen.

A wave of relief settled upon Dougal as he soaked in the pastoral scene around him. Behind his newly protected sightlines, it was first time he had truly felt peace since...*since when?* he wondered. There would no longer be any worry that a stray television screen or group of revealers would suddenly bring about the death image that had haunted him for so long post-DEP. Finally, he could go back to the blissful ambiguity that everyone once had before the pandemic.

Since, Ava's passing. His subconscious mind had diligently found the answer to the rhetorical question he posed himself. What followed was a flood of images and final moments.

"Oh...there it is." Ava had said that when she recognized the moment her death image had come to pass. He remembered the moment all too well. They were in their bedroom with the curtains drawn, as the light was too strong for Ava's sensitive eyes, yellowed from the jaundice of kidney failure—a last late gift from a virus that was thought to have been defeated a while ago. That whole afternoon she remarked she was experiencing intense déjà vu, that she knew the image was coming, the pieces were all falling into place. It was the image she had told him about months before when she had rolled over in bed to him after a day of pandemic fever and told him that a vivid image had just come to her, of a darkened room, with drawn curtains, amber light, and his face looking at her tired and filled with fear. At the time, he had dismissed the imagery as the warpings of a fever dream. It was still early and no one yet put much stock in the validity of death premonitions.

When the death image finally came true, before he could utter a multitude of comforting responses, Ava was gone. But that is not how it was supposed to happen. Ava was supposed to be the person he was going to grow old with, the person whom would share in the watching of each other die. To him, love had always been more than living with someone completely. It was also the very real choice of who he wanted to stick by to the very end. The person he loved enough to watch a slow death across the years and decades as time carved out thin lines in their face and age sucked away all the color and vibrancy of their youth. Until, one day, the person you loved, the person you have stood by for so long, would be gone in a final ending when the story had run its way through. All that would be left of their essence would be but a memory, a collection of images and movie reels that, like the real thing, would slowly begin to fade and degrade away with no hope of permeance—fleeting and eventually forgotten. Death...the finality of the word was hard to fathom still…it was not supposed to happen so soon, definitely not in the middle of the telling of the tale. There was supposed to be so much more time for them… they were supposed to end together…

He had lost himself in those first several months after. Every morning he awoke with the expectation of finding her there next to him, like she always had been. But, in those hazy moments of half-submerged consciousness, the empty place next to him crushed over his growing awareness like a tidal wave of reality. And, on the bad days, a flash of his own death image came in its wake. One that he had painstakingly tried to bury deep within himself. It was of no consequence though. The image was too deep; too seared in mind and memory. Any desperate attempts to thwart the unshakable shroud that had fallen over him were unsuccessful. After months of therapy, with a half-dozen suppressors, none of it seemed to work. At one point, he had even considered experimental neurosurgery to cut out areas believed to be associated with the death image. He was weeks away from the procedure when he first heard of the death cheaters.

And now, I have them. I can finally rest easy, he thought.

Off in the distance he could see a group of workers moving machines into place for the cultivation of the field. A slight haze fluttered across the scene quickly like a heat mirage. It warped the imagery in strange bends of light. It was all normal, he trusted. Just the machine doing its job.

The workers came back into crystal clarity. Behind his protected view from death, he pitied them—those who had to go through their day with their own images waiting to become manifest. In the post-DEP world, the veil of death became seared into the world consciousness. The lasting legacy of the pandemic was a society hyper-focused on death. No longer was one's death something relegated to be largely outside of awareness. What once only lurked at the back of the mind as a subtle influence over human actions had become tangible and in vivid detail for many.

The new prescience of death that had fallen upon the world had changed almost all aspects of daily life. In the first decade after the pandemic event, religiosity spiked through the roof; many believed the worldwide revelation of death to be a divine punishment by God. For so many that had been comfortably living in the present, the DEP brought an unwelcomed clarity to the mortality of their future lives. Though some took stock and treasured the moments they had left, many more doubled down on nihilism, self-indulgence, and hostility. Since death for some was many years out, people began to drink more, eat to excess, and engage in all varieties of risky behaviors. There were many who even strove to take back control of their lives and end them before their death image came about. These people sought out death, but typically never found it. Either the suicide lined up with their death image in some twisted turn of fate or, in most cases, they injured themselves into a state worse than death—bound to survive in a crippling existence of pain and misery until their death image eventually came about.

Towards the end of that first decade, crime was at such critical levels that society nearly collapsed upon itself. The world governments took drastic action and deployed mandatory mortality salience education for all children and adults to manage the terror of impending death. People were separated from society in 'Acceptance Institutions' until they could be certified with the requisite coping skills to accept the time and means of their own deaths and function within society. Because of all this, in the second decade post-DEP, entire industries had arrived surrounding every aspect of death images. People wanting to know the how and the time of their death went to death investigators that meticulously sketched out every detail of a person's mental image to be deconstructed and analyzed to pinpoint a year, a season, a day. It was risky business for individuals to manifest their death images into the physical world as, in some cases, the sight of the reveal of their death images brought about their own deaths. Unfortunately for some, their death images consisted only of a murky field of blackness or some blurry white vision. Without any details to rely upon, these people became known as 'unknowers' and were perceived by most as chaotic and unpredictable. For others—whose death image held within it an identifiable marker of future time such as a calendar or an electronic device's current date—a remarkable level of precision could be associated with their death visions. With many even able to establish exact dates of their demise, death dates.

Knowledge of the timing of your death changed many services to cater to people's exact or approximate death dates. Life insurance companies almost instantly became irrelevant. Funeral homes no longer could prey on those at a time of grief and ill-preparation. The entire dating industry reorganized itself to match people whose death dates closely aligned as no one wanted to be paired with a partner that would die decades before themselves. Preceded by weeks of 'living wakes,' it became not uncommon to wish a friend or co-worker a happy death day when they reached their death date. As with anything, businesses and government began to take advantage of this new reservoir of knowledge. Legislation in many places was drafted around death date privacy to avoid employers and service-provider discrimination. However, for public figures, it became common practice to disclose their death dates when running for high political office.

For many like Dougal, there was a retreat from anything to do with death dates and images. A large contingent of people—typically born pre-DEP—engaged in all manner of attempts to return to some semblance of death ignorance, to subjugate all forms of *memento moris*. From suppression therapies to hypnosis to neurosurgery, the desperate sought a myriad of services to suppress their death images. People were almost willing to do anything to get back to the way they were before; to cast back down death into the depths of their minds. The feeling was so pervasive that it forced every facet of media to offer content warnings for the entirety of their content so that people could avoid certain imagery. Though even with all these measures taken, it was never truly enough with the looming image in the back of your mind. The ever-present dread of death hung over you like a black shadow eliciting a wakeful restlessness of mortality that could never be soothed…but that was all behind him now.

Dougal tapped his death cheaters again to ensure that they were still in position. He felt the solid piece of machinery securely attached to the side of his head.

He let out a relieved sigh and rose to his feet.

It would be a long walk back home, he thought. Dougal estimated that it would be near nightfall before he got back to his apartment on the other side of the city. *A nice walk with peace, for once.*

~*~*~*~

The walk became tiresome sooner than Dougal had anticipated. After nearly an hour of trudging through dusty fields, rows of bean plants were still all he could see. He had followed the canal hoping to find a main road that would lead to the city. There had been nothing but rows of crops and rutted cultivator trails everywhere he looked. Eventually he came upon an abandoned water container and decided to take a rest.

Dougal sat and breathed in deep breaths of fresh air that smelled earthy and sweet. He had almost lulled himself into a daze watching the plants wave in the field like a green sea until a discordant sound broke him from his peaceful serenity. The sound was growing closer. He looked out into the field and did not see any cultivator approaching. There was only a small group of herbalists who were spraying some chemical over a field one hundred meters away. They wore protective suits from head-to-toe that covered them like spacemen visiting a strange planet. As he watched the workers, another distortion rippled across his vision. This time he thought he saw the faint outline of a small green blur of some creature. But it was gone before he could fully process what he saw.

That should not have happened, he thought. He tapped on the death cheaters again to make sure the storage cards were in place.

Soon his vision returned to their normal operation. The sound of a humming engine was nearly upon him.

The boat had come up behind him on the canal. It did not take long for him to recognize that its crew were the same goons he had escaped before. Each one wearing a silly leather jacket with a Bengal tiger face on the front. One of them was already pointing an alarming gesture his way that drew the boat to veer off from its path to the nearby bank.

Dougal swiveled his head in all directions for a route of escape. The spinning made for a nauseating mix of visual imagery as the augmented reality tried to keep pace with his swirling view. For whatever reason, the group of herbalists seemed to be his best means of salvation in his mind. Even if they could not ward off the goons, they might at least provide a good distraction. He looked back to see that a trio of beefy men had only just crested the canal bank carrying with them heavy clubs. Without a second thought, he began to run with all speed he could muster.

The leaves of the soybeans smacked at his sides as he rushed down the row towards the workers. Behind him, he could hear a greater disturbance of vegetation as the goons must have entered the field on their own. His legs and feet were sore from hours of walking and swimming. He did not know how much effort he could expend. What mattered was reaching the company of the workers who were growing closer with every bounce of his stride on the uneven dirt.

He had nearly made it to them, a mere few steps away, when he felt a root of some old plant looping around his foot. The world fell slowly in front of him as his face came crashing into the dirt. The side of his head hit a cold rock that had been sticking out of the ground like a bald scalp. The impact was abrupt and sent flashes of disjointed images across his vision. Images of displaced cavemen, a spaceman, and a green dinosaur...

Ugh, he thought, grabbing his head off the ground from a stone that had met it in the fall. He rose to his feet to find the herbalists around him with cocked heads covered in helmets looking strangely concerned. Unfortunately, the goons had also arrived with their clubs and were already trying to take over the situation.

"Back away now, this thief is no concern of yers. Go back to your planting." Spat the big goon with the missing eye.

Dougal looked them over still trying to get his bearings. The orange tiger on their jackets seemed to open its jaws in a mocking roar as they lobbed threats at him. His right hand was on his head feeling if any damage had been done to the death cheaters. His finger traced every millimeter of the rectangular implants and found nothing out of sorts.

It was a small relief.

The trio of goons held their clubs in a menacing fashion as the small group of herbalists had taken a few steps back away from any involvement.

So much for help, he thought.

"Give us the device or meet your death," cried the large goon, again.

A million thoughts ran through Dougal's mind, all of which were too fast for him to grasp. Nothing made sense. Yet, a growing familiarity like the feeling right before a moment of déjà vu was coming over him like a wave of hot air coming across the field of soybeans.

"This is not my death!" he screamed, slapping the side of the death cheaters in mocking victory. "I have cheated it and this will not be mine."

The one-eyed goon's frown almost looked like a smirk. The one beside him gripped his club tighter and looked to take a step forward.

Dougal took a step back. His muscles in his side tightened as they twisted in preparation for another flight. The tightening then turned to pain and confusion. Suddenly, he lost all energy to move at all. The rapid pounding in his chest had noticeably stopped and a wet sensation ran down his legs. Before he could react, his vision warped again. This time, the flickering persisted and distorted the scene in front of him. The scene, every aspect of it was like he knew it...like it always had been.

"No...it...can't...be," Dougal whispered.

His death image had arrived. But it could not be. Not with the glasses, it was not possible with them...right? Then a thought struck his consciousness cutting through everything else like a cold knife. He realized that somehow the death cheaters had become damaged and were malfunctioning. Either from the fall or a stray bit of dirt, something was causing the target image—the one they were supposed to monitor and augment—to display before him now. It was all there. A mix between reality and the death image that he had been trying to avoid and suppress for years. Three goons in loin cloths with clubs. Orange tigers tattooed on their chests. Herbalists looking like spacemen in their containment suits standing on a dusty spot in the field. And...a tiny green snake that flickered into the distorted shape of a small green dinosaur.

Dougal looked down to see a sharp object had pierced through his chest. The boat driver must have caught up to the party and stabbed him with some sort of fishing spear. The blood was oozing out of him with each moment that seemed to last for an eternity. Dougal looked back up at the men, knowing this would be the last image he would ever see. He never wanted to believe it; he had known for so long that it would be like this. It was his death image recreated perfectly.

In his final moments, time stretched out into a space of silent reflection, semi-disconnected from the world looming around him. In that bubble of space where no man or earthly force could touch him, he thought of death and how it was such a kindness that Death's face remained hidden. Though all must die someday, living in ignorance of that eventual end was a blessing. That living in hope was better than living in fear. But, like in all things born of this world, there is still an end, no matter what way we find to distract or delude ourselves of that eventuality. Death, even if cast to the icy reaches of our mind, was—like the rock that undid everything—still a stone-cold fact. It comes to devour everything long after the warmth of life has faded away.

The brief moment of reflection slowly began to fade before Dougal as the world now began to slip into blackness. It started at the edges of vision—a black void that encroached from areas long-held back by the direction of his gaze. He wondered, his thoughts now stretching further and further away, if the blackness had always been there, just out of view. It creeped forward until the last remnants of the image of death slipped away into nothingness. But then, after the blackness had faded the image away, a glistening smile appeared out of the darkness in a whirling tunnel of pristine light. It was hers! Ava's. And, in nearly an instant, the sight of her face made his death, his entire life, seem like some half-remembered daydream, soon to be long forgotten upon awakening.

Dream Traveler

With the last brown package sent down the conveyer belt, and no more behind it, Robert knew his shift was done for the day. He stepped back from his post—Package Route S2-3347—and let out a heavy sigh of relief that had been waiting to come out for the past few hours. The dull ache in the balls of his feet cried loudly in his boots from the hours that had weighed them down on the concrete floor. Their cry was only the loudest of many today. Yesterday, it had been his hips, the day before that, his knees, and before that a combination of neck and elbow. In his thirties, he knew his body could handle the work, but for how long, he wondered. Gus, a 35-year company man working in the adjacent packaging route, was in his fifties and he would still be gingerly walking out of the building on his bad knees by the time Robert got home that evening. Gus was quiet, but always nice to Robert and told him each time that the years sneak up on you. But for what purpose, he questioned himself in silence each and every time. Whose life was he changing by sending that can opener, branded by the company, but assembled in China for a fraction of the cost, down the line for the hundredth time. Thoughts like these always hit him like a wall after his shift. They waited for him like some logjam of packages, ready to be sorted and moved on their way without much of a second glance. There was little time for thinking when brown boxes needed to be pushed and pulled second-by-second.

Robert tidied up his stall the best he could for the next shift and headed out. The way was a winding maze of conveyor belts, trash bins, and orange plastic containers filled with odd assortments of packing materials. The smell of adhesive and the stable-like odor of manure that excreted from the cardboard boxes was everywhere. One fella remarked that there were enough corrugated boxes in the facility at any given moment that, assembled, they could be stacked to the moon. Thousands of boxes passed by in his queue every day, so he did not doubt it.

As he neared the exit of his little corner of the facility, he remembered how big it had seemed on his first day. It had taken him nearly two weeks to put the path to his station to memory when he started five years ago. Sounds of activity were everywhere, but never quite in view, making navigation through any part of the distribution center very difficult at first.

As he stepped onto the main forklift thoroughfare, Robert realized that he was still wearing his packing gloves. The heavy beige gloves clung to his fingers from the hours of sweat. Stuffing them both into his baggy jeans, he felt a hole that had formed in his right pocket. It would match the other one in the crotch that had been growing in size for weeks now. But there was no hurry to buy a new pair. Despite being surrounded by new stuff on a daily basis, buying new things was not really his thing. Most of his clothes were a decade old and he had some shirts still from his high school days. He knew he was an odd duck in that respect. Even the most traditional of folks he knew were receiving new packages on their doorsteps on a weekly basis. It seemed, in this one-click shopping era, the appetite for new things was nearly insatiable. It reminded him of the story his old high school biology teacher, Mr. Clark, would say about rats pressing down a lever to stimulate pleasure directly into their brains. They loved it so much—the instant gratification of it all—that they would forgo all other necessities until they eventually died of dehydration or starvation on their pleasure lever. What purpose would that serve, he always wondered. It never made sense to him. A deluge of ecstasy traded for your life.

Any pleasurable death was not so bad for a lab rat, he chuckled hard enough that he felt it in his groin. *Now, don't want to rip that hole any bigger.*

He looked around him, now walking on the main thoroughfare past rows-upon-rows of stacks that towered two-stories above him. Each one packed with carefully organized bins of products that varied from mundane toilet paper to the latest laptop computers. In between each, tiny people wearing reflective vest collected their items and pushed them in carts towards the sorting gates. The brief quiet in between shifts had already begun to be overcome by a steady rising humming and buzzing of machine activity.

Up ahead, near the rear exit, the brown packages of varying sizes were already moving in a zig-zig of metal conveyors, soon to be loaded onto an eighteen-wheeler and sped away to all the people clicking their little pleasure levers at home.

With a quick swipe of his badge, Robert busted through the two sets of double doors to finally exit the facility. An evening breeze of fresh air brushed against the side of his cheek in greeting. He looked up to see the long orange rays of a setting sun stretching across the horizon.

Robert sighed.

What seemed nearly at the horizon line was the employee parking lot.

A frown could not take full hold of his face. The walk would be nice in the evening air after a long day cooped up in the stale facility.

Ten minutes later, passed the line of trucks loading at the docks and the well-manicured landscaping, he reached his truck. It was the same one he had been driving since high school. Not much about it had changed besides the black paint turning greyer and the rust patches growing wider in diameter. With a slow turn of the key, the truck sputtered on with a bothered growl and was ready to go after a brief warm up.

The distribution center was located on the western side of the rural Pennsylvania town. It would be a thirty-minute drive east up the mountain ridge before he would be home. Robert turned on the radio to let it blabber on about another doomsday political event that would come and go like all the rest.

He rarely admitted to himself, but the real reason he suffered through the radio chatter was to feel like he had some comfort of human company in his life. During the day, the non-stop work on the line did not allow for much conversation with the fast pace of moving packages and cacophony of machinery. The meager thirty-minute lunch break yielded little opportunities, as well. Unless you knew someone outside of work, there was little by the way of conversation in the lunch hall—a makeshift space in the warehouse made up with a grid of picnic tables. No, as soon as the lunch tone rang, everyone's eyes seemed to turn from their work to their tiny phone screens. He often watched them stuff their vapid faces with sandwiches as their greasy fingers swiped in a rhythmic unison, almost like the guiding arms of the sorting machine back on the line. It made him long for his school days. A time he fondly recalled in which the school room facilitated forced interaction with peers his own age. At least then, there were people to talk to and share in all the troubles of a small-town high school education. Hell, he would even welcome the trite gossip again, if it meant there was someone who wanted to talk to him.

Yet, high school was the dead end of his educational aspirations. He had wanted to be a firefighter or a policeman, to make a difference in the world, but never had the grades to go to college. As he turned onto the parkway to bypass downtown, he could almost still hear his mama say that he was too busy runnin' and drinkin' with those Cooper boys instead of focusing on his studies at school.

"You trade short-term pleasures for your future, boy," his mom would say in a croaking voice, muffled by a lit Marlboro that was as much a feature of her face as her crinkled nose or receding hairline.

But dammit, if she had not been right, as she was about most things that only age, experience, and making your own mistakes can provide you. And she would still be squawking about such things if the three packs a day had not weighed her down into an early grave a couple years back.

Had it been that long? It was a terrible thing not to remember precisely the date of when your mama died of throat cancer. Not to be outdone, dad had preceded her in death a few months before in a mine collapse.

These blue thoughts made him want to pick up a rack of stones for old time's sake. A few cold beers when he got home would help him sleep and maybe get him away from all this sad nostalgia.

"Don't want'ya runnin' with those Cooper boys..." his mama's voice still hanging in his ear.

The memories of all the great fun he had with the 'Cooper boys' came over him like a creek after the first snow melt. Those boys were long and gone now. Terry was in prison for busting up a man accusing him of stealing a pack of smokes...which he had. Donnie Cooper went off to be in the service somewhere on the other side of the world. He was one of the lucky few who got to leave town. The youngest, Jimmy, could be found down by the interstate overpass on Mulberry and 5th street shot up on whatever had come up from the south. Jimmy was barely recognizable now. The meth had taken his teeth and opioids had taken the rest.

On the eastern edge of town, Robert stopped by a little gas station to pick up an eighteen-pack of Keystone Light. He threw the box of hunter orange cans into the bed of his truck and put it back in gear.

Dozens of boarded up houses passed by on his way out of town. They looked dilapidated and dead, like an appendage of the town that had withered and not quite fallen off. The town itself probably would have died if not for the distribution center coming in. It clung to the town like some sort of sick life support machine—keeping the last gasp at bay. The machine that both saved the town and was the cause of its demise. No one could count the number of hometown mom-and-pop shops that had closed due the company's never-ending success at lowering prices through efficiency and cheap labor. No one also seemed to care about their little town dying around them so long as they were getting their toilet paper for fifty cents cheaper.

It's hard to compete when the devil is giving you a steal. It will simply cost the soul of your town. But keep flying those old bars-and-stripes, true loyalty is found on the names printed on the cans in your cupboard and they surely don't say the good U-S of A.

The road that went up the mountain winded back-and-forth through a series of tight switch backs. A thin stone divider a few feet from his door was the only thing that separated the truck from barreling down to the valley floor below.

As he neared the summit, there was a small stretch of road which offered a view of Greenbrier down below. The town sat nestled on, and in between, a trio of hills with a branch of the Susquehanna River flowing through its center. Looking out over the little town, there was still enough sun for him to see the sleepy old buildings closing up their red-brick turn-of-the-century façades for the next day. In the dying light, the silhouettes of the town's half-dozen churches loomed prominent on the horizon. Their pointed steeples poked up into the sky in vain man-made attempts to pierce some view up into the heavens. Before he knew it, the town had slipped out of view over the ridge. All that laid ahead was a mountain-shadowed road descending into a thick a sea of green trees.

It was almost six by the time he reached his turnoff. The transition from the smooth asphalt to his gravel driveway rumbled his truck's tires sending up puffs of dust into the red taillights. The drive back winded for aways past a stream and field until the truck's headlights found the cabin home at the end of the lane.

The modest log home was of the two-bedroom type, more than enough for his meager needs. It was backed up against a patch of woods on the foot of a hill that led up into state game land. The house was as dark as he had left it in the morning. A few fumbling swipes of his hand found a switch that set the living room and kitchen aglow in a flickering dull blue light. And then, he went through the same motions he had performed every night for the last five years. They were the motions of a man living a life of quiet desperation—hollow, boring, and tired. To get up just early enough to slap some PB and J onto nearly-stale pieces of white bread and head out for the distribution center. And then, to put in eight hours of meaningless work that could be performed by mindless automatons so that there was still enough grease to keep the gears of capitalism turning. Only to return at dusk to the same empty house, eat a bite of microwaved frozen dinner, and then plop onto a twin-sized bed to carry on all over again the next day.

Life had become so routine that Robert could barely pick out a single day in the last year. It was as if all the mile markers had disappeared when your wheels stopped spinning and you realized you were no longer moving anywhere anymore.

At least that was true up until the previous night when he woke up shivering from the most vivid dream he could recall. It was strange because he usually did not dream much, or at least, he never remembered what he dreamed about when he woke in the mornings. Even for a dream, this one seemed strange.

In the dream, he found himself walking in a winter wood like none he had ever been to before. The trees were thinner and shorter than the ones he had run through with the Cooper Boys in Pennsylvania to sneak a smoke or guzzle a twelve pack. It looked like one out of Maine or New Hampshire that he had seen in travel guides.

A fresh blanket of snow had fallen, making mounds of glistening crystals in the boughs of the tree branches. A cold whoosh of air blew through the woods and he could actually feel it's bite as the chill snuck down his back. The time of day was late afternoon and, besides the rustling of branches, there was not a sound to be heard in the muffled whiteness. Every sense seemed to be active and he felt like he had an unprecedented degree of control for a dream that remained locked into a single scene.

Ahead of him, he noticed a set of little bootprints heading off down a slope in front of him. He followed them for a time down a path until he came to a clearing in the trees. It was as flat as a pancake with no signs of vegetation. The bootprints went out into the clearing and stopped abruptly around a dark hole.

Suddenly, a white crest of water splashed out of the hole, followed by another. On the second splash, he noticed a tiny red mitten reach above the waterline from someone who had fallen through a break in the ice.

Moving on pure gut instinct, he grabbed the longest branch he could find sticking out of the snow and slid on his belly across the icy pond. When he had reached within a few yards of the ice break, he shoved the branch out over the hole. It was not long before a flailing arm found purchase on the sturdy make-shift pole and clung to it tightly. Robert pulled on the branch with all his might until the small boy was lifted out of the dark waters and safely in the protective glade of trees.

"Gee, thanks, sir. You saved me," the boy said behind a face that was starting to regain some of its rosy color after appearing pale blue.

"You're welcome," he replied. "How did you get down into that pond in the first place?" He finally had time to look around to see that they were truly alone in this remote place. There was neither sign of house nor people anywhere around.

"Well, I was playing with my sled down that path there and it got away from me somehow. I tried running after it into this clearing and…" The boy took in a heavy gasp of air. "*Holy mackerel*, the next thing I knew I was head deep in water about to be sleeping with the frozen fishies." The boy finished, still catching his breath. He was buttoned up tight in a vintage double-breasted coat wearing equally old-looking galoshes that he must have borrowed from his grand-pappy.

"Say, do you live around here?" the boy asked, shaking out his soaked mitten.

"I am not sure where *here* is, but I don't think so." Robert looked around to try to get some sort of bearings but it was of no use.

"You're in Worcester, Massachusetts, mister. It's getting late though. I better get home soon or Ma won't let me listen to Captain Midnight," the boy said earnestly.

The reference to an old radio program made little sense to Robert. But, then again, kids nowadays were into all sorts of old vintage things. The internet provided that free of charge.

"Would you like me to walk you home?" he asked politely, still concerned the boy had suffered a trauma.

"I don't think so, mister. I feel fine enough to get-on-back to the house," the boy replied, turning to look up the path. Then, before the boy turned back...the dream was over and Robert woke up in the dark in his cold bed.

For a few moments, he could still feel the snowflakes melting against his cheeks.

Hitting the snooze button on his alarm, he laid there for a while longer wondering who was the boy and where had he been? These were not questions people normally asked of their dreams, but this one had been so vivid, so real that he began to question if he had actually experienced the event in some distant place and time.

Now, the following night, Robert found himself lying in bed wondering if another dream would come. One that would send him traveling to somewhere new, doing great things. These wistful thoughts faded quickly into the darkness around a paint-peeling ceiling. What followed were the usual monotonous images of work the next day. In what was a last conscious thought or a mumbled whisper, he wished he had purpose in his life. Some piece to latch onto.

The moment sleep took him, Robert could not say. The transition from the wide unfinished rustic pine boards of his cabin ceiling to the clean narrow white slats of a ceiling of a different place was seamless. One minute he was resting his eyes on his lopsided bed, the next he was in this new place. When his eyes opened again, he was still laying on his back, but now on a hard floor. The first thing he noticed was the intricate swirls and flourishes of leaf-like shapes that covered the crown molding and extended into the middle of the unfamiliar ceiling that hung high above him. He laid there motionless, wondering if he had awoken in one of Greenbrier's historic buildings downtown.

His first instinct was to look for a light switch.

Propping himself into a sitting position he examined the situation from his new perspective. He was in the middle of a large room with ceilings that hovered nearly eight feet above his head. His eyes dribbled across the four walls of the room, looking behind modest antique cushioned chairs, sofas, and wooden tables for a switch. But there was none to be found anywhere; only the odd candlestick holder, a bulbous oil lamp fixture, and a grand marble fireplace with the inscription 'Fletcher' carved in big block letters into the hefty mantle. In fact, there was not anything modern about the room at all—not one piece of plastic or trace of any kind of electronics.

I must be in a museum, he thought quietly to himself.

The only light in the room was seeping in from a sole window in the corner. The light was dim from what was probably a nearby street light and had an orange glow that seemed to be growing in intensity like the oncoming of a sunrise. Robert pulled himself to his feet and began to walk over to the widow.

As he crossed an ornate rug in the center of the room, a loud pounding sound resonated from within the fireplace.

He turned abruptly and approached the fireplace that was almost wide enough for him to fit his entire body within. Placing a hand against the sturdy mantle, he listened for the sound to come again.

A few moments later the pounding returned, now sounding more like knocking in quick, irregular patterns.

Robert noticed that the room had increased in brightness as he was drawn back towards the widow. The light outside now seemed to hit the side of the house with an orange intensity that danced in fluttering motions much like…like a…a flame.

In a moment of recognition, the faint scent of smoke came upon his nostrils on a draft passing through the mouth of the fireplace. Robert looked down immediately looking for some hint of a red spark or ember only to find the firewood very much inert and cold.

He crouched and stared through the fire box, passed the large wrought-iron andirons shaped like arrows to find the space very much empty and void. There was no masonry backing to the box. On the other side was an open space of a room of similar décor but half as large as the one he was kneeling in. It was also dimly lit save for the faintest of light escaping above a large wooden door on the opposite side of the room. The light flickered and rolled from a steady billow of thick black smoke escaping from a larger space in the doorframe.

The pounding sound came again. This time more desperate. It came accompanied by the faint screaming of children, little girls from the sounds of it.

Robert's thoughts raced out in front of him. There was a fire in the house, how large was unknown, where was also unknown, but any untamed fire in a house full of all of this woodwork would present a very real danger to anyone inside, especially little children who sounded in need of help.

"Hello? Can you hear me?" he yelled through the fireplace into the empty adjacent room. The sound of his voice seemed to become engulfed by the long void on its way to the door.

He listened for a moment. He heard a low rumbling sound beneath him. There was also the distant clamor of some sort of commotion coming from out beyond the window behind him. The urgency of the unseen children dissuaded any of his curiosities of the on-goings outside. Without response, he prepared to shout again, as loud as he could this time.

"HELLOO—"

Before he could vocalize the next word, the door in the adjacent room swung open. It let forth an invisible wave of heat that smacked him in the face like an oven door recently opened inches from his face. A cloud of smoke also began emptying into the room, growing darker and more ominous as he looked up at the ceiling. Within the grey smoke emerged three young girls, no older than six or seven. Each of them wore white nightgowns that covered them head to foot. The gowns were marred by a dusting of black soot around their square necklines.

"Who are you, sir?" promptly asked the tallest of the trio in a British accent. She held a candle out in front of the girls trying to pierce through the growing smoke.

"I'm Robert," he replied gently.

"The youngest girl who seemed to be wearing a white sleeping bonnet giggled for a few moments amidst the smoke-filtered firelight.

"You talk funny," she said eventually.

"Clara!" hushed the eldest in between hoarse coughs. Robert could feel the smoke starting to tickle the back of his own throat.

"And see how the sir is dressed," the middle child said, pointing a finger. "He is a Corinthian man, I'd say."

"Emma! Stop! We mustn't be rude to the man," the eldest snapped turning her attention back to Robert.

"Sorry, Abgail, I meant nothing by it, it's true. And sorry mister, I hope you can help us," Emma replied, almost going into a half curtsy.

Robert looked down at his flannel pajama top and bottoms not fully understanding their interest in his attire. If anything, these girls seemed to be the odd ones out in his eyes.

Seeming to trust Robert more in the situation, the eldest stepped closer to the fireplace.

"I'm Abigail Fletcher and these are my sisters. The alarm for a fire woke us from our sleep, but our chamber door would not budge and felt hot to the touch. Do you think you can help us, sir?"

Robert nodded and motioned for them to come to the fireplace.

"I think I can get you through here if I can move these andirons and massive logs out of the way."

He grabbed the large pieces of wrought-iron and pulled them towards the room in which he stood. The large logs that laid perfectly nestled within jiggled ever-so-slightly without much care to their relative displacement from the fire box. The heavy metal fixtures slid across the marble hearth with relative ease until they reached the greater floor where they began to dig into the fine hardwood.

It was enough to provide an opening for the three sisters to pass through into the larger room.

Once inside, the eldest marched to the only door in the room and seized the brass door knob. She immediately retracted in pain holding the palm of her hand like a crumbled flower.

"It's burning hot," she cried in between sniffles.

"All right, let's see if we can manage out the window then," Robert replied. "Come, now, hurry."

The three girls rushed to the window. The eldest reached for the latch but was unable to reach it inches away from her small fingertips. Outside, bells chimed out alarming tones against a cacophony of voices.

"I'll get it for you girls, hang on," he said, ensuring they all made it to the window from the rear.

"Look, Abgail! The fire brigade is here! And they brought ladders!" exclaimed Emma.

Robert reached the window, switched open the latch, and threw it wide open. The chilly night air poured in at his chest like a frigid wave bringing comforting relief.

After a few deep breaths of smokeless cool air, he finally had a chance to look out over the horizon. It was a city, but unlike any city he had ever seen. The night that hung over it was dark with only odd flames of candlelight flickering silently in the square windows of other old-looking buildings.

Robert's eyes fell down towards the street knowing, but not believing, what he would find there.

A group of people, in similar night dress as the girls, had amassed underneath a gas street light near a signpost that read "Peter Street" in fanciful script. Most of the onlookers stood in awe of the house that was completely engulfed in flames from the first and second floor.

Closest to the house was a group of men dressed in double-breasted coats with large belt buckles, knee-high black boots, and crested metal helmets. Some were carrying fire axes, others bits of rope, and several were lugging a hose in preparation of spraying the rooms directly below where they stood on the third floor so that another group could push a ladder into position. But these men were not any firefighters he had ever seen. The equipment did not come off any sort of motorized truck, but instead, off several horse-drawn carts and carriages. The largest of which, that carried the water and length of hose, was a wagon painted in bright red with 'London Fire Engine Establishment' inscribed in yellow and black lettering. The four sturdy Clydesdale horses that had pulled the wagon stood motionless in full view of the flames.

Robert watched quietly as if watching a film of people from a distant time. Yet, this film seemed real. The movements were smooth, the voices clear, and blast of flames were scorching.

It took a few minutes for the firemen to suppress the flames enough to push the ladder cart into position beneath them. The ladder slowly began to extend up to them on the third floor before eventually coming to a secure thud on the window sill just outside. Not much later a fireman, with a big bushy red beard and mustache was at the window motioning for the youngest girl to climb out. He took her in his arms and descended carefully back down. A few minutes later, he was back for the middle child. She gracefully stepped out onto the ladder next to him as the fireman did his best to keep her nightgown from flapping in the torrent of fire-fueled gusts of wind. The firefighter returned a third time for Abigail.

Before climbing out on to the ladder she leaned in to give him a kiss on his cheek.

"Thank you, Robert. We are indebted to you. I await to speak at length once all are safely on the street." She then hopped on the ladder with little assistance and proceeded down to meet the embrace of her awaiting sisters and parents.

Once the last girl was safely down the escape ladder, Robert turned back towards the fireplace to see a rush of flames creeping steadily across the adjacent room. He closed his eyes from the smoke and took what little breath he could.

When his eyes opened once more a fiery red trio of digital numerals stared back at him declaring the time to be half-passed six in the morning. He had returned to his bedroom. It was cool and quiet. Long gone were the tolling bells and shouting of English firemen. Only a faint scent of smoke lingered in the air before changing to the familiar scent of pine and dirty socks.

The next day was a Saturday and Robert could not shake off the dream he had the night before. It failed to fade like most dreams, sticking in his mind with all the details of a memory. Out of some sort of curiosity or merely to rest a confused mind, he went to the local library that afternoon. In the basement, past numerous metal stacks of old books, he found the microfilm stations. He then began to search through every archived London newspaper he could find that was in circulation in the early nineteenth century. He began to flip through page after page of the morning papers looking for anything about a house fire on Peter Street and the Fletcher sisters.

Hours had passed and he was almost ready to give up the search. Ready to concede that it was only a dream, when an article headline flashed before him, catching his weary eyes. It was from the eighteenth of March, 1833, on the second page of the *Morning Herald*. The headline read: "Friendly Phantom of Peter Street Saves Fletcher Children from Fire."

Robert slouched back in the metal chair that had long-since numbed his bottom in complete astonishment.

He quickly cross-referenced the date of the other London papers: *The Times*, the *Morning Chronicle*, the *Morning Herald*, and the *Morning Post*. Only The Times carried a similar story titled: "Guardian Angel Saves Three Tots from Inferno in West End." In both stories, the three Fletcher sisters—Abigail, Emma, and Clara—were said to have been saved by a mysterious "man in the fireplace" who aided in their rescue. The articles went on to describe that the man was seen by numerous onlookers, and firemen, but never rescued from the flames or a body recovered in the aftermath. As one witness who was quoted remarked, "The Scot in plaid simply disappeared."

Robert fell back into his chair hardly believing the account written in black-and-white before his eyes. It was all just as he had remembered. But how could it be? He could not have traveled to London in the night or definitely traveled back in time, could he? But, somehow, he was the friendly ghost or guardian angel described by very real people that were there so long ago. They simply did not know it was him, Robert, a guy living alone in a rural Pennsylvania town working at a package distribution plant.

That evening, for the first time in years, Robert went to bed with excitement for the work ahead. His new job was a moonlighting gig, one with purpose. Across some invisible veil he would be projected upon a universal conveyer to any time or space; a dream traveler delivering troubled souls at the moment of need and then fading into the ether once the job was done.

In his dream that night, Robert found himself on a long stretch of desert highway under a darkening purple sky. Tall dusty mesas lined the horizon like irregular boxes fallen from the heavens. Up ahead, a woman stood pacing in the distance, next to a steaming '76 Pontiac Firebird. When she first caught sight of him, she tried her best to hide a startled look.

"I don't know where you came from, but you are a Godsend," she replied, regarding him cautiously.

"Ma'am, can I help you?" Robert said simply, with a disarming smile.

House of
Many Corridors

What is that scratching upon the door, deep within this house of many corridors?

Yes, that is the one; I thought it to be sealed away ages ago. A passage longed to be forgotten but, long in memory. An account of it must persist; because to forget it in the passages of time could set the old door ajar. Though an overly attentive gaze I must also resist; to avoid breaking what has so carefully been barricaded and barred. Thus, I must leave my silent sentry, to only report on the faintest of cracks. Whose furtive glances ensures the doorway remains shut against a wondering mind or a surprise guest. I dare not think of what lies behind it, not now. Even cracking it for a peek could bring on that familiar flood of senses: those sights, those sounds. No, I fear all that would be too much excitement for me resting here in my cozy study, so pleasantly.

I have sat in this house of many corridors for what seems like a lifetime, but perhaps more. Some say they retreat to a place like this, *their place*. I have always been here though; this place is all that I have ever known. Since the beginning, when the first dawn of light hit the two large picture windows that empty into my study chamber—the only portholes to that outside world. For where else can the inner self go when at the seat of consciousness?

Only upon my death will I leave this place. To where, I am not certain—but I have imaginings that flitter through these endless halls. I try not to linger on such dark thoughts. Nonetheless, they loom over my study from time-to-time. Like a power surge dimming the lights. But, at the appointed hour of my departing, this house will not be left to any inheritance or buyer. It is a part of me and so it shall fade away with my last mortal thoughts.

The study in which I sit was the first room to be built in this house of many corridors. It resides at the front to view the world outside. It is a very fine room, well-appointed, with everything that I desire and need. Pictures adorn the walls and perch upon the cupboards to remind me of past versions of myself and ideal versions I sometimes wish that could be. Bells and chimes ring out repetitiously signaling reassuring thoughts and cues. On the writing desk, to-do lists remain scattered with some items scratched complete and others remaining unfinished. You will not see any rot and decay in this place, things remain as they were because dust never settles here and things do not age, not even me.

My study is where everything comes together. Two large windows provide views of an outside world. Light filters through the panes flipping and diffusing upon the fibers in the rafters until projected onto a flat viewing screen. Knowing no sense of time, the reflector reveals a blur of images melded from past, present, and future. Through floorboard vents, sounds echo up into the chamber, their trebled tones bouncing indefinitely off the walls. Large brass pipes drop off a potpourri of smells and odors to waft upon me in my seat at the room's center. And, at my steady hand, a series of levers and push-buttons offer up a multitude of interaction for acting upon the house and everything outside it.

This little study is more than some Cartesian theatre though, for a homunculus like me. There are psychodramas aplenty, and limitless content to satisfy every curiosity. Though spans of years and miles separate me within the outer world, across *these* corridors, time and distance know no bounds. Within a heartbeat, a memory can be dredged forward, so bitterly close, that it can still sting with the same pangs of a yesterday long past.

Most of the time I am focused on the daily tasks at hand. My life is a series of problems to work through in here. Every little challenge a whetstone keeping this place bright, shiny, and sharp. To go idle too long only invites the gloom that takes the luster out of everything.

I am the sole king of this place. It was the first thing I learned, to rule myself. A title born out of time-honed training and measured by discipline and self-control. Only then was I ready to attempt to navigate the countless causeways of an uncertain outer world. For it has been said, much more of life is based on our responses in here to what happens out there.

In here, nothing can touch me unless the defenses of this house allow it. But, when something powerful does slip through, touching us here in this inner sanctum, it can send reverberations that shake this house down to its very foundations—bringing about a warmly-scented personal paradise or our own cold inescapable hell.

I live like a hermit in here at times, but I am not alone. The butler of the house brings forth past triumphs and hides away every indiscretion. He is a doppelgänger of myself, sometimes shaped by what he brings me; at times weak and feeble, other times bold and witty. Memories, those encapsulated slices of existence that we store away into endless rooms, hold great power in this house. With the feelings that come in their wake, they know no boundary or sense of time. They affect every fabric of our being for as long as we allow them out of their rooms. They love to intermingle where visions and truth meet—making desires into reality and displeasures into myth.

The memories the butler brings to my screen are silent moving pictures that speak to my soul. And, if I am not careful, can unlock a cascade of other doors and corridors. I watch them, I feel them, I relive them sitting on my cushioned chair. At times sipping on cocktails of affirmation and, on other occasions, when the curtains are drawn closed, biting bitter pills of regret. Truth be told, it is often not even the real memories that touch me so deeply, but the ones imagined. The little what-ifs of possible futures or the what-could-have-beens of paths not taken. In this house of many corridors, there are many unfinished additions filled with imaginings and unrealized dreams.

Over the years a grand house of many corridors has been built around my inner study. With each passing year more corridors of rooms are added without nary the sound of a drill or saw. The rooms accumulate like softly falling snowflakes, each one a unique memory of a moment in time. The new rooms accept familiar and strange visitors alike. Many come a-calling. Some stay for a while, others leave out of view, and some take up residences in this place with a privileged lot having wings of their own. And then a special, trusted few have keys to secret rooms of my own. But only I possess the skeleton key. For there are doors it will open, deep inside of me; of memories, nightmares, and dreams that I wish no one else to see but me.

On some occasions, when I venture out from my study, the slatted floors of the corridors creak under cautious steps. The doors open on cue as I pass them by, to find little ageless dioramas of a moment in a memory from another time. When I wander still further, I pass the guest bedrooms made up for those as they were when they left but probably will never return—long-lost friends that have fallen out of reach. These rooms sometimes trigger other rooms to open, with connected moments or themes; and sometimes, entire corridors open, on ungreased hinges, to me.

My eyes often dart over the shoulder at a creak of a cracked door. What could it be I perpetually wonder? I must be careful not to trigger certain rooms or stroll down darkened corridors. Within them reside the shades of lost loves, departed companions, and bitter defeats. Sometimes I reach out trying to grasp them desperately, but only pull back shifting air. They are ghosts of my own making, haunting my footsteps here.

I live in a house of countless corridors. Yet, what I dread most are not the unpleasant visitors of times past. No, there are deeper and darker things which lurk in the recesses of this place—the unspeakable, the unmentionable, and unfathomable. They prowl beneath this place I have built; in the cellars, down around the catacombs, and other deep abysses I dare not explore.

In quiet moments, I sometimes hear their wispy echoes reach me in my seat so far above. They sound far off and remind me of foggy moments in childhood that I thought buried deep in the cellars of this house. Flashes of a time when voices whispered my name from a shadowy closet or a wretched hand was poised to spring out from under a bed. These terrors we somehow outgrew and left behind.

On some nights, I do sit and wonder whether we were closer to a universal truth in our youth. Unencumbered by the walls we build to guard us and bring comfort against the realities of a world we did not want to believe could be true. Barriers we built sturdy and firm against early corridors we wish to forget and never return.

I do my best to keep such imaginings underfoot and dare not grant them passage to halls of warm consciousness above. Though sometimes I find my thoughts do wander down into those deep, dark places, below the foundations of this place. Into a realm that underlies all other houses of every person who has ever taken breath. A weight tugs and pulls me down there, to sneak a peek beyond some opaque veil of mystery. A veil that has created an itch in the back of my mind. One I know probably should not be scratched. For when I do, I find things carved into the bedrock from a time I never knew. Ancestral memories of primal things, fantastical things, originators of myth and legend. Such knowledge on a cosmic scale that anything more than a peek could gobble us whole and rob our minds of any hope of returning to the realms of the sane—or ignorant.

In all my time here, I have merely snuck a peek or two at what lies beneath my feet many fathoms below. I dare not speak of them, even in the comforts of my study chamber. Even now I feel the specifics of which are slipping away brick-by-brick behind a wall of ignorance. To be forgotten long enough once again, until I have lost the reasons why I needed to forget.

I really must remember to write a note for myself not to go searching again for that revelational knowledge that lies deep in the recesses of this house. Knowledge of good and evil, of life's struggles, of entities of great power and dread. All of it is only a mind fissure away from being released. And to be face-to-face with those incomprehensible terrors would split this house down upon me in a torrent of madness, to never find my way back to my cozy study again.

There is really no need to consider those things further. Some knowledge should remain undiscovered and undisturbed. Therefore, I will just sit here in my study and note this all down and hope to keep the doors closed for a bit longer. There are plenty of other places to explore in a house of many corridors.

© SHANA RAMSOOK

ABOUT THE AUTHOR

Nathaniel J. Ratcliff was born in the small town of Chillicothe, Ohio in the winter of 1986. He began his writing career in high school by writing poetry for local library anthologies. From 2005 to 2009, he attended Miami University (of Ohio) and majored in psychology and political science before pursuing a Ph.D. in social psychology at The Pennsylvania State University, graduating in 2016. To date, his psychological research has yielded several peer-reviewed journal articles covering topics of memory, social power, leadership, and organizational behavior. Currently, Nathaniel works as a behavioral scientist at a not-for-profit research corporation in the United States. He resides in Northern Virginia with his wife, Shana, who has Ph.D. in child clinical psychology.

www.ingramcontent.com/pod-product-compliance
Lightning Source LLC
Chambersburg PA
CBHW031105030726
47496CB00002BA/399